Foursome

Foursome

JANE FALLON

HARPERCOLLINS PUBLISHERS LTD

Published by HarperCollins Publishers Ltd
First published in the United Kingdom in 2010 by the Penguin Group
First Canadian edition: 2011

HarperCollins books may be purchased for educational, business,
or sales promotional use through our Special Markets Department.

HarperCollins Publishers Ltd
2 Bloor Street East, 20th Floor
Toronto, Ontario, Canada
M4W 1A8

www.harpercollins.ca

Library and Archives Canada Cataloguing in Publication
information is available upon request

ISBN 978-1-55468-052-8

Printed and bound in the United States
RRD 9 8 7 6 5 4 3 2 1

Acknowledgements

Thanks as ever to everyone at Penguin, especially Louise Moore, Clare Pollock and Kate Burke; Jonny Geller, Betsy Robbins, Alice Lutyens and Melissa Pimentel at Curtis Brown; Charlotte Willow Edwards for her invaluable research and Rae Wilson, Jake Beckett and Ella Smith Fallon for answering her questions.

1

This isn't happening.

'I'm serious,' Alex is saying, except that he's had a few drinks so it comes out more like 'I'm sherioush', which almost makes me laugh, but then I remember the awful melodrama that I've somehow found myself starring in.

'You're drunk,' I say, getting up from the sofa to put more physical space between us. 'You should go to bed.'

Alex stands up and makes a move towards me. 'Just because I've had a couple doesn't mean that what I'm saying isn't true. It just means I've finally got the courage to say it. I love you, Rebecca. I always have.'

Oh God. There it is again, that statement that makes my stomach turn over and not in a good I've-been-waiting-for-you-to-say-that kind of way. More like I could be sick from a combination of the wine and the very idea that Alex is saying these things. Daniel, my husband, is asleep, by the way, upstairs in our bedroom. Why wouldn't he be? It's one in the morning and he's never had any reason to worry about leaving Alex and me alone together. Until now. Suddenly I'm angry with Alex. It's bad enough that he could be saying this at all, but with Daniel – the evidence if any was needed that I'm not available to be propositioned – asleep above our heads? Sweet, funny, clever Dan who has never been anything but loyal to both of us. I decide that I want this conversation to end now.

'Alex, you're being ridiculous. It's late and we're drunk and you don't know what you're saying. Go to bed, OK?'

Alex leans forward, puts his hand on my arm. I shrug it away. 'Don't tell me you don't feel the same,' he says, and for a second I think, Is this my fault? Have I somehow allowed him to think this might be true? Did I catch his eye and hold his gaze for too long one night after I'd had a couple of drinks? And then I realize no, definitely not, because I have never for a moment in our twenty-year friendship thought about Alex as anything other than a friend. Fancying him would be like fancying my brother. It has literally never occurred to me.

I ought to let him down gently. He's been through a lot lately – all of his own making, but nonetheless – and he's obviously losing his mind, but I'm angry with him. How dare he read something into our relationship that simply isn't there? How dare he be disloyal to Dan like this?

'Absolutely not,' I say, slightly too loudly. 'You're my friend, Alex. I'm not in love with you. I couldn't . . . just the idea of it . . .'

OK, I tell myself, he must have got the point by now, but I can't stop. I want to punish him. 'It makes me feel sick. I mean, really, it's . . . perverse. God, I could never . . .'

Alex looks like he's sobered up in an instant. 'Fine,' he says curtly. 'I get it.'

He turns on his heel and walks out, and a few seconds later I hear the front door slam. For a moment I start to worry about where he's going to go at one in the morning and without his coat, which is still draped over the back of one of the chairs, but then I think that's his problem. He's a grown man; he can take care of himself.

2

Rebecca and Daniel, Alex and Isabel.

It was the four of us for as long as I can remember. At least ever since Daniel and Alex, best friends since they were twelve, advertised for two flatmates to share their rundown, rented, second-year house in Windsor, and chose first Isabel and then me because they thought we looked like we might put out, as Dan once so delicately put it. Which we did in the end, although I'd held out till Christmas. We'd thought about advertising again once we had coupled up into two of the four rooms – we were students; we needed the money – but we liked it just being the four of us. We felt like a family. And that's how it stayed for the next two decades.

After college we rented flats in London, a few streets from each other, we had our weddings and then our babies in quick succession. We spent Christmases and birthdays and New Year's Eves together. We were a unit. We didn't need anyone else. Until a couple of months ago, that is, when Alex suddenly announced that he wanted out. There was no big drama – no one else was involved; he had just decided he needed to move on. He felt stifled, he said. Like he'd been in one place for too long and he needed to get out and see what else the world had to offer. He had left the girls – eight-year-old twins,

Nicola and Natalie – with Isabel, and he had moved into a new home, which was conveniently waiting for him only a few streets away so that he could still visit them. He wanted it to be civil, he said. He and Isabel could arrange times convenient to both of them when Alex could have the twins (although he pleaded with Isabel to let him visit whenever he wanted but she, quite rightly, wasn't going to let him have it all his own way). They would remain friends.

Of course, it wasn't really turning out like that. Isabel had fallen to pieces. She had always wanted to be married. That sounds bad. I don't mean for the sake of it, but she was one of those women for whom planning a wedding wasn't just about the day – she was as excited about the following forty or fifty years. She used to fantasize about being old with children and grandchildren and making jam in a house in the south of France with kids and friends and dogs running around all over the place.

Not that it should have made any difference – not that Isabel was even aware of it – but she and Alex *looked* the part. Both blonde and tanned and glowy, like the couple on top of a wedding cake. When you saw them together, you just thought, Oh yes, of course. And once she fell in love with Alex she embraced his family like they were her own, and they adored her in return. She was the daughter-in-law every mother would have wanted.

She had never questioned that she was in it for life. And Alex – or so I always thought – couldn't believe his luck that this beautiful, warm, loyal woman had chosen him. Maybe she mothered him a little too much, but he

5

was as complicit in that as she was. She had loved looking after him and he had loved being looked after. There had been no hints, no indications that anything was wrong. She had had no time to adjust to the fact that maybe her marriage wasn't as perfect as she had always thought. It was just over. Boom. One day it was there and then it was gone.

Alex wasn't faring much better. Faced with his new-found freedom he realized he had no idea what to do with it, and he was spending most of his time flopping around our little flat feeling sorry for himself. In any battle, it seems, you have to choose sides and with him spending so much of his time with us we were always going to look like we were on his, although that still makes me feel very uncomfortable. I know he's Dan's best friend forever, but it pisses me off what he's done. Not just to Isabel and the girls, but to all of us, our cosy little group. He might just as well have turned round and said, 'Sorry, you're all boring me.' I feel let down.

When I wonder aloud how Isabel is coping, or question what it was that drove him to make such a dramatic statement, he shuts the conversation down. It's only when I bring up the subject of the twins that he'll be drawn on the topic. He misses them – he doesn't know if he can spend a life away from them – but is that any reason to stay in a bad marriage? I never offer him any sympathy. He made his bed.

Dan loves the twins, as do I. Surrogate baby sisters to our two (Zoe, who is thirteen, and eleven-year-old William), they have been a part of our day-to-day lives for the whole of theirs. How could Alex do this to them? I ask him. How could he do it to Isabel of all people? I've sometimes wondered what Dan would say if I put my foot down, invited Isabel to stay with us, if I told him that I didn't want to see Alex, that I couldn't forgive him. Would he go along with me or would the history of their friendship still win out? It seems so unfair but, I suppose, that is hardly the point. The point is that Daniel and Alex are like brothers.

And this is how Alex repays him.

Before he made his grand declaration of love for me, before he said those three words that would change everything forever, the evening had started out fun.

I had taken him as my 'plus one' to the opening of a client's play. I say 'a client' like I mean *I* have clients. Actors and playwrights who hang on my every word when I offer up career advice. I don't. My bosses do. I am the assistant, recently turned full time when William started secondary school. Joshua and Melanie are the Mortimer and Sheedy on the sign beside the front door. Between them they represent about forty bit-part actors and 'personalities' whose smiling faces leer down at me from their 10x8s in the reception area, which is also home to my desk, and a handful of writers of varying degrees of competence and success.

I love my job. At university I studied drama and for several years after that I called myself an actress, despite the fact that all my paying work came from restaurants or telesales centres. I once played Cordelia in a production of *King Lear* that toured the Far East for six weeks. That was my moment. Otherwise I just sat and waited for the phone to ring, which it never did. To be honest, once I got pregnant with Zoe I couldn't wait to give it all up. I became a stay-at-home mum and I loved every second of it.

And then, when I got up the courage to go back to work, I found it was so much more fun for me to be working on the other side of the camera, so to speak. Not that there ever had been a camera, but you know what I mean. I have no real responsibilities, which suits me just fine. I don't want any. Basically I just pass on messages and keep diaries, arrange times for auditions and meetings, photocopy scripts and casting briefs. But I'm still enamoured with the world, thrilled by the possibilities every time the phone rings. The offers of TV work, the auditions for stage shows, the first tentative feelers from theatre companies about the rights to one of our writers' plays.

Truthfully, most of our clients don't earn very much. A few can sing or dance and make a good living on the regional musical circuit. A couple have turned to presenting. Our handful of actors audition almost every week and occasionally get a speaking role as 'second bank teller' or 'mugged woman' in *The Bill*. Our writers are mostly still waiting to find the Holy Grail that is highly paid TV work, beavering away on masterpieces that only a handful of people will ever read.

And then we have our 'stars'. The tiny elite who have managed to forge successful and lucrative long-term careers and who haven't yet been lured away to one of the bigger agencies. That happens to us a lot, you nurture someone, have faith in them when no one else does, and at the first sniff of fame they're off to ICM. Not even a thank you note.

Tonight's opening involved one of our still-loyal success stories – Gary McPherson – ex-soap opera actor turned leading man via a very public sex scandal involving class-A drugs and underage girls. Flushed with the success of his new-found media attention, Gary has landed the role of the Lothario brother in a revival of a 1930s farce, which, after a whirlwind regional tour, has, rather unexpectedly, ended up at a West End theatre on London's Shaftesbury Avenue for a limited five-week run. In reality it is filling in an unexpected period of darkness caused by the set for the new Andrew Lloyd Webber having been delayed. Needless to say, we don't mention that to the casting directors and critics when we call them up to ask them to come along. We simply say that Gary has a long-awaited West End role and that we would love them to come to the opening night.

Daniel has, over the years, been forced to attend far too many of these events and, at the last minute, he feigns a headache. It's too short notice to expect Isabel to find a babysitter so Dan suggests that I ask Alex to come along as my guest instead. It might cheer him up, I think, good idea. It's awful to see someone you care about so down, even if, as that critical voice in my head keeps on reminding me, they have brought it all on themselves.

My role in the evening isn't all jollity. I am required to schmooze at the opening-night party on the rooftop of the Century club. I have to make sure that Gary is paraded around and introduced to anyone who might be able to offer him work in the not too distant future. The plan is that I am to share these duties with my fellow assistant, Lorna. Did I mention Lorna? When I said that I loved my job could you see there was a 'but' coming?

'I love my job, but . . .'

That 'but' is Lorna. I love my job, but I wish I didn't have to share an office with Lorna. It's not that she's a bitch; she's just . . . annoying. Grating. Mind-numbingly irritating. She talks all the time. And I mean *all* the time. About nothing. There are very few things that wind me up as much as people who never know when to shut up. Who will fill every available space with tales of their journey into work or their 'hilarious' mishap in Morrisons yesterday or their views on the credit crunch. And, to be honest, when I said that she wasn't a bitch that wasn't entirely true. She can be. She is. And, in fact, she has been to me at times. But more of that later.

Anyway, Lorna is supposed to be helping me to wrangle Gary and we manage to share the burden pretty well for once, which I'm grateful to her for because I don't want to keep leaving Alex on his own for too long. He's a bit of a loose cannon and he's not good with talking to people other than Dan and me because, after a few exchanges, he will launch into his whole personal history: 'I've stayed in an unhappy relationship for years; I've tried, I really have. I don't know what I've done

10

wrong. I mean, don't tell me she's never thought about leaving?' He can't stop himself, but it's impossible not to notice the expressions on the faces of the people he's talking to; from sympathy through boredom to the fear that he'll never shut up. A master class in acting in three easy stages. So I try to go and check on him every five minutes or so and usually find him mooching about on his own near the free bar. He's drinking far too much lately.

'Are you OK?' I ask for the tenth time.

'I'm fine. I'm having a good time.' He knocks back what's left of his red wine and reaches for a fresh one. I can't stop myself from following his movement with my eyes. I'm worried he's going to get drunk and disgrace me.

'I've only had a couple,' he says defensively.

'I wasn't . . .' I start to say, and then stop because it's obvious that I was.

'Do you want to go?' I ask him. 'It's fine if you do.'

'No. Really. Sit and talk to me for a bit, though.'

I look around and Gary seems to be happily ensconced in a conversation with a well-known theatre director who has a predilection for handsome bits of rough, so I sit down.

'Tell me about your day,' Alex says. He always loves to hear the latest bits of gossip about the clients. The worse the better. So I tell him how Gary threw a fit because the producers forgot to send him a good-luck bunch of flowers, but they remembered the actress playing his sister who only has three lines.

'Gary has forty-eight lines,' I tell him.

'How do you know?' he laughs.

'He had me count them. But what he doesn't know is that in the original version of the play his character had eighty-three lines. They obviously cut some of them when they decided to cast him.'

Alex snorts and I feel a little ripple of pleasure that I'm managing to cheer him up. 'Didn't he notice?'

'No, he's never read the original. In fact, he never reads anything he's in. Just counts his lines and checks that his character doesn't die on page five.'

Alex is laughing a lot now so I start to tell him how Lorna has complained to Joshua and Melanie that her desk is smaller than mine, which is wrong because she's been there longer than me, so if anyone should have the bigger desk it's her.

'So I measured them,' I tell him. 'There's an inch in it. An inch!'

'You should measure everything, make a list of anything she has that's bigger than anything you have . . .' he starts to say, but Lorna herself interrupts and says that Melanie thinks Gary needs to circulate and that someone needs to rescue him from the predatory director.

'Can't you do it?' I ask. Isn't it obvious I'm in the middle of a conversation?

'I'm knackered,' she says, plonking herself down on the sofa. I get up, irritated.

'Oh, this is Lorna,' I say to Alex as I go off, and I know he'll get a kick out of meeting her because he's heard

12

me moan on often enough about how I can't stand her.

'God my feet are killing me,' I hear her say as I start to walk away. 'I only just bought these shoes yesterday and even though I take a six they only had a five and a half but I thought sod it they're bound to stretch and if I wait for them to get a six in it'll be ages and by that time I probably will have gone off them or I won't have anything to wear them to or something and anyway my feet are narrow so I sometimes feel like sixes are too big . . .'

You're not imagining it. There wasn't a single comma in her sentence. Not a moment where she paused for breath. I look round and Alex is just looking at her, one eyebrow raised in that way he has. Taking it all in so we can share a joke about it later. Smiling, I leave them to it.

We finally leave about one a.m. and we throw ourselves into a cab back to mine. It's just assumed that Alex will stay over. He hates his new place so he pretty much lives in our spare room at the moment. Besides, I'd guess he's hoping that Dan will still be up and he can drink some more and indulge in some self-flagellation ('Maybe I should have put up with being unhappy for the girls' sake. Am I being too selfish?'). It's in the taxi, though, that he starts behaving weirdly. I'm not sure if I'm imagining it, but I think I feel him looking at me a little too intently for a little too long while I'm staring vacantly out of the window. When I look round he gives me a slightly sickly sincere smile, which unsettles me for a moment.

It's worth mentioning here that there has never – not even for the most fleeting second – been any kind of frisson between Alex and me. Nothing. Not even when Daniel and I split up for a couple of months at the end of our first academic year of living together, and Alex and I were left alone in the house for the summer while Dan went back to his home town to work in his father's law practice and Isabel went off to fulfil a hastily made promise to go inter-railing around Europe with a girl-friend. Two and a half months by ourselves, an oversexed twenty-year-old boy and a newly single, heartbroken nineteen-year-old girl. Nothing. Not for either of us as far as I know. For a single second. Nothing.

Alex was always popular with the girls. He had that confidence that came from growing up knowing he was good looking, but his looks – he was slight, fair, pretty rather than handsome – were boy-band asexual rather than testosterone-fuelled manly. He was a teenage girl's unthreatening pin-up boy. He was also insufferably vain but in such a transparent way that it somehow became a virtue rather than an affliction.

'God, I'm gorgeous,' he would say whenever he passed a mirror, but he'd camp it up to make whoever he was with laugh. Everyone agreed that he really believed it deep down, but for some reason no one disliked him for it. People would roll their eyes and agree that it was just Alex being Alex. He was witty – that was his saving grace. And things happened when Alex was around. There was never a dull moment. He was always the first person on anyone's party list.

His looks have stood the test of time pretty well, actually. He still has a boyish quality, wide-eyed, smooth-skinned (I have no doubt that he moisturizes, and why not, it is the twenty-first century after all), with a thick shock of dark blond hair. I've just always preferred Dan's dark earthiness, that's all.

We adored each other, don't get me wrong. We always have. While Dan and I have everything in common – not just the surface things like tastes in music and what we like to do on holiday, but proper things, values and politics and how we want to raise the kids – Alex could always make me laugh. He's hands down the funniest person I've ever met. He can see the joke in everything – well, not so much at the moment actually; ditching his family seems to have affected his sense of humour. That summer, I remember, his favourite thing was to drag me to the local Pound Shop almost every day where he would pick out individual items and take them up to the assistant behind the counter one by one.

'How much is this?'

'A pound.'

'What about this?'

'That's a pound too.'

'Really? That's too expensive. What about this?'

Rolling her eyes. 'Everything's a pound.'

'And this?'

'Like I said, everything in this shop costs a pound.'

Every now and then he would turn to me and shout excitedly 'Hey, Bex, this is only a pound. Should I get it?' and then he'd turn back to the assistant and say, 'What if I buy two?'

'Well, that would be two pounds.'

'How about if I bought two of these?'

And so on. He got banned in the end. I guess you had to be there.

Both Dan and I have a tendency to take things too seriously, to worry about everything before it's happened so, for both of us, having Alex around has always been the perfect antidote to that. He's like a walking stress ball, or at least he was. A breath of fresh air. The bottom line is that he's one of my best friends. He's in the top three, after Dan but equal to Isabel. But that's all he has ever been. A friend.

So let's just say that I didn't see it coming. His declaration. We get back to the flat and I'm just thinking that maybe he's being a little bit weird. A little bit needy. And then, once we've established that Dan and the kids are all in bed, and we're sitting in the living room because Alex has insisted we open a bottle of wine anyway, that's when he tries to put his hand on my leg. I shrug it off, obviously, but in a way that I hope looks casual. I don't want to draw attention to it, make it real. But he puts it straight back on and I say, 'Alex, don't,' and that's somehow an invitation for him to blurt it all out. Great. My best night ever.

In the morning I struggle to get up for work. I'm feeling blurry. Fuzzy round the edges like a partly rubbed-out version of myself. I can't deal with getting drunk these days. I think my body's trying to tell me I'm too old. My head hurts. Dan is sweet, getting up with me and offering to make me coffee and toast, which I can't quite stomach. He's surprised that Alex isn't in the spare room and for a split second I think about telling him, but I decide against it. It was nothing. A momentary blip on Alex's path to post-Isabel enlightenment. But it still might make Dan feel uneasy and I would never want that to happen. Besides, I have absolutely no doubt that Alex – if he even remembers it – will be in the throes of a spiritual as well as a physical hangover. It's not every day you declare your love for your best friend's wife. I know he'll be feeling like shit, sweating about the prospect of me telling Dan what happened. I decide that the best thing to do is never mention it again. To anyone. Ever.

Thinking that, I realize that the only person who would appreciate the horror of what happened last night is Isabel, but I obviously can't share it with her. So I go to work without saying anything to anyone and just hope that it'll all go away.

3

Lorna is full of the opening night, prattling on about who was there and how great this is going to be for Gary, until we go through the papers and discover that of the five reviews we can only find one that actually mentions him and that's just to say that he was dreadful. He was, by the way, but what do they expect? This is a man who stood on a chalk mark on the studio floor and said his lines in the right order for most of his career. His greatest challenge was not to block one of the other actors from any of the three cameras that were running at all times. Actual emoting was out of the question. There just wasn't time.

I briefly feel sorry for Gary and then think, What the hell? He earned a fortune on *Reddington Road*; if he's deluded enough to really think he can act and risk his reputation then that's his problem.

Besides, I have troubles of my own. Not least of which is how to get Lorna to shut up. I want some peace to think through exactly what happened last night.

She's eating seeds while she talks. She's always on some health kick or other and she brings them in a Tupperware box and chomps on them all day. It's like sharing an office with a giant budgie: chat, chat, chat, peck, peck, peck. Maybe I should hang a mirror above her desk and hope she starts talking to her reflection so I can just turn off and ignore her.

'Didn't Melanie look fab?' she's saying in a voice that is making sure it's loud enough for Melanie, reading through a script in the room next door, to hear.

'Yep,' I say, one of my stock answers. The others being 'no', 'maybe', 'mmm' and occasionally 'really?', although that one is dangerous because it implies I want to hear more. In actual fact, it makes very little difference what I say – once that boat has sailed there's no stopping it. Lorna has decided to tell you something and she's going to get to the end of what she has to say regardless. I could probably put my head in an oven in front of her and threaten to turn on the gas if she didn't stop talking and she still wouldn't miss a beat. Trust me, I've considered it, and if I thought it might work I'd probably give it a go.

'I loved her dress! In fact, I tried on one just like it in Hobbs the other day but it didn't suit me like it does her. She has those curves,' she says. 'Like you, you have curves,' she adds as an afterthought, but in my case she manages to make it sound like a disease: 'You have a severe bout of curves. Take two aspirin and go on a diet.'

'And did you see the way Gary came over at the end and said thank you to me for organizing everything? He probably meant both of us, of course, but you were over the other side talking to your friend Alex . . .'

I am saved by the bell when the phone rings. Lorna has this trick she does where she manages to pretend

19

she hasn't noticed that the phone is ringing just long enough for me to answer it. Every time. This time, though, I am on it before the first ring ends. Anything to distract me from her wittering. It's the booker for a club in South London looking for someone to do a personal appearance at very short notice. I ask what the money is and then pass him through to Melanie who manages to palm him off with the presenter of a recently cancelled kids TV show who, she knows, needs the money so badly he'll agree to practically anything, including getting both abuse and glasses thrown at him by a load of drunk club-goers who were hoping to see someone they recognized.

Dan always says he doesn't understand how the agency keeps afloat. Tonight's job will earn us just forty-five pounds. But, I tell him, it all adds up. And forty-five pounds for a phone call lasting a couple of minutes is hardly bad going. I think sometimes he's a little embarrassed by the fact that our clients are so down market. I bet he'd love to be able to tell his friends I was working for the company that manages Ralph Fiennes or Dame Judy Dench. Proper actors.

He, by contrast, has a very sober and grown-up job as a solicitor specializing in family law. I'm sure he must have fantasies of running away and joining the circus, but if he has he keeps them to himself. I'm making him sound dull and I absolutely don't mean to because he's not. He's funny and kind and a fantastic father. Plus he has a romantic streak that pops out occasionally and which, even though I'm an old cynic and I would never admit this in public, makes me go weak at the knees.

He has a tendency to surprise me with things. Thought-ful surprises, not just the odd bunch of half-dead gerberas hastily grabbed at the petrol station. He once bought us tickets for the Eurostar to Paris. First class. But it wasn't the fact that he'd planned a weekend away in secret that really touched me, it was that he had thought of *everything*.

He'd arranged for the kids to stay with Alex and Isabel, asked Melanie if she'd mind if I had the Monday off, booked a taxi to take us to the station and one to pick us up from Gare du Nord, asked for a room with a terrace because he knows that I love to have somewhere to sit and look out when we go to a strange city, ordered cham-pagne and chocolates in the room. Everything. It must have taken hours of planning and although, to be really honest, I was knackered and my first thought was that I would rather have spent my days off flopping around the house doing not very much, his thoughtfulness blew me away. In the end we'd had the best weekend ever. Just the two of us reminding ourselves why we loved each other. It wasn't an isolated incident either. Over the years there have been hundreds of little surprises like that one.

I spend the morning drafting the new newsletter. We send one out to all the casting directors and producers three times a year, updating them on what all our clients are doing. This time Gary will, of course, feature heavily. It's a skill to make it sound as if everyone is massively success-ful and drowning in work, and yet might still be available if there were any jobs out there. I am giving it the once-over before I show it to Joshua and Melanie for approval when the phone rings again and another Mexican stand-off with Lorna begins. I have no idea whether she has a telephone phobia or whether she's just lazy. It's become a point of principle with me now. I just want her to answer the sodding phone. Just once. There will be five rings before it will automatically put itself on to answer-phone. Joshua and Melanie understandably go ballistic if calls go unanswered, but it always goes to the wire before one of us will relent and pick up. This time she's pretending to be engrossed in typing a contract so on ring three and a half I snatch up the receiver.

'Mortimer and Sheedy,' I say, trying to sound unflus-tered and not give away that I'm fuming because out of the ten or so calls we've received this morning I'd swear I've answered eight of them.

'Hey, you lost again,' a familiar voice says at the other end. Alex. He knows all about Phone Wars and it has always amused him to see who he'll get whenever he calls me at work. Thank God, I think. He hasn't taken offence at my rejection of him.

'Hi!' I say with genuine enthusiasm. 'How's it going?'

'OK,' he says. 'Not so good.'

'Oh. Are you having a bad day?' Post break-up Alex has bad days and not so bad days, but then I've always thought that Alex should have been the actor out of all of us. He's a drama queen. In a way that's always been part of his charm. An evening with Alex is never dull. He can turn the most mundane event into an epic comedy or tragedy. Plus he's the only person I know who can

22

make everyone feel sorry for him even though he's clearly the villain of the piece.

'Can you meet me for lunch?' he says. And then he drops the big one. 'I want to talk to you about what I said to you last night.'

I try to laugh it off. 'It's nothing. It's forgotten. Don't worry about it.'

'No,' he persists. 'It's not nothing. I need to see you.'

Clearly I'm boxed into a corner. He knows that I can't talk to him about this with Lorna listening in on the other side of the room. So I have to agree to have lunch with him although, to be honest, now that I know what's on his mind it's the last thing I want to do.

'It'll have to be a quick one,' I say. 'I'm busy.'

I suggest that Alex and I meet at YO! Sushi because it's fast and because if it all gets awkward I can bail out at any time without leaving loads of uneaten food on my plate. Something I'm genetically hard-wired not to be able to do. We both stare fixedly at the conveyor belt and I try to decide whether to wait for him to say what he's got to say or whether to try to head him off at the pass.

'Alex . . .' I begin, just as he starts speaking too.

'I meant it,' he's saying. 'I know you think it was just because I was drunk, but it wasn't. I'd been wanting to tell you for years. I never did, though, because of Dan . . .' He trails off. I know the idea of betraying Dan is not one he would ever take lightly.

'Alex, don't do this.'

'I just think that now I've said it, now you *know*, I have

23

to find out how you feel. I can't pretend it isn't there any more.'

He reaches over the table and tries to take my hand and I move it away, knocking over the soy sauce in the process. I fuss around, trying to mop it up.

'Why do you think things weren't right between me and Isabel? She didn't know but she must have sensed that my heart wasn't in it. Bex, you can't even begin to understand how hard it's been for me being in the same room as you and her and having to pretend that everything was perfect all these years . . .'

I'm angry with him again. I want this to stop. How dare he tell me this? This is not how our friendship is supposed to be. I decide that I have to shut it down once and for all.

'Alex, I meant what I said too. I have never thought of you like that and I never could. You're in a bad way because you've turned your life upside down, I understand that. You're going through something . . . some kind of . . . I don't know what . . .' I want to say mid-life crisis because that's undoubtedly what it is, but I know that he would take offence. '. . . breakdown. But this is not the solution. *I* am not the solution. It's never going to happen, OK? And what's more you're being disloyal to Dan. And let's not forget Isabel. Actually, you know what? I'm pissed off with you. I'm pissed off that you would put me in this position when you're meant to be one of my best friends.'

The conveyor belt is still chugging round but neither

of us has taken any food. He lowers his voice to a near whisper.

'I've felt like this for years. I just never had the courage. I –'

'OK,' I say, standing up. 'You have to stop this now. It's never going to happen and I never want to talk about it again. Let's just forget you ever said it and try to go back to the way we were.'

'I can't,' he says as I walk off, but I don't turn back.

4

Isabel calls me. I think about ignoring the call, letting her go straight to voicemail. I can't even begin to tell her what's been going on in my life. I never keep things from her but I know that this time I really have to. I hate not answering, though. To be honest, I feel like I've let her down a bit recently by consorting so much with the enemy. I haven't been as supportive as I could have been. It should be her spending every evening round at ours, not him, and I hate to think of her sitting in her big empty house miserable and needing someone to talk to. So I pick up.

'Hey,' I say. 'How's things?'

'Oh, you know,' she says.

'Do you want me to come over?' I say, and, although I'm hoping she'll say no because I'm halfway through cooking dinner and I promised to test William later on the speech he has to learn for his one scene in the class play, I'd hand everything over to Dan and go if she said yes.

'No, don't be silly. I'm fine,' she says. 'Maybe I'll see you at the weekend, though? I'm letting Alex have the girls on Saturday.'

'Definitely,' I say, making a decision to tell Dan that whatever Alex might want to do it's tough because I've made a date with Izz. 'We can spend the whole day together if you like.'

'Great,' she says, and she sounds so grateful that I feel even worse and when she asks me how I am I say, 'No, wait. First I have to say sorry for being such a crap friend and for not supporting you as much as I should have, and for not insisting that Dan kick Alex out.' It's a bit of an awkward moment because Isabel and I don't really do that soul-searching kind of stuff about our friendship. We've never needed to.

'It's OK,' she says, and she sounds like she means it. 'Dan is Alex's best mate so I kind of figured that things would be awkward for a while.'

'But you're *my* best mate. I should have put my foot down and that should have been that.'

'Bex, it's fine. But thank you.'

We say nothing for a few moments and then she says, 'How *is* Alex?'

'Actually I have no idea,' I say. 'He hasn't been around much lately. You've probably seen more of him than I have.'

'Well, yes,' she says. 'But the kids are always there.' She and Alex have worked out an elaborate child-share system, which Isabel thinks is grown-up and responsible of them. Alex, I know, thinks it is mean-spirited and immature. He wants to be able to visit the girls whenever he feels like it.

'Him leaving doesn't mean I don't still care about him,' she says. 'I want to know he's OK. After all, he is the father of my children.'

27

I'm not about to say, 'He's falling apart – and do you know how I know that? Because he's telling me he's in love with me.'

'He's fine, I think. You know Alex. Like I said, I haven't seen him for a while.'

And it's true. Alex hasn't been round for nearly two weeks. He and Dan have been out a couple of times and I've faked sickness or the need for an early night. I just don't want to see him at the moment. Dan has taken the fact that Alex has stopped using our sofa bed as a hotel as a good sign. He thinks it means that he is getting back on his feet, but I know otherwise. Luckily Dan has been snowed under at work and he hasn't really felt like going out much anyway, otherwise he might have noticed my reluctance or Alex's refusal of any offers to come round. I know it'll all blow over. Not for the first time I curse Alex for getting us all into this situation in the first place. Was life with Isabel really that bad that he couldn't just put up with it? For my sake, I find myself thinking, and then I remember that it's not all about me.

It's funny but when they were together, much as I loved them both, I often used to wonder what it was that Alex and Isabel saw in each other. Beyond the surface things, that is. They were such different people – Alex with his caustic wit and his egocentric universe, Isabel so much more gentle, but equally as entrenched in her opinions. They never agreed on anything, but their opposing viewpoints had got to be a routine so I guess I just never took them seriously. That was just how they were.

Alex is a writer and an impoverished one at that, and I know it used to drive Isabel crazy that he couldn't just get a job and write in his spare time. Which I guess I understood until they had the twins and he did all the house-husband stuff when Isabel went back to work. In fact, I used to envy her for the way that she could say goodbye to the kids in the morning, knowing that some-one who loved them as much as she did was going to be looking after them, and then not have to see them again until nearly bed time. Not that I didn't love staying at home with my two – I did. It was just . . . exhausting. Plus, Isabel loves her job (she's a graphic designer) and so it was no great hardship for her to go back to work. But I think she still made him feel bad about it. Emas-culated him, I guess. And I think she had a way of making him feel inadequate because he earned so much less than her (nothing, pretty much, if truth be told). Not deliberately. She would never have done that. But it was there between them, nevertheless. I always thought it wasn't really fair that she was doing exactly what she wanted but making him feel bad for trying to do the same.

And, to give Alex credit, he did use to have a job. Somewhere back in the dim and distant past he had a 'promising future in the City'. But he hated it, the stress and the cut and thrust of it all. He hated the hours and the dry soulless office. He earned an awful lot in a very short time and he nearly lost himself in the process. He'd finally told Isabel he needed to take some time out to pursue his passion and she had happily said OK. I assume she just never imagined he'd be no further on twelve years later.

Actually, I worry that Alex is a shit writer. He gave me one of his plays to read once – hoping, I think, that with my connections I could help him get it produced or, worse, give it to Joshua in the hope that he might see Alex's potential and offer to take him on as a client. God, it was awful. All middle-aged existential angst about being forced to settle down and have children. All, of course, thrown into relief when one of said children gets knocked down by a bus and nearly dies. Nothing that hasn't been rehashed a million times already by an army of male mid-life-crisis writers. Turgid, worthy, sentimental. He warned me it might make me cry and it nearly did, out of frustration because I had to finish it and because of the fear of what I was going to say to him about it (shit, clichéd and melodramatic not being the words he was looking for I suspected).

In the end I settled for 'very thought provoking' and told him that really I only knew people who made musicals and farces, not real theatre. Try the Royal Court, I said. I'm sure it's right up their alley but unfortunately I don't have any connections there. He sent it in and I assume they just sent it straight back after a cursory read because, truly, by page ten you knew it was a dog. Anyway, he didn't mention it to me again and I certainly wasn't going to bring it up. So, maybe Isabel was right all along, but it still felt mean to disabuse him of his dream and, besides, she earned enough to indulge him.

So, in all honesty, despite the fact that Isabel's my

closest girlfriend, I always thought in the back of my mind, that maybe Alex would be happier with someone else. And so would she. Not that I ever wanted that to happen. I loved our little clique. It couldn't have been more perfect that Dan's best friend ended up married to my best friend. And now they've split up I just want them to get back together. I want everything to be back to normal.

The 'who's a pretty boy' act is driving me especially crazy today. She's eating pomegranate seeds. Red juice is getting all over the papers on her desk and she's got stuff round her mouth like a two-year-old who's been chewing raspberry jelly. I hold my breath waiting for the next sucky noise followed by the little crunch. Part of the reason I find Lorna's dietary habits so mind-numbingly annoying is that she's tiny. There's not an ounce of fat on her eight-and-a-half-stone frame.

So partly, I guess, you might be forgiven for reading it as jealousy because I am on the fat side. Not 'you'll have to take the side of my house off if you want to get me out' fat but fat-ish. Plump. I have that trunky thing going on. Big tits, skinny legs but a big thick trunk in between with no waist, a fat stomach and absolutely no arse to speak of. Like a pillar-box with a head and two bits of string dangling down, someone once said to me.

Like all women blessed with a body like mine I have succumbed to dressing in a way that I despise – low-cut top to distract the eye with my cleavage, short skirt as if to say, 'Look, I can't be fat – I have skinny legs.' It kind

31

of works when you're twenty but at forty-one I know I have the potential to look like Bet Lynch. If I put on anything baggy, I resemble a marquee. So I've settled for blousy but with a lot of vintage and retro prints that I vainly hope will make me look interesting.

Lorna, on the other hand, is like an ironing board, which is not a good look either, in my opinion. Actually, she's like a bony ironing board. I imagine you could play the xylophone on her ribs (don't ask me why you'd want to). Everything about her is hard and angular and unfeminine. I may admit to an occasional pang of envy when I see those rare women who are both curvaceous and slim, but Lorna? No thank you. Give me lardy over skeletal any day. The point is that she doesn't need to diet. And she certainly doesn't need to keep going on about how big she's getting and 'look at my stomach' or 'have I got a double chin?'.

As well as Phone Wars she has several other weapons in her armoury. She's a master of work-avoidance techniques for a start. When I first started working part time I would go in on a Tuesday and she would usually give me a few tasks that she hadn't had time to complete the day before. I would diligently work my way through whatever Melanie and Joshua gave me to do and then, if possible, would help Lorna out too. There were a few occasions where there was simply too much and, at the end of the day, I would apologetically pass a few bits and pieces back to her. I soon started to realize that when I went back for the second time that week, on Thursday, the uncompleted tasks would still be uncompleted and would be piled up on my desk again.

OK, so this didn't seem like too much of a big deal until one day when Melanie asked Lorna why such and such a job hadn't been done and Lorna piped up, 'Oh, I asked Rebecca to do that. Has she not done it? I told her it was important.'

She never acknowledged what had really happened, even in private to me. And I was too new and unconfident to challenge her. Subsequently I would break my back to get through my own work *and* hers until one day, about three months later, after I genuinely hadn't been able to finish what she'd given me the previous Tuesday, and either Joshua or Melanie had queried it, I had simply said, 'Oh, Lorna, remember I told you I hadn't had time to do that on Tuesday. If you weren't going to be able to do it yourself, you should have told me then,' and I'd smiled sweetly at her as I'd said it. She'd got a little better after that.

Now I'm full time I'm wise to all her moves, but that doesn't mean she doesn't still try. Whenever I go out at lunchtime there's always a note on my desk when I get back as if someone has called to ask me to do something. 'Melissa says can you get her the pages for her audition on Friday,' was one. Most actors are happy just to be handed their scenes when they arrive at an audition, but Melissa is dyslexic so we always ask for her to get them a day early. It's common practice. I'm happy to call up and ask for them. The point is that Melissa didn't phone *me* to ask *me* to get them, she phoned to ask for *someone* to get them and, since Lorna was the one who spoke to her you would think that she would do it. But no.

Once she left me a note that said, 'Simon Harte called and asked if you could change the time of his costume fitting at the Shaftesbury to three rather than two,' and I absolutely knew that she was lying, because Simon Harte was a new client and didn't even know I existed yet. It must have taken her longer to write the note than it would have taken for her to phone and change the appointment herself. But, of course, that wasn't the issue. It's a power thing.

Lorna is forty-two and single. Occasionally she gets even more twittery than usual for a few days, and pays a lot of attention to her appearance, and I know it's because she's seeing someone. Then a couple of days later, inevitably, she'll look all teary-eyed and weepy so it's clear that it's all gone wrong. She spends an inordinate amount of time on her computer and I'm convinced she's checking out dating websites. I never ask her about her love life and, surprisingly, it's the one detail of her life that she doesn't feel compelled to burden me with, but I get the impression she's desperate to settle down and have kids. I imagine she scares off all the men she meets by asking them what their intentions are during the starter, and then moving on to their sperm count and whether there are any hereditary diseases in their families by dessert.

When I'm feeling generous, which isn't often, I feel sorry for her. She's not really a bad person. And I know that I lucked out when I met Dan otherwise there but for the grace of God and all that. Other times, though, I want to slap her and tell her it's all her own fault that she's on her own because she never effing shuts up. (I'm trying to wean myself off swearing, by the way, ever since I heard William, my youngest, telling his grandmother that his birthday present was 'fucking marvellous'. I tried to blame it on Grand Theft Auto, but William despises computer games.) She would drive any man crazy after five minutes, but, thankfully, I've never actually said this to her yet. Although I think evil thoughts about her I would never want to knowingly hurt her, or anyone else for that matter. So I try to hold my tongue. My biting but devastatingly witty comments remain in my head.

The fact that I am so intolerant is one of the things I dislike most about myself. It's a hard-fought contest because I am a master in the art of self-loathing. From the physical (my weight; my crêpy cleavage; my feet or more specifically my toes, which are short and stumpy; the bump in my nose) to the behavioural (my fear of change, my inability to do anything about my weight despite the fact that it makes me miserable, the way I always judge people before I meet them, my refusal to even pretend I can tolerate fools), I can find a million different ways to beat myself up about my failings. On a good day, when I'm being really honest with myself, I can acknowledge (only privately, of course), that I'm basically a good person. I'm a good wife, a caring mother and, usually, recent times with Isabel aside, a loyal and supportive friend. I give money to homeless people sometimes and I always sign up when I'm stopped by those charity muggers in the street. I just don't like people I don't know. Or idiots. Or my feet. Or Lorna, for that matter.

I've noticed that today she is looking quite smart, apart from the pomegranate detritus, so I'm guessing she's got a date tonight. Jim, forty, interests: listening, nodding and being bored to death. Would like to learn to play the xylophone. Well, good luck to her. Maybe once she does finally talk some poor bloke into submission she'll calm down a bit and shut up and do her job properly.

Actually, she's been making more of an effort looks-wise for a couple of weeks now. Plus she's been answering the phone, which is always a sign that she has a man on the go. Ever since I picked up once and it was her latest boyfriend and I told him she had just nipped out to the doctor's to get the results of her chlamydia test. I can't remember why. She'd annoyed me somehow. By the time she'd realized who it was I was talking to he'd hung up. It was no great disaster. She'd rung him back and explained and it had all been fine. He dumped her a few weeks later anyhow I seem to remember. I found out when she came in all red eyed with no make-up on one day and Phone Wars commenced again.

She's chattering on, of course, and I realize I haven't heard a word she's said for about an hour now, so I do what I always do, which is nod and smile and pretend I'm agreeing with whatever it is I've missed. Then I notice she's getting up and putting her coat on so I realize I've agreed to her going for lunch first even though it's meant to be my turn. Fine. It's an hour's peace either way.

I use the time to call Zoe on her mobile. I can tell she's

with her friends because she doesn't say anything that gives away that it's her mother she's speaking to.

'Hey,' she says when she answers.

'Hi, sweetie. Are you OK?'

'Mmm hmm.'

She's not exactly forthcoming so I cut to the chase. 'Have you seen William today?'

Zoe's worst nightmare has come true. Her uncool little brother has landed up at her school and I'm expecting her to keep an eye on him at break time.

'No,' she says, reverting to her thirteen-year-old self and giving the word two extra syllables.

'Well, could you maybe look out for him in the canteen?'

William is nowhere near as socially confident as his sister. He's – how can I put this? He's . . . a bit weird, people who don't love him as much as I do might think. He's into science and history and he likes to dress a bit like a nineteenth-century fop. He hates his name being shortened and always corrects people if they call him Will. He's a total one-off and I adore him for it. What he's not is ready for the social fascism of the Barnsbury Road comprehensive. I worry about him.

'Just try and have a sneaky look out for him,' I say. 'Check he's OK.'

Zoe says nothing.

'Oh, and eat some lunch,' I add just before she says a hurried, 'Later,' and hangs up.

Zoe, like Lorna, is on a permanent diet. Like Lorna, she is as skinny as a rake and I keep myself up at night

37

imagining her wasting away to nothing then years of force-feeding followed by an early death from a weakened heart. I have a tendency to indulge myself in worst-case scenario fantasies about the people I love. It's a defence mechanism, I think. If I torture myself by imagining how I'd cope with the bleakest possible horrors, then I figure I can deal with whatever shit actually does occur. I force myself not to think about William spending his dinner hour alone or, worse, being bullied by gangs of older boys. I can't call him. We bought him a phone when he started his new school two weeks ago and he lost it on day one. He loses everything.

By the time I get home in the evening both the kids are there, limbs intact, and no one's fighting. Zoe even helps me cook dinner for once, which makes me think she wants something but I stop myself from asking what it is – 'Are you pregnant?' being perhaps a slight over-reaction to your daughter offering to peel the potatoes. William is in one piece and is talking about his new friend Sam who is in his class and who, apparently, has a micro-scope set up in his bedroom to examine dust for bed bugs. Great. That'll help William on his entry into high society. Still, I tell myself, at least he has a friend. Dan is on his way home early, his last appointment having been cancelled. All is right with the world. And then my mobile rings. William picks it up.

'It's Uncle Alex,' he says, and before I can say anything he answers.

I'm thrown into a momentary panic. I haven't spoken to Alex since our lunch. Probably the longest period of no communication we've ever had because even when one of us is on holiday he and Dan talk all the time and I usually pop on to the phone to say hello.

'Bed bugs,' William is saying. 'They live off the dead skin you leave on your sheets. Millions of them.'

I think about leaving the room as if I have to go to the toilet, but I know that William will only follow me and there's no way I can explain to him that I don't want to talk to his favourite uncle. Too late, anyway. William is holding the phone out to me.

'Mum,' he's saying impatiently. 'Wake up.' 'Wake up' is one of William's favourite expressions. He thinks it's hilarious.

'Hi, Alex,' I say, trying to sound friendly but business-like. 'How are you doing?'

'Great,' he says. 'Fantastic, actually.'

Really? He does sound cheerful, in fact, something that has been missing for the past couple of months or so.

'That's good,' I say cautiously. I hope it's true. I hope he's come out the other end of whatever he was going through and that he feels like his old self again. Maybe he'll see sense, move back home and we can all write his recent behaviour off to temporary insanity.

'Really,' he says. 'Actually, Rebecca, that's why I'm ringing you.' He pauses for dramatic effect. 'I've met someone. A woman.'

'Gosh,' I say, sounding like a schoolgirl from the 1930s, but I don't know what else to say. I don't know how I feel. I should be delighted for him but a part of me wants to say, 'Hold on, what was all that crap about you being in love with me, then? Why did you just put me through that?' I momentarily consider whether I might be jealous, whether any part of me was actually getting off on the fact that he wanted me, but the answer is definitely no.

'Well?' he says.

'Alex, that's brilliant. I'm really pleased for you. Honestly.'

'Are you?' he says, and I think I detect a tiny hint of disappointment there.

'Absolutely.'

'Good,' he says. 'Because I was worried because of . . . you know. I wanted to apologize, by the way, for putting you on the spot like that. I've realized now it was just an aberration, fear of ending up on my own, something like that.'

'Exactly,' I say. 'So, who is she?'

'She's great,' he says, and he's brimming over with enthusiasm so I forget everything that's gone on between us and I feel genuinely happy for him. It'll be good to have the old Alex back.

'She's kind and clever. And she gets me. She's really supportive about my writing.'

Implicit in that last statement is the fact that I was not. I change the subject. 'Where did you meet her? More to the point when can *we* meet her?'

'Oh, you already have,' he says with a hint of triumph.

'Really? Who? Tell me?' I'm hoping it's that nice Nadia from the girls' school. The teaching assistant.

She's single, or at least she still was when William left in the summer. I think he asked her to marry him on the last day.

'It's Lorna.'

I feel my heart quicken a little. 'Lorna?'

'Your Lorna from work.' He gives me a moment to let the full horror sink in. I'm speechless. My mouth opens and shuts without anything coming out.

'I knew you'd be surprised,' the master of understatement says. 'We met at that opening night, remember?'

I do, of course, remember. How could I forget that I thought he'd find it funny?

'Anyway,' he carries on. 'I liked her so I decided to call and see if she fancied a drink.'

I know what he's doing. He's so deluded that he thinks this will tip me over the edge so that I have to admit that I love him after all. Well, fine, two can play at that game.

'I really am pleased for you,' I say. 'I know you think she and I don't get on, but if it makes you happy . . .'

'Oh, she told me she's tried to get along with you.'

I bite my tongue. How dare she? She's made no effort, ever, to be anything other than mean-spirited and difficult. But I'm not going to let him see he's getting to me.

'Enjoy yourself. You deserve some happiness. We'll see you soon.'

That'll teach him. I wonder how long he'll be able to keep it up or whether weepy red-eyed Lorna will be back at her desk tomorrow in place of the more glamorous alter ego. But then he plays his trump card.

'Yes, you will. In about an hour, in fact. Dan just invited us over for dinner.'

He pretty much hangs up before I can respond although truthfully I have no idea how I would have responded if I was given the time. I call Dan immediately.

'What the fuck . . .?' Swearing embargo out of the window. This is too serious.

'I know, I know,' he interrupts. 'But what could I do? He asked me if he could bring his new girlfriend over and I said yes before he told me who she was. At least that explains where he's been the past few weeks. I was beginning to think I'd done something to upset him.' That's so typical. Dan always assumes that he must be to blame for everything even though he never puts a foot wrong.

'Oh God,' I say. 'Anyone but Lorna.'

Dan has met Lorna a couple of times over the years so he knows where I'm coming from. He laughs. 'I know. But look at it this way. Alex is just dipping his toe back into the water. He just needs to have a bit of fun to help him back in the game.'

'Fun? Lorna?' I can't stop myself saying.

'Maybe that's the wrong word. Just think of her as a stepping stone. She's a transitional step on the way to some fantastic woman he's going to meet in the future.'

I grunt. 'He had a fantastic woman already. He doesn't deserve another one.'

'We can make it an early one,' Dan says, ignoring my last comment. 'Only make one course and make it something we can shovel in and get rid of them by nine.'

I laugh despite myself. 'Soup,' I say. 'That way we don't even have to wait for them to chew.'

'Perfect,' Dan says.

Rebecca and Daniel, Alex and Lorna. It doesn't even sound right.

5

So, here they are standing on my doorstep. Alex and Lorna. Holding hands like love's young dream. He has a smug expression on his face that says 'see what you've made me do?' while she is smirking at me triumphantly.

'Hi,' I say with as much enthusiasm as I can muster, which isn't much. 'Come in.'

Dan is all smiles. 'Hi, mate,' he says, getting Alex into a bear hug before he can even take off his coat. 'Hi, Lorna.'

He couldn't look happier for them. I know he has reservations too, but he's determined not to show them. He's so desperate for his friend to be back to his old uncomplicated, cheerful self that he'd be happy if Alex went out with Myra Hindley so long as she made him smile. I stand slightly paralysed by the front door. Am I really going to have to invite Lorna into my home? Into my life?

Too late.

'Come on in,' Dan is saying. And he manoeuvres them through to the living room. At least, that's what he tries to do. Lorna has other ideas and follows me into the kitchen.

'I bet this is a surprise! I've been dying to tell you,' she gushes, as if we really were friends, the kind who never keep secrets from each other. 'Only we thought we should wait a few weeks. Alex thought you might find it a bit . . . you know.'

'No,' I say defensively. 'A bit what?'

'A bit awkward, what with us working together.'

Oh, so not awkward because he only just finished telling me I was the love of his life, then? I'm angry. I know exactly why he's doing this. It's pathetic.

'He wanted to tell you himself but then he said he had to wait because things had been a bit funny between you lately so he didn't like to call you.'

Great. So Alex is already confiding in her about me although not, of course, the whole truth. That would be too much to hope for. I decide not to rise to the bait, which though unintentional is just as infuriating.

'So, when did you get together?' I ask in an effort to be friendly.

'Well, we met at Gary's opening – you know that. After all, you introduced us!'

There's an implied exclamation point at the end of her sentence as there almost always is.

'And then Alex called me at work the next day and asked me if I wanted to go out!'

The day after I told him I wasn't interested. The day we had lunch and he told me all over again that he was in love with me. What a coincidence. I almost feel sorry for her.

She's still talking. 'I can't believe you didn't notice anything. Didn't you wonder why I'd started going out for lunch every day?'

'No,' I say. 'I didn't.'

Thinking about it, she has been going out more than usual. Usually she brings her lunch with her – crispy lettuce, Ryvita, carrots, the noisiest diet food she can find – and sits crunching at her desk. She always insists I stay and answer the phones while she eats because she's on her break, so I have to sit there counting the seconds between bites, cringing every time she lifts a bit of food to her lips.

'Anyway we've been spending all of our time together and I know it's only been a few weeks but I think it might be serious. You know, I think we might end up moving in together or something!'

I'm chopping salad. I have a knife in my hand. It's tempting. Instead I say, 'Do you want a glass of wine? Dinner'll be ready in a few minutes.'

Just get them fed, get them out of here and then Alex can feel he's made his point and hopefully we can all get back to normal.

Of course dinner goes on for hours. Alex is so hell bent on showing me how over it he is, how happy with his new love, that he's the life and soul of the party, and Dan is just so relieved that he matches him drink for drink and they guffaw away at each other's stories until at one point the kids, who have eaten early and then gone to Zoe's bedroom to watch TV, come in and William says, 'Are you still here?'

'More to the point, are you still up?' Dan says, looking at his watch.

'Well, there was no point trying to sleep with all the racket you're making,' Zoe says, and she's got a point. God knows what the neighbours downstairs think.

Lorna is a bit drunk too and laughing uproariously at everything Alex says, funny or not. He's in storytelling mode and regales her with all sorts of tales about our exploits that I would rather she didn't know. He tells her about the time only a couple of months ago when we'd all been out for a boozy dinner and drunk way too much, and I fell down the kerb getting into the taxi and then couldn't get up again I was laughing so much.

'I think she called in sick the next day,' he says. 'Food poisoning.'

'Oh,' Lorna says, wide-eyed. 'I remember when you said you had food poisoning! Well, next time I'll know that just means you've had a few too many!'

I try and laugh along with them, but the truth is I'm embarrassed. Like everyone does when they call in sick, I remember that I'd made a big deal of going into what I'd eaten, trying to make it sound genuine. Protesting too much, Dan always calls it. He says I should just call up and say I'm not coming in, I don't feel well, without going into all the details because that's where you get caught out. And he's right, clearly.

'I always thought you were such a goody-goody,' Lorna says. 'Joshua and Melanie are always going on about how hard you work and aren't you great.'

'And don't even ask her what she'd been doing the night before she called up and said she had a migraine that time,' Alex says, and I say, 'OK, Alex, I think Lorna's

47

heard enough stories about my sick days. Can we change the subject?' I can't even remember what incident he's alluding to but whatever it is I don't want to share it with the group. I start to clear the table and even collect glasses, which, I think, says very firmly that dinner is over. No one makes an effort to move so I give Dan a look that he can't fail to ignore.

'Right,' he says, standing up. 'I've got an early start in the morning so I'm going to throw you out now.'

Before they have a chance to protest he busies himself getting coats and opening the front door, practically herding them outside. Lorna gives me a hug, which unnerves me, and says thank you so much for dinner and I'll see you at work tomorrow.

Alex smirks and says, 'Maybe we could all go out at the weekend?' and I want to punch him.

'He's just doing it to piss me off,' I say to Dan as he closes the front door.

'Why would he do that?' Dan says, bemused, and of course I can't tell him why so I just shrug my shoulders. 'He obviously likes her,' he adds.

'It won't last,' is the only parting shot I can muster as I stomp off to bed.

6

It's *Spotlight* time for our actor clients, which means that I am having to ring them all to hassle them for a head shot to go into the casting directors' bible. That way, if anyone is looking for a young leading man or an older character actor, they will see our boys lined up side by side with the great and good, and they might actually think about auditioning them. Some of them are too tight to shell out for a new photo each year so they stay looking forever twenty-seven when, in actuality, they are coming up for forty. Others favour a montage of pictures of themselves wearing a variety of hats as if this shows their versatility. And a few are guaranteed to straight out refuse to pay for the service so it's my job to try and persuade them that it's in their interests. Usually this involves offering to pay the cost for them up front and telling them they can reimburse Mortimer and Sheedy when they have some money coming in. Which for some of them will be never.

It's a time-consuming task and so I decided to come in early today to make lists and try to get ahead of the game. It's easy to lose track of who I've spoken to and who I've just left messages for, let alone what they are intending to do. So I'm letting myself in the front door, tall skinny wet latte in one hand and a Danish in the other when this is what I hear coming from Melanie's office:

'. . . and then she couldn't get up because she was laughing so much, and, of course, she was really drunk. Isn't that hilarious? I mean, I always thought Rebecca was so prim and proper.'

Laugh, laugh from Melanie. Melanie has a snorty laugh that I could pick out of a line-up if I had to, although I'm struggling to imagine a scenario in which that might be required.

'Me too.'

'And Alex said that in the end it took him and Daniel *and* the taxi driver to get her into the taxi . . .'

Enough. Humiliated, I back out of the front door and then open it again noisily, rattling my keys and coughing like I've spent my life down the pit. Lorna emerges from Melanie's office, big innocent smile on her face.

'Oh hi. We were just talking about you.'

'Right.' Hardly genius, but I don't know what else to say.

'That was a great night, last night. I had a really good time.'

'Good.'

'Wasn't that funny when . . .'

I interrupt her. 'I have to concentrate, sorry,' I say, sitting at my desk and staring intently at whatever is lying there. A list of what I had intended to buy from M&S on the way home the previous evening, I think it is. I stare at it for way too long, to make my point. Eventually she sits down and turns her computer on and I figure it's safe to look up again.

I'm finding it hard to shake off my irritation, though, and stupidly I open up the whole channel of communication again.

'Lorna,' I say, trying not to sound as irritated as I am, 'I'd rather you didn't discuss my personal stuff with Melanie or Joshua. They don't need to know about me getting drunk and falling over.'

Now I've started I can't stop.

'And, just for your information, that happened months ago and was a complete one-off. Now they'll think it happens all the time. Like I go out every night and drink myself stupid.'

Lorna is looking at me like a puppy who has just been told off for chewing up the carpet. What? What have I done? I'm innocent!

'I heard you,' I say, as if that isn't obvious. What am I, clairvoyant?

'I just thought it was a funny story,' she says, all big eyes.

I'm terrified she's going to cry on me. She has a habit of turning on the tears when it suits her. She does it all the time with Joshua in particular. It always works. It somehow seems to make him forget she's a forty-two-year-old woman with a mortgage and an eating disorder, and he comes over all paternal and completely forgets whatever it was he was having a go at her for. I put it down to the fact that his only daughter left home last year to go to university and he's feeling a bit unneeded.

51

Anyway, I need to divert the tear train before it gets to the station because there's no way I'm going to be getting on board.

'Fine,' I say. 'I was just saying, maybe in future, you know . . .'

'OK,' she says in a pained voice. 'I'm sorry.'

'I said it's fine. Don't worry about it, OK?'

So she sits snivelling at her computer for a few minutes and then flounces off in the direction of the ladies,' almost bumping into Joshua who is coming out of the kitchen, clearly having given up on waiting for one of us to offer him a cup of tea.

'Are you all right?' he says, all concerned.

'Yes, I'm OK,' Lorna says in a voice that manages to convey 'no, I'm not, that nasty bitch upset me'. Joshua shoots me an accusatory look. Round one to Lorna.

Lorna has been at Mortimer and Sheedy for ten years, since she was thirty-two. She had been drifting around in a variety of secretarial jobs and junior management positions ever since she left college, never finding anything that made her feel passionate, until she walked into the little attic rooms of Mortimer and Sheedy for an interview and fell in love. Now she had found her niche she was fiercely ambitious. She decided that she would stay there for three years or so, learning everything there was to learn about contracts and castings and how to keep clients happy as well as earning them money, then look for a position as an agent at one of the larger, better known, theatrical agencies. But before she knew it

Mortimer and Sheedy felt like home, Joshua and Melanie like family. Now she couldn't imagine working anywhere else, even if it meant that her career had stalled. How do I know this? She told me, breathlessly recounting the whole story of her life, in the first thirty seconds of meeting me, while I nervously sipped my bottle of water and waited for my interview. I was going back to work for the first time since Zoe was born, seven years before. I wanted to work two days a week from nine thirty till six, and I wanted my office to be on the Piccadilly line. Those were the only criteria. I would have walked the streets if the hours and location were right. William had just started school and I wanted a no-pressure job where a day taken off because a child had a temperature wouldn't be viewed as a disaster.

Like Lorna, I guess I never realized how much I would come to love what I do. I've been here six years. Six years of listening to her prattle on. Sometimes it feels like a lifetime.

We sit in subtext-laden silence for most of the afternoon. Lorna in the wounded corner, me in the righteously indignant. As you know, I take no pleasure from upsetting her but it does, at least, shut her up. Which means that I can get all my calls and callbacks made and, by five thirty, I have cajoled all our boys into parting with their money and I'm heading out the door. Lorna has barely looked up from her work all day and I'm feeling bad so as I leave I smile and say, 'I'm sorry if it came across like I was angry with you earlier. I really wasn't having a go. See you tomorrow.'

She looks up at me, Bambi eyes moist, poor-me smile, and says, 'Oh, that's fine. It's forgotten. Bye, Rebecca,' in the most insincere way possible.

Dan and I spend a blissful evening in front of the TV while William crawls around looking for baby spiders with an old magnifying glass he's found, and Zoe sits on her bed, iPod on, oblivious to the world. I try to explain the frustration of my day to Dan but it's hard without sounding petty and about ten years old. After all, what am I really saying? I had a go at Lorna because she was talking to Melanie about me and then she got upset. I can't seem to get across the passive aggressiveness of her, the way that I know the whole situation is being manipulated to make her the victim and me the aggressor. That's the whole point of Lorna. She's good at what she does. You have to be there to really appreciate it, to take in all the nuances. To realize that although she's not actually doing anything wrong she's doing *everything* wrong because of the way in which she does it. I try to imitate her little girl voice, her watery-eyed half smile, her ever so subtle accusations, but I only succeed in making her sound like Little Nell and me like the hunchback bully chasing after her.

'You know we're going to have to see them at the weekend,' Dan says eventually.

'I know,' I say. 'I'll be good.'

And I mean it. I do. I will try.

I get to work before her in the morning and I'm pottering around making coffee, minding my own business, when Joshua sticks his head round the kitchen door and asks me if I have a moment. I think about saying no. Someone asking you if you have a moment is almost never a good thing. But clearly I am doing nothing much so I offer him a coffee, which he accepts and then I follow him into his office.

Joshua has this avuncular thing going on. He's only fifty-three but as soon as I'm in his presence I forget that he is a mere twelve years older than me and I revert to being six. I want him to tell me I've been good. I put it down to the fact that he has white hair and a kind, craggy face, prematurely aged from years of smoking twenty-odd Silk Cut a day. That and the fact that I have always been in awe of authority. If a policeman so much as says hello to me, I become grovelling and subservient despite the fact that (1) I have never done anything wrong and (2) he is probably young enough to be my son. With the doctor I'm even worse. She must only be my age but I always find myself apologizing for wasting her time, practically doffing my cap in deference to her greatness. Before I go in I always give myself a pep talk. Be confident. Be demanding. If she tries to brush off the importance of your symptoms, insist on your right to have tests. So she spent four more years at university than you. So what? It never works. I know without a doubt that one of these days I am going to die of some trivial ailment left untreated because I was too much of a wimp to question her judgement.

'So, how's things?' Joshua asks, and I immediately feel nervous and put on the spot. What things?

'Oh, fine,' I say. 'Good.'

We sit there in silence for a moment while he tries to summon up the courage to say whatever it is he really wants to say to me. Joshua hates having to engage in the trivia, the office politics. I look at my hands and out of the window at the attic rooms above the shops across the road.

'You know how much we value you, Melanie and I,' he says, and my heart sinks. This doesn't sound like he's about to offer me a pay rise, which is a shame because I was intending to ask him for one, one of these days. Only after I'd spent a week on an assertiveness course obviously.

'Thank you,' I say, although for what I don't know.

'You're an integral part of this company. The clients all love you.' OK, so maybe this is starting to sound a bit better. At least it doesn't sound like he's about to give me my P45 and then show me the door.

Joshua's still talking. 'It's just, well, sometimes you can be a little – how shall I put this? – abrupt.'

'Abrupt?' I have no idea what he's going on about. He's just said the clients all like me and I know that I have good relationships with the producers, directors and casting people I have to deal with. Some of them have become more like friends – work friends, not real friends, of course – ones I'll have a coffee or a quick drink after work with. Often I pick up good tip-offs about upcoming productions.

'Not . . .' he says, and then runs out of steam a bit.

'Well, let's put it this way. I think Lorna sometimes finds you a bit domineering . . .'

I miss the rest of what he's saying because all the blood has rushed from helping my ears to work and into my brain to try to calm it down before I explode. So that's what this is about. Lorna must have gone crying to Joshua last night after I'd left. Boo hoo. Rebecca's bullying me.

I cut Joshua off. 'So Lorna's complained about me?'

'No, no, of course not,' Joshua lies, flustered now that he might have made the situation worse. 'I just noticed that she seemed a bit upset yesterday, that's all.'

I resist the temptation to ask him why he would think that Lorna's state of mind might have anything to do with me if she really hasn't said anything. There's no point. He's clearly protecting her. I can't win except to take my telling off and get back to work.

'Well, if I have upset her I can't imagine why,' I say. And then I add, 'I mean, I certainly didn't intend to.'

'I'm sure you didn't. It's just . . . you know what she's like . . .'

Yes I do. Conniving, manipulative, lazy, need I say more?

'. . . She's very sensitive. I'm only saying this to you and not to her because I know you won't get upset. I just think you should make more of an effort to get along.'

He must be able to see that my face is going purple because he adds, 'Both of you, I mean. Not just you. I hate to have an atmosphere in the office. It's not good for business.'

I take a deep breath. This is so unjust. But I know I have nothing to gain by snapping at Joshua.

'Of course,' I say. 'I'm sorry you think there's been a problem. There really hasn't.'

He smiles his Uncle Josh smile. 'I expect she was just overreacting,' he says, thus giving away that Lorna did indeed lodge a complaint.

'How are you getting on with *Spotlight*?' he asks, subject well and truly changed.

'All done,' I say, and I manage a smile. 'No problems.'

'Nice work,' he says, and looks down at some papers on his desk. I take my cue to leave.

Back in reception Lorna is taking off her coat. She's five minutes late as usual. She gives me a big innocent smile.

'Morning,' she says breezily.

'Oh, hello,' I say in a manner that I hope is slightly menacing but not so much so that it would stand up in court.

7

It's Friday evening. Fabulous, wonderful, no work for two whole days, I-can-do-anything Friday evening. Even though these days I rarely do anything on a Friday evening other than cook and watch TV with Dan and the kids I still always feel that rush of excitement as I leave work. The world's my oyster. Anything is possible. I have all the time in the world and no one to tell me what to do with it. You know, of course, what I'm about to say: except for this weekend. This Friday evening has been hijacked by the enemy. We are going to a restaurant with Alex and Lorna. I am entering my own personal hell.

The table is booked for seven thirty and Lorna has been fussing all day about what am I wearing and what time should we get there or should we meet up somewhere else first for a drink (no). You'd think she'd never been to a restaurant before.

The kids are going to spend the night at Isabel's. Zoe is furious. At thirteen she thinks she is old enough to stay home on her own and I have to explain to her for the hundredth time that she is (I'm lying), but what she is not is old enough to look after her brother. William, in typical mad-inventor fashion, has a tendency to get absorbed in things. Tiny details that most mere mortals would brush past without a second thought – trying to discover why an ant took a particular route along the kitchen windowsill, for example, or why the light coming through the window is refracting in a certain way, fascinating stuff like that – and he will forget that he has left the bath running or some baked beans frazzling in a saucepan. He's a walking hazard.

William, unlike his sister, is happy to go and see the twins. He's alternately besotted in a quiet, hopeless way with each of them. I always know when his allegiance changes because he will start saying, 'Natalie/Nicola is much cleverer than Nicola/Natalie,' or, 'Nicola/Natalie has much nicer hair than Natalie/Nicola.' He mooches about after his current chosen one with a lovesick expression on his face, and tries to engage with them by showing them frog spawn or, once, some hedgehog droppings ('See those shiny bits? That's where it's been eating beetles.') and the girls tend to just scream and say, 'You're gross,' and run away.

They never fall out, though, because William never takes offence, he just keeps plodding along his devoted path with the dogged, slow persistence of a zombie after its human prey. And the girls love the fact that he will always do their bidding in any way they want – fetching them drinks, doing their chores and, on more than one occasion, allowing them to play 'dress up' with him, which means he comes home in full make-up and wearing their clothes. Isabel and I have wondered before whether we should put a stop to it, whether the girls are bullying him, but we've come to the conclusion that they're not. They're always sweet to him; they always say please. If he ever refused one of their requests, I think they'd be fine, it's just that he never does. He doesn't seem to mind. He'll make some dominatrix a lovely husband one day.

By seven we're ready to go out. Alex has taken the kids over to Isabel's for us so he can have a quick visit with the twins before he has to pick Lorna up. I sit at the kitchen table trying to summon up the energy to move.

'You look nice,' Dan says as he comes in, although he makes the mistake of starting to say it before he's put one foot through the door so he can't possibly have seen what I'm looking like. I decide to let him off.

'Thanks.'

'Ready?'

'Yep,' I say, not moving.

'Taxi's here,' he says, and I reluctantly drag myself off my chair. Dan kisses the top of my head.

'Cheer up,' he says. 'It could be worse.'

'No,' I say. 'It couldn't.'

I can hear her talking as soon as I walk in.

'. . . and the thing is that I don't know whether you just think it tastes better because you know how expensive it is or whether it actually does I mean someone could give you the really cheap nasty version if there is such a thing I'm not sure there is and you'd still probably say it was great . . .'

61

I assume she's talking about the glass of champagne she's waving around in her right hand. We make our way over.

'. . . I mean would you really know the difference . . . oh, hello.'

She and Alex stand up and we all do that half-hearted kissing thing. I'm struck by the fear that Lorna might start expecting me to kiss her on the cheek when I see her at work first thing every morning.

'That's an interesting dress you have on,' she's saying. 'I didn't know what to wear so I just dug out this thing I haven't put on for about a year but I'm not sure about it now . . .'

Interesting? When was interesting ever a compliment when it came to clothing? I tune out. Butting in on Dan and Alex's conversation about Arsenal is neither possible nor desirable so I amuse myself by giving Lorna a critical once over. Actually, she's looking pretty good in the dress, which is very fitted and unforgiving in a way I could never carry off. I always forget that Lorna is, in fact, rather pretty. When her face is still, which is never, you notice her big eyes, which are dark brown and doe-ish and the fact that her mouth is wide and quite full (she has a big mouth, no kidding). Mind you, if I ate nothing but bird seed I'm sure my features would start to seem larger as my face got smaller. She has a bit of a crooked nose but not in a bad way, in a way that stops her face from seeming too bland, too regular. Her hair is a disaster, thin and wispy and unloved but all in all she's in the top, what, thirtieth centile of looks.

I like to do this with people, rate them out of a hundred. I don't know why. Most of the people I know, I have decided, score between seventy and eighty, which means there must be some seriously unattractive people around that I haven't come across yet. I have put myself in the bottom of the sixties but with the potential to improve. Alex is in the seventies but I have placed Dan right up in the eighties, bordering on the nineties. It's subjective, of course. I once decided Angelina Jolie was only just in the top fifty per cent but that was right after she started collecting babies and I was finding her self-righteousness really annoying.

The waiter comes to usher us through to our table. I have already decided that the best way to get through the evening is to let Lorna talk and only answer when necessary. I have warned Dan of the perils of telling her any funny anecdotes about me and my misbehaviour for fear they will be broadcast round the office, so now he's scared to say anything. But that's OK, because Lorna is in full flow, telling us about the time she went on a cookery course and Aldo Zilli was running it and he kept singling her out and wasn't that just typical? Lorna is one of those people who always thinks she is the most important person in any room. Of course Aldo would pick her to slice the aubergines because she's so amazing and hilarious. The more prosaic explanation that maybe she just happened to be the person standing closest to him would never occur to her. Dan, trying to be polite, is making things worse by saying 'wow' and 'really?' and sounding like he's impressed, but I just let them get on

63

with it and eat my food, which is fantastic by the way. Halfway through the meal he asks me if I'm feeling all right.

'You're very quiet,' he says, concerned.

'I'm fine. Just enjoying my Dover sole,' I say, and thankfully Dan leaves it at that. But then the meal takes an altogether more stressful turn. Alex, I am convinced, has been looking to make mischief ever since we arrived and, finding that it's all going fairly smoothly, can't resist throwing a spanner in the works.

'Hey, Rebecca,' he says out of nowhere. 'Tell Lorna about the email thing.'

'Oh no,' I say, trying to make light of it. 'She doesn't want to be bored with that.'

I give Alex an imploring look that says 'please don't,' but he just smirks at me. Dan, who knows what's coming, tries to step in and help, but all he can manage is, 'God, this sea bass is delicious,' which does nothing to halt the oncoming juggernaut.

'Well, *I* will, then. So . . .' Alex says, turning to Lorna and taking a big hammy deep breath. 'You won't believe this . . .'

The email incident is not one of which I am proud. It was funny at the time, don't get me wrong. Reliving it gave me, Dan, Alex and Isabel several drunken evenings of hilarity, and all of us – Alex included – would laugh until tears rolled down our cheeks. Now, suddenly, it doesn't seem so side splitting. It seems a bit mean-spirited and childish, not to mention a flagrant breach of some-one's privacy and, probably, for all I know, against the law. I'm hesitating before I repeat it. You'll laugh. That's everyone's first reaction. But then, like everyone else, you'll say, 'You really shouldn't have done that.'

OK, here goes . . .

A couple of years ago I was looking for something on Lorna's computer in the office. Legitimately. She was off sick or something and I needed to find a copy of a contract she had been sent that had suddenly become urgent because the client was due to start the job in two days' time and Joshua hadn't even clapped eyes on it, let alone approved it. So, with Joshua's blessing, I went into Outlook and scanned through her in box looking for something that might pertain to the document we needed.

I found it pretty easily and was about to click on it when I noticed that the message above came from someone called Les and had the intriguing subject line 'stiff as a board'. No, I chastised myself. Don't open it. But it was during one of those periods when I suspected Lorna was having one of her dating-agency romances, and curiosity got the better of me. That and the fact that I thought I might get a funny story out of it, something to make the others laugh down the pub. I have to say, I hadn't bargained on *how* funny, but anyway. To cut a long story short, I opened Les's email and read a detailed description of, as the title suggested, his rather overexcited feelings the morning after they had clearly had a night before.

'Can hardly walk,' he'd written poetically. 'Scared to stand up from behind my desk in case somebody notices.'

So far, so funny. I mean, come on, who wouldn't laugh? This is the point, obviously, where I should be telling you how I then printed off the document I needed, turned Lorna's computer off and never poked my nose into her personal life again. Unfortunately that's not exactly what happened. In fact, what I actually did was to look backwards for the previous missive from Les to see if that also contained anything juicy. This one was entitled Re:re:re:re:re: etcetera. That one email promised to detail the whole history of their relationship, stretching over nearly two weeks of correspondence. Before I could stop myself I had pressed print and the whole thing was chuntering out of the big printer over by my desk. I added the requested contract to the pile and switched off her computer. When the printer went quiet I stuffed the incriminating pages into my bag and forgot about them till Joshua and Melanie went out for lunch, leaving me alone.

I started at the beginning. They'd clearly not been going out for long at that point and the emails still had the flirty mixed with matey tone of a burgeoning relationship. I scrolled down, only half concentrating on what I was reading. Bored, I was about to put the whole lot in the shredder when I saw it. Overnight their communication became loaded with sexual references and heavy-handed eroticism, which said to me that they had finally got it on. Blushing, I read through all the 'I loved it when you . . .'s and the 'next time I'm going to . . .'s. It was oddly fascinating but also completely ludicrous, which, let's face it, everyone's cyber pillow talk would be when read in the cold light of day. Laughing, I picked up the phone. This was too good not to share. I tried Isabel but she was engaged, Dan was in a meeting, so I called Alex.

'Guess what Lorna calls her clitoris,' I asked as soon as he answered.

'Do I win a prize?'

'Her bean.' I could hardly get the word out. Alex snorted.

'Did she tell you this?'

'No, I . . . well, I saw it on an email.'

'No!' he said, mock horrified.

'I know,' I said. 'I'm not going to look at any more.'

But I read him some of the choicer passages and he pissed himself laughing and then, later, as we perused the dinner menus, Alex made me rehash it all again for Dan and Isabel's benefit. To give myself credit, I hesitated because once the immediate moment was over I started feeling a little bit guilty. Not to mention the fact that while I knew that Alex with his cruel streak would find the whole thing hilarious I wasn't nearly so sure about Dan or Isabel.

Alex pushed me. 'Go on,' he kept saying. 'Honestly, you have to hear this.'

So I told the whole story again and, at one point, when I got to the bit about going back through Lorna's old emails, Dan said, 'Oh no, don't go there . . .' But, to be fair, they both laughed because it was hard not to. It was just so . . . ridiculous. All evening Alex kept repeat-ing the phrases in a stupid voice that he reserved for whenever he talked about Lorna, and then, when the waiter came over to tell us the specials and the soup of the day was White Tuscan Bean we all sniggered at once like a bunch of ten-year-olds.

It was cruel, of course it was, but, in my defence, it was a victimless crime. There was no way I was ever going to let Lorna know what I'd seen. I certainly wasn't going to make a habit of reading her mail. It would remain an in joke between four friends who would never share it with anyone else. Until now, it seemed. If Alex really was as fond of Lorna as he was trying to have us believe, would he really risk hurting her by letting her know we had all of us – him included – been laughing at her behind her back?

'Well?' Lorna is saying, waiting breathlessly for Alex to tell her whichever hilarious story he seems to think she'd love so much.

Alex looks at me. 'Actually,' he says. 'I'll save it. It's not that great a story.'

I sigh an almost audible sigh of relief. Lorna's not giving up that easily, though.

'No,' she squeaks. 'You have to tell me now! You can't just give an anecdote a build up like that and then not tell it!'

'Oh, Alex,' Dan leaps in, seeing an opening. He's clearly not quite worked out what he's going to say next, though, because he grinds to a halt almost immediately.

'Erm . . . I've been meaning to say to you. Did you see that . . . erm . . . that article in the *Guardian* about

68

that new car? The one that's all electric but it's a sports model?'

I have no idea where this came from. Dan has no interest in cars. Alex has no interest in cars. But it manages to divert attention from the email fiasco for a moment. And because Alex has clearly also decided to bail out he goes along with the car conversation for just long enough for Lorna to lose interest in the previous topic.

I can breathe again. The guilt that had washed over me when I thought that Alex was going to tell the whole embarrassing story means that I feel better disposed towards Lorna for the rest of the meal. I try to smile and nod while she talks. I even think about trying to join in the conversation myself, but there seems little point; she doesn't actually seem to need any feedback. The rest of the meal passes off uneventfully and, thankfully, at ten it is all over with no one feeling in the mood to suggest going on anywhere else.

At home Dan and I go through our usual routine. A quick debrief over a glass of brandy, bed, read for five minutes then lights out. He is asleep almost immediately as he almost always is. These days, like most couples with many years and two children behind them, bed is primarily for sleeping. I look at him fondly in the half dark, but I can't shake the image of Alex and Lorna in the smug first flush of coupledom. There's no denying that their physical attraction is real, whatever Alex's underlying motives might be. His hand on her knee, her rubbing his thigh as she told some story or other. It unsettles me a bit, and I wonder if it does Dan too, this blatant display of sexual chemistry. It makes me feel inadequate, un-exciting and unexcited. I briefly think about waking Dan up, telling him I've got a sudden urge, take me now, but I know he'd just be confused, wonder what had got into me and if I was OK and the moment would be lost. So I just cuddle into his broad back and try to sleep.

8

Isabel is sitting at a table by the window, nose in a paperback. She looks so exactly like, well, like Isabel, that I almost burst into tears as I rush across the café to greet her. We haven't set eyes on each other for nearly a month and, as I get her in a bear hug, I realize just how much I've missed my friend. We've talked on the phone, of course, but with Alex staying at ours for all that time we got out of the habit of inviting her round. The intensity with which she returns my embrace and the fact that she won't let go even when I've clearly relaxed my arms tells me that she's missed me too. We eventually break apart, ignoring the stares of a weasely-looking young man in a nylon suit, who I think is hoping he's about to see a live stage show of *Emmanuelle*.

'So,' she says as I sit down. 'How have you been?'

'I'm fine,' I say. 'Well, work's a bit . . .' I realize that I can't even begin to explain the whole story so I witter on aimlessly. Eventually Isabel asks the question she always asks.

'So, how's Alex? Is he OK?' she asks.

I've agonized about this. On the one hand Isabel will be horrified and hurt to discover that Alex is already seeing someone else. On the other, the fact that it's Lorna might even amuse her. I know that someone will tell her

71

once the grapevine moves into action and I decide that it's better if that someone is me. I leave out the part about Alex making a pass at me obviously. I want her to take him back if he ever sees sense and she's hardly going to do that if she thinks he's that disloyal.

'He's obviously doing it just to prove some kind of a point,' I say, although it's hard to justify what point without telling her what I really think. 'To himself, I mean. That he was right to leave or something. God knows.'

Luckily my instincts were right and the pain is outweighed by the comedy value. Isabel manages a smile.

'I don't know,' she says, 'maybe he likes her.'

'But this is *Lorna*,' I say, my voice rising an octave. 'He can't really like her.'

'Oh God, do you think he's calling it the bean yet?'

'And that's another thing. He nearly told her that story. I mean I have to work with her. What if he tells her and then she tells Joshua or Melanie . . .'

Isabel laughs. 'I doubt she'd want to admit to it to anyone.'

The conversation slows to a halt for a moment. Isabel looks at me.

'Rebecca,' she says hesitantly. 'Why do you think he left? Really?'

'I have no idea,' I say. I'm not about to tell her that he now claims he never really loved her after all. 'I always thought you seemed so happy.'

She sighs. 'I don't think it was ever as good as you thought it was. Not for years, anyway. We argued all the time when we were on our own. But don't all couples? About money, mostly. Him getting a job . . .'

'But . . . I always thought . . . I mean, you do OK, don't you?' I ask. 'You're doing something you love and I guess he just wanted to try and do something he loves too. And when you had the girls, I mean, I was always so envious of you that you could just go back to work knowing he was happy to stay with them.'

'I didn't want to go back to work, though,' she says, and a look of irritation passes over her face. 'I wanted to stay at home and do the new-mother thing. But even then he refused to think about looking for a job.'

I'm shocked. I had no idea. It had all seemed like such a perfect twenty-first-century solution to me.

'I cried all day every day in the office,' she's saying. 'But Alex insisted that if he got another job it would be a slippery slope and then he'd never have any time to do any writing.'

'Gosh,' I say. 'I didn't realize.'

Isabel is on a roll. 'And, to be honest, I have no idea when the last time he actually wrote something was.'

'I thought you loved your work,' I say, rather lamely.

'I do. But I would have liked to opt out for a while. Or I'd like to have been able to be part time so at least I could spend some time with my daughters while they were little. Tell me,' she says, 'do you think Alex is a good writer? I mean, you read something of his once. Do you think he's ever going to become the next Alan Bennett?'

I blush. I don't want to be too disloyal to Alex but she's got a point.

'I guess not,' I say. 'No.'

'He's been trying for twelve years. And at no point during that time did he even think, Well, maybe I could work part time, do my bit for the family, and write on my days off. Because he never cared that much. It was all about him having a nice life, pottering around all day and chatting up the mums on the school run.'

I'm about to say that doesn't sound like Alex when I realize that, of course, it does, so I keep my mouth shut.

'The whole writing thing is like a diversionary tactic. If he says that that's what he's doing, then no one questions why he hasn't got a job. No one's got the faintest idea whether he ever actually writes anything or not. He can play the tortured artist. But even with all that I never thought about leaving. We were in it together. We'd promised. And I loved him.'

'Why did you never tell me any of this?' I say, irrationally hurt that she hasn't confided in me.

'Because,' she says, 'you know, you always thought it was all so perfect, the four of us. You were always saying how amazing it was how it had all worked out. I don't know. I didn't want to be the one to disillusion you, I guess.'

She's right. I did always marvel at our luck, that the four of us had found each other. We were a perfect unit, like those two sets of Siamese twins who happened to fall in love in Russia or somewhere.

I try and take this all in for a moment. Isabel sips her coffee and looks at me, willing me to understand.

'I'm so sorry, Izz,' I say. 'If I'd have known . . .Well, actually, I don't know what I would have done if I'd have known. Tried to convince you that it was all in your head, maybe, that nothing was really wrong. That would have been helpful.'

She laughs. 'You probably would have succeeded. You can be very persuasive when you get a sulk on. And he'd still have left.'

I feel like we've exhausted the topic for now. There's so much more I want to ask her, but I think it'd be pushing my luck so I change the subject.

'How are the girls doing?'

'Oh, you know,' she says. 'They're miserable. They can't understand why he's done it.'

We make plans to get the kids together so that the twins can engage in a bit of William baiting, which will cheer them up. There's a big old elephant in the room, which only I can see, which is Alex's declaration of love to me. I wonder briefly whether knowing that about Alex might actually help her in some way. Make her see that he's not worth pining over. But it's not worth the risk. And, besides, if I tell her, then I'll have to tell Dan and I don't see how that would be beneficial to anybody. Uncomfortable as I am with keeping a secret from him – beyond hiding his Christmas and birthday presents I'm not sure I ever have done – in this instance I know that it's the right thing to do. In Dan's case ignorance is bliss.

Back in the office Lorna looks at her watch as I walk in.

'I thought you were coming back at one thirty,' she says for the benefit of Melanie, who is also in the room. It is now one thirty-four, by the way. I am four minutes late. Arrest me.

'I'm meant to be meeting Alex,' she says. 'I don't know if it's worth it now.'

'Tell you what,' I say. 'Why don't you come back at twenty to three. It's really no problem. Is it Melanie?'

'What? Oh no,' Melanie says. 'Just work it out between you, so long as everything gets done.'

'There,' I say to a sulky-looking Lorna. 'Crisis averted.'

Over dinner I tell Dan that I had lunch with Isabel, but I skirt around what she told me about the state of their marriage. I'll save that for later, once the kids are out of the way.

'Did she say anything about Nicola and Natalie?' William asks, fish finger poised in front of his mouth, little finger aloft like a duchess with a tea cup. I smile at him.

'She said they're fine. But they're sad they haven't seen you for a while so I thought we might go over there at the weekend.'

The way his face lights up you'd think I'd told him he'd won the Nobel Prize.

'Excellent,' he says.

Zoe looks at him. 'God, you're sad,' she says, but he's too happy to retaliate.

9

Somehow in the chaos of everything that's been going on I'd forgotten about IT. The holiday. Every year since I can't remember when, we have all gone on holiday together. Rebecca and Daniel, Alex and Isabel and then, as they arrived, the four kids. In the summer we go away in our couples like normal people and the rest of the time we hang around each other's roof terraces and gardens and local parks. But the autumn half term has become *our* time. The group. We book ahead, getting together for an evening in the early summer to argue about where it'll be this year. We've done Madeira and Lanzarote, Crete and Rhodes, Center Parcs and Euro Disney.

This year, on an evening in late May, we decided on the Amalfi Coast, where it should be warm though not hot and where we could force some culture down our children's throats and then get pissed on cheap red wine in the evenings. Cleverly we booked it there and then. Six nights in Sorrento. In the subsequent fighting over who was getting to keep the house and the dog, no one has even thought to argue about who gets the holiday. We've all forgotten. At least, that is, until one night when I wake up in a cold sweat and realize that we have got to cancel it. Now. While we can still get some of our money back. Before it just becomes accepted that we're going. Or at least, some of us are.

I shake Dan awake.

'Dan,' I say in a stage whisper. 'Wake up.'

He groans. There's nothing Dan hates more than being disturbed when he's sleeping, but this is an emergency.

'What? What's wrong?'

'We have to cancel Sorrento. I think we only have a couple of days left. Can you do it tomorrow?'

Dan booked it on his computer. He has the reference number, the details of the travel company, all that essential stuff. It makes sense for him to be the one to cancel it. He sits up. Once he's awake, he's awake.

'You woke me up for that?'

'I was scared I'd forget. We can't afford to lose the deposit.'

'It's OK,' he says. 'I think Alex still wants to go. I guess he'll bring Lorna.'

I snap my bedside light on so he can see exactly how serious I am.

'No,' I say in a tone I'd ordinarily reserve for a naughty dog. Down boy. 'No, Dan, no. Are you f . . . reaking mad?'

'Did you just say freaking?'

'I'm being serious.'

'But freaking?' He looks at me, realizes I am not in the mood to laugh. 'Oh, for God's sake,' he says. 'She's OK.'

I can't believe this is happening.

'What about the kids? They haven't even met her yet. It could damage them for life watching their father frolicking on the beach in his swimming trunks with some bikini-clad woman who's not their mum.'

'I don't think anyone's going to be frolicking on the beach in their swim wear in October,' he says in that pedantic way he has sometimes.

'That's not the point,' I say, getting desperate. 'The point is that this holiday is for the kids. If anything, it should be Isabel who comes with them, not Alex.'

'You want me to tell Alex that we'd rather go on holiday with Isabel than him?'

'Why not? He's the one who's ruined everything. Look, just cancel the holiday, OK?' I say, turning over so my back is towards him. 'We can go somewhere else, just us and Zoe and William. Maybe take the girls along too. But no Alex. And no Lorna.'

'Fine,' he says in a way that makes it clear that it's anything but fine.

'Whatever,' I retaliate, channelling Zoe.

The next morning we get ready in huffy silence. We still walk to the tube station together as we do every day and I wait until I'm about to disappear underground, leaving him to catch his bus, before I say, 'Don't forget to cancel the holiday,' and then I practically run off before he can respond.

The upshot is this. Dan calls Alex to let him know the holiday is about to be cancelled. Alex says, hold on a minute, I still want to go and, by the way, I'm taking

79

Lorna. Dan, being Dan, says fine. He calls the travel company and tells them it's going to be two adults only. No children, no Dan and Rebecca Morrison.

'So,' he says to me as I'm cooking dinner that evening. 'It's all sorted out. Where do you want to go instead?'

He comes up behind me and snakes his arms round my waist, his way of trying to end our dispute. I'm not playing, though.

'We can't go anywhere,' I say. 'I can't have the same week off work as Lorna. So now the childless couple gets to go away in half term and we get to do precisely nothing because we can't take the kids out of school.'

'Shit,' he says, 'I didn't think of that.'

'No,' I say. 'You didn't, did you?'

Actually, Lorna being out of the office for a week turns out to be as good for me as having a holiday. I don't edge along from Piccadilly tube station every morning, my shoulders hunched up around my ears. I can relax knowing that for a whole week there's no question of dinner or a trip to the pub or a cosy night at home with the four of us.

Dan and I suddenly remember why we like each other so much and cuddle up on the sofa in front of the TV contentedly. Just the two of us. Neither of us mentions Alex or Lorna for fear we'll break the spell.

At work, I have no doubt, I am less defensive, less inclined to sulk. Without question more productive because without Lorna there to play Phone Wars with I answer each call happily, on the first or second ring. I can't be helpful enough.

Isabel has taken the girls to Cornwall for the week. She calls me to tell me that I would love their hotel because it's run by someone who used to be a children's TV presenter in the 80s and that he still wears his trade-mark red glasses and uses his catch phrase – fabbo! – at every opportunity. She is amusing herself by refusing to acknowledge that she knows who he is, which, she says, he is clearly waiting for. As the days go by, he is becoming more and more frustrated and saying 'fabbo!' way more often than necessary. Soon, she says, he will no doubt produce the battered old kangaroo puppet who used to be his sidekick and then probably break down and say, 'Don't you remember me?' and start crying. I laugh and ask her to take a photo if he does.

Otherwise, she says, to be honest, it's depressing. It's great watching the girls having a good time but some adult company in the evenings wouldn't go amiss. Once the twins are in bed there is nothing to do but sit in the adjoining room and watch TV.

'I may become an alcoholic,' she says, and she laughs, but I know she's miserable.

'I might join you,' I say.

We promise to meet up as soon as she gets back.

'Say hi to Dan from me,' she says as she rings off.

'OK,' I say. 'Bye.'

Melanie and Joshua are being very secretive. They keep closeting themselves away in one or other of their offices for 'talks'. If I didn't know better, I'd think that they had a thing going on. Actually, that's not such a ludicrous idea. I suspect that he would in a heartbeat if she was up for it, but she has a handsome, attentive, successful husband and a very professional attitude towards her work, which means, I think, that she would never mix business with carnal pleasure. He, on the other hand, is a bit of a randy old dog who would probably never say no. I like him, though, don't get me wrong. There's a certain old-fashioned, gentleman-cad quality about him that I find quite endearing. He's very theatrical, very luvvy and utterly harmless.

Anyway, clearly something is afoot because no one ever really shuts their doors at Mortimer and Sheedy, unless they're with a client. In fact, the last time I can remember was when the Gary McPherson scandal broke and that didn't last for long because Lorna and I were having to fend off calls from the *Sun* and the *Mirror* within minutes so there was no point anyone trying to pretend it was a big secret.

I'm running through the client list in my head, trying to imagine who might have done what and with whom when they emerge, all smiles and everything goes back to normal.

'Everything OK?' I say to Melanie later. She's never very good at keeping secrets.

'Of course,' she says. 'Why wouldn't it be?'

The week passes way too quickly and before I know it I'm dawdling along Jermyn Street from the tube station, shoulders up, braced for the inevitable.

'Oh, Rebecca, we had such a great time!' she says, the minute I walk through the door, and then proceeds to tell me every minute detail of that great time, starting with the second they set foot in Gatwick Airport and ending, well, I don't really know, because I've long since switched off. Nearly an hour has gone by when I look at my watch, and that and the fact that she seems to have stopped talking tells me that she's probably reached the end of the journey home.

There's a pause.

'Good,' I say. 'I'm glad you had a good break.'

Luckily that seems to be all that was required and she sets off again about what has she missed and has anything happened and what's the goss?

'Nothing,' I say. 'Nothing has happened, you've missed nothing and there's no gossip. Sorry.'

That shuts her up for a moment and then thankfully Joshua arrives and she follows him into his office and rehashes the whole thing again.

While she's been away I have been steeling myself. The third time the phone rings and she pretends to be fascinated by some speck of dust on her desk, I answer but then, once I have put the person on the other end through to Melanie, I take a deep breath.

'Lorna,' I say, and she looks up, eager as a puppy for some interaction. I almost bottle out.

'This thing with the phones . . .' I start, and then realize that I'm not quite sure where I'm going even after rehearsing this moment in my head for a week.

'The phones?' she says, like she hasn't quite under-stood me right.

'Yes, you know, the way you never answer them.'

'I do,' she says. 'What are you talking about? I'm always answering the phones.'

'No,' I say. 'You don't. At least, you only do when you have to, when I don't give in first.' Now I say it out loud it does sound a little paranoid.

'I've been away for a week. I have to catch up with what I've missed. I've just been concentrating, that's all. I haven't even noticed the phones have been ringing. How many times have they rung?'

She's getting louder now. Loud enough so that Joshua and Melanie will be able to hear every word. I want to tell her to keep her voice down, but that'd be like a red rag to a bull. I'm beginning to wish I'd never started this.

'I'm not talking about today,' I say, and then, as if by magic, the phone bursts into life. Lorna leaps at it, answering before it has even managed to get one full ring out, looking at me triumphantly as if to say, 'See how wrong you are?'

I wait for her to finish. I'm not sure how to get back on the subject without tipping her over the edge, but in the end I don't have to. I never really understood what passive aggressive meant until I met Lorna. She's the living embodiment of it, all innocent little baby face but she will never let things go. Underneath all that pitiful feyness she's like a pit bull.

'So, what were you accusing me of before I answered

the phone?' she says, putting a great deal of emphasis on the last four words. I can see the water gathering in pools in the corners of her eyes. I know that once it's released, once it finds its way down her cheeks, it will be impossible to stop. At least, not before Joshua notices, she'll make sure of that.

Still, I knew it would be like this. Now I've started I have to finish because I don't know when I'll have the courage to bring it up again.

'I wasn't accusing you of anything,' I say evenly. One of us has to remain calm. 'I was just saying that you have a habit of waiting for me to answer the phone rather than picking it up yourself and I'd be grateful if we could share the load a bit more, that's all.'

I can see it, one tear struggling to force its way out, clearing the way for its hundreds of brothers and sisters to follow.

'I don't know what you're talking about,' she says, ramping up the volume another notch. 'I've been on holiday. Why are you attacking me the minute I walk back through the door?'

'I'm not . . . forget it. There's no point carrying on this conversation. Let's just forget it, OK?' I say.

'No,' she says. 'You can't just accuse me of something and then try to pretend you haven't.'

'I shouldn't have said anything,' I say. This is how it always ends if I ever try to say anything even vaguely critical to Lorna. I should have learned my lesson by now.

'No,' she says again. 'You must have meant it. You've

obviously been festering away about something the whole time I've been off . . .'

'What's going on?'

Oh great, now the cavalry has arrived in the form of Joshua on his great white charger.

'Nothing,' I say. 'Everything's fine.'

'Rebecca thinks that I deliberately don't answer the phones,' Lorna says, and right on cue the watery army starts its way down her face. 'She thinks that I wait so that she has to do it. That I pretend to be busy when I'm not or something.'

She gives way to big noisy sobs. Once again I am the school bully. I wonder if anyone cries like that when they're on their own, wailing and moaning, when they don't have an audience. I doubt it. Joshua puts a paternal hand on Lorna's shoulder.

'Rebecca?' he says.

I take a breath.

'I think,' I say, 'that sometimes Lorna holds back from answering the phones in the hope that I'll do it, yes. Even when I'm clearly in the middle of something and she isn't,' I add for good measure.

Surely he can see the sense in what I'm saying. From his and Melanie's point of view they just want the phones to be answered promptly and by someone who sounds like they're happy to be there.

Lorna gives another well-timed sob and Joshua turns back to her to be confronted by the full force of Niagara Falls. He looks at me again, disappointment in his avuncular eyes.

'Honestly, this has got to stop.'

Once he's gone back into his office she looks at me and smiles nervously.

'Sorry,' she says. 'I didn't mean to get you into trouble.'

I turn back to my work without answering. When the phone rings a few minutes later she answers it on the second ring.

When I get back from lunch Lorna, Melanie and Joshua are all standing there with their coats on. I feel pathetically left out when they all trip off to a restaurant together. Not that I want to have lunch with the bosses – in fact, they've offered many times but I always make an excuse – it's just that my worst and most paranoid instincts take over when I am not invited but Lorna is. And guess what? This time it's actually not paranoia. This time I'm right to worry because when they come back Lorna looks like the offspring of the Cheshire cat and the one that got the cream. Smiling cat squared.

'Oh, Rebecca,' she says before she even takes her coat off. 'You'll never guess what's happened!'

As it goes, I don't even need to try because she barely pauses for breath before she carries on.

'I probably shouldn't tell you. I think Joshua and Melanie want to tell you themselves, but if I don't share it with someone I'll burst and I can't raise Alex on the phone.'

OK, it's going to be bad. My mind leaps to the obvious – she's pregnant. She's having Alex's baby and all of our lives are going to be inextricably linked forever. The twins are going to have a little brother or sister who is the product of Alex's ill-judged relationship with the devil. Although exactly why Joshua and Melanie would want to be the ones to break that to me I can't quite work out.

'I'm going to be the new agent,' she's saying, but I'm having trouble processing the words. There has been a lot of talk lately about how there are now too many clients for Joshua and Melanie to handle between them, and how, perhaps, at some point in the future, they might begin to think about getting another pair of hands, expanding the agency. It always sounded very vague and very far off and I had always assumed that they meant bringing someone in from the outside. Someone with experience and a few loyal clients of their own to bring to the table. Someone who wasn't Lorna.

I tune back in.

'I'll start off just helping out with the people we've got. And maybe I might take some of them over completely, the less successful ones, probably. I can even bring in clients of my own. In fact, they want me to start looking for promising new people right away. They said they'd been thinking about offering it to me for ages but they just had to make sure they had it all worked out properly, you know, because, of course I'll get a raise . . .'

It's not that I'm jealous. I'm not. I've never been ambitious. I don't want any more responsibility. I don't want some discontented actor calling me on a Sunday morning to complain about how hard he's being worked. My dressing room is six inches smaller than hers or so and so got given six weeks off last year to do panto but they won't even let me book a holiday. Oh no, what is eating away at me is far worse than mere envy. It's the fact that suddenly my working life has changed forever. Lorna is going to be my boss.

10

'I'm going to have to look for a new job,' I say to Dan as he's opening a bottle of wine in the kitchen. The second honeymoon period is most definitely over. One day spent with Lorna and I'm back to my old irritable glass-half-empty self.

'Don't be ridiculous,' he says. 'You love your job.'

'I used to.'

'Where else are you going to find something as flexible? Where they'll let you take a day off just because it's one of the kids' sports days and not count it as part of your holiday allowance? Where they'll buy you champagne on your birthday and get you free tickets to the theatre?'

'I know, I know,' I say, and when I'm being rational I do know that I'm on to a good thing but I'm just not sure it's possible that it can feel like that ever again.

'I mean, it's up to you,' Dan says, ever reasonable. 'I'm just saying.'

'Can't you have a word with Alex?' I know I'm talking rubbish but I feel like I'm in a bad film. Why is this happening to me?

'And say what? Could you dump your girlfriend because she's ruining Rebecca's life?'

Despite my misery I laugh. 'It'd be a start,' I say.

*

As luck would have it Alex and Lorna want to celebrate Lorna's new found success and, who do they want to celebrate with? Their best friends of course. So at seven thirty all four of us are sitting in the bar of the York and Albany waiting for our table. Alex is raising his glass, proposing a toast.

'To Lorna,' he says, all smiles. 'Congratulations and good luck. You'll need it now you're Rebecca's boss.'

He looks at me, victorious. Touché. Lorna laughs out of all proportion to how funny his remark was.

'I'm sure we're going to be fine,' she says. 'After all, I know all her tricks now. Ha ha ha.'

Hilarious.

Lorna's new duties are effective immediately. Although we are still sharing a work space in the reception – waiting while Melanie negotiates with our landlord to acquire the office next door so that the new hot shot can have her own room – we both know that it is now out of the question that Lorna be expected to answer the phones. No one needs to say anything; it's the New World Order. She's now way too important. At least, in her own opinion. Without anyone to play Phone Wars with I expend far less energy just picking up the calls as and when they come than I did trying to avoid answering them.

Lorna spends all day calling around everyone she has ever met and telling them that she is now 'AN AGENT!' Then, once she knows that Joshua has called the four least successful and therefore least likely to complain clients to tell them the good news that Lorna will be looking after them from here on in, she calls them too and says isn't it great that she's now 'THEIR AGENT!' She instructs me in all seriousness that I am to make sure to tell anyone who calls up enquiring after any of her four clients (I won't hold my breath), that those clients are under new representation and that, if they wish to discuss those clients, they must speak to Lorna and Lorna alone. I resist saying that no one has called up about any of those four clients in living memory, except when one of them had failed to pay their rent and their landlord tried to track them down through us.

In addition to her extensive client list Lorna will now be representing all of our boys and girls for voice-over work. In between phone calls she studies old contracts and badgers Melanie with questions, making copious notes in the brand-new notebook she is now using to keep track of her enormous empire.

By lunchtime I am exhausted from watching the energy she uses up doing not much really. At a quarter to one I stand up and put on my coat.

'I'm going to lunch,' I say. 'Are you OK to wait?'

'Oh,' she says. 'No. I mean, I think you're just going to have to pick up a sandwich and bring it back here from now on. I can't be worrying about coordinating my lunch break with yours any more. Not now I'm AN AGENT!'

'I can't do that every day,' I say. 'What about when I need to go shopping?'

'I don't know,' she says haughtily. 'You'll have to speak to Josh or Melanie about it.'

I'm momentarily knocked off course. Did she just call Joshua Josh? I've never even heard Melanie call him that. I force myself back on track.

'What's more, I'm sure I must have a statutory right to some fresh air or something,' I say, rather hysterically, but I can't help myself.

'Like I say, talk to Josh or Melanie. All I know is that I need to be able to take people out to lunch as and when I want without consulting you.'

'Who are you having lunch with today?' I ask, somewhat aggressively.

'That's beside the point.'

'No, it isn't. It is the point. If you have a lunch meeting today, then I can understand why you might want me to stay in the office but, if you haven't, then I don't see what difference it makes to you if I go out first and you stay and answer the phones and then you go out when I get back.'

'It's not my job to answer the phones any more,' she says.

I breathe in slowly. 'I know that. All I'm saying is that if someone needs to be here at all times to answer the phones then surely we need to work something out between us rather than you just telling me I can't take a lunch break any more.'

'I didn't say you couldn't have a lunch break, I just said that from now on you need to take it at your desk. There's a big difference. So, you'll have to get a sandwich and come straight back because I have to go out at one.'

'This is ridiculous,' I say, and I move towards the door. 'You can't tell me what to do.'

'Actually,' she says, 'I think you'll find I can.'

I go out anyway and, even though today I don't really have anything to do, I make sure that I stay out for a full hour, sitting in the grounds of St James's church, trying to concentrate on reading *Metro*. I make sure I'm back several minutes before my hour is up; I don't want to give her any ammunition. She is sitting there angrily, bent over some papers on her desk. I don't even bother asking what happened to her lunch date because I know she never had one.

As soon as Melanie gets back, I ask her if I can see her for a few minutes. While Lorna has Joshua wrapped around her little finger I still have hope that I can appeal to Melanie's more rational personality.

'I was wondering,' I say, once she has closed the door, although I have no doubt that Lorna will be listening, 'what was going to happen now about things like who's going to answer the phones at lunchtime?' I have already decided that I am not going to stoop to Lorna's level of tale telling. No 'she said this' or 'she did that'.

'Well, why can't you just carry on as normal?' Melanie says, clearly not very interested in having this conversation.

'Erm . . .' I say. 'Great, OK, if you think that's what we should do.'

'Good,' she says, riffling through papers on her desk.

'Do you think . . . well, could you mention that to Lorna if you get a chance? Just so that we all know where we are.'

'Fine,' she says, and I don't want to push it so I leave it at that.

Dan is meeting Alex and Lorna in the pub, but I have the perfect excuse in that I promised to take William and Zoe over to Isabel's and, of course, there's no question that we could all join up. Isabel doesn't seem to be home so I let myself in and I get the kids a drink from the kitchen. It's a beautiful house, a Victorian terrace with as many original features as you could wish for, bought, of course, with a mortgage based on Isabel's income because Alex doesn't have one, although I'm sure he stumped up the deposit saved from one of his not inconsiderable City bonuses. It's feeling a bit unloved at the moment, though, not so much like a home. It's amazing how one person's absence can do that, take some of the life out of a place. Usually it smells of freshly baked bread and Diptyque candles and all the other little touches Isabel used to do to make it feel homely. I guess she doesn't feel like bothering at the moment.

I hear her key in the lock. The twins bowl in before she does and they don't even raise an eyebrow at the sight of us already making ourselves at home in their kitchen. It has always been such a common occurrence.

'Sorry I'm late,' she says once the kids have all gone off to the twins' room. 'He'd taken them swimming.'

'Without telling you?' She nods. 'He can't do that.'

95

'I'm scared to make too much fuss,' she says. 'In case he starts demanding that the girls go and live with him. After all, he has been their primary carer for most of their lives.'

'Only till they were old enough to go to school,' I say. 'He wouldn't do that, surely?' I'm not sure I have a firm grasp on just exactly what Alex would or wouldn't do these days, actually. He seems to be capable of just about anything. 'And anyway I can't believe any court would put two kids with their father rather than their mother.'

'It happens all the time,' she says. 'And why not? Sometimes the father can look after them better.'

'Not this time,' I say. It worries me, though, this talk of who will get the children.

'Are you going to get a divorce, then?'

'He wants to,' she says. 'He says it'd be better for everyone, a clean break.'

'Gosh,' I say. Gosh seems to have become my new favourite word in my self-imposed swearing embargo. Golly! Jeeps! Crikey! 'That seems so final.'

Isabel laughs unconvincingly. 'I think that's the idea.'

So that's it. Just like that all hope for the future is lost. I'm not so pessimistic that I think Alex asking for a divorce is going to mean that Lorna is in my social life forever. I have no doubt that he'll get bored soon enough, once he's made his point, but it's definitely the end of an era. The end of 'life as we know it'. Alex and Isabel are finished and there's no going back. Deep down – well, not even that deep, to be really honest –

I was sure that Alex would come to his senses and go home. It just never really occurred to me that he wouldn't. And I think that Isabel thought it too. Rebecca and Daniel, Alex and Isabel, that's just how it is.

I'm feeling depressed by the time I get home.

'Alex is going to ask Isabel for a divorce,' I say to Dan, thinking he might understand.

'I had a feeling he would,' he says. 'I suppose it makes sense. A clean break.'

'That's what she said. Aren't you sad about it, though?' I ask accusingly.

'Of course,' he says, putting an arm round my shoulders. 'But things have to change.'

'I don't see why,' I say.

'Because that's how life is. It doesn't matter if you don't like it.'

'Not everything. Not us,' I say, feeling suddenly needy.

'No stupid,' he laughs. 'Not us.'

Oh God. Any minute now I'm going to start asking him if he still loves me and making him promise he'll never leave me. I get a grip quickly. There's nothing more guaranteed to frighten even the most loyal partner off than asking for reassurance that they're not going anywhere.

It's like he can sense my insecurity (which hardly makes him telepathic; it's oozing out of me, all over the nice smoked-oak floor) and, being Dan, he adds, 'You're stuck with me, I'm afraid,' so that I don't have to 'fess up what a pitiful wimp I am.

'I know,' I say, a well-rehearsed routine. 'If only we hadn't had the kids, I could still be young, free and single.'

'Well, free and single at any rate,' he says, and we laugh like we always do, safe in the knowledge that everything's OK in our little world.

Dan never suffers from insecurities. Or, if he does, he keeps them to himself. He knows that I love him and that's good enough. He doesn't need me to keep re-assuring him that I haven't changed my mind. He'll take it as read that it's still true until I tell him it isn't. I envy him his certainty.

11

Lorna is on a mission to find new clients. To justify her position as AN AGENT! She comes in a few more minutes late every day, rolling her eyes and waiting for me to ask what she was up to the night before that made her late getting up this morning. In the spirit of trying to pretend I'm being supportive I oblige for a few days and I listen to her breathless descriptions of the amazing new acting or writing talent she has unearthed. Nothing much ever seems to come of it. It usually turns out that her discoveries have already been discovered by somebody else months ago and they already have representation, but she still makes sure we all know about her dedication and her commitment to the cause. After a couple of weeks she does find an actress fresh out of drama school who seems to have some promise and a young would-be TV writer who has written, as she says, 'a lovely short film,' and she signs them up proudly and sets about making them superstars. At great expense she has cards made that say 'Lorna Whittaker. Artist and Writer representation. Mortimer and Sheedy' with the office address and phone number and she hands them out like Maundy money to anyone who so much as looks in her direction. I'm a little disappointed that her cards don't simply say 'I'm AN AGENT!!'

although I guess written down it wouldn't have quite the same impact as it does when she says it out loud.

Her new clients – Mary the actress (actually her name is Mhari but Lorna has persuaded her to change it, telling her that no one will be able to pronounce it and therefore will never ask her to audition for anything for fear of making themselves look foolish. Mhari, being new to the profession and filled with gratitude for having been given the chance to be represented by the great Ms Whittaker herself, readily agreed and consigned her cultural heritage to the dustbin without a second thought) and Craig the writer – seem sweet and naive enough to believe they have made an astute career move by signing their lives – and fifteen per cent of their future earnings – over to her. To be fair, though, Mortimer and Sheedy, despite being small, does have a good name and if it's known for anything then it's known for bringing on new talent. Melanie and Joshua are well respected. The name will look good on their CVs.

I read Craig's short film script when Lorna is out at lunch one day and it's really not bad. Plus Lorna, it has to be acknowledged, is like a dog with a bone on the line to one of the script editors at *Reddington Road*, trying to persuade them that Craig is just the kind of fresh young talent they need to nurture through their new-writers scheme. It pays off. They commission him to write a dummy episode – shadowing a real storyline – for no money, but with all the care and attention given to it as if it was the real thing. If he does well, they might give him a real script to write, one that will actually go on air, that he will be paid real money for – no promises. I have to grudgingly admit that Lorna's pulled it off on this occasion. It's the kind of break every inexperienced writer dreams about. I suspect that Alex, though he pretends to turn up his nose at soaps, indeed at TV in general – heaven forbid you actually get paid good money for writing something that will reach five million people – would kill to be given the chance.

Mary is a harder prospect. There is nothing tangible to show a casting director. She has never done anything on tape. Still Lorna pulls favours and gets her an audition for a one-line part in a new fringe play. Nothing comes of it except that Marilyn Carson, the casting director, sends back word that Mary reads well and that she'd certainly see her again for something or other in the future. Meanwhile Lorna advises her to take any old job she can find in any tiny above-a-pub theatre so that people can come and watch her in action. I find myself thinking that's exactly the advice I would have given her, which is rather disconcerting. Maybe Lorna has found her calling after all. Although what do I know about the way to get a young actress noticed?

Meanwhile, I am struggling to keep up, doing both my own job and the one Lorna so recently abdicated. She can see I'm overworked. We're still sharing the reception space while she waits for her new office to be painted (baby blue), so there's no way for her to miss the fact that I have too much to do. Still she sticks to her guns. If I am on a call and one of the other lines rings, she will sit there ignoring it, staring at me as if to say, 'Well, go on, answer it; that's your job.' We desperately need to bring in someone to replace the old Lorna, but no one seems to be mentioning it. I resolve to have a word with Melanie as soon as I get a moment. Of course, I am terrified they'll bring in someone even worse, although that's hard to imagine, but I'm going through my usual 'maybe it's better to stick with the devil I know' routine even though the devil I know is no longer doing the job.

We pass the day sitting at our desks, me resentful and sulky, her perky, feet up on the desk, reading. I am juggling two phone calls and conscious of the fact that Joshua asked me to make him a coffee fifteen minutes ago when Lorna gets up and sashays across the room to me, dropping a piece of paper on my desk. The paper is covered with a handwritten scrawl and across the top in capitals the words 'PLEASE TYPE' scream out at me. I look up questioningly, but she's halfway out the door with her coat on.

By the time I have dispatched the two callers (courier company – 'why haven't you paid your bill,' and actor client – 'I'm lost on my way to an audition') she's long gone. I look at the sheet of paper. I turn it over. Maybe what Lorna really meant to give me is on the other side. It's blank. I scan the words for further clues. It seems to be a CV for Mary. Age, height, attended the Central School of Speech and Drama from September 2006 to June 2009, two small-time productions in profit-share theatre as well as a couple of months doing Theatre In Education since. It would take about three minutes to input it on to my computer. That's not the point. The point is that it would have taken Lorna about three minutes to input it on to *her* computer too. Now I'm sure she's taking the piss. I consider going in and talking to Melanie about it, but I feel like all I do is moan and complain these days. I decide to put the paper back on Lorna's desk. If she wants me to type something for her, she can damn well look me in the eye and ask me to do it face to face. I prop it up on her keyboard where she can't miss it and settle back down to work.

'How are you getting on?' Joshua asks me as he walks through reception on his way out to lunch. 'Not too over worked?'

'Erm . . .' I say. 'Well . . .'

He's gone before I can say anything even if I had decided to. Joshua never really wants to hear the answers to questions like, 'How are you?' or, 'Any problems?' He likes to be able to tell himself that everything in his kingdom is in order.

Sixty-seven minutes later Lorna breezes back in. I have my coat on, ready to go out. I look at my watch as she walks straight through to the kitchen to make herself a coffee. At least she didn't ask me to make it for her, that's something. I wait until I hear her coming back and then I call out, 'I'm going for lunch.'

I'm nearly through the door when I hear her say, 'Oh, Rebecca?'

I force myself to stop. 'I'm going to be late,' I say, although I have no plans beyond a sandwich in St James's Square.

103

'I left something for you,' she says, not even apologetically. 'Did you see it?'

'Oh,' I say. 'Yes. I put it back on your desk.' I'm not going to offer up the fact that I haven't typed it up as her note asked. If she wants a fight, then she can start it.

She smiles. 'Good.' That's it. Good. I wait for her to say thank you, after all she doesn't yet know that I didn't carry out her request. But no. No 'thank you'. Just 'good'. I hear her shuffling papers around on her desk as I leave and I have to stop myself from laughing. It's either that or kill her.

When I get back exactly an hour later (I'm not stupid, I know she's timing me, desperate to catch me out) she's sitting there waiting for me with a face like thunder.

'Hi,' I say, smiling.

She launches straight into it. 'I thought you said you had typed that CV up for me.'

I feign confusion. 'No, I said that I saw the piece of paper you left on my desk . . .'

'Which clearly said "please type" across the top . . .'

I take a deep breath. 'Lorna,' I say. 'At no point has anyone told me that I was now to be your assistant as well as having to look after Joshua and Melanie on my own and deal with all the general office stuff. If you're really snowed under and you want to ask me to do something for you, as a favour, then that's one thing. And, if I have time, then I'll be glad to help. But if you're going to start treating me like I'm here to do your admin then that's another matter entirely. It's not happening. I've just had my workload doubled as it is.'

She's turned a funny shade of purple. 'Of course you have to do things for me,' she says, almost hissing. 'You're the *assistant*.'

'I'm Joshua and Melanie's assistant. I'm the *general* assistant. I'm not *your* assistant.' I can't say it any clearer than that.

'I'm going to speak to Josh about this,' she says, and I say, 'Good. You do that. I'll be interested to hear what he has to say.'

12

It's the twins' ninth birthday and, in an effort to fool them into thinking that everything is just fine, Isabel has organized a party to which she has invited not only me and Dan and the kids but also Alex and Lorna. We have all been told to be on our best behaviour, to keep any simmering resentments to ourselves, to save any arguments we may be fermenting for another occasion. Isabel knows how I feel about being in the same space as Lorna any more often than I have to be, but, the way I see it, the night is going to be infinitely harder for her, with her children trying to come to terms with their father's vile new girlfriend, not to mention the loose cannon that is Alex, so I resolve just to keep quiet and to be there for my friend.

The party is to take place on a Sunday afternoon in the house formerly known as Alex and Isabel's. In order to try to minimize the trauma caused by meeting their scary new surrogate mother figure at the event, and thereby ensuring that they will never be able to celebrate a birthday again without serious therapy, Alex has arranged to take both the girls and Lorna out to lunch the weekend before. Lorna, who now seems able to switch, in a worryingly accomplished bipolar fashion, between Nazi boss and best girly friend, has been quizzing me for days about what she should wear and what, exactly, eight-, about to be nine-, year-old girls like to talk about. I'm tempted to lead her down the wrong path ('They hate animals, loathe them. Tell them about the time you ran over that puppy,' or, 'They're obsessed with serial killers, the more gruesome details the better'), but I decide it would be unfair on the twins, who I adore. I tell her – truthfully – that they're into Barbie and Miley Cyrus and clothes and dogs and gymnastics. It's hardly rocket science, they're eight-year-old girls after all, but she looks gratefully at me as if I just gave her my last twenty-pence piece. The fact that I've made her happy irritates me so, to unsettle her a little, I tell her that the girls are identical and that the worst faux pas she could commit would be to mix them up. She blanches, nervous again. Actually the truth is that once you've known Natalie and Nicola for more than five minutes it's almost impossible not to know which is which. Nicola is lively and confident; Natalie is quiet and introverted. That and the fact that Natalie's hair barely reaches her shoulders while Nicola's cascades down her back. They are very much their own people and along with that, very early on, came the announcement that they would never dress the same or have the same haircut. I don't share this piece of vital information with Lorna, though. Let her sweat for a few days.

Isabel, who has been hearing stories about Lorna for years, will also be meeting her for the first time when she drops the twins off at the Pizza Express in Islington.

'Just don't think about the bean,' I say when she calls me to say she's on her way.

'Honestly,' she says, 'I thought I was taking the moral high ground inviting her to the party, but I'm not actually sure I'm ready to see him with somebody else.'

It's so like Isabel to be trying to do the grown-up thing. I knew that she had been agonizing over whether or not to invite Lorna, but I also knew that Isabel being Isabel she would decide to try to be gracious. The way she sees it Alex is the one who has behaved badly, but there is no reason why she shouldn't be civil towards Lorna. If it had been me, I would have told Alex that he could bring his new girlfriend over my dead body or, even better, over hers. And probably once I'd said that Isabel would have taken me aside and calmed me down and told me to remember that the only thing I had control over, the thing to hang on to at all costs, was my dignity. Isabel has always been the person I've turned to when I know I'm working myself up into an irrational frenzy about something. She's my voice of reason.

I don't really know what to say to her. I can't even imagine what it would be like to see your not-quite-ex husband with another woman. Knowing it is one thing, being forced to witness it is something else altogether.

'Of course it's going to be hard,' I say. 'But you're doing the right thing.'

I'm not at all sure I believe what I'm saying, but it sounds like the appropriate response. 'Plus, it's Lorna,' I add. 'So at least you're not going to feel inadequate next to her.'

'Rebecca,' Isabel says disapprovingly, but I can tell she's smiling.

*

'She looks like she needs to eat something,' is the first thing Isabel says to me afterwards.

'Tell me about it,' I say. 'So . . . what else?'

'She seemed nice enough. A bit territorial with Alex.'

'She's insecure,' I say. 'It's the root of all her neuroses.'

'Maybe we should feel sorry for her?' Isabel asks, and I snort.

'We're all insecure,' I say, which makes her laugh.

Isabel says that Lorna seemed to be making a big effort with the girls for which she is grateful although when quizzed later Nicola said that she was 'nosy' and Natalie had complained that Lorna 'talked too much'.

'Do you think Alex is happy with her?' she asks.

I brush off the question. 'They deserve each other.'

On Monday Lorna is all 'Nicola this' and 'Natalie that' like all three were in the same class at school and have just declared themselves best friends forever. I let her ramble on, though, because it beats her telling me what to do. After a while I tune out and it feels quite comfortable, like the good old days when she talked about herself incessantly and I ignored her but that was the extent of our interaction.

William is beyond excitement about the party and by Wednesday he has already picked out an outfit: his pageboy suit from his uncle's wedding last year, along with a rather foppy ruffled shirt, which he blackmailed us into buying for him on holiday once. He has decided to accompany this with a blue tie.

'Don't you want to wear something a bit more casual?' I ask, although I know what the answer will be. 'You might be running around. How about your tracksuit?'

'It's a party,' he says very deliberately, as if I'm a little slow. I know that he has visions of himself, cocktail glass in one hand, cigar in the other, wooing either Nicola or Natalie, whoever is his current favourite, with his sophistication.

'Well, it's up to you. I'm just saying.'

He has been agonizing over what to buy them for a gift. He has a budget of two pounds fifty each and for this he means to get each of them something that will demonstrate how much he understands and values their individuality. He finally settles on a hairbrush for Nicola and a book on identifying beetles for Natalie.

'Does she like beetles?' I ask. I find it hard to imagine.

'Of course she does, that's why I'm getting it for her,' he says, sighing at my stupidity. From his choices I deduce that Natalie is the current twin number one in his eyes.

Zoe is being allowed to bring a friend from school to the party because the girls would be devastated if she wasn't there, but I know that it's very damaging to her self-image for her to have to spend too much time in the company of eight- and nine-year-olds. I have bribed her by saying that she and her friend Kerrie can retire to Isabel's spare room and play on the Wii once the cake has been cut and 'Happy Birthday' sung. She tells me I

110

owe her big time because she has agreed to make an appearance at all.

As far as grown-ups go there will just be me and Daniel, Alex and Isabel. And Lorna. All the other parents will drop and run, making the most of an afternoon where they've managed to fob off their children on someone else. I always look forward to the twins' birthdays. I love kids' parties. Well, those where I know most of the kids involved anyway. But, this time, there's a dark cloud hanging over the event. A skinny, seed-eating, talkative black cloud. OK, I never said I was good at similes.

We somehow pass the week leading up to the big day fairly uneventfully. I manage to bite my tongue and she manages to do her own job without trying to palm the bits she can't be bothered with on to me. Her new office is nearly ready so I can see a light at the end of the tunnel. When I am on my own with Melanie one day I get up the courage to ask what is going to happen in the future. I figure that things do need to change and maybe I should start acclimatizing myself to that now. Who knows, if they bring in someone to do Lorna's old job, then maybe we could divide up the work completely. I could work for Joshua and Melanie, they could work for Lorna. I'd never have to deal with her again. And it's even possible that they might employ someone I'd like, an ally. Maybe I won't have to try to find something else to do with my life after all.

'Yes, we must talk about that,' Melanie says when I

collar her, and then she gets straight back on the phone, leaving me thinking, Isn't that what we could be doing now?

So I come up with a plan of sorts. My job is untenable as it is. We need a replacement old Lorna. If they don't replace her, I can't stay because I have too much to do and spending my days trying to find ways not to take orders from new Lorna is definitely not good for my health. If they do replace her and they take on someone I don't get on with, I can still leave. I might as well see how it pans out. My new year's resolution – if I believed in new year's resolutions, which I don't – this year was going to be to try to embrace change. Mind you, I decide this pretty much every December and come January 1st I have usually forgotten all about it. Maybe that could be the first change I embrace, remembering that I have made a resolution. Anyway, I have decided, why wait until January. I'm determined to start now. No one seems to be listening to me so I go direct to the person I think they might listen to.

'You need to get an assistant,' I say to Lorna when she's grudgingly making herself a cup of tea. 'I mean, I'd help you out if I could (yeah, right), but I'm snowed under looking after Joshua and Melanie on my own. I just don't have the time.'

She looks at me suspiciously, but she can't see the catch in what I've said so she relaxes.

'I know,' she says. 'They told me they'd take someone else on but they seem to have forgotten all about it.'

'Well, you need to talk to them again,' I say. 'After all,

you're an agent now; you need to be spending time on your clients, not doing your own filing.' All six of her clients, without a paying job between them. I have no idea what there is to file. Still, she takes the bait as I knew she would.

'You're right,' she says.

'I mean, it's not fair,' I say, winding her up a little more. 'I don't know how they expect you to really make a go of it with no support.'

'Plus, it looks bad,' she says. 'If people ask who my assistant is and they get told I don't have one.'

'Exactly,' I say.

So the next thing I know there's an advert going in the *Evening Standard*. General assistant wanted for Theatrical and Literary Agency. I think about adding 'ability to listen to drivel for eight and a half hours a day an asset,' but then I want there to be lots of applicants. In these days of unemployment I figure we'll be inundated with responses despite the fact that there's no mention of the salary, which is, to say the least, basic. Melanie and Joshua will be looking for somebody to fall in love with the idea of the job in the way that me and Lorna did. In a way they see it as a vocation. I feel better now I've set things in motion. One way or another this will sort itself out. It will be my task to sort through the applicants and to prepare a short list for interview so I am confident that I can eliminate a lot of the potential nightmares. Questions I resolve to ask them on the phone before I decide whether they are suitable:

- Do you talk all the time regardless of whether or not you have anything to say?
- Do you have a power complex?
- Are you so desperate for a relationship that you will consider any man, however unsuitable for you?
- Do you eat iceberg lettuce/celery/sunflower seeds?
- Do you eat at all?

I'm actually looking forward to it.

On Sunday I get to the house early. Alex is taking the girls off to Gap Kids to buy them birthday outfits, his gift to them, and while they're out Isabel and I are going to decorate and make pizzas and fairy cakes. It's like old times except that Isabel's heart is broken and her husband is going to be coming to the party with his new girlfriend.

It's the first time I have seen Alex and Isabel together since the split although, of course, they have seen each other regularly for child-handing-over duties. Isabel seems nervous, wanting to give off the impression that she's over him but unable to do so convincingly. Alex actually seems unruffled by her presence. He's looking good. Relaxed. I suddenly wonder what he's living on. Is Isabel still paying the mortgage on the house and giving him pocket money? Is she paying the rent on his flat? Or is Lorna keeping him? Maybe that's the attraction. He certainly isn't bringing in any money himself. I'm glad when he leaves with the girls. I don't really enjoy being around him these days. There's a growing list of things I want to start a fight with him about.

'You two seem to be getting on OK,' I say to Isabel once he's gone.

'We are,' she says. 'He's stopped trying to pick arguments with me at least.'

'Maybe he can move on from his transitional woman soon,' I say, forcing a laugh.

'You know what? I'm glad he seems happy; it's far better for the girls. I don't have to like her.' I'm not sure if I believe her or not.

'It'd just be nice if he could pick someone I didn't work with. And who wasn't a complete bitch.'

Isabel tells me that she is going to start looking for a smaller place soon and sell the house so they can share the profits. I look around sadly, so much of our shared history is in this house. Isabel went into labour with the twins in this very kitchen. The four of us were having dinner at the time, curry to try and speed her along. I sat on the kitchen floor with her and timed contractions while Alex ran around like a headless chicken and Dan hid in the living room.

'It's a shame,' I say, knowing she'll know what I mean.

'It is,' she says, concentrating far too hard on putting the finishing touches on one tiny cake. 'But we have to be practical. It's only a house.'

'How is Alex managing,' I ask tentatively. 'For money?'

'Don't ask,' she says, and I know that that means she is still paying his way.

*

115

All too quickly Alex and the girls arrive back with Lorna in tow. Then Dan turns up with our two and Kerrie and, before I know it, there are eighteen eight- and nine-year-olds causing havoc all over the house. Usually at these parties the grown-ups take it in turns to sit in the little downstairs TV room drinking spritzers and weak lager while the kids take over the living room and do whatever kids do, with hands off supervision from one adult. This time the dynamics are all over the shop so Isabel and I stay with the children the whole time, while Alex and Dan pop in and out every now and then to see what's going on. I am dreading the part when the visiting kids go home and ours all crash out in the bedroom when, traditionally, we all get pissed together. Somehow that doesn't seem like such a good idea this year.

At one point Lorna leaves Alex and Dan to it and comes to join the party. It's such an inappropriate gesture, even if well intentioned, that I don't know what to do. I want to tell her to go away and leave us alone, but I don't want the kids to pick up on a bad atmosphere so I at least sacrifice myself to keep her away from Isabel and I listen to her drivelling on about how Natalie reminds her of herself when she was little and hasn't Nicola got lovely hair and isn't William the spitting image of Dan for about an hour without strangling her, which is, I feel, quite an achievement.

William is the only boy and, as such, is alternately adopted by the screaming masses as some kind of pet and then spurned by them as a pariah. It's like watching a microcosm of a rioting mob. It's impossible to see from the outside why the mood changes, it just suddenly does, and every one of the group picks up the cue at the same time just as if they had been given an order. My poor boy is utterly bemused by the shifting tides, but he valiantly battles through, somehow knowing the good times will come again as they always seem to. I have to stop myself from steaming in to rescue him. By seven thirty, when the first of the parents comes to collect their offspring, he has been a servant, a dog, a horse, a pampered baby and the groom at several play weddings.

Zoe and Kerrie are nowhere to be seen, presumably holed up in Isabel's spare bedroom. I can't blame them for not wanting to spend the whole afternoon in the middle of this mayhem. It's exhausting.

Suddenly it's quiet. Kerrie, the last to leave, is promising to text Zoe as soon as she gets home. What they can have left to talk about I can't imagine. Our kids are staying the night here as they always do on these occasions and, while the shattered twins go off complaining to have their baths, William and Zoe are dispatched to the TV room with sandwiches and Coke and the promise of an hour's TV before bed (William) and two hours for Zoe. The five of us reclaim the living room and flop on the sofas, temporarily ceasing hostilities because we are so knackered. Lorna, of course, is holding court.

'Aren't Nicola and Natalie funny the way they're so different I mean I said to Nicola you should be a journalist when you grow up because you know how she likes telling tales and she said I want to be a nurse stupid it's Natalie who should be a journalist and . . .'

Isabel stands up suddenly, as if remembering exactly what the situation is.

'Actually, maybe I should phone for cabs.'

'No,' I say, pulling her hand so she sits again. 'We'll stay for a bit.' I want to say that Alex and Lorna should go. Surely if they had any kind of awareness they would offer. But, of course, they don't.

'Why don't I get some drinks?' Lorna says, oblivious to the tension. 'What does everyone want?'

Isabel looks at her open-mouthed for a second as do I. Lorna starts collecting our glasses as if she were the gracious hostess.

'No!' Isabel says, snapping back to life. 'I'll do it. Thanks, though, Lorna,' she adds in an effort to be nice. I don't know why she's bothering. OK, so maybe Lorna thought she was helping in some kind of misguided way, but her lack of social awareness is staggering. She's got Isabel's husband and now she's acting like she's taking over her home too. Or, at least, that's how it seems to me.

'I'll help you,' I say to Isabel, practically snatching the glasses out of Lorna's hands.

Dan settles down, as if in for the long haul.

'Let's all get pissed,' he says.

In retrospect this was not a good idea.

13

OK, so here's what I remember. Nothing. I woke up this morning in my own bed, but with no idea how I had got there. I'm aware that my head hurts and that I feel sick and that something bad has happened although I can't see through the fog to recall what exactly that is. My first thought is Dan. Oh God, please don't let me have started a fight with Dan. I do that sometimes when I'm drunk and I start to get irrationally irritated about the fact that he's so placid, that he never rises to the bait.

I look around. There's no sign of him but his side of the bed is rumpled so we clearly both slept in the same room, which is a good omen. I groan and roll over, looking at the clock. Eight forty-five. Isn't it Monday? Don't I have a job to go to? I try to pull myself up to a sitting position, but my body won't play ball. I'm scared that if I move I'm going to vomit and, looking down, I see that the washing-up bowl is beside the bed filled with God knows what, but it must have come from me.

Thankfully, just as I'm about to burst into tears of despair, Dan comes in, dressed and ready to go out and, what's more, he's smiling or at least he's not looking like he hates me.

'How are you feeling?' he asks, and sits on the bed.

'Oh God. What happened? What did I do?'

'You don't remember?' he says, which makes me feel worse. So there is something that I should be remembering.

I shake my head but even that small movement makes me feel queasy.

'Did we have a fight? Was I mean to you?'

He strokes my head. 'No, of course not.'

'What then?' And then it hits me like a ten-ton truck. Lorna. 'Oh God,' I say. 'Lorna.'

'Yes,' Dan says. 'Lorna. But don't worry too much about it. She was drunk as well. We all were. She probably won't even remember.'

He clearly doesn't know Lorna.

'You do,' I say.

'I stopped drinking before the rest of you because I knew one of us had to be in control enough to call a cab.'

'Tell me what I did.'

Dan kisses me. 'I'll have to be quick; I'm going to be late for work."

'Just get it over with.'

'You just told her what you thought of her I guess. Nothing that you haven't said about her to me but I'm not sure you ever would have intentionally said those things to her face . . .'

If I didn't already feel sick before then I would now. 'What things?'

'You know, that you think she's desperate, that she's only with Alex because she'd have any man at this point, that she's annoying . . .'

'Oh God. OK, stop. Don't tell me any more. Oh God,' I say again, and I bury my head in the pillow.

120

Then I remember Alex. 'What did Alex do?'

'Let's just say I'd keep out of his way for a while,' Dan says, and I want to think that he's joking, but I know he's not. 'There's nothing you can do about it now so there's no point beating yourself up,' he carries on, and I notice he has a sneaky glance at his watch.

'It's OK,' I say. 'Go to work.'

'It's just I have a meeting at nine forty-five. Otherwise . . .'

'It's fine. I'll be fine.'

One thing I know is that I can't call in sick. In my absence Lorna will answer the phone and, of course, she will know that I'm not ill at all. Well, I am but not in a way that it's acceptable to miss work for. Besides what would I say to her when she picked up? Once Dan has left I drag myself out of bed and stand under the shower without even bothering to wash properly. If I leave in ten minutes, I'll only be about fifteen minutes late for work. I'll be useless, I'll probably smell and my pores will be oozing vodka, but at least I'll be there. I can decide how I'm going to handle the situation when I'm on the tube.

The fact is that I genuinely do feel awful. For all my going on and on about Lorna I know that she didn't deserve this. No one would. I've never been the kind of person who feels they have the right to tell other people what they think of them. Who sees it as some kind of virtue – 'at least I'm honest' – when actually all they are is rude. I wouldn't want anyone to do it to me so why would I feel I could do it to anybody else? I can be cutting, but only in my own head or to Isabel or Dan to make them laugh. I've never been a bully; I hate those people. I'd never want to be the cause of anyone's misery. There's only one thing I can do and that is to offer up a genuine and abject apology as soon as I get to the office. I'll try to explain to her that it was more about me and the loss of my secure little family than it was about her. I'll grovel. I may not like Lorna, but I truly want to put right whatever I've done wrong. Then later I'll have to think about calling Alex and making peace with him. And Isabel to apologise for ruining the night. One step at a time.

On the way to work memories come flashing back like lightning strikes. I catch an image of Lorna crying, one of Alex's furious face, Isabel, bless her, trying gently to tell me to be quiet, to go home. I hear myself telling Lorna she has an eating disorder, that she needs psychiatric help. I force myself to block out the flashbacks by concentrating on just how shit I feel in the present, which isn't as hard as you might imagine given how sick I feel and the jolting of the tube carriage. At one point I gag and put my hand over my mouth, and the bloke next to me changes seats, rolling his eyes at a woman opposite as he goes.

Before I've even put my bag down I am saying, 'Lorna, I am so sorry.'

She looks at me with an expression that could freeze water and says nothing.

'I was drunk. I'm an idiot. I didn't mean those things I said. Any of them. Really.'

Still she doesn't speak, but I can't seem to stop.

'I've been thinking about it. I was threatened, I think, by having you come into our little social circle. I was worried that it would change everything forever and I hate change. It's ridiculous, I know. And it certainly doesn't excuse what I did but it maybe explains it a bit.'

Nothing.

'Say something, please. I can't take back what I said, but I want you to believe I am truly sorry. Please say you accept my apology.'

Finally she opens her mouth. 'I'm busy, Rebecca,' she says. 'I really don't want to listen to you.'

'But,' I say, 'you have to. I need to get this sorted now. I can't get through the day with the cloud of my bad behaviour hanging over me.'

Lorna's eyes narrow. 'Really? I have to?'

'I don't mean that you have to. I just mean please will you? I feel really bad. Please just let me apologize and then we can move on.'

'You smell terrible, do you know that?' she says, getting up and going to the kitchen. 'For God's sake, don't let any of the clients see you like this.'

I consider following her, crawling in on my hands and knees, beating myself with a stick, anything, but right at that moment Joshua comes hurtling out of his office as he always does.

'Morning,' he says, en route to make himself a coffee. 'How are you today?'

'I have a hangover, I'm afraid,' I say weakly. There's no point even trying to disguise the fact.

123

'Hair of the dog,' he barks without missing a stride. 'Morning,' he shouts to Lorna as he arrives at the kitchen and then she pushes the door shut and I know that they are talking about me.

As the physical hangover starts to recede I am left with the spiritual one, twice as powerful and ten times as distressing. I'm a bad person. I know that when I have a few drinks too many I have a tendency to show off, to act brave and hard and like I couldn't care less what anyone thinks of me. And I also know that the next day I am always full of regret and shame. I am too old to behave like this. But still I allow it to happen. I say yes to one glass of wine after another even when I am in the company of someone I have been secretly fantasizing about putting in their place. Even when I know, as I accept glass three, that this would be a terrible idea. Suddenly I'm confident. Overexcited by my own fabulous quick tongue, my ability to make bystanders gawp at my straight-talking bravery, to make my enemies appear *that* small. Usually, on balance, I get away with it because comedy outweighs cruelty by a significant margin – like I said before, I'm not naturally mean. But then I've never felt about anyone the way I feel about Lorna. It was a stupid thing to do. Immature. A look-at-me moment from someone who usually hides in the shadows.

Lorna lets me suffer all day. And who could blame her? I offer her a weak smile every time I catch her eye, which she makes sure isn't often. At one point she calls Alex and talks about me right in front of my face as if I wasn't there. She puts on a stage whisper as if I'm not meant to hear, but she's on her mobile so if she cared that much she could just leave the room.

'Well, I'm hurt, Alex. I mean, no one likes to hear these things about themselves.'

I bury my head in my work and try to pretend I can't hear.

'No, no,' she's saying. 'I'm sure I'll feel better later. You know me, I'm thick skinned.'

I decide I don't need to put myself through this and so I walk out and sit in the ladies' for five minutes until I'm sure she will be finished. And, while I'm there, I decide I might as well have a good cry because I'm miserable and I feel ill and I hate myself. I can't go home feeling like this. If I let it drag over into another day, I won't sleep and getting through to her tomorrow will be even harder once she's dug her heels in even further. I have to resolve it. Much as I would love a world where Lorna and I could ignore each other for the rest of our lives that isn't the world I live in. She's one of my bosses and the girlfriend of my husband's best friend. Even if I didn't feel so bad I would have to sort things out. The only thing I can think to do is to wait until the end of the day in the hope that Joshua and Melanie leave before Lorna does and then beg. Corner her when she has no audience to play to and hope that I can appeal to her better nature. If she has one. I have no option.

The afternoon drags on and on. Every time she stands up I'm terrified she's going to reach for her coat and leave for the day. I keep my head down, determined not to make things worse before I can make them better.

Eventually both Joshua and Melanie head for the door. Lorna scrambles for her bag, intent on avoiding being left alone with me for a second, but I've started before she can even sling it over her shoulder.

'Lorna,' I say, edging over to the door in case she makes a run for it. I've pretty much decided I'll rugby tackle her if she does. 'Can I talk to you?'

'I'm going to be late,' she says, stuffing one arm into a sleeve of her coat. 'And I don't think we have anything to talk about anyway.'

'It'll only take a minute. Please just hear me out. There's nothing I can do but apologize. I'm really sorry. One hundred per cent honestly sorry for the way I behaved. I can't emphasize enough how much I know I'm in the wrong. And I don't expect you to say that it's fine or it's forgotten. And I know we're never going to be great friends. But could we maybe try to move on? Get back to how we were?'

She stands looking at me disdainfully for a moment.

'What? You reading my personal emails and sharing the details with your friends?'

I'm so taken aback I can't think what to say.

'Alex told me last night,' she adds, throwing her trump card on the table. 'I always knew you were a bitch, but at least I thought you were professional.'

'Lorna, I . . .' I run out of steam pretty quickly. There's nothing I can really say now to defend myself. Thanks, Alex. At least now I know where your real loyalties lie. As if there was really any question that any of them still lay with me.

'In fact, Alex talked a lot about you. Like how you would have hated whoever he went out with now because you've got no interest in him being happy – you just want your cosy little foursome to stay the same. It's always about you.'

I'm fuming but I don't want to let her see it. Partly because I don't see what good it would do, but also because I don't want her to think that she's struck a nerve. Which, of course, she has. I try to make light of what she's said, forcing a fake laugh. 'That's ridiculous.'

She ignores me. 'He also said that Isabel used to say you were too clingy. That it was oppressive the way you always wanted to do everything with them, just the four of you. He said it was one of the few things they agreed on by the end.'

She pauses to take in the effect her dart has had and, if she thinks she's scored a direct hit, she's right. I try to tell myself that she's making it up to hurt me or that Alex was just feeding her what he thought she'd want to hear, but the truth is it's not out of the realms of possibility. I know that there were many occasions when either Alex or Isabel or even Dan said something along the lines of 'shall we invite so and so' when we were arranging a birthday dinner or even just a night down the pub and, thinking about it now, I realize that I was always the one saying no, it's more fun with just us. I feel warm tears spring up in the corners of my eyes and I try to hold them in, which, of course, is impossible and one escapes and rolls traitorously down my cheek. I flick my head to one side, hoping it'll fly off, hoping she won't notice, but

I catch a glimmer of a smirk on her face. She knows she's got to me. This isn't quite going to plan.

'You see, Rebecca, things don't stay the same forever. Loyalties shift. You have to earn friendship. You can't just assume that because you were close to someone once you'll always stay that way whatever. Especially if you don't respect their choices. You've made Alex choose between you, his friend, and me, the woman he's in love with, and, you know what, he told me there's no contest.'

She's gathering up her stuff again to leave in triumph. I'm lost for words, floored by the things she's said, which I guess is the effect she wanted. Payback for my savaging of her last night. It's understandable. But I'm hurt and I can't help but want to fight back.

'Lorna,' I say, without really thinking through what I'm going to say next. 'Alex is . . .' I pause. I have to remember I'm trying to make things better here despite everything. 'Just . . . it's not as straightforward as you think. Don't buy into everything he says, OK?'

Lorna snorts. 'Alex and I are together now whether you like it or not.'

'Who Alex chooses to go out with is nothing to do with me,' I say, trying to get back to the point. 'But given that we are bound to keep having to spend a lot of time together maybe we need to try to work out a way to be friends.'

She sniffs. 'We're never going to be friends, Rebecca. But Daniel will still be Alex's best mate and so we'd still all have to see each other even if we didn't work together. I'd never get in the way of Alex's friendship with Dan,' she says, implying that she might well get in the way of his friendship with me, such as it is these days.

'Fine,' I say, giving up. 'I've tried, OK?'

And I have. I've tried to atone for my sin, but she's not going to let me. There's nothing else I can do other than try to be nice, try to kill her with kindness. That doesn't last for long.

'Alex was right,' Lorna pipes up as I am putting my coat on. 'You've got self-esteem issues.'

I stop dead in my tracks. 'Excuse me?'

'He says you've always been insecure. He says that's what makes you lash out at people. You think that you're being funny, but no one else does. It embarrasses people. He says he hates being around you after you've had a few drinks.'

OK, that's it. Resolution gone.

'Oh really? And did Alex have anything else to say?' I've gone from the defence to the offence. Supplicant to aggressor. She blinks momentarily like she's nervous she's woken a hibernating bear, but then she remembers that she holds all the good cards, or so she believes.

'Yes, actually. He said he felt sorry for Dan. Backed into his small corner of the world because you never want to do anything new or meet anyone new . . .'

I've stopped listening because the scale of the betrayal, the slap in the face from someone I thought of as family, is overwhelming. OK, so she might be exaggerating. She might be embellishing to add to the hurt, but there's no doubt in my mind that the heart of what she's saying did indeed come from Alex. Did I really hurt him that much when I rejected him? I can think of no other reason why he'd want to punish me in this way. Lorna is smirking a victory smile and I want to wipe it right off her face. Forget trying to get along; I want to wound her like she's wounded me. If she wants to play dirty, then so can I. I speak before I have a chance to censor myself, even though a small voice inside my head is already telling me to stop. Don't. Say. It.

'Is this the same Alex who keeps telling me he's in love with me?' I say, and then I stand back and wait, pleased to see I've got her attention. She gives a little snort of derision, but it's not confident. I want to make certain she's understood exactly what I'm saying.

'The Alex who told me he'd been in love with me for years? On the day – the very day – he first asked you out. In fact he got in touch with you about an hour after I'd rejected him yet again. After I'd told him that there was no chance, I could never be interested and asked him to please leave me alone. Coincidence, isn't it?'

She's looking at me open-mouthed, trying to work out whether or not I'm bluffing. I'm relying on her having as many insecurities as me, even if they're better hidden.

'Didn't you ever wonder why he just called you like that, out of the blue? Didn't you think it odd that you've only been seeing each other for two months and he's already telling you he loves you? Or do you really believe that you're that irresistible?'

Lorna is red in the face. 'You're pathetic,' she says through gritted teeth.

'Am I?' I say, secure in my victory.

'As if Alex would ever fall for you,' she adds, looking me up and down.

'Why don't you ask him?'

There's nothing more to be said so I pick up my bag and sweep out of the room.

'You know what?' Lorna shouts after me. 'Your real problem is that you have a complex about the way you look. You're fat and unattractive and you can't deal with the fact that I'm neither of those things.'

She screams this last sentence, determined to ensure that I hear every word, which, of course, I do but so does Mary who I find hovering on the doorstep as I open the front door.

'Oh,' she says. 'I was . . .'

'She's in there,' I say, indicating the room behind me.

'It's just . . . I'm meant to be meeting her for a drink and a chat, that's all.' Clearly Lorna had forgotten that she'd arranged to see one of her only clients in her rush to get away from me earlier.

'Go on in,' I say. I think about adding something like 'we were just reading aloud from a new play'. Something that would explain the shouting and the personal insults that Mary must have just witnessed, but it sounds lame and untrue and, besides, why should I get Lorna off the hook. She's Mary's agent; she can explain why she was shouting things like 'you're fat and unattractive' at a colleague. A subordinate, no less.

*

As I travel home on the Piccadilly line, it begins to sink

131

in exactly what I've done. I don't feel bad for losing my temper with Lorna. She asked for it. I tried my best to apologize to her and she wouldn't accept. She goaded me and pushed me until I snapped and, to be honest, I would have had to be superhuman not to have risen to the bait.

But the one thing that I should have kept to myself, that I never should have told anyone if I wasn't going to tell Dan, was that Alex had declared himself in love with me. I'm not so much worried about how that piece of information might make Lorna feel as I am about Dan. I made a decision to keep Alex's declaration – Dan's best friend's betrayal – to myself, and having made that choice the only other thing I had to do was to stick to it. It was one thing not to tell Dan at the time. It's a whole other issue for him to find out about it months later because I've blurted it out to someone else. I try to decide what to do next. I could go home now and tell Dan right away. 'Oh, by the way, I forgot to mention it but a couple of months ago Alex told me he was in love with me. He asked me to leave you. I don't know why I didn't think to tell you before. It must have slipped my mind.' He'd want to know why I hadn't told him at the time, though. He'd feel like Alex and I had been secretly colluding behind his back somehow, keeping the truth from him. He'd be devastated by Alex's disloyalty. Their bond precedes even mine with Dan. It's indestructible. Or so he's always thought. I can't be the one to take that away from him.

I try to work out the odds of him finding out if I don't tell him. Lorna is obviously going to go straight to Alex and accuse him. But there's no way Alex is ever going to want Dan to find out. And I imagine that Lorna is going to be conflicted between her desire to hurt me and her reluctance to tell a story that, after all, paints her in quite a humiliating light.

By the time I get to Caledonian Road station I've decided to take my chances. If Lorna is so vindictive that she'd be prepared to hurt Dan – who has never been anything other than sweet and welcoming to her – then I will simply tell him the whole truth. I'll sell Alex down the river because, actually, I've realized I have no reason to protect him any more. He's betrayed me in the most fundamental way. If we ever were really such close friends as I thought we were, then we certainly aren't any more.

Dan is happily supervising the kids' homework when I get in, rather later than usual. He's letting them have the TV on while they do it, which he always does, although he knows I don't approve. I decide to let them get away with it. I'm hit by a wave of love for my little family so strong it nearly flattens me. I put my arms round Dan's back and kiss the top of his head five or six times in succession.

'What was that for?' he says.

'No reason,' I reply, but I don't let go of him.

14

There's an eerie calm in the office next morning. I don't
know what I was expecting. That Lorna would come at
me like a banshee, scissors in hand, or that Joshua would
call me in to say that this time I really had overstepped
the mark, but everything seems pretty much like normal.
Lorna is a little red eyed, like she hasn't slept much but
we edge around one another, not speaking, not even
making eye contact, which suits me just fine.

The great day has come for her to move into her
new office. Melanie asks me if I'll help pack up Lorna's
stuff and I oblige, slinging everything into boxes like a
possessed woman. The quicker she moves the better for
me. By lunchtime she's gone.

Today is also the day that I have decided to select the
likely candidates from the applications we have received.
I need an ally. I have already weeded out and discarded
the no hopers but the pile of potentials is still too large.
Sitting in blissful solitude I read through them all carefully, looking for clues. Anyone who seems too pleased
with themselves gets put straight on the reject pile. As
does anyone who comes across as too ambitious. Joshua
and Melanie are looking for some continuity. They want
someone who will be happy to remain an assistant for at
least three or four years, not just someone who will use

us as a stepping stone to greater things. I have to keep reminding myself that it's important I look for someone who will make Joshua and Melanie happy as well as me. They need to be bright, willing, friendly and eager to learn as well as sane, able to listen and with a BMI of more than twenty-two.

By the end of the day I have made a shortlist of five and I've called them all and arranged for them to come in and be interviewed.

The idea is that I will give them a sort of pre-interview, ostensibly to explain the ins and outs of the job ('You'll be doing general office duties, answering the phone as well as working exclusively to Cruella de Vil in the next room there.') but really so that I get to check them out. Then I'll send them through to meet with Joshua, Melanie and, of course, Lorna. They all sound quite nice on the phone and I feel a momentary blip of guilt that one of them will be sentenced to work for the boss from hell, but I manage to get over that pretty quickly. I leave for the night feeling optimistic. What's more, Lorna and I have managed to pass a whole day without exchanging a single word and the company didn't fall to pieces, Joshua and Melanie didn't even notice and everything has been done that had to be done. I'm desperate to know what happened last night, whether Alex and Lorna have had a fight about my bombshell, whether it's just confirmed to them that they are right to unite against me or whether he's managed to convince her that I was just making it up, but I can never ask.

*

135

I've completely forgotten that it's William's big day. The first time since he has been at secondary school that he's invited a friend home. He and Sam seem to be doing some kind of chemistry experiment in the kitchen while Zoe, huffy that she had to walk home from school in the company of two – as she puts it – freaks, rather than just the usual one, is holed up in her room texting furiously.

'Hi,' I say to Sam. 'I'm William's mum.'

'Pleased to meet you,' he says, holding out his hand stiffly for me to shake, which I do, but then I don't really know what to say so I settle for, 'Well, don't make too much mess,' and leave them to destroy my beautiful Italian marble worktops.

With no children for company and no kitchen to start dinner in, I sit by myself in the living room waiting for Dan to come home. I'm not particularly good at being on my own when I have things on my mind. I have a tendency to brood and to dwell on all my failings and the many ways in which my charmed life could implode. By the time Dan walks through the door I'm almost desperate to know what, if any, fallout there's been from my set-to with Lorna.

'Have you spoken to Alex today?' I say as casually as I can, having forced myself to wait for him to get changed and grab a beer from the fridge. (Seen through the partially opened kitchen door: two small boys covered from head to foot with what looks like flour and something ominous bubbling away on the cooker.)

'No,' he says, and he pops his can and, feet up, picks up the newspaper and starts to read.

So that's that. For now.

For a couple of days Lorna and I carry on in the same state of denial – not of the problem between us but of each other's existence. We speak only when I have to put a call through to her. She says 'hello' and I say 'so and so is on the phone'. I don't even wait to hear if she wants to take the call or not, I just put them straight through. I've barely clapped eyes on her either. Now that she has her own office she rarely seems to leave it except to shut herself in with either Joshua or Melanie or, I assume, to go to lunch. Obviously all question of us sharing the lunchtime duties until her replacement arrives has gone out of the window because that would mean us communicating and that's not about to happen any time soon. So I have taken to sticking the phones on to voicemail and running to the sandwich shop in the alley round the corner to grab something to eat at my desk. I know the end is in sight.

Today is interview day. Five women and one man are coming in to give it their best shot. They're a mixed bunch – a mother returning to work, two recent graduates, a financial advisor who wants to start again in a new direction, a redundant PA and an older woman whose youngest child has just gone off to university leaving her feeling adrift in the world. Actually, I'm not sure what Joshua and Melanie will make of that last one. I have a feeling they're expecting some young thing they can mould. But I strongly believe you have to give everyone a fair chance, regardless of age or experience. You never know what valuable skills you might unearth.

The first, Marie, turns out to be a little disappointing. She's the mum trying to get back into work now that her daughter has gone to school – a situation so like my own that I'm desperate to like her, but she has an Estuary whine with the added pseudo Australian implied question mark at the end of every sentence which, I think, would send me crazy after a couple of hours. She seems keen enough, but she's also a bit dull. I get the feeling she'd be as happy working in an accountant's office as for a theatrical and literary agency and I think it's important that whoever gets the job be as in love with our world as we all are. As I send her through to meet the triumvirate I mentally cross her name off the list. Then comes Annie, the financial advisor who is a bit up herself and who doesn't make me feel confident that she'd really take kindly to being asked to make a cup of tea, and Amita, the recently redundant PA (executive PA as she reminds me several times like I'm supposed to know the difference) who seems like a know-it-all. I imagine she would have a rigid code about what exactly was and was not in her job description (cue Phone Wars 2). Several times she says things like, 'That wasn't how we did it at MacReedy's,' which is the insurance company she worked for, and I have to bite my tongue to stop myself from saying, 'Do you know, I couldn't give a toss how you did things at MacReedy's, actually.' When I show her the filing system – which I agree might leave something to be desired – she says, 'I'll have to reorganize that,' and I decide I hate her.

I'm trying to explain to her that the way things work here is the way we all like it when the phone rings. I'm having to answer all the calls while talking to the candidates and, in a way, it's helpful because it gives them a good idea of what's involved in the job. I set up an audition before their very eyes. I take a call from someone at *Reddington Road* who tells me that one of their writers has keeled over sick and they've decided – for this read they're desperate and everyone else is busy – to promote Craig to writing a real episode. I deftly sidestep a call from someone at a casting newsletter, which takes money from our acting clients in return for supplying pointless information on projects that are barely even half ideas yet, let alone starting to cast. No, I tell them, none of our writers or directors have anything interesting in the pipeline. One slip, let one piece of premature information go, and the office will be inundated for weeks with photos and CVs from hopeful actors and actresses looking for a non-existent job. After each call I talk through what just happened with whoever I'm with and the best way to deal with it. The fourth time I'm just relieved that I can stop listening to Amita tell me how crap we all are.

'Let's see what this is,' I say, enjoying my role as mentor. 'Mortimer and Sheedy,' I say into the phone in my best sing-song voice.

'So, are you happy now?' a man's voice barks at me in such an aggressive tone that it takes me a moment to work out who it is. Alex. I'm so taken aback by how angry he sounds that I don't say anything. I'm aware of Amita looking at me.

'No point trying to pretend you're not there,' he growls after a moment's silence. I snap back to life.

'I'm busy, Alex.'

'You got what you wanted, OK? Lorna's finished with me.'

I should be elated. Surely this is the answer to all my prayers. But I never intended to be the root cause. I don't want to be the one who gets the blame for my wish coming true.

'I'm sorry, OK?' I start to say, my voice lowered, but he's not interested in my side of the conversation.

'You're a vindictive bitch, Rebecca,' he says. 'I hope you can live with yourself.'

I want to say, 'Hold on, did you or did you not tell me you were in love with me and had been forever on the same day you first asked Lorna out? Did you or did you not ask her out just to spite me? So don't ask me to believe that I have been responsible for breaking up the greatest love story ever told,' but Amita is looking at me expectantly so, of course, I can't. Instead I say, 'I can't talk about this now. We'll discuss it all when you're feeling a bit more rational,' and I put the phone down.

'Are you allowed to have personal conversations in the office? We never were at MacReedy's. It was deemed to be unprofessional. Quite right too, in my opinion,' Amita says pompously, and I hate her even more.

I try to get back on track, but I'm so rattled by the venom in Alex's voice it's hard to concentrate. Luckily I am saved by Annie's departure. Melanie shows her out and then I introduce Amita and sit back down to wait for the next one to arrive. Melanie and I have been going through an elaborate thumbs-up/thumbs-down ritual behind each of the candidate's backs and this time I jerk my thumb down several times like a vindictive Roman emperor, trying to convey just how unsuitable Amita is.

Amita is followed by the first of the two graduates, Nadeem, who is desperate, he tells me, for a break into the industry. He loves theatre and he's completely in awe of the whole place. I like him. I like graduate number two, Carla, as well. She's quiet, keen to learn, unsure of what direction she wants to take, but interested enough in what we do to give off a very positive vibe. Neither of them has any experience of anything, really, but they both get a tentative thumbs-up as they go in.

But it's Kay I really warm to. I've done her a disservice assuming she was about to be pensioned off. She's only in her mid-forties I realize when she walks in; she just had her children early. In her twenties, before she had her first child, she worked briefly in a theatre box office. She didn't much like the job, she tells me, but she loved being able to sneak in and see all the new productions. She never really thought about a career because she had always known she wanted to have kids and stay at home to look after them. Now she feels like she's got no purpose in life. No longer needed as a mother, marriage long since over. She wants to put herself first for once and work in a field she knows she'll love. She doesn't care how lowly the duties, she just wants to feel part of something again.

141

She's down to earth and smart. I find myself wanting to burst into tears all over her and tell her the ridiculous mess I have got myself and everyone else into. I feel like she could be a friend. I can see myself sharing the reception with her very happily. My thumbs are up almost before she's even turned her back.

Once Kay has gone Melanie, Joshua and Lorna closet themselves away with the door shut and it's all I can do not to put a glass against it and listen. I'm desperate for them to want to know my opinion and, thankfully, Melanie still values me enough to come out and canvas it.

'We're stuck between Kay and Amita,' she says. 'We thought you might be able to help us make up our minds as you seemed to have pretty strong opinions on both of them.'

God, Amita's in the running? How did that happen? I go through to the other room. Lorna won't even look at me and, after my conversation with Alex, I'm nervous of catching her eye too so the atmosphere is even more tense than before.

'Well?' Joshua says. 'What did you think?'

I measure my words carefully. 'I like Kay,' I say. 'She seemed bright and motivated. I think we'd get on,' I add. Surely they don't want to bring in anyone else I'm going to be feuding with.

'And I got the impression you weren't so impressed with Amita,' Melanie says. I nod. I need to make sure that whatever I say comes across as a negative rather than a positive.

'She's rather . . .' What? Efficient? Experienced? Conscientious? '. . . I got the feeling she might be a bit of a job's worth,' is the best I can come up with. 'I'm not sure she'd be happy to muck in and do whatever was needed.' Mucking in has always been a big deal at Mortimer and Sheedy.

'Mmm, that's what we were afraid of too,' Joshua says, and I assume the 'we' means him and Melanie because she nods. 'You were keen on Amita, though, weren't you Lorna?'

Great, now I've unwittingly pissed all over another of Lorna's bonfires. It doesn't surprise me that she favours Amita, though. She wants a high-powered assistant; it'll add to her status.

'Yes,' she says, and I'm forced to look at her so as not to seem rude. I'm shocked by what I see. I'm used to red-eyed, newly single Lorna, but this version looks like she has been crying for days. Either the tears or lack of sleep have forged little dark gulleys under her eyes. I'm not sure that she has any make-up on and her hair is a mess. Guilt makes me look away again.

'I think we could do with some updating. Things don't always work as efficiently as they should here,' she continues, and I know that what she is really implying, not very subtly, is that I am shit and they need to bring in someone who can put a rocket up me. However, she hasn't thought her reasoning through. About the worst thing you can say to Joshua is that Mortimer and Sheedy needs bringing into the twenty-first century. He doesn't even own a mobile phone. I

143

stay quiet, not wanting to aggravate her more, and wait.

'I think we muddle along OK,' Joshua says, and I know they're going to make the right decision. Right for me at any rate. In reality Mortimer and Sheedy could do with shaking up; it would probably be more efficient, bring in more money – it just wouldn't be such a nice place to work.

'Let's give Kay a month's trial,' he says. 'Lorna, do you want to call her and tell her the good news?'

I breathe a sigh of relief. Sometimes Joshua being an overbearing old patriarch is exactly what's needed.

As I leave the room Lorna gives me a look of such intense loathing that I almost flinch. Back in reception I reflect back on what's happened. I'm surprised, actually, that Lorna dumped Alex. I knew I had hurt her and I guess I knew – maybe at the time I even hoped if I'm being really honest – that what I told her would cause problems between them, but I didn't think she had it in her to end any relationship. I have always assumed that her red-eyed days were caused by whatever man she was currently dating seeing sense. Running for the hills before it was too late. I guess she never felt as strongly for Alex as she tried to make out. If the usual pattern is anything to go by, she'll be weepy for a couple of days and then move on to the next. With Kay hopefully arriving next week to be a human buffer between us, things should settle back down pretty quickly.

Alex is a different prospect altogether. I don't know if there's a way to get our friendship back on track and at this point I don't even know if I want to try. I've seen sides of him these past couple of months that I really don't like. Sides that I hardly even recognize. He bears almost no resemblance to the funny, up for anything, irrepressible joker that I was so close to for so long. I know he's angry with me and I understand why. I've betrayed the fact that he propositioned me, something that I'm sure he believed I would always keep secret. He'll get over it. But whether or not I'll get over the fact that he hit on me in the first place, and the way he's behaved towards me since, that's another story. Not to mention the way he treated Isabel. I'll never forget some of the things he's said to me, his petty planned revenge asking Lorna out, feeding her stories about me, jeopardizing my job really.

I don't know, maybe our friendship was never real in the first place after all if he could try to hurt me like that. Now it's all over I feel a bit overwhelmed by everything. Actually I feel like I want to cry. Like I've been holding it in all this time and now I can let it go. But I'm not going to be that person who sits sniffling at her desk waiting for someone to ask if she's OK. At least I'm going to try not to be. Sometimes it's easier said than done.

15

Dan is spending the evening down the pub with Alex. He announces this as I walk through the front door.

'He and Lorna have split up,' he says. 'He sounds in a bad way. Do you mind?'

'Of course not.' I kiss him on the cheek to demonstrate just how much I don't mind.

'Why don't you come?' Dan says. 'You're always good at cheering Alex up. He'd love to see you.'

Not quite as much as you'd imagine, I think, but I say, 'What about the kids? It's too short notice to get someone to watch them now.' I try to sound like I'm disappointed. Actually I'm nervous about Alex pouring his heart out to Dan. If he drinks too much, who knows what version of the truth he might tell him. But I'm also hoping that this might be it. One night of drowning his sorrows and then move on. Lorna is out of the picture forever and Alex and I can stand back and see exactly what the fallout is.

Zoe, William and I watch TV for a while but I'm finding it hard to concentrate. By the time Dan gets home I'm practically pacing up and down the living room expectantly.

'So,' I ask, 'how was he?'

'He seems to have taken it quite badly,' Dan says, picking at the leftovers of my penne arrabiata. 'I think he actually liked her.'

I snort. Luckily Dan doesn't notice. I'm hesitant to ask my next question, but I have to know so I brave it.

'Why did they . . . you know?' I can't look at him.

'Split up? I don't really know to be honest.'

I breathe out again, slowly.

'It was her, I know that much. He said it was all a big misunderstanding; she overreacted. So I said, well, in that case you can sort it out, convince her she's wrong about whatever it is. But he wouldn't listen.'

'Maybe he's just being dramatic,' I say, overwhelmed with relief that I'm not having to defend myself. 'You know what he's like.'

'I hate seeing him like this.' Dan pours us both a glass of Merlot.

'It was bound to happen,' I say. 'It's too soon after Isabel for him to settle down again. Maybe she was just meant to be his transitional relationship and now he'll be ready to meet someone more . . . suitable.'

Dan laughs. 'Someone you'll like, you mean.'

I smile at him. If only it was that simple, that Alex would meet someone nice and everything could go back to normal. 'Exactly,' I say.

As secrets go mine isn't a particularly big or bad one, but I hate it just the same. I try to reassure myself that it's for Dan's sake, for the sake of his and Alex's friendship, but it still sits uneasily with me. I was always the one who put her hand up in class when the teacher asked whose fault something was. I think I remember once, in junior school, taking the blame for having pushed Pauline Cooper into a puddle when it wasn't even me. It was Andrew Eldon. But I couldn't stand the suspense when our form teacher, Miss Harding, asked who had done it. It wasn't that I was trying to get Andrew Eldon off the hook (cue much playground taunting of 'you love him, you want to kiss him'), I just wanted to break the tension. I've never been afraid to face the music. Mine or anyone else's. Until now that is. And that's because the person who would be most hurt by the truth coming out isn't me, it's Dan, and I won't allow that to happen. So I make the appropriate faces that agree that it's sad that Alex and Lorna have broken up and that I feel sorry for Alex, but deep down I let myself start to feel optimistic. OK, so mine and Alex's relationship isn't going to just repair itself any time soon, but with Lorna out of the picture at least I am only going to have one person who hates me in my social life. I suppose that's not bad going.

Isabel calls me just as I'm arriving at work the next morning.

'Did you know Alex and Lorna have split up?' she asks after we've got through the niceties.

'I did,' I say. 'Who told you?'

'The girls. They're delighted.'

I laugh. 'How is he taking it?' she asks before I can say anything else. Despite everything, Isabel's first concern is still always for Alex.

'Oh, you know,' I say. 'I don't think he's that bothered.'

'Really?' she says, fishing. 'I thought he seemed quite fond of her.'

'He'll get over it,' I say harshly.

I realize that things at work aren't going to cruise back to normal quite as smoothly as I'd hoped when I arrive at the office and Joshua and Melanie are waiting for me in reception, looking like two policemen sent to break the bad news.

'Morning,' I say nervously, and busy myself around my desk, waiting for whatever it is they are going to say.

'Have you got a minute?' Joshua says, and shuts the door to the corridor so I can't escape. I briefly wonder what they would do if I said, 'No, I don't actually. I'm busy; you'll have to make an appointment.'

'Sure. What's going on?' I sit down behind my desk. Joshua and Melanie look at each other. They obviously haven't worked out their routine – who is going to be good cop and who is going to be bad. Joshua looks at the floor, thus indicating that as the senior partner he is handing the reins over to Melanie.

'The thing is, Rebecca,' she says, once she's got the message. 'Lorna has spoken to us about something and we felt that we needed to hear your side of the story. She's very upset.'

I'm momentarily taken aback. I had a feeling that whatever was wrong Lorna would have been behind it, but surely 'Rebecca told me that my boyfriend doesn't love me' wouldn't stand up in an industrial tribunal. I

149

don't trust myself to say anything constructive so I just say, 'Right . . .?' and wait to see what Melanie will come up with next.

'She's made a complaint, an official complaint I suppose you'd call it . . .'

I want to jump in, but I stop myself. What does she mean an official complaint? What is this? ICI? Since when did Mortimer and Sheedy have a procedure in place for official complaints? I can feel myself going red. I take a sip from my bottle of Evian water and try to look calm.

'And while you know we love you we have to take it seriously. There's been a lot of tension between the two of you and it's making for a terrible atmosphere.'

Melanie stops like she expects me to say something.

'What has she complained about?' I ask, and I know it comes out more aggressively that I meant it to. Melanie hesitates and I feel a bit sorry for her. I shouldn't make this any harder for her than it already is. I try to soften my expression, but my face doesn't want to play ball. Joshua, clearly tired of waiting, decides to cut to the chase.

'Lorna believes that you have been looking through her emails when she's out of the office and sharing personal details from them with other people.'

Wow. That wasn't what I was expecting. That truly is a low blow. OK, if that's the way she wants to play it.

'What?' I do my best hurt/confused expression (and thank God for my three years' training on the Royal Holloway drama degree course). They look a bit confused

150

by my lack of a confession. I'm usually only too willing to own up to my own failings.

Melanie smiles nervously. 'She said that this friend of yours that she's been seeing, Alex, he told her.'

'Alex and I fell out a while ago,' I say, doing my best to maintain eye contact. I will myself not to look down and to the left, which, I think, indicates that you are lying. Or is it down and to the right? Anyway, I try to keep my gaze as steady as I can and say, 'He can be very bitchy. I imagine this is his way of getting back at me. To be honest, I never thought he would be this vindictive, though.'

'So it's not true?' Joshua says, and he looks relieved.

'No! Of course not. I would never do anything like that.'

'Well, that hopefully clears that up. I'm sorry we had to ambush you like this, but it's just that Lorna seemed very upset and we're duty bound to keep everyone happy,' Joshua says pleasantly.

'Did she say what personal things I was supposed to have looked at?' I can't help saying. I can't resist the idea that one of them might have to say, 'Oh yes, she told us that you told your friends that she refers to her clitoris as "the bean".'

Neither of them bother to answer that one, but Melanie says, 'What a horrible thing to do. He doesn't sound like a very nice bloke.'

'Apparently they've split up,' I say. 'I think that's why Lorna seems so unhappy at the moment probably. It's nothing to do with anything between her and me.' I try to say this in a way that I hope implies that Lorna is maybe feeling a little more irrational than usual and might be prone to a few wild accusations of her own. Joshua, who is never comfortable when the conversation approaches anything like personal, heads off into his office. Case closed. Melanie, though, is curious and wants the gory details, which I don't want to share with her.

'Like I said,' I say when pressed, 'Alex and I aren't really getting along at the moment so I only heard through Dan. I've no idea what happened.'

'Well, it sounds like it's for the best,' she says, and then thankfully goes off to get on with her work. I give thanks too for the fact that my bosses are so low octane, so trusting, both so wanting all to be right in their little world that they have all the investigative powers of . . . well, of two middle-aged theatrical and literary agents who really don't want to be bothered. I feel bad that I basically just lied to their faces. I'm not a good liar. I never have been. To be honest, I don't want to be. It's not a skill that I ever sought to acquire. New Year's resolutions – must learn knitting, Italian and how to be deceitful. But it's survival of the fittest now.

A few minutes later Lorna arrives conveniently ten minutes after her usual time. As she passes by the door to reception I'm sure she smirks in my direction so I wait with bated breath while she shuts herself in with Melanie. After a few moments I can hear a raised voice and, by the slightly hysterical tone of it, I'd say it was Lorna. I can't make out what she is saying, but

I can imagine. A few minutes later I hear the door slam and she flounces out. Like the coward I really am, I pick up the phone and pretend to be deep in conversation until she's safely back in her office. Round one to me.

I'm still trying to decide what to do about Alex. When he called I told him that I would ring him back later and, of course, I didn't. I couldn't. I don't know what to say to him. If I leave things for too long, I worry that we won't ever be able to act normally around each other, that there will always be an atmosphere. I pick up the phone and dial before I have a chance to change my mind. He answers immediately and my heart starts pounding out of my chest. I need to say something, anything, to start trying to rebuild bridges. Not because I believe I can ever be friends with him again; I'm not that naive. But because Dan of course is, and we need to find a way to operate around each other that allows that friendship to continue.

'Alex . . .' I say, but before I can carry on he butts in, 'I've got nothing to say to you.'

'I know things are messed up between us,' I say, 'but you have to believe me when I say that I had no intention of breaking up your relationship. I know you must be feeling awful about Lorna –'

'You know what, I liked her,' he says viciously. 'I know it doesn't suit you to believe that, but I did. She was never going to be the love of my life but that was for me to decide, not you. I don't really care that she's dumped me, to be honest, but what I do care about is that she dumped me because of you. Who the fuck do you think you are?'

'We need to –' I start to say, but then I hear the blank tone, which tells me he's hung up on me.

A few weeks ago I'd have been elated by the fact that Alex and Lorna are no more. Maybe now he'd get a grip, realize what he'd given up and go back to Isabel. I never doubted that she'd have him. Now it's nowhere near that clear cut. I'm not sure I'd wish this new Alex – this aggressive, spiteful version – on anyone. Well, anyone I like.

Isabel and I meet for a drink after work. We fight our way through the crowds in the Red Lion in Kingly Street and manage to find two stools near the open fireplace that at first seem like a godsend but, as we start to sweat, it quickly becomes clear why no one else has nabbed them. We decide it's still preferable to standing in the crush, though, and edge them away from the fire as much as we can without encroaching on anyone else's space.

She's looking good. Better than she has in weeks, actually, and it's not long before I find out why.

'I've met someone,' she says breathlessly, almost as soon as we've sat down. 'I've been dying to tell you, but I thought I should wait until I'd seen him a couple of times, you know, just in case it was a non-starter.'

I'm rendered speechless momentarily. She's met some-one already? How did that happen? I always thought that your options would narrow dramatically as you hit your forties. All the decent people would be married or at the very least settled down. Those that would be left would be single for a reason – sociopaths or, God forbid, psychopaths. Mummy's boys and 'too scared to come out' gays. But it seems I'm wrong. There are the newly divorced to contend with and the 'missed the marriage boat because I was concentrating on my career' brigade. A whole demographic I had never even realized existed.

Isabel's new man is one of the recently separated, soon-to-be-divorced masses. They met, she tells me, at a parents' evening at the girls' school. He was queuing to see Miss Farley Evans, the year six form tutor; she was flapping around like a disorientated homing pigeon trying to find the table where Mr Leach, one of the year four tutors, had set up shop. He pointed her in the right direction. She said thank you and, because he was handsome and polite, flashed him her best grateful smile. He asked her whose mother she was and they fell into conversation.

'Where was Alex?' I interrupt. Alex may be many things, but he's a good father and he never misses a parents' evening.

'Having some crisis with Lorna,' she says, rolling her eyes. 'He cried off at the last minute. In fact, it was right around the time they split up so I guess he does have an excuse.'

'Mmm . . .' I say, non-committal. 'I suppose so.'

'Is he OK by the way?' she asks after a moment, and I shrug and say, 'Who cares?' which makes her laugh again.

'Anyway,' I say. 'Back to your new man. What's his name?'

'Luke. He's in the middle of a divorce, hence being at parents' night on his own because they can't bear to be in the same room yet, apparently. He has a ten-year-old son and he works in finance doing something I don't understand.'

'And then what?' I ask. 'Let me live vicariously through you. He told you where to find Mr Leach, then what happened?'

'He asked me if I fancied a drink afterwards and I said yes.'

'Really?'

I have never known Isabel single. Well, only for a couple of months and not for at least twenty years. I can't imagine her saying yes to a drink with some random man she's only just met.

'I figured what was the worst that could happen? The teachers at the school all seemed to know him. If he'd turned out to be a maniac, he would have had trouble covering his tracks. So we went to this pub down by the canal and we had a good time. Then he asked me to see him again and I said OK.'

'And?' I say expectantly.

'And the second time we went for a meal. La Petite Maison.'

'I've always wanted to go there,' I say enviously. 'Then what?'

She looks a bit coy, not a look I'm used to on Isabel. 'Then . . . nothing.'

I shriek and a couple at the nearby table look round and give me disapproving stares. 'No! You didn't!'

'Shh,' she says, looking over at them as if they know what we've been talking about. 'No, we didn't. But he did kiss me and then we sat in his car for a bit. You know . . .'

'Izz!' I say. 'The second time you met him? And I'm assuming this is the first person since Alex?'

'Of course,' she says, indignant.

'What was it like? No, I can't ask you that, you're my friend. Don't tell me.'

'I wasn't going to. Anyway, then he took me home and that was that.'

'So, next time . . .? I assume there is going to be a next time?'

She smiles. 'I'm seeing him again on Monday. He has to go away tomorrow on business for a few days. He goes away a lot for business. Switzerland and Brussels mainly. And New York. I'm hoping that at the very least I'll get a few good holidays out of it.'

'So, on Monday?'

'On Monday we're going out to eat again, and then I am hoping that he'll come round to mine, yes.'

'Oh my God! Well, good for you,' I say, and I mean it. This is a good sign. If Isabel is seeing a new man, then there's no way she's still thinking about getting back with Alex.

'I'll keep you posted,' she says. 'Although it'll probably all be over next time I see you. He'll have got bored or met someone else . . .'

'Think positive,' I say. 'There have to be some good men out there and Luke might just be one of them.'

157

'I thought Alex was,' Isabel says, looking deep into her glass. 'I wouldn't have stayed married to him for so long if I didn't. If I hadn't thought we could make it all all right somehow. If I hadn't thought he wanted to make it work as much as I did.'

'Yeah, well, we all make mistakes,' I say, and I pick up our glasses and head to the bar to get us another drink.

I'm a little bit the worse for wear, I realize, as I weave up the Caledonian Road from the tube. Isabel and I have always done this about once a month, left the kids with their fathers and blown off steam together in the pub for a couple of hours. Usually I stop after three glasses because I can't trust myself to get home in one piece otherwise, and because I am trying these days, in a half-hearted fashion, to stick to the recommended government guidelines for unit consumption. But, to-night, I allowed myself one extra because there was so much to catch up on. I'm not exactly drunk, but I don't feel entirely clear headed either. Dan will have fed the kids and corralled them into bed by now, so all I have to do is stay awake and keep him company watching TV for an hour or so, until it's a respectable time to turn in. I haven't eaten but I'm past caring. I might just have another glass of wine, I think daringly, as I round the corner into our street.

I let myself in and head straight for the living room, treading carefully so as not to wake the children. Dan always finds it funny when I've had a few too many so

I don't even try to disguise the fact when I walk in. Tonight, though, I realize, sobering up pretty quickly, he doesn't seem too amused.

I stop in my tracks when I see his expression, which is, to say the least, serious.

'Are you OK?' I say.

'Lorna was here.'

'Lorna?'

'She said she had something to tell me. I think she was disappointed that you weren't here to witness it.'

'What?' I say. 'What did she have to tell you?' Actually I have a pretty good idea, but the way Lorna is acting at the minute it could be anything. Dan smiles a weak smile at me. 'She was trying to convince me that you'd told her Alex was in love with you. That he'd made a pass at you one night a couple of months ago, right before he asked her out.'

He looks at me, willing me to say it's not true. I can't.

'Dan . . . he did . . .' I say, reluctantly.

Dan looks so confused I have to go over and hug him. 'Alex . . .?' he says, pulling away.

I nod. 'He was drunk, he didn't know what he was saying. I was going to tell you, but I figured it was just the drink talking and that he'd be feeling terrible about it once he'd sobered up. I didn't want to cause any problems between you, that's all. I thought it was best all round to just pretend it never happened.'

'Except that you thought it was meaningful enough to tell Lorna about it? She says you told her Alex couldn't really be in love with her because he was in love with you.'

He's right. I did say exactly that to Lorna and I'm not going to lie about it now to Dan, but maybe I can protect him from the whole truth.

'I did say that to her, I'm afraid. I was angry. She's been being awful to me at work and I guess I just snapped. I just wanted to hurt her.' Even as I say this I'm aware that it sounds so pitiful, so unconvincing.

'It's just,' he says, 'that it makes me feel a bit stupid, you know. Like you all had a secret. Like I was the only one who didn't know that my best friend was trying to sleep with my wife.'

'I'm sorry, Dan. I thought not telling you was the right thing to do. I didn't want to hurt you.'

He takes a long sip of his drink. 'Could you just tell me exactly what happened now? Don't spare me. Let me be the judge of what I am and what I'm not able to deal with, OK?'

'OK,' I say, and I tell him the whole story of that night, leaving nothing out, not even the fact that Alex asked me to leave him. When I get to that part Dan's face takes on an expression I have never seen before. Part anger, part devastation. I hesitate, unsure whether to continue. I put my hand on his arm.

'Carry on,' he says. 'What happened next?'

I'm thankful that I can be completely, one hundred per cent honest about my reaction to Alex's proposition. I tell Dan word for word what I said, at least as far as I can remember. The look of relief that passes across his face gives away the fact that he was terrified that I might have responded, that something might actually have happened between Alex and me. It hadn't even occurred to me that he might think that. That he hadn't just been sitting here all evening worrying about his best friend betraying him but his wife too. I reassure him again about the unequivocal nature of my rejection. 'Not,' I say, 'for a single second. Not even for the tiniest fraction of a second.'

I put my hand on his knee and he picks it up with one of his. 'Well, that's something,' he says. 'And how did he react to that?'

'Like I said, he was drunk and I guess he felt humiliated. I told him to go home. Do you remember? You wondered where he was in the morning.'

Dan nods and then he looks right at me. 'And that was really it? There's been nothing since?'

I could keep the rest to myself. That had been what I was intending to do at first and, in retrospect, I should probably have stuck to my plan but then Dan notices my slight hesitation and says, 'The truth, Rebecca. Please,' and it hits me like a bolt of lightning that my loyalty is to him and him alone.

'No . . .' I begin hesitantly. 'There's one more thing. He called me the next day and asked me to meet him for lunch so that we could talk about it.' I stop for a moment as I see Dan's face turn pale.

'So this time he was stone-cold sober?' he says, and I nod. 'I guess so. I had to agree only because I couldn't talk to him on the phone in front of Lorna and I needed to make sure that he'd got the message loud and clear. You do understand, don't you?'

'Yes,' he says, anxious not to make me feel bad. 'He put you in a difficult position.'

'So I met him at YO! Sushi. Because it's open and public, no whispering in corners. Repeated what I'd said the night before about there being no chance and me not being interested. I was angry with him for what he was trying to do to you. We argued, we didn't even eat, I just left.'

'And he was still trying to tell you that he was in love with you? Still trying to persuade you to leave me and go off with him?'

'Yes. I'm so sorry, Dan.'

'It's not your fault,' he says, and he kisses me to show me that he means it. 'It must have been awful for you.'

'It was, to be honest. I hated having a secret from you. I just thought, well, your friendship with Alex is so important to you. I didn't want to be the one who ruined it.'

'You haven't. He has.' Dan's expression has hardened and for a moment I allow myself to wonder what he might do, what might happen next.

'And that's why you were so cynical about him and Lorna?'

I nod. 'He called and asked her out right after we had that lunch. It just felt like a childish way to get back at me. He knew how much I disliked her. And then five minutes later we're meant to believe they're in love.'

'I feel sorry for her,' Dan says, ever reasonable, 'if he's used her like that. Don't you?'

'I suppose so,' I say unconvincingly. 'It's complicated. The minute I start to think she might not be that bad she does something to make me hate her again.'

'Alex is the only villain in all this.'

'Shit, Dan. I really am sorry. I should just have come out and told you straight away.'

'Is this why he left Isabel, do you think? Because of how he felt about you?'

'I think so. At least, that's what he said. I haven't told her either,' I add hurriedly. I don't want him to think I've been talking about this behind his back and neither do I want him to bring it up with Izz. 'I think it's much better all round if she never knows.'

'I agree,' he says.

'What are you going to do?' I say.

'What do you think I'm going to do? I'm going to fucking kill him.' He looks at his watch. I look at mine. It's ten to eleven. 'Now?'

'No,' he says. 'Now I'm going to ring him like everything's normal and I'm going to invite him round tomorrow night. Then I'm going to kill him.'

'Figuratively,' I say. 'With words, I mean. Not literally.'

'Figuratively,' he says, and laughs grimly. 'Although literally is tempting.'

16

Now that the truth is out there, messy and complicated though it is, I actually feel like a weight has been lifted off my shoulders. Whatever Lorna felt she was going to achieve by telling Dan what I'd told her has backfired in a big way. She must have thought that Dan would be angry with me for keeping a secret from him. I can't believe that she did it to hurt him; he's never been anything but friendly and welcoming to her. She's mean, but she's not that mean. Maybe she wasn't thinking at all, she just wanted to get it off her chest. Throw it out there and see what the fallout would be. Or, most likely, she wanted to wound Alex. Destroy the one thing he supposedly valued above all else although, of course, that's debatable. She probably didn't even consider the other casualties that might occur.

I don't say anything to her when I see her at work the next day. I won't give her the satisfaction. We do find ourselves having to speak at one point, though, which is a shame because it was all going so well on the mutual ignoring front. While Lorna is on the other line I take a call from one of the script editors on *Reddington Road* asking why Craig hasn't shown up at their story conference. I have no idea so I put them on hold and I quickly dial Craig's mobile. Luckily he answers so I ask him how far away he is; what time he thinks he will get there.

'What are you talking about?' he says. I can hear loud music in the background and the occasional clanking of metal.

'Where are you?'

'I'm at the gym,' he says. 'What about *Reddington Road*?'

'The story conference,' I say. 'They called last week about booking you for a real episode.'

'You are joking?' Craig says. 'Nobody told me. Are you telling me I'm meant to be there now?' His voice is getting a little high pitched. I don't know what to do now. Unless Craig has some kind of degenerative memory-loss disease, clearly Lorna has fucked up and failed to tell him about the most momentous event in his short career so far. I need to do some damage control.

'Craig,' I say. 'Don't panic. There must have been some kind of mix up. I'll get to the bottom of it and call you back. But the good news is that *Reddington Road* want you to write an actual episode. That's great, isn't it?'

'I'd better not have missed a meeting,' he says, panicked, despite my asking him not to be. 'Not on my first job.'

'Keep your phone on,' I say. 'I'll find out what's going on.'

Lorna is still on the phone so I get back on to the *Reddington Road* script editor and I tell her that Craig is really sick. That his girlfriend has just told me he's half delirious with the flu and that she didn't realize his meeting was today otherwise she would have called to let everyone know. The editor is a little irritated still – 'I had to stick my neck out to get them to take a chance on him,' she says, but she's reasonable enough to accept the excuse. I tell her that Lorna will call her as soon as she's off the phone so she can figure something out.

I can't hear voices as I approach Lorna's closed office door so I wait for a moment before knocking and putting my head round. Maybe her call has ended in the twenty-five or so seconds it has taken me to walk here from reception. I open the door and see Lorna sitting staring off into space, the phone's handset lying on the table in front of her. She jumps when she notices me then picks up the phone and puts it back on its cradle nonchalantly as if sitting in your office with the phone off the hook all morning is an acceptable way to operate.

'You should knock,' she says.

'I did,' I say. There really isn't time for us to get into an argument, though, so I add, 'I guess you didn't hear me.'

'Well?' she says. 'What's so important?'

'*Reddington Road* have just been on the phone. They want to know why Craig hasn't shown up at the story conference.'

A look of total panic flickers across her face quickly before she can paper over it and, I have to admit, I'm relieved. There was a moment there when it crossed my mind that maybe I was the one at fault here. Could I have forgotten to give Lorna the original message about Craig? I remember speaking to them and I feel pretty sure I remember sending her an email about it, but there are so many messages to be passed on it's hard to be certain. Thankfully her look confirms that I did. She's not about to take the blame, though.

'What story conference?' she says, and she tries to look like she's getting angry at me rather than like she knows she's messed up.

'*Reddington Road*,' I say calmly. 'Don't you remember? They called last week and offered Craig an episode. I emailed you about it.'

'I didn't get any email,' she says. 'Otherwise I would have made sure Craig had all the details. I mean, we haven't even discussed an offer for him. Why would I allow him to attend a story conference?'

It's all coming back to me. 'That's what the message said. That someone had dropped out and they needed him to fill in at very short notice. They gave the date and time of the story conference and said his fee would be their lowest rate, the one for writers with no experience. They said you should call them if there was a problem with that or just to confirm that it would be OK. I wrote it all out.'

'I told you,' she says. 'I didn't get the message.'

'Could I just have a look on your computer?' I say. 'I know it's there.'

She puts her hand over her mouse protectively. 'You must have forgotten to let me know and now I'm going to have to call Craig and explain and then try to persuade *Reddington Road* to give him another shot.'

'I told them he was sick,' I say. 'And that his girlfriend didn't let us know.' There's no point me trying to argue

167

with her any more. She's decided she's not going to take responsibility and that's that.

'Fine,' she says curtly. 'I'll see if I can salvage the situation.'

I turn on my heel to leave, but I can't bear just to let her put all the blame on me without saying anything in my own defence. 'I did email you,' I say as I leave. 'Oh, and, Lorna, it might help if you didn't sit here with the phone off the hook for hours on end. That way you could actually speak to people rather than rely on messages.'

She ignores me. 'Oh, hi, Craig,' she says into the phone as I shut the door. 'I am so sorry. Rebecca never gave me the message . . .'

And I know that when I check my sent emails there will be one from me to her detailing the whole thing, but that if I look at her in box next time she goes out there will be no trace of any message from me on the subject.

I have to admit that it's unlike her, though. Craig getting this break is a big deal, the first real job any one of her clients has got under her patronage. I would have expected her to have dealt with it with great efficiency and then to have been unbearably smug around the office. The phone thing strikes me as a little weird too. How long had she been sitting there like that? I had tried to put at least three calls through to her in the past couple of hours and had got the engaged signal each time. Has she spent the whole morning sitting there with the phone off the hook, staring into space?

I spend the rest of the day waiting for some kind of ramifications. I'm hoping that even Lorna isn't stupid enough to go to Joshua or Melanie with this one because, although I can't prove that she ever received my email, I can show that I sent it. It seems that she's worked that one out too because nothing more happens. Fine. She's won her small victory; she's saved face with her client and hopefully managed to retain the commission. She knows she's in the wrong but, so long as she never tries to use it against me I can live with her rewriting of the truth. From Monday I can pass all messages for her over to Kay. There will be no reason for us to communicate at all.

Dan has told Alex that I am going out for the evening in order to entice him over to the house. In reality I'm worried about what is going to happen between them so I am going to be hiding out in the bedroom, finger poised over the 9 key on my mobile in case it all kicks off. The kids have been packed off to Auntie Isabel's for the night in order to avoid seeing their father murder his best friend, their honorary uncle. Dan is on edge, hyped up with adrenalin and anger. He tells me that he could barely stop himself from calling Alex all day, screaming down the phone at him that he knows all about his betrayal. His fury worries me, but what actually bothers me more is what will replace it when it's gone. When he realizes that he's lost his buddy. The friend he's spoken to several times a day every day for nearly thirty years. I can't imagine Dan and Alex's friendship surviving this or, if by some miracle it does, ever being the same again. And I don't really know what Dan is going to do without it.

'Don't go crazy,' I say to him just before I retreat to the bedroom with my glass of wine and bowl of pasta. 'Just get it all off your chest and you'll feel better.'

He's pacing up and down the hallway like a circus tiger waiting for his chance to bite the face off his trainer.

'Stay put,' he says. 'I don't want you having to get caught up in this any more.'

'I will,' I say obediently. I have absolutely no desire to see Alex.

'This is between me and him now,' Dan says, pushing his hair back from his face. I notice he's sweating. 'I've known him since my first term at secondary school, can you believe that? And he does this to me.'

'I know,' I say. 'Calm down.'

'I am calm,' he says in a way that only someone who is most definitely not calm can. 'I can handle it.'

The doorbell rings and I give Dan a quick kiss before he goes to answer it.

'I love you,' I say as I shut the bedroom door.

I hear Alex's cheery, 'All right, mate,' and then the next thing I hear is a thud and a crash and I forget all about the fact that I was intending to hide, and run out into the hall to see Alex lying on the floor with blood pouring from his nose and Dan standing over him looking like he doesn't quite know what just happened.

'What the fuck . . .?' Alex is saying, wiping the blood from his face. Then he sees me. 'Oh.'

Dan, who clearly learned to fight in some kind of

seventeenth-century school for polite combat, helps Alex to his feet before starting to hurl accusations at him. Alex, to give him some credit, takes it and waits for Dan to shout himself out before saying, 'I've totally and utterly fucked everything up, OK. I know that.'

'Just tell me this,' Dan says. 'If Rebecca had said yes, would you have gone through with it? Would you have broken up my marriage?'

Alex looks at the floor. 'I guess so. I hadn't really thought it through. I was never intending to actually do anything about it and then it all got too much for me and next thing I knew I'd left Izz and . . . well, it just came out. And once it had I couldn't take it back. It was a mistake.' He looks at me with complete and utter disdain. 'I realize that now. A total and absolute mistake.'

Dan says nothing for a moment and then says, 'So you might have broken up my marriage and then decided it had all been a big mistake. Does that make it any better?'

'No. Of course not. I just mean . . . Well, I didn't want you to worry that I still think I'm in love with her. Because I don't. I'm not.'

'Oh, that makes it OK, then,' Dan says sarcastically. 'Let's all go back to normal. Hey, let's book a holiday together.'

'There's nothing I can say except that I'm sorry. I can't change what happened. I'm just saying if no one had told you about it then it would have blown over naturally, that's all.' He looks at me accusingly.

I say nothing.

'Rebecca didn't tell me,' Dan says. 'Lorna did.'

Alex looks taken aback for a moment. 'When did you see Lorna?'

'She came round here to tell me what a good friend you were. I take it this is the reason the two of you broke up?'

Alex throws a half glance my way. 'Rebecca was the reason we broke up.'

'You expect me to feel sorry for you?' Dan says. 'You've lost your girlfriend of five minutes. I nearly lost my twenty-year marriage.'

'No,' I say quickly. 'You didn't.'

'But that's what he hoped would happen. What he was trying to make happen. My best friend.'

'Dan,' Alex says. 'I don't know what to say to you. It was a mistake, a huge fucking great mistake and I'm going to regret it for the rest of my life. I just want – I need – to know that there's a chance we can get past this. You're my best mate. I . . .' His voice cracks and for a second I almost feel sorry for him, but I have to say I get over it pretty quickly. 'I don't know what I'd do without you.'

He waits for Dan to say something and when he doesn't Alex says, 'Please, Dan. Can we talk about it? Something . . .?'

'I told you I've got nothing to say to you. I don't want to hear from you. I don't want you to call me, OK? Now go. Fuck off. I mean it.'

'Dan.' Alex doesn't move. He looks lost. Dan – who

I have never seen this angry before in the whole time I've known him – is looking like he might be sick.

'That's it, Alex. If you really feel as bad as you say you do, then fuck off and leave me alone because that's what I want.'

Alex still doesn't move so Dan shouts, 'Now!' in such a loud voice that I momentarily find myself wondering what the neighbours must be thinking. Alex finally takes the hint and goes. He looks at me briefly as he leaves, but I look away because I just don't know what else to do. This has all got so out of hand, so crazy.

Dan is shaking so I put my arms round him and try to tell him that it will all be OK although I don't really believe it will be. How do you replace a thirty-year friendship just like that? I know how much Dan loves me, but I also know he needs more than just me in his life. I pull out of the hug and it hits me that Dan is crying, which floors me. I put my face against his and we stand like that for a while. Eventually I say, 'I'm sorry.'

He looks at me. 'None of this is your fault,' he says for the second time. 'It's all down to him.'

17

I have to decide how much I'm going to tell Isabel about what has been going on. Although obviously we're never all together any more she's bound to pick up that Alex and Dan have had a big bust-up somewhere. We have other mutual acquaintances who will realize something is wrong soon enough and report back. Alex and Lorna are both loose cannons careening around out of control. After what has happened with Dan I'm not in the mood for keeping secrets any more, but I'm also not prepared to steam in and tell her that her marriage was a sham for the most part. Dan and I talk it over before I leave to pick up the kids on Saturday morning. I want his approval for whatever I do next. We decide on a slightly rewritten and altogether more palatable version of the truth and I steel myself to try and crowbar it into the conversation in as natural a way as I can.

Isabel has always been the mother of the group, despite the fact that she's also its only career woman. She's the kind of woman who has always seemed to have it all – the job, the house, the beautiful twins, the doting husband (OK, so we were all wrong about that one) – but you couldn't begrudge her that because she was so sweet and kind and thoughtful. Even her good looks are forgivable because she's blonde and soft and pretty in a way that it's impossible to find threatening. She always thinks the best of everyone until she's proved wrong – the polar opposite of me. And she's propped me up so many times I can't even remember. I just always know she's there when I need her. She would do anything for anybody, never forgets a birthday or an anniversary, is both a good mother and daughter and for twenty years was a devoted and supportive wife. To say she doesn't deserve what has happened to her is like saying that having your puppy put down because he sneezed once was a bit harsh. Which is to say it's an understatement. I'd do anything to prevent her being hurt even more.

William is sitting on a pile of cushions on one of the kitchen chairs when I let myself in, napkin tied round his neck like a bib. Nicola and Natalie are taking it in turns to 'feed the baby' and spooning some kind of porridgy breakfast cereal into his mouth.

'Hi, girls,' I say, and I kiss my youngest on the top of his head. 'Having a good time?'

'He's being a very good baby,' Natalie says, and she pats him on the head and then kisses him too, which explains why he seems to be going along with it so happily.

'I think the baby's got wind,' Nicola is saying as I head out of the kitchen looking for Isabel. 'Let's burp him.'

Zoe is lying on the sofa in the living room texting as usual. 'Hi, Mum,' she says without looking up.

'I'm going to chat to Auntie Isabel for a bit before we go,' I say. 'Are you OK?'

'Great,' she says. 'Will you drop me off at Kerrie's on the way home? She wants to go shopping.'

'Sure.' I wait for her to say, 'You and Auntie Isabel can come in here and talk and I'll go in the other room,' but she's thirteen so she doesn't. I retreat.

'Where is Auntie Isabel by the way?' I say as I leave and Zoe shrugs. 'Dunno.'

Eventually I find her upstairs making one of the beds so I pitch in and help, looking for a way to casually bring up the subject of Alex.

'Oh, did I tell you Alex left you because he's in love with me?'

'Guess what? Dan punched Alex in the face last night and then told him to fuck off out of our lives forever. And all because of me!'

Maybe not.

Izz is telling me about how Zoe spent the evening teaching the girls all the lyrics to the whole of Lily Allen's back catalogue. On the one hand I'm delighted that my surly teenager bothered to spend time taking notice of her two young non-blood-related cousins. I remind myself that Lily Allen is a good role model: a strong, independent, successful young woman who is actually famous for something other than taking her clothes off. On the other hand, though, the idea of my two adorable little surrogate nieces running around the playground singing 'I want loads of clothes and fuck loads of diamonds' but without the irony doesn't seem like such a great idea. Still, Isabel seems to think it's funny so I guess that's all that matters.

'They idolize Zoe,' she says, and I find myself apologizing. I'm sure Isabel doesn't want them acting like sulky adolescents any sooner than is going to happen naturally.

'Don't be stupid,' she laughs. 'They're a nightmare already. Look at what they're doing to William.'

I take a deep breath. 'Izz,' I say, 'you know Alex and Lorna broke up?'

She nods.

'Well, there's a bit more to it than I told you before.' She looks at me, curious. 'Nothing bad,' I say. 'At least not really.'

And I tell her the whole story, leaving out the part about Alex telling me he'd been in love with me for years and that that was the reason he couldn't stay with her any more pretty much. I manage to make it sound like a ridiculous drunken pass, a one-time thing. An embarrassing but not devastating revelation.

She laughs nervously. 'God, do you think he's been having some kind of mid-life crisis?'

'Definitely,' I say. A mid-life crisis that has apparently been going on since he was in his twenties. I have to make it sound like what I said to Lorna was wildly exaggerated, which luckily Isabel thinks is funny.

It's a little more difficult to make Dan's reaction sound reasonable when I am downplaying Alex's bad behaviour so radically. Isabel knows that Dan is not, by nature, jealous or irrational. He's never hit anyone before. He's barely ever raised his voice.

'I think it's a bloke thing,' I say, clutching at straws.

177

'They take loyalty between mates so seriously. You've seen all those war films where they take bullets for each other. I'm sure he'll calm down.'

I'm not sure about this last statement at all, but, anyway, it seems like the only way to get off the subject of Dan's seemingly out of proportion aggression. Thankfully she buys it.

'Poor you and Dan,' she says, rubbing my arm. 'Getting mixed up in our mess.'

'We'll live,' I say. 'Have you spoken to Luke?' I ask after a few moments, once I think it's safe to change course.

'I have,' she says, and she looks like an excited adolescent. 'He called me from Zurich yesterday. Are you still OK to have the girls on Monday night?'

'Of course. Me and Zoe are going to teach them how to smoke crack.'

'Don't even joke about it.'

'So, what did he say? Switzerland is a barren wasteland without you?'

'Something like that. No, he just told me what he's been doing and then we chatted about all sorts of stuff. He's really easy to talk to. He was at some function or other but he stood outside in the snow and we talked for about an hour.'

I can't help envying her the excitement of it all. Not that I'd trade Dan in for anyone, but there's that feeling of being alive when you first meet someone, of being young and a little bit out of control, that's pretty overwhelming. Isabel even looks different. She's lost a couple of pounds, not that she needed to. Her skin's glowing. She's animated. As much as anything – nice as I'm sure Luke is – I assume it's from the validation that she's still an attractive woman, the possibility that there are men out there who will be interested in her. Smart, intelligent, good-looking men at that. At least I assume he's good looking. Who cares anyway so long as he's nice to her and she has fun.

'Well, he'd better appreciate how lucky he is,' I say, and I give her a hug.

I wake up on Monday morning feeling that at least the world can move on now. It couldn't really have turned out worse than that Dan ended up the major casualty in all this, but at least now everything is out in the open and we can all start picking up the pieces.

When I arrive at the office ten minutes early Kay is standing on the doorstep looking smart and scrubbed up in that 'first day on a new job' way.

'Hi,' I say. 'You're keen.'

'I always was a swot,' she says, smiling.

We go upstairs and I show her round the little suite of rooms and where to put her coat. I make her a coffee in the tiny kitchen and talk her through how Joshua and Melanie like theirs.

'What about Lorna?' she says. I have already decided that I have to be grown-up about Lorna as far as Kay's concerned, so I just say, 'Black, no sugar,' and leave it at that. I even manage not to roll my eyes as I say it. I show her which is her desk and then talk her through the phone system. I don't want to overload her so I give her a file with all our clients' CVs in so that she can familiarize herself with who's who – given that she won't have heard of ninety per cent of them before – and I tell her that I'll answer all the calls this morning, but that she should listen in to get more of an idea of what goes on.

When Lorna arrives she is forced to come in to reception to say hello to Kay, so I make a big point of being really smiley and happy to see her. I know she thinks I will have had a weekend from hell after her visit to see Dan on Friday night, but I am not going to give her the satisfaction of looking miserable. The look of confusion that passes over her face when I cheerily ask how her weekend was is priceless. She wants to make a good impression on Kay, though, so she has to respond in an equally matey manner.

It's the first time I've been in a room with her for more than a couple of minutes since she and Alex split up, and I can't help but notice that she's looking even more skeletal than usual and that the dark circles round her eyes seem to have moved in permanently. She looks like she's aged and it occurs to me that she's really taking the end of the relationship hard. Loathsome as she is, Alex used her very unfairly. I have no doubt but that he accelerated the relationship cynically, and he made her genuinely believe he had fallen in love with her. Partly, no doubt, it was easy because she's always been so desperate for someone to love her. Well, she's better off without him whether she realizes it yet or not (not, I'd

180

say from the red rims round her eyes). Once she gets a bit of distance from the relationship I'm sure she'll be able to see it for what it is more clearly. And when that happens, I decide, I'll try to talk to her about everything that's gone on. I'll see if we can clear the air and at least pretend to get along.

There's big excitement in the office today because we have a new client. And not just any old client. Lorna is the golden girl because she has somehow convinced the uncrowned but universally acknowledged queen of prime time Saturday night TV, Heather Barclay, to join Mortimer and Sheedy's humble little stable.

Supposedly – and I hear this from the skinny horse's mouth itself because Lorna, while in no mood to share her good news with me, is revelling in showing off to Joshua in front of Kay – Lorna met her at a mutual friend's short-film screening at BAFTA a few weeks ago. She (Lorna) introduced herself to Heather and flattered her that she was capable of far more worthy and challenging work than merely reading someone else's words off an autocue. Heather confided that she felt she had been pigeonholed as the nation's slightly bland sweetheart and that she didn't believe her current agent knew how to help her broaden her horizons. She was with one of the bigger, flashier agencies and she didn't feel like anybody there was hungry enough to really be prepared to work hard on her behalf. They were happy for her to just coast along doing the same old stuff so long as they could keep on taking fifteen per cent of her quite considerable earnings.

'So I told her,' Lorna says, seemingly loving having an attentive audience hanging on her every word (Kay and Joshua, I mean, obviously. I am pretending to get on with my work), 'that I was an agent who was so hungry she was almost starving!' She laughs at her own joke here although, of course, the irony is that she does actually look like she's starving at the moment. Literally.

'And I told her all about Mortimer and Sheedy. Then, to be honest, I forgot all about it until she phoned me over the weekend and she said she was going to tell Fisher Parsons Management today that she wants to leave. She's coming in at three o'clock to talk about exactly what she wants to do next.'

Actually, I feel like there's something flat in the way Lorna is delivering her story, despite the jokes and the self-congratulation. Like she's going through the motions, showing off because it's expected of her rather than because she's getting any pleasure from it.

'Good girl,' Joshua says, as if he was talking to his pet lurcher. 'And obviously you'll be looking after her?' There's a question mark in his voice that makes me think that he's hoping Lorna will say, 'No, she's coming to be represented by you,' but, of course, that doesn't happen. I guess that even while he's delighted on behalf of the company to have acquired a big fish, he's a little jealous that he didn't net her himself. Lorna, of course, has no intention of handing over the big prize.

'Yes,' she says. 'She said she felt like we really clicked.'

There's no denying that poaching Heather is, indeed, great news for Mortimer and Sheedy. The more money the company brings in the better for all of us. Very few of our clients earn the big bucks. We rely more on the slow but steady. Heather's arrival will not bring about an immediate change in our fortunes, though. In fact, there's no guarantee that it ever will. The way it works is that Heather will continue to pay commission to her previous agents, Fisher Parsons Management, for all jobs which predated her defection to us. So, if she spends the next five years hosting her hit game show, *High Speed Dating*, we'll earn nothing. Ditto if she continues to front *Celebrity Karaoke*. Lorna's job is to find her new projects, to negotiate brand-new deals. And that may not be as easy as it sounds, especially since Heather has delusions of gravitas. Still, even if she never earns a penny for us, she will still be a great poster girl for the company. And, because celebrities attract other celebrities like moths round a candle, the chances are that we will acquire a few more A-list clients in the next few months.

Kay is understandably impressed with her new boss's brilliance.

'Wow,' she says, once Lorna and Joshua have left the room. 'Heather Barclay.'

'Yep,' I say, not quite trusting myself with any more. The truth is that Lorna has pulled off quite a coup and I'm finding that a little irritating.

'She just went up and talked to her at a party,' Kay continues. 'That's so cool.'

'Yes,' I say. 'Isn't it?'

I take Kay round to the Red Lion for lunch and I ask her if she has any questions so far. She does and they're all quite insightful and the kind of thing you ought to ask, so I'm feeling good that I backed the right horse. I'm enjoying the fact that I can mould her into my ideal co-worker. ('Don't ever let the phone ring more than three times. In fact, while you're still learning the ropes the most useful thing you can do is answer as many calls as you can, get a feel for who's calling and why.') Kay is so happy to be back at work, so grateful for the opportunity, so keen to do well that she absorbs everything I throw at her, like a Vileda super mop. I'm careful to be fair. I make it clear to her that we share the chores and the responsibilities. I'm not trying to dump the jobs I don't like on her just because I probably could. She already gets the rough end of the deal by having to work for Lorna.

Lorna is poking about in reception when we get back, which always makes me nervous. She looks at her watch.

'You need to stagger your lunch breaks in future,' she says, looking at Kay. 'You can't both be going out together; someone needs to be here at all times to man the phones.'

'Oh,' Kay says, and looks worried.

'My fault,' I say cheerily. 'I checked with Melanie and she said it was fine because she wasn't going to be going anywhere.'

'Well, you should have let me know,' she says grumpily.

'Yes, I suppose I should,' I say, refusing to rise to the bait. 'Oh well, never mind. No harm done.'

If Kay wasn't there, we would probably have a row about now. Her accusing me of being insubordinate, me hurling accusations at her that would include being patronizing and high handed. As it is she merely mutters under her breath and retreats to her office to prepare for the big meeting.

Heather seems nice enough when she comes in, although she does that thing where she's very friendly until she realizes I am only a humble assistant and then she switches to polite but disinterested. I make her a cup of tea while she is waiting for Lorna to get off the phone and I hope that she isn't put off by the wall of photos of people she probably doesn't even recognize who make up our clients.

The meeting clearly goes to plan. Heather reiterates her decision to sack her current representation and join us. Once she has left, Joshua produces a bottle of champagne from somewhere and insists that we all sit in his office and have a glass to celebrate.

'Don't get ideas,' I say to Kay, smiling. 'This doesn't happen every day.'

She laughs and Melanie asks her how she's enjoying it so far.

'It's great,' Kay says. 'I think I'm going to love it here.'

Silently I hope she's right.

18

It's a relief to have Nicola and Natalie already causing havoc in the flat when I get home. It will give Dan something to focus on other than his fight with Alex. He was very down all weekend, preoccupied. Tonight he won't have the luxury of being able to brood because he'll be forced into playing Mousetrap or boxing on Zoe's Wii Fit.

Isabel has already been and gone, dropping the girls off into Zoe's dubious care and racing back round to Liverpool Road to prepare for her date. Luke is taking her to Nobu and then – I am in no doubt that Isabel is hoping at least – back to hers for the big moment.

I send her a text – 'Don't do anything I wouldn't do' – and she calls me almost immediately and says, 'I'm terrified.'

'Just lie back and think of England,' I say, and she laughs.

'I haven't been naked in front of anyone other than Alex since I was, what? Twenty?'

'I've seen you naked.'

'You know what I mean. I don't look like that any more. I look like a forty-year-old woman who's had twins.'

'That's because that's what you are. What's wrong with that?'

'It's just . . . it doesn't all look as good as it used to.'

'Luke has kids, doesn't he? Presumably he coped with having to see his wife with no clothes on after she had them.'

'They're separated, remember?'

'Isabel. If you are going to tell me that Luke left his wife because he didn't fancy her any more once she had children, then I am going to forbid you from ever seeing him again.'

'No! Of course not. I don't know what I mean. I'm just nervous about . . . you know . . . doing it.'

'Listen to yourself. You're a beautiful, funny, intelligent, successful woman. He should be so lucky.'

'I know, I know. I'm pathetic.'

I'm not letting her off that easily. 'Don't you think he's feeling nervous too? I doubt he's in the same shape he was when he was at college, but do you care? No. And neither does he about you. And if he's that shallow that he's put off by the odd stretch mark then he's not worth knowing. OK?'

'Yes. OK.'

'Try to enjoy it. It's meant to be fun, remember.'

'Fun. Yes. I'll try to keep that in mind.'

'Go and have a glass of wine before you go out. And call me as soon as he's left in the morning. The minute he leaves, OK?'

I find myself thinking about it a lot later on. Not Isabel and Luke having sex. That would be weird. Not to mention that I have no idea what Luke looks like so I would have to make up my own image, avatar-like, to project into the picture. No, I can't stop myself from wondering what it would be like to be with someone other than Dan. Now, at my age. I know exactly what Isabel meant when she said she was nervous, despite my giving her a hard time about it. It would be so exposing, so much more revealing and potentially humiliating than when we were young and confident. But also thrilling and daring and invigorating. Not to mention the ego boost, that someone had looked at you now, exactly as you are with all your wobbly bits and lines round your eyes, and thought, Phwoar.

A part of me, a part I'd rather not acknowledge, is envious. But I know that if I were her there's no way I would be taking my own advice. I would be crawling back into my safe shell and not risking the rejection. And, by the way, I am not looking for any kind of a change. I am very happy with the way my life is. I just find it a bit unnerving, being surrounded by all this rampant lust all of a sudden, that's all. It's not what I'm used to in my friends. It's making me feel, what? Inadequate? Boring? Left out?

It suddenly occurs to me that when I met Dan I was so self-assured. Of course, I was also about nine stone. I have a horrible moment of insecurity when I wonder what he thinks about the way I look now, whether he notices that I've let myself go a bit or whether he just sees the woman he loves, and embraces all the changes. Whether underneath it all he's watching Alex and Isabel and wishing he could run off and have wild abandoned passionate sex with someone new. No, I tell myself. Not

Dan. He's probably thinking about how awful it must be to have to remember to hold your stomach in and not to breath through your mouth because you've been eating garlic. And I feel the same. I do.

As soon as I have dispatched the kids off to school the next morning – giving Zoe strict instructions to walk the girls right up to the front door 'and make sure they go through it' before getting on the bus with William – I call Isabel. I know I should be waiting for her to ring me and I'm taking a chance that Luke might still be there. I'm guessing that she won't answer if he is. But she picks up on the third ring and it doesn't sound like she's in the throes of passion.

'So,' I say as soon as she says hello. 'How was it?'

'Oh,' she says, not sounding at all like the earth has recently been moving. 'It was great. I think. It was all over quite quickly.'

'The first one always is,' I say as if I have any idea. 'You just have to get it out of the way and then, once all the awkwardness about taking your clothes off is over, you can really take it slowly the next time. Right?'

'That's just it,' she says. 'There wasn't a next time.'

'Not even this morning?'

'He didn't stay the night. He came back and it was all going really well and then he said that he had to get home. He said he had a meeting early this morning and he needed a change of clothes.'

'Oh. Right. Well, that's understandable, I suppose. It

189

would have looked a bit presumptuous if he had turned up for your date clutching a clean suit.'

'I know. I guess I just felt a little disappointed. I'd built up this whole scenario in my head of me cooking breakfast for him and it really being a chance for us to get to know each other better . . .'

'Did you ever actually ask him if he wanted to stay the night? Before you got home, I mean?'

'No. I suppose I didn't. I just assumed . . .'

'You know what? Maybe it's a good thing. I can't imagine facing someone I hardly know over cornflakes and toast in the morning. Especially after . . .'

She laughs. 'You're right. The reality probably wouldn't have been that romantic. Anyway, he's asked me if I want to go out again later in the week so I guess it must have been OK.'

'Only OK?'

'No. It was better than OK. And next time it'll be fantastic.'

'So he didn't take one look at you with your clothes off and run a mile, then?'

'No,' she says coyly. 'He didn't.'

'Do you need me to have the girls again? I'm happy to.'

'It's OK,' she says. 'Alex wants them to stay at his.'

'You've talked to him?'

'Of course. Only about logistics. He didn't mention anything about falling out with Dan. And I wasn't about to bring it up.'

'How did he sound?' I say. Despite all of my angry

feelings towards Alex I don't like to think of him cut adrift.

'A bit miserable to be honest. Flat.'

'Well, it's his own fault,' I say.

'Some of it,' she says. 'Not everything.'

When we say goodbye I start to feel incredibly sad. How have we got to this stage where Isabel is sleeping with someone new and Alex has had a whole other relationship start and finish? Where Dan couldn't care less about whether Alex is OK or not? It feels bizarre that all of our shared history, that bond that was so important to all of us, has come to count for nothing.

Despite Lorna work feels like a welcome distraction to real life at the moment and I feel my mood lighten as I go up in the rickety old lift towards our attic rooms.

Kay is already there, kettle on, and we chatter amiably while we wait for the day to pick up speed. She takes a message from Craig who is calling to say he is safely on his way to his script meeting and then I pass Heather over to her so that she can leave a message for Lorna too.

'What did she want?' I ask when Kay has put the phone back down.

'To find out if Lorna has called the BBC to set up a meeting yet.'

'Blimey. She's keen.' Strictly speaking, Heather has to give Fisher Parsons Management three months' notice and we would have to share commission with them on any new jobs, which we set up for her in that period. In reality it's a grey area and one that's notoriously hard to police. Everything takes so long that even if Heather met with the Head of Light Entertainment at the BBC tomorrow (or the Controller of Entertainment Commissioning as I think they are calling themselves these days. I try not to get distracted by wondering how much it cost to replace all the headed notepaper when that change came in) and they offered her her own series on the spot, it would still be months before contracts were signed and production begun. And by that stage who's to say when that original meeting actually happened? Besides, Heather is under contract to ITV for the next year and a half so it all feels a little irrelevant.

'So just email Lorna all the details you have, including the time of the call. And then file the email somewhere. Don't delete it.'

Kay nods, taking it in.

'And, if it's important, deliver it verbally when you get a chance too.'

If she wonders why I am hammering the point home so violently, she doesn't say. I just want to make sure she's covered herself.

Later, when Lorna comes in – the twenty-five minutes late that has become her custom these days – looking watery eyed and lank haired, and hyped up on disappointment and lack of food, I hear my protégée deliver the two messages in person and I'm glad my lecture hit home.

At lunchtime, while Kay is out getting a sandwich and doing some shopping, I answer another call from Craig.

'How did it go?' I know that he's been a mess of excitement and anxiety in the run-up to his first real commissioning meeting.

'Great,' he says. 'Except that the script editor mentioned that they'd never heard back from Lorna about my fee so I still don't have a contract.'

Really? What is going on with that woman? I try not to sound as exasperated as I feel. 'There must have been a mix up. I know she was trying to call them,' I lie. 'I'll get her to try them again today and we'll get it sorted. Don't worry.'

'Only Hattie, that's the script editor, she said they can't go ahead if it's not all agreed. Just in case Lorna turns round and asks them for a fortune or something. I told her I'd write it for nothing . . .'

'It won't come to that. She's on the phone at the moment, but as soon as she gets off I'll talk to her and one of us will call you back, OK?'

'OK,' he says reluctantly.

I wait a few minutes but Lorna's line is still engaged so I send her an email marked 'Urgent!!!'. I watch for her light to go out to tell me she's off the phone, but after fifteen minutes it's still lit up. It occurs to me that she might be doing her trick of sitting there with it off the hook again so, even though I could wait for Kay to come back in thirty-five minutes' time, I decide that for Craig's sake this needs to be dealt with now.

I steel myself to approach the closed door of her office. I listen outside for a few moments, but I can't hear her talking so I knock and wait for her to tell me to come in. Silence. I knock again. I'm sure I would have heard her if she'd gone out, and her coat is still hanging on the hook in the hall. I knock once more and then open the door. Lorna is at her desk, tears streaming down her face, eyes swollen.

'What?' she says aggressively. I notice that her phone is lying on her desk again. I decide to try to ignore the state she's in and just act businesslike. She clearly didn't want me to see her like this. I tell her about Craig as briefly as I can.

'I spoke to the producer,' she says defensively. 'I said he'd accept the minimum.'

'Well, maybe someone there messed up. They obviously didn't make a note or pass it on or . . . whatever.' I just want to get out of the room as quickly as I can. 'Perhaps you could ring them and put it straight? Craig's terrified they'll get someone else to write it.'

'Fine,' she says.

'OK. Good.' I start to retreat, but it's incredibly hard to ignore someone who seems to be having some kind of nervous breakdown right in front of you, however much you dislike them so, before I can stop myself, I say, 'Are you OK?'

'Next time,' she says, 'if you knock and you don't hear me say come in, then don't come in.'

'You're the boss,' I say sarcastically. That's the last time I try to be nice.

When I get back to reception I see the light by her phone line go off and on again. I know I shouldn't, but I flick the switch that allows me to listen in on her call and I clamp my hand firmly over the mouthpiece so she can't hear me breathing. Someone answers the phone with the words 'Reddington Road' and Lorna asks for one of the producers by name.

'Kate,' she says as soon as she's put through. 'I'm so sorry. I completely neglected to call you back about Craig Connolly. I know he had his script meeting this morning and I just wanted to confirm that, of course, he'll do it for the minimum. He's just thrilled to have the break.'

'Great,' Kate says. 'I was worried there was a problem there for a moment. Especially as he had already had to miss the story conference . . .'

'He was ill,' Lorna jumps in. 'But he's very confident that he's up to speed with everything and he's raring to go. And, again, I can't apologize enough,' she adds. 'It's entirely our fuck-up. To be completely honest, I didn't get your message, but anyway . . .'

'No problem,' Kate says pleasantly. 'I'll get Emma to send the contract out today and you tell Craig he should just get on with it.'

I wait for Lorna to hang up before I put my phone down too. I assume that when her light goes on again she's calling Craig to tell him the good news, but I decide to call him myself later to reiterate it. Just in case.

I can understand why she didn't want to admit to me that she had messed up but her behaviour seems so extreme. I know that, lazy as she can be on occasions, her promotion means everything to her. It's given her the status she's always wanted and I can't believe she's going to mess it all up now. Can this all still be fallout from her bust-up with Alex? Did she really believe they were going to get married and have babies and live happily ever after? It's not beyond the realms of possibility. Alex is an attractive and funny man. He was professing his love for her within about five minutes of their starting to go out. Why wouldn't she believe him? Why wouldn't she fall in love with him back? Just because I know that he was stringing her along doesn't make it any less real for her.

19

In one fell swoop Dan's and my social life – such as it was – is over. Gone. Kaput. We still have Isabel, of course, but she doesn't want to leave the girls more often than she has to after all the upheaval there's been in their lives lately, and on the nights when she does she understandably wants to see Luke. There are other more casual friendships, couples we know through the kids or from the local pub, people Dan works with, but they're the kind of friends you exchange Christmas cards with and chat to for ten minutes at parties; none of them are people we've ever felt the desire to spend whole evenings with.

In desperation to get Dan out of the house and to take his mind off things I write a list of all our possible new best friends and try to feel enthusiastic about arranging an evening out with any of them.

'Anna and Kelvin?'

'Mmm,' he says, non-committally. 'They're OK.'

'How about Sharon and Patrick? We had a good time with them at that school barbecue.'

'He's a bit of a know-all.'

He's right. 'You're right,' I say, crossing them off the list. 'Not them.' I scroll further down the list of names. 'Oh, what about Rose and Simon? They're fun.'

Dan sighs. 'Do we have to? They're nice enough but I just don't feel like trying to force a connection with someone. Friendships happen naturally; they're organic.'

'I know that. But you have to interact with people in order to allow a friendship to develop organically. All I'm saying is why don't we see if Rose and Simon want to have dinner? We might have a good time. If we don't fall madly in love with them, then it's no big deal. It's just a night out, Dan, that's all.'

'Maybe in a couple of weeks,' he says. 'I don't feel like it at the moment.'

'Things aren't just going to go back to the way they were, you know.' I brush the hair away from his eyes the way I'm always doing to William. 'Trust me, if there was a way for that to happen I would have found it by now.'

He shrugs. 'What's for dinner?' he says, and that's the end of it.

It's quiet in the office. I'm reading a script that's been sent in for Gary McPherson. It's a two-minute scene in a film – a cameo, I'm sure Gary would call it, but actually it's just a very small part. It's one of those cockney geezer gangster movies that are like something set in the 1950s but with added guns and swearing. I'm quite enjoying it, actually, although I'm pretty sure it'll go straight to DVD because there's no budget and the cast is like a who's who of the nineties. Still, Gary needs the work and I'm sure Joshua will persuade him to say yes.

Kay is typing something or other on her computer and Joshua, Melanie and Lorna are all in their separate

198

offices with the doors shut doing whatever it is they do. I'm drifting off, something I often do when I'm reading scripts in the office and I usually don't realize until I've read the same page three times. It's one of those dull days where it already feels like it's getting dark at about two thirty, which doesn't help. Plus I ate way too much at lunch because I got a take-out jacket potato with beans and cheese from the café round the corner and then stuffed in a whole Kit Kat. I feel my eyes shutting and I have to force myself to open them again.

'Jesus,' I say to Kay. 'I'm falling asleep here.'

I barely get the words out before I hear the front door bang open. Both Kay and I nearly jump out of our skin. I get up and walk towards the door to the corridor to see who's coming for a visit just as a very unsteady-looking figure staggers through it towards me. We nearly collide and, as I'm about to apologize, I realize that it's Alex and, not only that, but he's blind drunk.

'Ah, there she is,' he shouts. He's acting like Oliver Reed on a chat show, all fake bonhomie and talking like he's addressing the Albert Hall without a microphone.

'My favourite woman in the world. The love of my life.'

I take a step back. I notice that Kay has stood up and is looking anxiously in my direction.

'Rebecca?' she says. 'Is everything OK?'

'It's fine.' I turn my attention back to the figure reeling in the doorway. 'Alex, what are you doing here?'

'I've come to see you. Can't I visit my friend in her place of work?'

'You're pissed,' I say, stating the blatantly obvious.

'Ooh, well observed.' He's talking way too loudly and my main preoccupation isn't 'what is Alex doing here drunk, at my place of work, in the middle of the day?' – it's that Joshua or Melanie might hear him and come out to see what's going on.

'I think you should leave, OK?' I say, although I know I'm fighting a losing battle. Alex has come to make a scene and he's not going to leave till he's done so.

'What should I do?' Kay says. 'Shall I get Joshua?'

'No!' I say, panicked.

'I'm Rebecca's friend,' Alex says, extending a hand to Kay, which she takes like it was a hand grenade with the pin pulled out. 'Surely she's told you about me?'

'I don't . . . I've only been here a couple of days,' Kay says nervously.

'I'm also Rebecca's husband's best mate,' he says, like that's any kind of explanation. 'Or, at least, I was. And I used to go out with the lovely Lorna. Oh, and before that me and Bex had a little thing, didn't we, Bex?'

'No,' I say firmly, 'we did not.'

'Rebecca's kind of the reason me and Lorna broke up and Dan is no longer my best friend. Isn't that right?' He looks at me, eyes unfocused. God, he really must have been knocking them back.

'Ignore him,' I say. 'He's drunk and he's talking bollocks. I'll explain later.'

'Oh, go on, explain it all to her now. I'd love to hear the whole sad little story from your perspective.'

I've had enough of this. 'Really? Would you really like

to hear my version of what's happened, Alex? OK, here goes. You ready?' I look at him and he sways a little. 'This, Kay, is the story of mine and Alex's relationship. We were friends for twenty years. Like he said, he was my husband's best friend and his wife was – still is – my best friend. But recently Alex left his wife – out of the blue – and he told me he was in love with me. That he'd never really loved his wife because he'd always been in love with me. He even asked me to leave my husband – his closest mate, remember – and go away with him. I said no. Obviously. I told him I wasn't – that I never have been – interested in him. And then he asked Lorna out and he used her, basically. Luckily she saw sense and dumped him.'

'When you interfered and fucked it up,' Alex says aggressively.

'And he and Dan are no longer friends,' I continue, ignoring his interjection. 'Understandably. So basically he got what he deserved all round. And he's bitter about it – mostly about getting caught, I think – but it's all his own fault. He's the architect of his own downfall and that's what's really killing him.'

I stop and look at him to see if my words have hit home. It's hard to tell. He puts a hand on the corner of Kay's desk to steady himself.

'I think that's a pretty fair analysis, isn't it, Alex?'

'You know why I've come here?' he says.

'Enlighten me.'

'You think you can ruin my life,' he says. 'Fine. It works both ways, though.'

I have no idea what he means, but I'm not going to give him the satisfaction of looking concerned.

'You're so smug,' he says. 'You're so certain your relationship's perfect, that your whole life is perfect.'

I don't say anything, mostly because I don't know what to say. I feel uneasy about what's coming next.

'You think Dan's as certain? You think he's never wavered?' A hint of a smirk starts to creep across his face. 'You think there haven't been times when he's been bored of you or had his head turned by someone else? Ask him about Edinburgh. Ask him what happened when we went away for the weekend.'

My heart nearly stops. What is he talking about? There can't be anything Dan has kept from me. He and Alex went to Scotland for a couple of days about four years ago. They thought it would be fun to go hiking in the day and drinking in little old pubs in the evening, and Isabel and I were only too happy to let them go and play. I quickly scan my memory for telltale signs that anything was wrong, that Dan was unhappy or different in any way when they came home, but there's nothing.

'You're so full of shit,' I say, and Alex smirks that fucking annoying knowing smirk again.

'Fine,' he says. 'Don't believe me if you don't want to.'

Kay has walked over to stand beside me as if we'll look more intimidating timesed by two.

'OK,' she says, and I can hear a waver in her voice. She's not to know that Alex isn't given to violence. 'It's time for you to go.'

'Who's your Rottweiler?' Alex says to me, laughing to himself at how witty he is.

'She's the person who's going to scream the place down if you don't leave now. She's also the person who is going to call the police,' she adds, two threats being better than one.

'It's OK,' he says. 'I'm leaving. I've said everything I came to say.' He starts to back off and then turns to Kay as an afterthought. 'Can you believe I ever thought I was in love with that?' He looks me up and down theatrically. 'I mean, look at her. What a bitch.'

He moves again and I'm willing him to leave. Just get out of here. God knows what Kay must think. He's on his way to the front door. Backwards for maximum smirking potential. He's almost there when it opens and Lorna walks through and bumps straight into her ex. Oh God. I'd forgotten about her. She stops dead in her tracks when she realizes who it is.

'Alex . . .'

Alex turns a little unsteadily. 'Oh, hi, Lorna.'

She's turned completely pale. In fact she looks like she might faint. There's a glimmer of hope in her voice that she doesn't even try to disguise. 'Did you come to see me?' Alex almost double takes, as if he's just remembered that this is where she works too.

'No. I came to see Rebecca.'

I actually feel sorry for her. He doesn't even care enough to pretend. Or he's too wrapped up in his own personal drama to even register her distress. Either way, Lorna is clearly not at the top of his agenda. It's as if

203

the look on her face once he's delivered this blow sobers him up suddenly, though, and he notices for the first time just how bad she looks.

'I mean, obviously I was going to say hi to you too. See how you were. How are you?'

'Have you got time for a coffee?' she says, unable to keep the desperation out of her voice.

Alex indicates Kay who is looking utterly bemused. 'Well, old Goebbels over there threatened to ring the police unless I left so . . .'

Lorna looks at Kay. 'Alex is a friend of mine.'

'Fine,' Kay says. 'It was just getting a bit out of hand. I didn't know what else to do.'

'You did right,' I say. I don't want Kay to be dragged into this mess any more than is necessary. Lorna shoots me a look that is, to say the least, hostile.

'Alex is always welcome to come and see me,' she says.

'Actually,' Alex pipes up. 'I can't stay. Another time, Lorna, OK?'

Her face falls. 'Just for ten minutes. We really should talk.'

I know that, painful as this scenario would be for her under any circumstances, having to have this conversation in front of me must be agony. I move backwards towards reception and I indicate to Kay that she should do the same.

'What the hell's going on?' she whispers as we back off.

'Shh,' I hiss. I want to hear what the outcome is.

'I told you I can't, OK. I'm busy. I have to go.'

'No,' Lorna says, a strangled cry. 'Look, just come and talk to me. Just for a minute. In private. Please.'

It's tragic the way she's begging. It's obvious that she never thought it was really all over for her and Alex. She probably believed that he would come running back, tail between his legs, and they'd patch everything up. Emerge stronger with me as the common enemy. She had clearly never reckoned on the fact that Alex just didn't care enough about her to go through that whole dance. He used her; he found that he actually liked her more than he thought he would which made the whole thing easier. But he didn't love her. He didn't feel the way he allowed her to believe he felt. The way she felt about him.

'I'm leaving, OK?' I hear the front door go and then Lorna says, 'Please, Alex,' but he doesn't reply. I hold my hand up to Kay, telling her not to talk yet. A loud sobbing begins in the corridor. The phone starts to ring so I wave to Kay to answer it. I have to deal with Lorna before her wailing brings either Joshua or Melanie out of their offices. They mustn't see her like this, out of control.

I know I have to do something.

'Come on, Lorna,' I say. 'Let's go back to your office.'

She shakes off the hand I've put on her arm to speed her along.

'Get off me,' she says way too loudly. 'Leave me alone. This is all your fault.' I try to edge her through the door, but she's not having it and it's too late anyway because Joshua appears, face like thunder.

205

'What in hell's name is going on?' he barks. 'I can't hear myself think.'

'It's nothing,' I say. 'Lorna just isn't feeling well,' I add unconvincingly. Luckily Kay saves the day by popping her head out from reception and saying 'Joshua, it's Mike O'Reilly on the phone for you.'

'Put him through,' he says gruffly. 'And whatever the problem is sort it out.'

Lorna, who has been jolted back into the real world by Joshua's appearance allows me to manoeuvre her into her office. I shut the door. I don't really have any idea what I'm going to say to her, but I have to say something. I steer her over to her chair and she sits down. Tears are still streaming down her face and she makes no attempt to wipe them away. I hand her a tissue from a box on the bookcase.

'Do you want me to get you a drink or something?'

'Just leave me on my own.'

It's tempting. 'Lorna, he's not worth it. Alex. He's a user. He used you.'

'What the fuck do you know?' she shouts, and I think, OK, maybe it wasn't such a good idea to come in here. We seem to be about to have the row that's been brewing between us for months. In fact, she's going to make sure we do.

'I know Alex. I've known him since I was twenty, remember?' I talk quietly, hoping she might mirror my tone. No such luck.

'Well, according to you he's been madly in love with

206

you all that time and you didn't realize so you couldn't have known him that well, could you?'

Touché. 'I know him a lot better than you do. And he's not worth wasting your life for or messing up your job for, for that matter.'

'What do you mean messing up my job?' She stares at me accusingly. 'How dare you.'

'You've been a bit . . . well, let's just say your eye's been off the ball lately. I'm not having a go, I'm just saying . . .'

'Oh, I see what this is,' Lorna says angrily. 'You're jealous because I got promoted and you didn't so you're trying to undermine me. What do you think they're going to do, get rid of me and promote you now? There's no way Joshua and Melanie think you're up to it.'

She thinks this will hurt me, but I couldn't care less. 'I'm not after your job. I wouldn't take it if they offered it to me. I don't want the responsibility. But I know your work is everything to you. And, honestly, you're good at it. Most of the time. Really you are. And I don't think allowing your personal life to get in the way is something you would ever do if you were feeling rational.'

'So poor little Lorna who has nothing in her life other than work, no family, no boyfriend, needs to make a success of her career because otherwise what has she got? Nothing?'

'That's not what I'm saying. I was trying to say that at some point you'll get over Alex and you'll wonder what you ever saw in him and, at that point, you don't want to look around and see that you allowed him to ruin your career too. You might not care at the moment, but you will again.'

'If I had ever wanted your career advice, I'd have asked for it. And, as I haven't, then you can safely assume that it's of no interest to me whatsoever.'

'That's fine,' I say. 'I've said what I had to say. I've tried, OK? It's up to you how you live your life. It's nothing to do with me.'

'I couldn't have put it better myself,' she says haughtily. 'Now please get back to work before I have to make a complaint about you.'

'Another one?' I say facetiously.

'Yes,' she says. 'Another one.'

20

Before I can even fully digest what Alex has said to me I feel I owe Kay an explanation, so I stick the phones on to voicemail and take her to the pub. If they don't like it, then fuck them. I'm past caring. Actually, that's not true. Before we go I creep in to see Melanie, who is on the phone, and do a mime that I hope indicates that Kay and I are going out, is that OK? She smiles and nods so I'm taking that as a yes.

Kay is shaken up to say the least. I buy her a glass of red wine and then try to fill her in on the broad strokes of my complicated relationships. I try to keep to the facts – or at least, an abridged version of them – and I don't offer up my opinion of Alex or Lorna. I'm worried she'll judge me unfavourably when I get to the part about telling Lorna about Alex's declaration of love to me, but she just nods and takes it all in.

'He seems awful. I'm sorry, I know he's your friend and everything . . .'

'He is awful,' I say. 'I've realized that recently. I can't believe I thought I knew him.'

'And,' Kay says. 'I know it's none of my business, but what do you think about those things he was saying about your husband?'

'I don't know,' I say, and I mean it. I can't believe

there's anything about Dan's past that I don't know. 'I think he's clutching at straws. Making something out of nothing to try and hurt me.'

'That's what I think too. Not that I even know Dan, but it all feels too convenient. You've hurt him so now he's going to hurt you. Ignore him. Don't even bring it up with Dan because that's what Alex wants.'

I know she's right, I'm just not sure it's that easy.

Back in the office it doesn't seem like Lorna even noticed we were gone.

'Shall I go and see if she's OK?' Kay asks, a little nervously.

'Just go in and offer her a coffee or something.'

A couple of minutes later Kay comes back again, shaking her head. 'She doesn't want anything. She looks terrible, though.'

'Just leave her to it, then,' I say. 'She knows we're here if she needs anything.'

The phone rings and Kay picks it up straight away. 'Hi, Heather,' she says cheerfully and then, 'Oh no, did she not?' She looks at me and pulls a face. I look at my phone. Lorna's line is lit up. 'It must have slipped her mind. I'll remind her again. Yes . . . yes . . . I'm sure you are. Well, I'm very sorry. Like I said, I'll remind her . . .' She says goodbye and hangs up.

'Lorna still hasn't called her,' she says. 'She sounded a little irritated to say the least.'

'Who can blame her? Email Lorna and then as soon as she's off the phone go in there and tell her again. Offer to get Heather on the line and put her through,' I say.

210

Kay does as she's told, but then comes out of Lorna's office again saying, 'She said she'll call her in a minute. She's in the middle of something.'

'Did she look like she was in the middle of something?'

'No. She was just sitting there staring into space.'

'Oh, for God's sake. I'll tell her she has to do it now. Heather's going to leave us and go somewhere else if she doesn't feel like she's getting enough attention.'

I go to lift up my phone to call her just as her light goes red to show she's engaged. Maybe she's calling Heather now.

'Shhh a minute,' I say to Kay and I pick up anyway and do my old trick of covering the mouthpiece with my hand.

'. . . only said it because it was her. It upset me so much, but I didn't mean it, Alex. I didn't really want to break up with you, you know that, don't you?'

Oh God. There's no response so I assume it's Alex's answerphone she's talking to. I sit there, paralysed. I should put down my phone, this is none of my business, but I'm scared she'll hear the click and know someone was listening. Besides, I can't quite tear myself away from the scene of the accident. I'm like a rubber-necker going past a motorway pile-up. I should just speed up and keep moving, but I'm transfixed.

'. . . I just wanted to punish you because I was hurt. But I know that she was exaggerating. I know you loved me really. And now I've ruined it. You have to call me back. Please, Alex. I don't understand why you wouldn't stay and talk to me today. I don't understand why you won't answer my calls. Please phone me back. Please. I love you. Bye.'

I wait to hear her phone go down before I hang up mine. Kay is looking at me expectantly.

'Oh,' I say. 'It wasn't Heather.'

I don't offer up any more information and luckily she doesn't ask. This feels like too personal a thing to share. I'm at a loss what to do next, to be honest. I try to focus on the immediate problem. Lorna needs to speak to Heather. In fact, I have no doubt, she needs to take one step back first and speak to the Controller of Entertainment Commissioning at the BBC and then report to Heather on the outcome of that conversation. Today.

I sit with my head in my hands for a moment trying to decide how I am going to force a hysterical woman into making a phone call. Even if I do I'm worried she'll sound half insane to whoever is on the other end. Probably the professional thing to do, the grown-up thing, would be to go in and speak to either Joshua or Melanie and ask their advice. Tell them that Lorna is behaving a little oddly and ask them to step in. It's their reputation she's messing with, after all. But by doing that I would also be basically telling them that she hasn't been doing her job properly. I'd be pointing out something that they definitely haven't cottoned on to yet. That Lorna is falling apart in front of our eyes and is incapable of acting in a professional manner. I can't bring myself to do it. She's been kicked enough already without me joining in, taking a swipe at the one thing she does usually have control of in her life. The constant that is always there while the stream of unsuitable men comes and goes. Her career.

I can hardly believe I am thinking like this, but she doesn't deserve it. She's mean and crazy and vindictive and insecure but, even so, she shouldn't be going through what she's going through now. So the only choice I have is to keep on at her until she makes those calls and just hope she can hold it together enough to talk sense when she does. Or at least that's what I think until Kay takes a call from her.

'Don't forget about Heather,' Kay says into the phone. 'She sounded annoyed.'

'Lorna's going home for the afternoon; she's not feeling well,' she says to me when the call ends.

'What about Heather?' I say.

'She said she doesn't feel up to talking to anyone today. She'll call her tomorrow. She did sound terrible, actually.' Kay, understandably, doesn't realize how serious the situation is. Clients like Heather Barclay don't sit around waiting for their agents to feel well enough to do things on their behalf. Especially not when they've been lured away from their previous representation with promises of dynamism and great things.

'She has to get back to her today. Even if it's only to lie and say she's been chasing the Controller of Entertainment and he hasn't called her back. Although that would sound like either he didn't think Lorna was important enough to speak to or he wasn't interested enough in Heather to want to follow it up. If he was, wouldn't he be falling over himself to call back and arrange a meeting?'

Kay looks a little flustered, like she doesn't know what I expect her to do about it and, truthfully, I don't really expect her to do anything. There's nothing she can do. I was just thinking aloud. Lorna wouldn't listen to her anyway; she's barely given her the time of day since she arrived.

I hear the outer door click quietly like someone doesn't want to be heard and I realize that it must be Lorna getting her coat. I'm out of my chair like a greyhound after a rabbit.

'Lorna,' I say, and she jumps. 'I know you're not well and I'm sorry to ambush you, but you really do need to talk to Heather today. She's not happy and I'm worried that she'll just go somewhere else if she doesn't feel like she's your top priority.'

'Kay can ring her and tell her I'm ill,' Lorna says, and she grabs her coat off the hook.

'And what about the BBC? What can we tell her about that? Does she have a meeting? Are they interested?'

'Tell her what you like. I'm going home.' She leaves before I can do anything about it even if I could think what to do.

'Shall I do that, then,' Kay asks, 'call Heather and tell her Lorna's gone home sick?'

'That won't explain why she didn't call her yesterday or this morning. Oh God. This is ridiculous.'

I run through my options. It seems to me they're severely limited. Tell Joshua and Melanie. I've already dismissed that as too risky. Call Heather and tell her Lorna's sick and there's no news from the BBC, but won't that leave her with an unanswered question about what exactly Lorna has been doing on her behalf for the past twenty-four hours? That leaves me with only one route to go down. It seems like the wrong road to take in so many ways but I don't see what choice I have.

'I'm just going to use Lorna's office for a while.' I say to Kay. 'Make a few calls. Don't ring Heather yet. I'll let you know what's going on later.'

Luckily Kay is still so new she doesn't have the where-withal to fling herself across the doorway to stop me, which would probably be the sensible thing to do. She doesn't yet know that what I'm doing could be deemed stupid or maybe just career suicidal.

'OK,' she says.

I sit at Lorna's desk and take a deep breath. I know the number of the BBC by heart – I am always being asked to call people there on Joshua or Melanie's behalf. I pick up the phone then I realize I have no idea what the name of the Controller of Entertainment is so I have to spend a few minutes on Lorna's computer look-ing it up. I'm not even tempted to look through her emails. The less I know about Lorna's life the better, I've decided.

Armed with the name, I dial.

'Niall Johnson's office, please,' I say to the person who answers, and, next thing I know, a woman with a pleas-ant voice is telling me that that's exactly where I've got through to.

'Could I speak to his assistant, please? It's Lorna Whittaker from Mortimer and Sheedy.' I'm taking a chance that Lorna will never have spoken to Niall, but as she only became a fully fledged agent a matter of weeks ago it seems like a pretty fair chance to take. And if he answers, 'Hey, Lorna, long time no hear!' I can always say that his assistant got it wrong and that I am, in fact, calling on behalf of Lorna. If I say that up front, I know he'll never take my call, though.

'Can I ask what it's about?' she says, and I say, 'Heather Barclay. I've taken over her representation. She's asked me personally to call to see if she can set up a meeting with Niall. Confidentially, of course,' I add, thinking that this will whet his appetite.

'Hold on,' she says.

I feel a little sick while I wait for her to come back on. Then I hear a click. 'Lorna, you're on with Niall.'

'Hello,' he says, thankfully not in a tone that indicates they've ever encountered each other before.

I try to sound breezy and confident. I'm AN AGENT! I have a client he wants. He's more scared of me than I am of him. Or is that spiders?

'Hi, Niall! It's Lorna Whittaker from Mortimer and Sheedy. We've taken on Heather Barclay and she's looking to move on to bigger things! See beyond her ITV contract! And we were hoping we could come in to see you to talk about the future!' I find myself mimicking Lorna's rather gushy, exclamation-mark-ridden way of speaking.

'Heather's leaving ITV?' he says. 'Interesting.'

Oh God, is she? I don't really know. 'It's just between us for now, of course. She just wants to explore what other opportunities there are out there.' That sounds like the kind of thing I've heard Joshua and Melanie say to people on the phone.

'OK,' he says. 'Well, let's say we have lunch? That should set some tongues wagging.'

'Great!' I say, my voice pitching up an octave. 'Give me some dates and I'll check when she's free.'

'I'll have my assistant Colette ring you with my diary. I assume you'll be joining us too?'

'Oh . . . um.'

'I think you should be there,' he says. 'In case we get down to talking strategy. That way we avoid any Chinese whispers, not to mention me having to have the same conversation all over again.'

What the hell, I think. In for a penny. 'Of course! It'll be a pleasure. Tell Colette she can speak to Rebecca in my office if I'm not around. And thank you for your time. I look forward to meeting you!'

'You too,' he says. 'Goodbye for now and tell Heather we love her.'

He rings off and I sit shaking in Lorna's chair for a good three or four minutes. My legs feel like jelly. It's too late to back out now. I've set something in motion and I couldn't stop it even if I wanted to. I just have to hope that Lorna gets her act back together soon, in time for her lunch with Niall Johnson at least.

I gather myself together and then I flick through Lorna's Rolodex to find Heather's number.

'Finally. Where the hell have you been?' she says when she answers.

'Oh, hi. It's not Lorna, it's Rebecca. Her . . . erm . . . I work with her. We met. You won't remember. Anyway, Lorna asked me to call you. She's really unwell – she's been ill for a couple of days now, actually – and we've made her go home, against all her protests.'

'Oh,' she says, not sounding too concerned for Lorna's welfare. 'I wondered why she hadn't called me back. Is she OK?' she adds as an afterthought.

'She will be,' I say. 'She just needed to admit that she was ill and take some time off. She's such a workaholic,' I add, and then wonder if that's overkill. 'Anyway, she asked me to let you know that Niall Johnson is really excited about the prospect of you doing something for . . .' I remember the cardinal sin. Never make a celebrity feel like the hired help. '. . . I mean with him. He wants to take you for lunch. I'm just waiting to find out when he can do, but Lorna asked me to check when you're free too.'

'Mondays and Tuesdays really. The other days I have rehearsals or taping. Did she really say he sounded excited?'

'She did. And he also said, "Tell Heather we love her."'

'Excellent.' All of Heather's former irritation seems to have dissipated with the news that she's in demand.

'So, we'll find a Monday or Tuesday that Niall can do and I'll call you back. You might not hear from Lorna for a few days because we've insisted she take to her bed

218

and turn her phone off. If you need anything in the meantime, feel free to call me. Rebecca. In fact, let me give you my mobile number.'

I spell it out for her and she seems to go off happy.

Back in reception I tell Kay to put any calls from Niall Johnson's office through to me, even if they ask for Lorna. I want to hug her when she just says, 'OK,' and doesn't ask me why. I spend the whole afternoon willing Colette to call. I don't think I could go through with pretending to be Lorna once she's back and sitting in the room along the corridor.

At about four thirty Kay finally tells me in a loud stage whisper that Niall Johnson's office is calling.

'For Lorna or Rebecca?' I say.

'Lorna.'

I hadn't really been conscious of making myself sound like Lorna when I spoke to Colette before, but now I make an effort to repeat the performance I gave for Niall earlier. Just in case she and Lorna ever meet. Although, if they do then what Lorna sounded like would be the least of their problems given that Lorna would have no memory of ever having spoken to her before. As soon as this is all arranged, I tell myself, as soon as Lorna is back at work, I'll explain to her what I've done and why. Obviously I'm hoping that she will understand, even be grateful to me for the way I've covered her back. But, hey, this is Lorna we're talking about here.

Anyway, back to the task in hand.

'Hi, Colette!' I say. Think exclamation marks. 'Thanks

for calling me back so soon!' Kay is looking at me strangely.

'OK,' Colette says. 'I have Niall's diary in front of me. What dates were you looking at?'

So I explain that it has to be a Monday or a Tuesday and that really works in my favour because Niall doesn't have one of those free for another couple of weeks. Surely Lorna will be back to her old self by then. 'Let me just check my schedule too.' I say the date out loud and look at Kay meaningfully. She seems to take the hint and quickly looks something up on her computer – hopefully Lorna's diary because that's what I was trying to communicate to her. A couple of clicks later she nods to me, which I take to mean that Lorna is free that day.

'Where would Heather like to go?' Colette says. 'Niall says he'll leave the choice to her.'

How the hell do I know? 'Oh, let's say the Ivy,' I say, naming somewhere I've always wanted to go myself. I can't imagine either Lorna or Heather having a problem with that.

'The Ivy it is,' she says. 'I'll book it now and confirm with your office a few days before.'

'Great!' I say. 'Tell Niall I'm looking forward to it!'

'Rebecca,' Kay says when I put the phone down, 'I know I'm new here, but I'm assuming that what's happening today isn't normal.'

'I'm sorry, Kay,' I say. 'I'm putting you in a really awkward position. But I didn't know what else to do. I need to be able to trust you to keep this to yourself. That's all.'

'You know I will,' she says, and I believe her. 'But it's making me very uncomfortable to be really honest.'

'Just know that I'm doing it for Lorna's own good. And for the good of Mortimer and Sheedy. Hopefully she'll be fine in a couple of days and that'll be the end of it.'

'OK,' she says. 'Jesus, what a day.'

'I know.' I nod and then I remember the earlier drama, the one that set this one in motion. In all the excitement about Lorna and Heather and Niall I'd completely forgotten about Alex and his drunken rantings.

At home I find myself looking at Dan, searching for, what? Some four-year-old guilty secret that is etched on his face? I'm trying not to ask him about it. That's exactly what Alex wants, for me to be suspicious and jealous. For Dan and I to argue and start to question one another. I'm hoping not to play my assigned role but I also know that if I don't say anything there's a danger it'll start eating away at me and that could damage things between us even more. Plus, I feel like I have to tell Dan about Alex coming to the office. Keeping a secret from him definitely isn't a good idea, I've learned that lesson. And, if I tell him any of it, then I should tell him all of it. I'm winning the argument with myself. I want an excuse to bring up what Alex said with Dan and I've found one. Dan asked me to be straight with him about all things concerning Alex and so I will. It won't look like I'm accusing, I'll just be reporting what Alex said to me and then waiting to see what Dan has to say about it. I won't get worked up. I won't show him that underneath it all I'm terrified that there might be some grain of truth behind Alex's accusation. I'll just put it out there and see what happens.

I try to be extra nice to him over dinner. William is telling some interminable story about an experiment they did in physics to prove whether certain things are classed as solids, liquids or gases. He's talking about particle vibration and thermal energy and God knows what else. I'm finding it hard to concentrate.

'Take this ketchup,' he says, waving his Heinz-covered knife at us. 'What would you say it was?'

I'm not sure what answer he requires so I say nothing while Dan says, 'Tasty,' which he knows is guaranteed to drive William crazy.

'No!' William says. 'Is it a liquid or a solid?'

I make an effort. 'Oh, liquid, of course, anyone knows that,' I say, knowing that he's only asking this question because this answer, the obvious one, is clearly wrong.

He's triumphant as I knew he would be. 'Not necessarily,' he says smugly. 'It may be an emulsion because it's a mix of two unblendable liquids. Or some would say it's actually a colloid, which is a chemical mixture where one substance is evenly spread through another.'

'Wow,' Dan says, feigning interest. I catch Dan's eye. He smiles as if to say, 'Isn't our son amazing?' I smile back but then the moment is broken by Zoe saying, 'For God's sake, William. I am literally going to slit my wrists if you don't stop talking soon.'

William, good natured as ever – he's definitely his father's son – simply says, 'Sorry,' and shuts up.

Dan laughs. 'So, let's hear about Mum's day.' Zoe groans and I almost join in. I really don't want to talk about the day I've had over dinner. I scrabble around for anything to say that doesn't involve some kind of trauma but, between Alex and Lorna, there really isn't anything.

'Oh, you know. It was OK,' is all I can come up with.

'Come on,' he says. 'There must be something to tell us about your glamorous celebrity-filled life.'

'Well, I spoke to Heather Barclay.' Thankfully this has the desired effect as Zoe suddenly comes to life and she and William demand to know what Heather was like.

'I met her in person the other day too.'

'No! Is she skinny?' Zoe says. 'How skinny is she?'

'Too skinny,' I say. 'Don't go getting any ideas.'

'Is she pretty?' William says.

'Yes,' I say. 'In a too-skinny kind of way.'

'Is she nice?'

'She's OK. I imagine she might be a nightmare if you got on the wrong side of her.'

'Wow, Mum. That's so cool,' Zoe says. 'No one else at school's mum has a job where they get to meet famous people.'

'Archie Samson's dad *is* a famous person,' William says, naming a boy in the year above him whose father hosts a current-affairs programme.

'So?' Zoe says. 'Archie Samson's dad does the news. This is Heather Barclay. Can you get me her autograph?'

'I don't know,' I say. 'Probably. Let me wait till she's been with us a bit longer.' It doesn't feel like now is the time to be asking Heather Barclay for a signed photo.

'And one for Kerrie.'

'And one for me,' William says.

'And one for me. With kisses on,' Dan says, which makes me laugh despite my nervousness.

Once the kids have finally gone to bed, or at least, in Zoe's case, her room, I say to Dan, 'Do you really want to hear how my day was?'

He realizes immediately that something's wrong. 'What? What happened?'

So I tell him about Alex and his face goes pale. I don't spare him any of the details; I don't care how bad a light I paint Alex in any more. I never want him back in our lives in any capacity. I don't exaggerate, but I want Dan to know exactly how badly he's behaving.

'And then,' I say, trying to sound matter of fact, 'he said something about Edinburgh. Ask you about Edinburgh. Said that I was wrong to be so certain my marriage was perfect.'

I pause so I can take a good look at Dan. I'm hoping he'll laugh or just look confused. He does neither. In fact, he looks panicked, caught out. I feel my heart pounding in my throat. I bite my top lip to stop me from saying anything, from screaming at him to tell me what it is. It's up to him now.

Dan sighs audibly and then takes my hand, which is never a good sign in this kind of situation.

'Dan . . .' I say, barely able to speak above a whisper. I realize now that I have to know. There's no rewinding back to blissful ignorance. There's no more convincing myself that Alex was lying. There's no shutting the box now without looking at what's inside. I have to hear what it is Dan might have to tell me. Because now I know for certain that he does have something to confess.

'Just tell me. Whatever it is, get it over with.'

'I'm so sorry, Rebecca.'

With these four words I feel the floor drop out of my world. My safe cocoon that I've spent years constructing around myself starts to unravel before my eyes. I want to take my hand back. but Dan holds on to it tightly. I wait to hear what he has to say next.

'When Alex and I went to Edinburgh there was this woman . . .'

'No, Dan . . .' I can't stop myself.

'Nothing really happened,' he says quickly. Now I'm confused.

'What do you mean?'

'She was staying in our hotel and we got talking to her in the bar. She was there for some conference with a load of work colleagues. She just . . . She made it really obvious she liked me. And I nearly went for it. I don't know why. I'd never even thought of doing anything like that before, but we'd been having a bit of a rough time . . . I don't know, there's no excuse. Anyway, I talked to Alex about it. I told him I was thinking about it . . . I guess it was my mid-life crisis.'

He stops and looks at me like a dog waiting to be punished.

'And that's it? That's really it, that you thought about it?'

He nods.

'Nothing happened? You didn't . . . kiss . . . or anything?'

He looks at the floor. 'Yes. We did. But only for a few seconds. In the lift. She invited me back to her room and I went. That's the bit I'm really ashamed of. But as soon as I got there I knew it wasn't what I wanted. I couldn't have gone through with it. So I left. I didn't even get her number and we left the next day. I'm sorry. I should have told you at the time, but I felt so bad and I was scared I would have ruined everything . . .'

I can't help myself. I laugh. It's not even remotely funny and I know that when I have an off day I'll probably torture myself with the details. (What did she look like? What was so special about her to make him even contemplate it? Did he tell her about me? How was our conversation on the phone that night? Normal, as if nothing had happened? Did he tell me that he was missing me? That he loved me?) But the truth is I am so relieved I could cry. And he's right, we were having a bit of a rough patch. Nothing serious, nothing even tangible really, just one of those phases you go through from time to time when you're crashing into each other rather than connecting, when for a few days or even weeks you suddenly find one another's habits so mind-crushingly irritating that you have to hold yourself back from picking a fight. All couples have them. They blow over eventually, but I remember this one in particular because it started when we were on holiday. Just the two of us, without the kids, for the first time in years. Suddenly we were together twenty-four hours a day, but it was like we couldn't remember how to be together. Everything was wrong. In fact, that was part of the reason why I was so keen for Dan to go to Scotland with Alex straight afterwards. I felt like we needed a few days apart from each other. He's right, it's definitely not an excuse, but it actually could have been so much worse. And I resolve never to give Dan a hard time about it. Ever.

'That's really it?' I say, and he looks me right in the eyes and says that yes, that's it, but that's bad enough, isn't it?

'Dan, it's fine. I mean, it's not fine but it's OK. I'd be lying if I said it didn't upset me at all, you going to her room and . . . But, anyway, in the greater scheme of things it's nothing. A tiny blip. And you're right. Things weren't going so well at the time.'

'I still shouldn't ever have got myself in that position.'

'You made a mistake. Not only that but you stopped yourself from making a much bigger one. We're all allowed a wobble. We're all allowed to question our relationships once in a while.'

'Except that you never do. Do you?'

'I've had my moments,' I say, although I can't remember when I ever have. 'I want us to forget about it,' I say. 'Let's just put it in the past and move on. It's fine, Dan, really.'

227

'Really?' he says, and he looks so relieved that I think he might cry.

'Really.'

Maybe if Dan had told me about this another time I wouldn't have taken it so well. In fact, I know I wouldn't. It would have felt like an enormous betrayal. I would have been confused that Dan could even start to behave in a way so unlike the Dan I thought I knew. (Dan flirting? It's impossible to imagine. Don't go there, I tell myself. Don't allow yourself to blow it up into something bigger than it is.) My insecurity rating would have shot up (was she thinner stroke younger stroke prettier stroke funnier than me?) and I probably would have picked at it, beating myself up with the details, until I had driven Dan away completely. As it is I'm pretty sure I can lock it away and forget about it. Almost. I allow myself one tiny moment of neediness.

'Dan? Since then . . . I mean, we're OK, aren't we?'

'God, yes,' he says, hugging me so hard I can barely breathe. 'It gave me a wake-up call about what I nearly threw away. God, Rebecca, when I think that I could have lost you and the kids. You believe me, don't you?' He holds me at arm's length so that he can look at me and I say yes, I do, of course I do, and I mean it. I know from his reaction, from his guilt and shame over what, in the end, was nothing, that there's no danger of him being a repeat offender.

'I'm just curious,' I say a couple of minutes later, 'but what did Alex say about it?'

'He told me to go for it,' Dan says, looking even

more apologetic at having to hammer another nail into the coffin containing my friendship with Alex. 'Actually,' he adds, reluctantly, 'he said that if she'd been coming on to him he definitely would have gone for it, no question.'

I interrupt. 'Even then?'

Dan nods. 'He said he felt trapped by having been in the same relationship for so long. That there was no harm in seeing what else was out there.'

'Jesus, Dan, really?'

'Obviously I know now that he was hoping we'd fall apart and then he could be free to pursue you. He'd been with other women too, before that.'

Alex? Really? 'And you knew?'

'He knew I didn't approve.'

'And you didn't tell me?'

He shrugs, miserably. 'He asked me not to. And to be honest I was afraid that if I did you would have either killed him or felt you had to tell Isabel.'

'Too right I would. And don't you think that it might have been better for her to have realized her marriage wasn't perfect earlier? When she was younger and it might have been less daunting to go it alone?' I can feel myself getting angry. It's this boys' club thing. This idea that friendships between blokes are more important than anything else.

'Maybe. I'm just telling you how it was,' he says, sensing that I'm losing it and no doubt afraid that if I lost my temper right now he wouldn't get off so easily about Edinburgh. In fact, maybe that's part of the reason why

I'm feeling so angry about Alex. I was so determined not to kick off at Dan that I was suppressing all my hurt and anger about what he'd done. I have to remember what the real issue is here, though. Alex is trying to rock my marriage and I mustn't let him. And, anyway, it's not like Dan and Alex are going to be covering each other's tracks in the future.

'I know,' I say. 'It just makes me so angry on Isabel's behalf.'

'And rightly so.'

'We won't tell her about . . . you know . . . the other women. Agreed?'

He nods.

'What a mess,' I say, and Dan says, 'I really am sorry,' again. 'For everything.'

21

There's no sign of Lorna in the office next day. Neither does she ring in to tell anyone she won't be there. I ask Kay to find an excuse to call her – 'don't let her think you're checking up on her' – which she does and she gets an earful in the process. We tell Joshua and Melanie that Lorna has called in sick and then I set about doing some damage limitation. Thank God Lorna has so few clients, but I still have no idea what half of them are up to and what crucial meetings or auditions they might be missing as we speak. I decide to ring them all to tell them that Lorna's been unwell for a few days and to ask if there's anything that needs doing. They'll just think I'm being overly conscientious, which is fine by me. Before I do I ask Kay to run me through all the phone messages she's taken for Lorna since she arrived, in case there is anything urgent that needs a response. It's unlikely, I know, except that before Lorna keeled over she was on a roll, trying to breathe life into even the most comatose careers.

As well as the people she has taken on herself since she became AN AGENT! – Mary, Craig and Heather – Lorna was handed the floundering fortunes of four others who Joshua and Melanie no longer had the stomachs to look after, but who they also couldn't get up

231

the courage to sack. They are: playwright Joy Wright Phillips who once won a young writers award and subsequently had her play staged by the Donmar as part of a new-talent season, but who seems to have been suffering from writer's block ever since; actors Samuel Sweeney and Kathryn Greyson who tick along with varying degrees of success in regional theatre and, very occasionally, on TV; and 'personality' Jasmine Howard who is really a gossip-magazine journalist, but who has found her niche as a pundit, willing to give her views on anything from female circumcision to why she loves the 1980s, so long as the money is right.

I call Samuel first because one of the messages Kay took for Lorna a few days ago was from a casting director asking him to come in and read for a small part in hospital drama *Nottingham General*. It's the first he's heard of it, but he seems completely unfazed. The audition is the day after tomorrow, he's free and the fact that it's such short notice makes no difference to him. He won't be given the scenes until he gets there anyway. It's a process he's used to.

'Oh great,' he says genuinely. 'My car's MOT is due so I could do with the money.'

Next I pick Jasmine who I figure is the one most likely to actually have something going on in her life.

'Did she ring Phil?' she says.

'Phil . . .?'

'Phil Masterson, the producer of *London at Six*,' she explains in a tone that suggests I'm an idiot for not knowing which Phil she's referring to.

232

'Oh. I have no idea, I'm afraid. Was it urgent?'

'She's meant to be ringing him every week to see what topics they've got coming up. It was her idea, but I haven't heard from her since she suggested it. There's no point having good ideas if you're not going to follow them through. I said to Joshua when he asked if I minded going over to Lorna that it was fine, but she'd better be good –'

'Let me check,' I interrupt. 'She probably called him before she was taken ill and then didn't have a chance to tell anyone about it. She did get taken ill very suddenly.'

'What's wrong with her?'

'Um . . . they're not sure yet, actually. She just collapsed. They're doing tests at the moment.'

'She probably just needs to eat more,' Jasmine says, a woman after my own heart. 'She's way too thin. Don't you think she's too thin?'

'Oh, but she had all these symptoms, fever, nausea, a headache. Pins and needles.' OK, Rebecca, shut up, you're protesting too much. 'Listen,' I say. 'Let me see what I can find out and I'll call you back, OK?'

I give Kay instructions to go through Lorna's book for the past two weeks to look for Phil's name. Lorna, Joshua and Melanie all have these books where they write down every call they make and the gist of the conversation. It's to cover their backs, really, and it works.

Once when Joshua got into a fight with a TV producer about the finer details of a very complicated contract they were trying to negotiate for one of his actress clients, he had me go right back through his book highlighting every

233

conversation they'd had about it. It took me hours. Later I'd heard him on the phone – 'On the twenty-fourth of May you agreed that my client could have second billing above the titles and be on a shared card with no more than two others in the end credits. Why would I have agreed to a five per cent drop in the episode fee otherwise?'

He'd won his corner in the end and the producer had had to concede. He would never have had the leverage, he'd said afterwards, if it hadn't been for his meticulous – and more importantly contemporaneous – note taking. Recall after the event was never going to be as accurate.

It feels a little intrusive to be doing forensic tests on Lorna's book without her permission, but I figure we have no choice. Kay does the deed – again, I assure her that I will accept all blame if necessary – while I call Kathryn Greyson who is sweet and says, no, there's nothing much going on, but that she will call me if she needs anything. She's in the florist where she works three mornings a week. I can't actually remember the last time she had an acting job.

Lastly it's playwright Joy Wright Phillips. She takes an age to answer and then, when she does, I realize from the confusion in her voice, that she was still asleep.

'What time is it?' she says, clearly irritated at being disturbed. I check my watch. 'Quarter past eleven.'

'Oh,' she says. 'I had a late night. I was writing,' she adds unconvincingly.

I tell her about Lorna and she says that, no, she wasn't expecting anything to be happening. Nothing was ever going to happen until she had finished writing something.

I know all about Joy's writer's block even though she tries to pretend it doesn't exist so I say, 'I don't know how you do it. I'd never have the discipline. I think if it was me I'd write first thing. Before I even got dressed or had any other distractions.' What I know about it I don't know, but I feel like I ought to say something to help get Joy her mojo back. 'That way you get it out of the way. It's not hanging over you for the rest of the day. And I'd work on a computer that didn't have the internet so I wouldn't be tempted to check my emails every five minutes or spend all day on Facebook. Anyway . . .' I've run out of words of wisdom so I decide to shut up.

Joy doesn't really respond so I just say goodbye. I know what Craig and Heather are up to so that just leaves Mary. I decide that I can allow myself a quick coffee break. I feel like I've achieved an awful lot already this morning – apart from actually doing my own work, of course, that's piling up on my desk. Kay seems to have finished scrutinizing Lorna's notebook by the time I get off the phone.

'Well, the good news is that there's nothing else really in here that hasn't been dealt with,' she says, waving the book at me. 'The bad news is there's nothing really in here at all. She's hardly made any notes in the past couple of weeks.'

'No mention of Phil Masterson?'

'None.'

I decide that Phil is not urgent and that he and Jasmine

can wait for a couple of days. That way, if Lorna comes back and looks like she's got any intention of actually doing anything, then she can call him herself which would be much easier all round.

Kay and I sit and drink our coffee in silence, staring off into space like two shell-shocked soldiers. I feel quite proud of myself. Everything is under control, all of Lorna's clients are happy, everyone is where they are meant to be and no one is any the wiser. This feeling lasts for, oh twenty-odd seconds, until I answer the phone and it's Mary who seems to be in tears. I tell her that Lorna's sick, blah blah, and I ask her what's wrong.

'I bumped into Marilyn Carson this morning. She's casting that new production of *A Doll's House* that Elizabeth O'Mara is starring in – and she asked me why I wasn't at the audition yesterday. So I told her that I didn't know anything about it and she said that's a shame because she thought there was definitely a little part in there for me and she'd even suggested they look at me for Nora's understudy. Understudy Elizabeth O'Mara? Can you imagine? And I said, well, maybe they could see me today or over the weekend; I'd cancel anything that got in the way. But she said they'd already given the part to some other girl because they start rehearsal next week. She said it was a shame because she liked me in my final-year show and it was only a few lines so she thought the director would definitely take a chance on someone new. In fact, he has. The girl they've picked has almost no experience at all. And it's a big regional tour and then almost certainly coming into the West End. A proper paying job, Rebecca. And everyone knows the star always misses a few matinees deliberately to give the understudy a go. Nora? Can you imagine?'

Oh shit.

'Calm down, Mary,' I say. 'Do you want me to ring Marilyn Carson?'

'There's no point. Like I said, they've offered it already.'

I have absolutely no idea what to do. I make more elaborate excuses for Lorna, but Mary's not really in the mood to listen. To a seasoned old pro like Samuel this would be a tiny insignificant blip. One of a thousand parts that have slipped through his fingers over the years for one reason or another. But for Mary it's a major catastrophe. Marilyn is the only casting director she has even met so far in her short career.

I know exactly how she feels. In my brief incarnation as an actress-cum-waitress-cum-telesales person I would view every audition as a watershed, the break I needed to really launch me into, at least, being able to drop two of my professions. Every disappointment hit me like a high-speed train and I would fixate on who they had actually given the role to and why. Every other young actress's triumph was an opportunity missed.

Mary knows that doing a few lines in *A Doll's House* and maybe, if she was incredibly lucky, taking the lead in the odd matinee in front of an audience reeking with disappointment that the woman they had really come to see was apparently sick, wasn't going to change her life. But it would have been a validation of her decision to call herself an actress, and at her fledgling stage of the game the importance of that can't be underestimated.

'Listen, Mary,' I say. 'You just have to write this one off to bad luck. I'll call Marilyn anyway, just to make sure that she knows it's our mess up, not yours. You just have to look ahead to the next audition.'

I don't really know what else to say to her.

'There is no next audition,' she says. 'Marilyn is the only casting director who's ever even agreed to see me. Why should anyone else? I have zero real experience.'

'I'll tell you what, we'll find you an audition for something else, OK? I promise you I'll get you in with another casting director if it kills me.' Kay is looking at me, eyebrows raised. I shrug.

'Leave it with me,' I say to Mary.

'Don't go native,' Kay says once I've put the phone down. 'You're covering Lorna's tracks, remember? You're not actually meant to be doing her job.'

'What else could I say?' Fucking hell, Lorna.

For the first time today my newly burgeoning sympathy for Lorna wavers. I have to remind myself that, really, this is all Alex's fault, and remembering that spurs me on.

'Well,' I say to Kay. 'What castings do we know are coming up? I'm going to get Mary in to see somebody. How hard can it be?'

I know Marilyn at least to speak to. I must have spoken to her a hundred times over the years.

'Oh, hi, Rebecca,' she says in a friendly voice. 'How are you?'

'Good,' I say unconvincingly. 'I'm just calling to apologize about Mary Fitzmaurice.' I go into the whole poor Lorna's sick routine and, of course, Marilyn's absolutely fine about it. Why wouldn't she be? It's not her who's missed out on a job.

'The thing is, Marilyn, I need to get Mary into another casting. This has knocked her confidence a bit. Do you have anything else coming up?'

'Not really. I'm doing *Journey's End* next, which is all boys . . . but tell her not to worry. I'll have her in again next time there's something relevant. She shouldn't panic.'

'I know. But you know what it's like. Thanks, though.'

I follow my call to Marilyn with five calls to other casting directors who are apparently also looking for people at the moment. No one is very interested in seeing an actress who has no track record and who they've never met. I agree to let them all know when there's something they can see her in and they all agree to see her for a quick general meeting after that if they think she's any good in it. I tell them she's great even though I've never seen her act, and then leave it at that. It's something.

While I'm talking to one of them, Paul Seeborne, Joshua comes into reception and hovers around looking for something in one of the filing cabinets. I'm in full flow – 'We think she's got great potential as a young character actress. She's got something of Samantha Morton about her, that edginess . . .' – when I realize he's there and I stop abruptly and say, 'Anyway, I'm sure

Lorna will get back to you as soon as she's back,' which must confuse Paul enormously because, so far as he's aware, he has nothing he needs to be talking to Lorna about. 'OK, well, thanks. Bye,' I say, and I put the phone down before he can respond. Joshua shows no sign of having witnessed anything untoward so I figure I've got away with it for now. I really must go and hide in Lorna's office before I make any more calls.

'Settling in OK?' Joshua says to Kay, not really interested in the answer.

'Yes. It's a real eye-opener,' she says, smiling at him. 'An education.'

'Good, good,' he says, and he rushes off again, thankfully with no idea of what she's referring to.

By the end of the day I'm exhausted. I feel like I need to be taken home on a stretcher and put straight to bed, but instead I'm heading off to Isabel's because we arranged a girly night in days ago and I haven't the heart to cancel.

The girls, with no William to torment, are the model of sweetness and good behaviour. They help with the vegetables for dinner and then, once we've eaten, sitting around the big kitchen table, they offer to load the dishwasher. I tell Izz about my day while they clear up and fetch us glasses of wine like two mini waitresses. I'm much more interested to hear her news, but I know I have to wait for the twins to decamp to their room at the top of the house before I can bring up the subject of Luke.

Isabel lives in a proper house – three storeys and a cellar that, while not enormous, could fit our little flat into it several times. Despite that, the girls have always insisted on sharing a room, so Alex knocked down the walls between two tiny attic bedrooms and now they inhabit the top storey like a pair of very loud mice. They go off promising not to watch too much TV and to come down promptly at half past eight to say goodnight, and Isabel and I move into the comfortable sitting room, taking the bottle with us.

'I don't really understand why you're helping her out,' she says when I've finished bringing her up to date with events at the office, including a version of Alex's drunken visit. 'She's always been horrible to you.'

'I know, neither do I really. But she's completely fallen apart and I just think if she loses her job then she's got nothing. She might be vile sometimes but no one deserves to be treated the way Alex treated her. She's heartbroken. And I suppose I feel responsible in a way. If I hadn't introduced them . . .'

'Well, I hope she's grateful.'

I laugh. 'She won't be.'

'Don't get yourself in deep water, will you?' Isabel says, suddenly serious. 'It's all very well trying to cover up her fuck-ups, but if she doesn't come back in a couple of days you're going to have to come clean with Joshua and Melanie.'

'I will.'

'Promise?'

'Yes,' I say. 'She'll probably be back tomorrow anyway,'

241

I add, although I don't believe it. I can't imagine Lorna just pulling herself together and breezing back in somehow.

'So . . .' I say to her once we've exhausted the subject of Lorna. 'How's love's young dream?'

She smiles. 'It's good. I'm having fun.'

She and Luke have been out again since I last saw her, this time to a small local bistro. They had gone back to hers again, only this time Luke made sure she was aware that he wasn't going to be able to stay over before they left the restaurant.

'He had to get to St Pancras first thing to get on the Eurostar,' she tells me, 'so he needed to get home and pack.'

'Where does he live?'

'Miles away. He's taken a flat in Teddington while he waits for the divorce to go through and they decide what to do with the house. He did ask me if I wanted to go back there, but it seemed crazy when we were just round the corner from here. And, besides, I would have had to come back here before work to get ready anyway.'

'Fair enough. But it was fun? You had a good time?'

'Definitely. He makes me feel . . . I don't know . . . desirable and all that stuff. I need that after Alex. He never really made me feel attractive.'

I nod. 'You do.' The more I hear about Isabel's marriage to Alex the more I'm amazed that I could ever have been so blind.

'I hope that Alex is OK, though,' she says, veering off the subject. 'I mean, being drunk in the day, getting aggressive. It's not like him at all. I'm worried about him, now he's got no one . . .'

Isabel still has a tendency to look wistful and concerned whenever Alex is mentioned, which after the way I now know he treated her is pretty laughable.

'Tell me more about Luke,' I say, wanting to get her off the subject. It makes me uneasy. She needs to move on and, surely, Luke is the perfect vehicle to move on in.

'His son is called Charlie. He's ten. I haven't met him yet, but I've seen his picture and he looks cute. He lives with his mum in Highgate. They moved from round here last year, but the school agreed that Charlie could stay on. He has ADD, I think, so he would have found it hard to settle in somewhere new and he leaves next year anyway. Luke's forty-four. He's got brown hair. Lots of hair, actually. And brown eyes and a really sweet smile that he does all the time, like he knows something funny that no one else does. He's into music and films and stuff, and cars, although I told him I couldn't drum up any enthusiasm about that so he doesn't go on about them. He's funny and clever and I fancy him like crazy.'

'He sounds perfect.'

'He is. He's perfect for what I need at the moment. He's great; he's helping me feel way better about myself, but I'm not in any hurry to move in with him and settle down.'

'Well, you have only known him for three and a half weeks.'

'You know what I mean. I don't think he's going to

turn out to be the love of my life necessarily, but I really like spending time with him and he's doing my ego no end of good.'

'Well, you never know,' I say. Funny, clever, handsome, kind – that sounds exactly like the man Isabel should be getting serious with. 'I'm so happy for you, honestly.'

'Oh, and guess what?' She sits back and smiles at me triumphantly. 'He's asked me if I want to go to Munich with him for a couple of days.'

'No! Are you going to go?'

'Definitely. He'll have meetings during the day, but I can potter around and amuse myself, and then we'll have the evenings together. And the nights.'

'Perfect. I bet you any money you come back thinking that he might be the love of your life after all.'

'Maybe.' She smiles. 'I'm trying to decide what to tell Alex. I need to ask him if he'll have the girls.'

'The truth,' I say. 'I'd love to see the look on his face when you tell him you're going away with another man.'

'Mmm,' she says. 'Maybe.'

'Sod him. It'll do him good to see that you're moving on while he's still a mess.'

'Yes, I suppose so.'

'And if he gives you any problems you know we'll have the girls. We'd love to.'

'Thanks.' She gives me a quick hug.

'So, when can I meet him? Luke?'

'Once we get back from Munich. I reckon that's make-or-break time. If we still like each other once we've got through the snoring and the morning breath and the accidental wind breaking and whatever else, then I think we'll be able to say we're a proper couple.'

'And that's just you,' I say, laughing. 'I wonder what his faults are.'

'Funny,' she says. 'You're very funny.'

I don't tell her about Dan and the woman in Edinburgh. I feel like if I do it will make it real, something that has to be analysed and talked about. I seem to be keeping a lot of secrets from her lately.

22

It's been four work days and Lorna is still not back in the office. She hasn't called in at all and the only reason we know she's still in one piece is because I make Kay ring her every day to check. She has taken to screening her calls, but Kay stays on the line saying things like, 'I'm going to keep talking until you pick up,' or, today, 'If you don't answer, I'm going to call nine-nine-nine and have them come and break your door down,' which results in Lorna picking up and screaming, 'You're so sacked,' into the phone.

Kay, who has been getting braver by the day, is completely unfazed by this. 'I hope you feel better soon,' she says. 'If you're not here tomorrow, I'll call you again to check you're still OK.'

Joshua and Melanie are getting a little concerned, but Kay and I are going into overdrive to assure them that all is OK. Lorna calls us every day with pages of instructions for what needs doing, we tell them. All of her clients are happy.

I have no idea how long we can keep this up. You can get away with one week off work and have people believe you just have some kind of bug that the doctor has told you is highly contagious. Any longer and they're going to start worrying that there's something seriously wrong with you. So far I have placated Joshua and Melanie by telling them that what is up with Lorna is a kind of gastric flu, very debilitating and involving lots of vomiting and needing to stay within a few feet of the toilet. I've made the symptoms sound so revolting that they have stopped asking and have indicated that they'd rather not know the details.

The truth is that all Lorna's clients do seem fairly happy, although for how long is another matter. Samuel got the part on *Nottingham General*. (Man who has been in a car accident caused by his own negligence, in which a young woman was killed, briefly comes into contact with one of the regular doctors whose sister has just died in similar circumstances. Cue much blame and emoting.) When the casting director calls us to tell us the news she also lays out the details of the offer – number of days, fee, billing and travel expenses – and I tell her I'll run it all by Lorna and Samuel and get back to her.

It all looks fair enough to me but, just to be sure, I dial Lorna's number in the hope that I can check with her. Samuel is her client after all. She doesn't answer so I leave a message, knowing she'll never call me back. I check through the files and it seems comparable with what other clients have been paid for similar jobs – but I know that I can't make this decision on my own. Melanie is leafing through a script in her office so I go in and hover until she looks up and sees me. I show her the offer.

'I don't want to disturb Lorna, so I thought you could have a look. It seems OK to me, but . . .'

She looks through it. 'The fee seems all right,' she says. 'That's what I thought.'

'Everything else is fine. They don't mention whether they'll pay his overnights if the days end up being consecutive, though, and as the dates aren't set in stone we should clarify that.'

She must notice my terrified expression because she says, 'Do you want me to do it?'

Yes. Please. Yes, I do. But I worry that if I start inviting her or Joshua to get involved with Lorna's clients while she's absent then the whole charade is going to be exposed. I need them to think that everything is under control. The thought of having to negotiate even on such a small point is making me feel sick, though. 'No. It's fine. I can do it if you're OK with that.'

She smiles, relieved not to have any extra work dumped on her. 'I'd say, with that one caveat and if Samuel's happy, then it's fine. Let me know if you need me to do anything else, though,' she adds in a voice that really says, 'I'm busy. Please don't bother me with this again.'

I call Samuel and tell him and he's happy, which makes life a whole lot easier. If I had to go back and ask for more money, I think I'd take to my bed like Lorna.

Then I take a deep breath and call the casting director back. 'We're just a little concerned about overnights,' I say. 'If the days end up being consecutive, will they pay for his hotel?'

'Let me check,' she says, and I wait anxiously for her to call back. If she says no, I'm not exactly sure what

I'm meant to do. Turn the job down? Roll over and say fine? Put my foot down and insist and risk them saying 'we'll cast someone else then'? Thankfully five minutes later I get a call back saying it's fine, it's the norm for them to pay overnights when necessary but, if it makes Samuel happy, they'll add it to the contract.

'Great,' I say. 'Let's do that.'

And that's it. It's that simple. I have done a deal for a client all by myself. Well, almost. Six years after I joined the company and I have actually done something more than just pass on a message or arrange a time for an audition. I am feeling pleasantly smug and proud of myself and then Kay passes Marilyn Carson to me and she raises my mood even further.

'I've just been speaking to Kate on *Reddington Road*,' she says. 'And they're bringing in a new young family – mum, dad and two babies. Early twenties. They're looking for unknowns but they don't want to put the word out because they'll be inundated with everyone who's ever fancied themselves a soap star. I told them about Mary and I said you'd bike something over to them this afternoon.'

'Marilyn, that's great,' I say. 'But she doesn't have anything. She's never done anything on tape.'

'Oh,' Marilyn says, sounding disappointed. 'Nothing? Well, I'll have to tell them, but there's no way they'll meet her without seeing anything first . . .'

I know there's no chance Mary will get the part but if I can at least get them to see her it'll make her day.

'Wait,' I say. 'What if we could get her in here this

morning and just film her reading something. Would that be any good?'

'Great idea,' Marilyn says. 'Just find a scene for her to read. Anything.'

I get her to tell me a bit more about the role – vulnerable working-class mum, we'll find out later she's a victim of domestic violence, sweet and caring in the face of adversity, soft-spoken but tough underneath.

'It sounds just like Mary,' I say. 'Without the spousal abuse bit at least.'

'Exactly,' she says.

I tell Marilyn I'll keep her posted and I get Mary on the phone. She's at her waitressing job, but luckily all the staff, pretty much, are actors and they have an agreement that they'll cover for each other in emergencies like this so she tells me she can be here in an hour. Meanwhile Kay and I scour the scripts that are lying around the office for something suitable for her to read. We find a scene in Gary's cockney geezer film where a young mother is arguing with her gangster boyfriend that seems perfect. I call Isabel who I know is working from home today and I tell her I am sending a bike for her DVD camera.

When Mary arrives we sit her in Lorna's office and point the camera at her. Kay agrees to read the boyfriend part. I have literally no idea what I'm doing but I figure what's the worst that can happen? Either Mary gets an audition or she doesn't. We do the scene three times and Mary seems great to me, but what do I know?

I get Kay to run off a copy of the DVD, and bike it

straight over to the *Reddington Road* studios in Streatham. It's only once we've done that that it occurs to me I should maybe have asked either Joshua or Melanie for their advice before I went ahead, but I got completely carried away in the moment and it's too late now so Kay tells me there's no point worrying about it. We sit nervously, waiting to see if anything will happen.

It doesn't. At least, not today. No doubt Kate has hundreds of DVDs to wade through, I tell myself. I'm all hyped up, though, and at the end of the day I don't feel like going straight home so I ask Kay if she fancies going to the pub for a quick one and, when she says yes, I call Dan just to check whether he minds giving the kids their tea, which, of course, he doesn't. He's always pretty easy going about that stuff but, at the moment, he's trying even harder than usual to be nice to me.

Kay and I head over to the Crown and Two Chairmen and I get a vodka and tonic for her and a large white wine for myself. Even though we share a work space it's the first time we've really had a chance to sit and chat about personal stuff because it's been so crazy since she arrived.

Kay lives alone in a small house in Shepherd's Bush. Her husband left when her youngest son – now eighteen – was only three and the elder one seven. It seems amazing to me that she's brought the boys up on her own for all that time. Their father has only been in their lives sporadically. I wonder if she's lonely, but it seems rude to ask. She's very open about the fact that she's returned to work because she was feeling un-needed at home, though. She didn't know what to do with her time with no sports kits to wash and only the one bed to make. She has a tendency to talk about her sons rather a lot but, rather than being annoying, it's endearing. She's obviously so proud of them and the job she's done bringing them up. I get the feeling she doesn't hear from them very often, which is heartbreaking, but, I guess, that's what happens when your kids go off to college. One minute you're involved in every last detail of their lives, feeding them, picking up after them, arguing about who gets to watch what on TV and the next – nothing. You're lucky if you get a five-minute phone call once a week.

I really like Kay. There's something just very down to earth about her. I'm tempted to offload all my problems, but I worry that she'll think I'm a drama queen or else some kind of emotional trauma magnet. I don't know her well enough yet anyway, but I'm feeling like, I'm hoping, that one day we might be friends. And I've started to appreciate that I need more friends.

We resist the urge to have a second drink.

'I have important deals to do tomorrow,' I say, and she laughs.

As I make my way home I realize that a tiny part of me is hoping that Lorna doesn't come in again in the morning.

Dan has dinner and wine ready when I walk through the door. He gets me in a bear hug. 'Tell me all about your day,' he says, kissing the top of my head and, for once, I do have some pretty interesting stuff to tell him.

Isabel is panicking about what to take to Munich.

'What if we go somewhere posh both nights? I need to take two entirely different smart outfits,' she says when she phones me for the third time.

'Do you think he's going to care what you're wearing? I don't think that's why he's invited you to go with him.'

'What about a jacket? Do I need a jacket as well as a coat?'

She witters away like this on and off all evening. I have no doubt that the clothing anxiety masks a much more fundamental nervousness about the whole trip. This is a big step for Isabel and Luke. A test of how they get on cut off from their normal lives. Of course, Luke will be out all day so it's not quite the full 24/7 experience, but they'll get a pretty good idea whether or not they can stomach each other's habits and peccadillos. The thought of having to go through all that again sends a shiver down my spine and I reach out and rub Dan's arm and make apologetic faces about the fact that I am on the phone again.

I like the sound of Luke, though. He's arranged a car with a driver to take Isabel to the airport so she doesn't have to worry about fighting her way there on the tube. He's bought her two guide books, and he's marked up pages where he found interesting places she might want to visit while he's working.

'Just suggestions,' he said, apparently, when she commented on it. 'I don't want you to think I'm trying to tell you what to do.' Plus, he tells her, he's booked a hotel with a spa in case she'd rather just relax. He's very concerned, she tells me, in case she finds it dull having to amuse herself all day.

'He sounds really nice,' I say to her. 'One of the good ones. You should hang on to him.'

'I know,' she says. 'I'm starting to really like him.'

Alex, she tells me, seemed a little taken aback when she told him her plans. 'I actually think he was upset. Genuinely.'

I scoff. 'I should hope he is upset after the way he's behaved.'

'Maybe,' Isabel says reluctantly, 'but I don't want him to be unhappy, though. I mean, it can't be good for the girls for one thing.'

'He's manipulating you. You know what he's like. Luke sounds like a much nicer guy. Don't let worrying about Alex stop you from having a good time with him.'

'I won't,' she says.

I tell her to have fun, to let her guard down, to just go with it and see what happens. All advice I would never heed myself. She promises to ring me once Luke has gone off to his first meeting and I tell her to remember she deserves this.

I nearly have a seizure when the alarm goes off at six thirty and then I remember that I decided to go in extra early today, to catch up with all the things I'm meant to have done for Joshua and Melanie in the past week. There's no point jeopardizing my own job just to save Lorna's.

'Sorry, sorry,' I say to Dan while I flap around trying to turn it off. I'm in the office by five past eight. It's amazing how much you can get done when you have no distractions and by the time Melanie breezes in at twenty-five past nine I've caught up with all the essential stuff, plus I've read through a casting breakdown which was emailed in and I've made a note to suggest Kathryn for one of the roles.

Melanie takes her coat off and then comes and sits down in Kay's chair, which makes me nervous.

'Are you all right?' I say, trying to act like everything's normal.

'Rebecca, what is really going on with Lorna?' she asks. I have been dreading this conversation because of my inability to lie convincingly. I nearly spill it all out, it would be a relief actually, but I don't know where that would leave Lorna, so I decide to offer up the half truth I have been rehearsing for this very occasion.

'She's not really got a virus,' I say, and I try to look Melanie in the eye during this part, the true part. 'I told you she split up with Alex?' Melanie nods. 'Well, she's just taking it pretty hard, that's all.'

'I thought she dumped him?'

'She did, but I think she thought he'd come running back. And he hasn't. In fact, he's being really mean to her. She just couldn't face being around people because she keeps bursting out crying . . .'

'Oh God, poor Lorna,' says Melanie, who is basically a kind person. 'Why didn't she just tell me? I'd have understood.'

'Um . . . I think she was worried about looking un-professional – you know what she's like. And she didn't really think Joshua would understand . . .'

'But she's OK? When you've spoken to her how has she seemed?'

OK, so here comes the lying part. 'She's getting there. She hates being off, but she thought that if all her clients thought she was sick then it would give her a bit of time to get herself back together. She's across everything . . . It's just like she's working from home really. She's just doing everything through me instead of directly.'

Melanie nods. 'I thought it might be something like this. Should I call her?'

'No!' I say, far too loudly, before I can stop myself. 'I promised her I'd keep it to myself. If she thinks you or Joshua know, she'll feel she has to come back and I think she needs a few more days. Sorry, Melanie, for . . . you know . . . having had to tell you a white lie.'

'Don't worry. Just so long as she's OK and everything's under control. How's Kay fitting in?'

'Great,' I say with genuine enthusiasm, relieved the subject has changed. 'She's being a great help.'

Mary has got an audition. Someone called from *Redding-ton Road* to book in a time for her and I think they were a little taken aback by how excited I was. It's only an audition, after all. I was probably the fiftieth person

256

they'd called already about the same role. I don't care that the chances of her getting the job are probably a hundred to one, she has an audition. I told her I'd get her one and I did. Mary is as delighted as I am – which is a relief because I suddenly realized I should have actually checked she would want to go up for a soap before I agreed that she would see them on Monday morning. Her time is eleven ten which makes me think they are seeing people every ten minutes, six people an hour. Mary has never been to a TV casting before so she asks me what to expect and, thankfully, I know because we have clients who go on them all the time.

'They'll probably put you on tape. They'll give you a couple of scenes when you get there so make sure you arrive at least twenty minutes early to look over them. Someone will read with you and then they'll chat to you a bit. Honestly, it'll all be over before you know it.'

'Thanks, Rebecca,' Mary says, excited. 'And thank Lorna for me, won't you?'

'Of course.'

I'm on the phone to Isabel. It's hard to concentrate with Kay talking loudly in the background. ('Lorna, pick up, pick up, pick up. I'm staying on here till you do.') Izz is babbling, excited about her and Luke's first whole night together.

'We went to this amazing restaurant which must be about five hundred years old. The building, that is. And we had a bottle of champagne and oysters and all that clichéd romantic stuff, but it *was* romantic. And he'd bought me a book – *The Count of Monte Cristo* – because we were talking about it the other night and it's his favourite but I've never read it. And then we went back to the hotel and it was just . . . anyway. I thought I'd never be able to sleep because I'd be uncomfortable being with someone new, but actually I felt so relaxed with him. Not that we slept that much . . .'

'OK,' I interrupt, 'that's enough of that. No details. I'm squeamish, remember.'

'Well, I'll just say it was fantastic, then. And then this morning we had breakfast together in the room before he had to go off to his meeting. And he'd asked for them to put flowers on the tray . . .'

'How lovely.'

'I've decided I really do like him. He's kind and thoughtful and responsible. All the things that Alex isn't.'

'He sounds like a grown-up,' I say. 'And Alex is still a child.'

'Exactly.'

'So, what are you going to do today?' She tells me about a few places she's hoping to visit. It's freezing, apparently, but the Christmas markets are in full swing so she's going to brave the snow and wander around those to find some little gifts for the girls. I realize that I haven't heard her sound this unreservedly happy for years.

'Have a great time,' I say. Out of the corner of my eye I can see Kay flapping her arms at me, panicky. 'I've got to go.'

Isabel promises to call me once they get home tomorrow to give me the full low-down.

'What?' I say to Kay once I've hung up.

'She's not answering,' she says. 'Not even when I threatened to call the police and the fire brigade and to send Joshua round.'

'Oh, for God's sake,' I say. 'This is ridiculous. What do we do now?'

'You know her better than me, but . . . I'm sure she's fine. She probably just got sick of me phoning all the time.'

'I don't even know her address,' I say. God, is that really the case? I've been working with Lorna for six years and all I know is that she lives in Maida Vale somewhere. I don't even know the road, which given Lorna's propensity for talking about herself all the time is pretty astounding.

'It'll be in a file somewhere,' Kay says. 'Or Melanie might have it. Tell her you're sending flowers. What are you going to do, go round there?'

'I don't know. What do you think?'

'Leave it a couple of hours and I'll try her again. She's probably nipped out to the shops. After all, she's not really sick, is she?'

I'm grateful for Kay's calm presence. Rationally, I'm sure Lorna is fine. She's probably listening to her answerphone messages and laughing at how she's got us both running around. But a small part of me, the part that always gets out of control imagining tragedies and disasters, keeps offering up all kinds of less comforting explanations.

'I wonder if she's got any family,' Kay says, and I realize I don't really know that either.

'She might have a sister somewhere,' is all I can offer up although I can't remember why I think that might be the case.

I decide I need to do something as a distraction so I call Phil Masterson and, when I say why I am calling, I get put straight through to him.

'So,' he says before I really have a chance to explain, 'you must be psychic. One of our guests has just pulled out for tonight's show and we were in the middle of making a list of who else might be available. I'd forgotten about Jasmine. She'd be perfect. Is she free? We'd have to get her picked up around four fifteen.'

I look at my watch. It's half past two now. 'Gosh, I don't know. Let me check. What's the topic?'

'The use of mitochondrial DNA as evidence. Do you think Jasmine has strong opinions on the use of mitochondrial DNA as evidence?'

'Jasmine has strong opinions on everything. Let me check that she's available and I'll call you straight back.'

'Fantastic,' Jasmine says when I call her to let her know they want to book her. I tell her what the topic is and she says, 'What the fuck is that?' That's the trouble with Jasmine, she likes you to think she's an intellectual but really she hasn't got a clue. It seems immaterial to her, though; so long as she's on TV, even if she's making a fool of herself, she's happy.

'Isn't it from your mother only? Something like that?'

I know this because I spend a lot of time watching trashy real-life crime documentaries on cable. I also know that you can find minute traces of blood on carpets and soft furnishings using something called Luminol, even when they've been cleaned over and over again. You never know, it might come in handy one day. 'Look, if you still want to do it I can do an internet search and email you whatever I find.'

'Great,' she says, 'will you?'

'Check your email in half an hour.'

'Oh, and, Rebecca,' she says as I'm about to hang up, 'what are they paying?'

'I don't know yet. What do you usually get?'

'They'll try and palm you off with three hundred and twenty-five, but don't let them. I should be getting four hundred. I'm a name and who else are they going to get at this short notice?'

'OK,' I say a little nervously, although I'm careful not to show her that. Why is nothing ever straightforward? Why does no one ever make an offer that is acceptable in every detail? 'I'll try.'

I leave the obligatory message on Lorna's answerphone. She has still never called me back about Samuel's *Nottingham General* deal, so I don't hold out much hope. Before I call Phil back I check Jasmine's file and discover that the last time she did the show – a year ago – she only received £300.

'All you can do is try,' Kay says. 'If they say no, then she can take it or leave it. It'll be up to her.'

She's right but my mouth still feels dry when I get Phil

back on the phone. Suddenly it seems really important that I can do this. I want to be able to go back and tell Jasmine that I, Rebecca Morrison, have personally got her a £400 fee for a job for which she should really have been paid about £75 less.

Phil is delighted that he has someone – anyone, I imagine – to fill the hole in his line-up.

'So,' he says, 'the standard fee is three twenty-five now. I'll arrange the –'

I interrupt. 'The thing is, Phil, Jasmine is going to have to cancel another engagement to free herself up for this. We need to get her four hundred, really.'

Phil sounds taken aback. 'No one gets four hundred.'

'Well, that's what she feels she needs to make it worth-while.' I have no idea how stroppy to get, how far I'm meant to push this.

Phil sighs. 'Our top rate is three seventy-five. And I mean that's our *top* rate. That's what we'd pay Jonathan Miller or Stephen Hawking . . .'

'Well, I could try her with that,' I say. 'She might be OK as it's your ceiling.'

I'm sure Phil must want to tell Jasmine to go to hell but he's a desperate man with a live show going out at six and no guest.

'Call me back as soon as you can,' he says, not quite so matey now.

'God, that's great,' Jasmine says when I tentatively break the news. 'That's their top rate.' I stop myself from saying, 'Why did you tell me to ask for more than that, then?'

'Don't forget to find that stuff for me will you,' she says. 'I want to look like I know what I'm talking about.'

That would be a first. I finalize things with Phil, and then Kay and I spend twenty minutes researching mitochondrial DNA on the internet. I email Jasmine the salient points and then I realize that half an hour has gone past and I haven't even had a moment to worry about Lorna. Kay goes through the whole routine on Lorna's answerphone again, pleading, cajoling, begging Lorna to come to the phone to no avail.

By four o'clock I have decided to leave early and go round to Lorna's flat to try to find out what's going on, if we can find her address, that is. No business ever happens on a Friday afternoon, most people seem to go off early to their homes in the country or wherever it is they go. I have my mobile; I'm not going to miss anything. I decide that I need to get Melanie on side, though.

'I was hoping I might pop round to Lorna's,' I say. 'Take her a few things so she doesn't feel too out of the loop.'

'Good idea,' Melanie says.

'Only I forgot that I didn't have her address and rather than call her back and disturb her again I thought maybe you had it.'

She does and she writes it down for me and says of course it's fine for me to go now – it's work after all. And, in fact, I should take a taxi on expenses because I must have stuff to carry. I thank her and once again I feel shitty that I am keeping so much from her. I take up her offer of the taxi, though. Having to go and see Lorna is bad enough – I'm not having it encroaching on my Friday evening.

23

Lorna's flat is in one of those redbrick Victorian mansion blocks that line the streets near Maida Vale tube station. There's an intercom at the front door, but I'm pretty confident that if I ring the bell and announce myself when she answers then she simply won't buzz me in. There's a part of me – quite a big part of me, actually – which is thinking that if she does answer then I could just run away without saying anything. I would have achieved what I came for, which is to find out if she is still in one piece and she would be none the wiser. Tempting as it is, I know that's the coward's way out, though.

I wait for someone else to come along and then make apologetic noises about having lost my keys. They let me follow them in without any questions and I walk on up to the first floor and flat number 132. I can hear the TV on inside. I knock loudly and then stand to one side so that she can't see me if she looks through the spy hole. I haven't even worked out what I'm going to say to her if she does answer – oh good, you're alive, well, bye, then – maybe.

It has obviously never occurred to Lorna that I might know where she lives let alone turn up on her doorstep because she answers almost immediately. She's probably hoping it's Alex, here to declare that he's changed his mind and that he's loved her all along. She looks a fright. She's still in her dressing gown for a start, never a good sign at a quarter to five in the afternoon. She looks gaunt and her hair is uncombed and sticking out in odd directions as if she's just got out of bed. There's a musty smell coming from inside her flat like no one has opened any windows or taken the rubbish out in days. She doesn't even bother to hide her disappointment, not to mention her disgust, when she sees me standing there.

'What do you want?' she says in a flat voice, and I say, 'I just wanted to check you were all right. You didn't return Kay's calls.'

'Well, now you know. What? Did you think poor pathetic Lorna's probably topped herself because she has no life? Sorry to disappoint you.'

'I've told everyone you have a virus,' I say. 'Everything's under control. All your clients are fine – in fact Jasmine's on *London at Six* tonight – but you might want to think about coming back to work after the weekend, because otherwise it's going to get hard to explain where you are, OK?' I think about telling her what is going on with Heather and Mary but it would require too much explanation and she doesn't look like she would start showering me with gratitude.

I'm backing off. It's obvious she doesn't want me here and I don't want to be here so the best thing I can do is leave.

'Let me or Kay know if there's anything that needs doing.' I turn to go.

266

I can only imagine how much it irks her, but as I'm walking away, she says, 'Rebecca.'

I stop and turn round.

'How's Alex? Have you seen him?'

'No,' I say. 'I haven't. Look, Lorna, you need to forget about Alex. He's not going to have a sudden change of heart and he's not worth all this. Like I said . . .'

She bangs the door shut in my face. Good, I think. That went well. I flag down a taxi outside and, once we're on our way, I call Kay.

'She's fine,' I say. 'If you call being anorexic, mean and crazy fine.'

Kay laughs. 'She's her usual self, then?'

'Basically.'

'Do you think she's going to come back any time soon?'

'I have no idea,' I say, and I don't.

Dan and I are spending our fabulous Friday evening having dinner with Rose and Simon. I have finally persuaded him that we need to interact with other people at some point if we want to stand any chance of having a conversation with anyone other than Isabel and the kids in the next fifty years. To be honest, I'm dreading it myself. They've seemed like nice enough people the few times we've met them. They're the best possible new-best-friend candidates of all the people we know. It's just that we don't know them that well so the evening will probably be awkward. We'll tiptoe around each other trying to discover our common ground and maybe, just maybe, we'll find enough to make all four of us want to meet up again. It's important that we like both of them equally. We don't want to get into one of those relationships where we feel duty bound to see someone, but every time we do we're going, 'She's so lovely; it's a shame he's such an arse.' There also needs to be absolutely no hint of any attraction between any of the parties involved. If Rose gets flirty with Dan once she's had a few drinks, or if Simon tries to hold my gaze across the table for too long, then they're not the kind of people we want to invite into our lives. It's complicated, this couples-friendship thing. At least, it is for us at the moment because it feels like there's so much riding on it. For Rose and Simon it's probably just an excuse for a night out and some nice food. They have no idea they're being auditioned for Best New Friend Couple 2010.

It takes me ages to get ready. I want to look nice but not like I'm trying too hard. I change my outfit twice and, at one point, take off all of my make-up and start again. I try to remember what Rose and Simon do for a living. He's in recruitment, I think, something a bit dull but very well paid. Rose works for a charity, but I can't remember which one. Some obscure illness maybe. She'll probably think that what I do is absurdly trivial. They have a daughter in William's class, Lily, who seems like a nice girl. She came up from the same junior school as him, in fact; that's how we first met them. At the beginning of the summer all of the kids in William's year who were going on to Barnsbury Road spent a day familiarizing themselves with the big school and the parents were invited along for the first hour. Rose and I clicked immediately, I remember, both anxious about whether our children would cope. Lily isn't eccentric like William, but she's a quiet and nervous little thing and Rose was worried she'd be overwhelmed.

'How's Lily Freshney settled in at school?' I ask William when I go into his room to say goodbye, having given the babysitter strict instructions not to let him turn on any kitchen appliances unless she's going to be in the room with him.

'She got an A plus in the maths test,' he says, and that's it, that's as much intel as he can give me, despite the fact that he has spent the best part of the last five years sitting in the same classroom as her for six and a half hours a day.

'She's clever, then?' I ask, and he shrugs. For him, getting an A plus in maths just means you're normal.

I think they have two younger children too. Harry and Fabia, something like that. A boy and a girl, anyway.

I force myself to resist the urge to say to Dan, 'Let's call and tell them one of us is sick and we can get a takeaway and cuddle up on the sofa, just the two of us.' I have to remember why I am doing this. Dan has been moping around the house for weeks now. Although Simon can't be expected to replace Alex overnight I at least want to find him someone he can pop out for a quick beer with or phone up to talk about the football – something which I'm ill equipped, not to mention unwilling, to do.

'Come on, then,' Dan says as we're on our way out. 'Let's get it over with.' And then, thankfully, he laughs.

We're meeting in a new Moroccan place on Upper Street, all purple velvet and low-slung seats. There's loud jangly music – presumably meant to be North African – which always drives me crazy. The waiters and waitresses all look like they're dressed to work in some kind of Arabian Nights theme park.

'Jesus,' I say to Dan. 'Whose idea was it to come here?'

'Yours,' he says helpfully.

Rose and Simon are already there, squatting down on the foot-high banquette like two gnomes on toadstools.

'I would get up,' Rose says as we reach the table, 'but it would take me about half an hour and I don't think I'd ever be able to sit back down again; my knees wouldn't take it.'

Dan and I try to manoeuvre ourselves on to our seats, which involves first stepping down into a kind of trough. I nearly fall on to the table in the process, which, luckily, I find as funny as the other three.

'Sorry,' I say. 'We haven't actually been here before.'

'It's interesting,' Rose says, and she is so obviously trying to be nice, but without being able to think of a single positive thing to say, that it's very endearing.

'It's awful, isn't it?' I say. 'I can admit it.'

Just then the waitress comes over – a dead ringer for the genie in Aladdin – and says, 'Bonjour,' but with a pained expression like she knows the whole thing is ridiculous.

'Actually, why don't we just go to the pub? We can get something to eat there,' Simon says, and the rest of us seize on that like it's the greatest idea anyone's ever had.

I must try to remember always to book a shit restaurant whenever we are going out to eat with people we don't know well because it certainly did break the ice. We have a good time in the end. We stay till last orders and drink too much. We seem to laugh at all the same things. Rose and I find we have a shared interest in the theatre and she asks me loads of questions about my work and the clients and who I think the hot new writers are. We agree to go and see something at the Royal Court together, although we don't actually arrange a date.

The charity she works for is to do with inoculating children in Third World countries (I don't know where I got the obscure disease idea from, although some of the diseases they're immunizing them against seem pretty obscure to me so maybe that was it) so she travels a lot and that gives us stuff to talk about too.

I keep an eye on Dan and Simon and they seem to be chatting away quite happily and laughing at stuff. Overall it's a fun evening. Obviously not as easy or relaxed as spending time with Isabel and Alex before it all went awry – they were like family; you could not speak for hours and no one would get offended – but nice enough that we agree to do it again. In fact, I'm thinking of inviting them over for dinner with Isabel and Luke. That way it'll take the pressure off Luke being held up for the approval of Isabel's best mates.

'That was fun,' I say to Dan as we make our way home in a cab, a little bit worse for wear.

'It was,' he says. 'I like them.'

'Me too.'

Rebecca and Daniel, Rose and Simon. Maybe.

24

Isabel stops over on her way back from the airport. Alex will have dropped the girls off at ballet and she has an hour or so to kill before she needs to go and pick them up. If ever a woman could be described as glowing, then Isabel is it. Even Dan notices, which is saying something because Dan has basically no observational skills whatsoever. He could never be a witness. Even if a burglar walked over to him, took off his balaclava and introduced himself by name, Dan would still have trouble picking him out of a line-up the next day.

She gives me the edited highlights of the past twenty-four hours, which include a bit of shopping, a sixteenth-century castle and the entire plot of a Mills and Boon novel. Luke has proved to be romantic, not to mention insatiable on top of his other qualities. Actually I do ask her to, in fact, never mention that again. But, such is Isabel's state of euphoria that whatever I say I can't seem to get it into her head that I don't want to hear the details of her sex life. She's my friend. I don't want to be forced to imagine her . . . well, you know what.

I put to Isabel my dinner plans with Rose and Simon and she's delighted. She wants to show Luke off. She has told him all about me and Dan, of course, and, she hopes

I don't mind, about Dan and Alex's falling out. Luke suffered badly where friends were concerned in the separation from his wife, because most of their coupley circle was made up of people she knew before they were married. They had always tended to socialize with her friends, he told Izz, because his mates were scattered all over the country while his wife's had, by chance, all settled in London. Great, I think, he can join our little tentative new circle. I hope I like him. I daren't even think that I might not and, to be honest, seeing the effect he is having on Isabel I don't see how I couldn't.

'Sound him out for next week,' I say. 'We can do any night, that's how sad we are.'

Later in the day Isabel calls me, not sounding anywhere near so happy.

'It's Alex,' she says when I ask her what's happened. 'He was there when I went to pick the girls up and . . . this is going to sound crazy . . . but he asked if he could come back to the house with us and then, once the twins had gone off to their room, he started begging me to take him back.'

'You are kidding me.'

'He said he had realized finally that he'd made a huge mistake and he misses us so much . . .'

'Not to mention you just went away for a few days with another man. It's just a knee-jerk reaction. It's textbook.'

'I don't know. I don't know what to think. He's asked me to at least think about it. Not to say never, which, of course, I never would because he's still my kids' father so . . .'

274

Oh no.

'Think about what you really want. You told me you were never really happy with him, remember.' Not that she knows the half of it, of course, because we chose to protect her from the full horror of his declaration to me and, let's not forget, all the other women.

'Don't worry. I'm not about to take him back.'

She's saying the right words, but I'm not sure they sound that convincing. Well, that's something, I suppose. I couldn't stand back and watch Alex mess up Isabel's life again just because he couldn't bear to be on his own and he'd been rejected by the woman he supposedly really loves and his best friend. And I can't even think about the nightmare of having him back in our lives after everything that's gone on. Although, if she did go back to him, what would be the alternative? Lose Isabel and the girls too?

'Isabel, he's manipulating you. He's guilt tripping you about the girls and being on his own and God knows what.'

'I know. I know all that. Like I said, I have absolutely no intention of taking him back. I'm just concerned about him, that's all. I've agreed to let him spend more time with the girls because he misses them like crazy. And they miss him, obviously. You know,' she says, 'I thought you'd be all for me getting back with him, getting our cosy little group back together. I guess him hitting on you and then falling out with Dan has really changed the way you feel about him.'

'You could say that. Just don't let him inveigle his way

back into your life. Of course he should be able to spend more time with Nicola and Natalie because it'll be good for them. But don't let him use that as a way of trying to spend time with you too.'

'I won't. I'm just worried about him, that's all. Don't be too hard on him.'

'He's an adult. He'll cope. And look at how far you've come now . . .'

'Rebecca, listen to me. I said I have no intention of taking him back. Stop going on about it. I wish I hadn't mentioned it now.'

She's right. I'm lecturing. I just want to make sure she's really got her guard up. Alex is insidious. If he gets it into his head that he wants her back, then he'll work on her and work on her till she relents.

'Sorry. I was getting carried away. I'm just protective of you, you know that.'

'Besides everything else,' she says, 'I have Luke now.'

'You do. And he sounds like a prince in comparison to Alex.'

'He is. Which reminds me. How about Tuesday for our dinner? He says he can't wait to meet you, although I think really he's terrified.'

'It'll be fine. I'm just going to ask him what his intentions are . . .'

Isabel laughs. 'You have to be nice. Don't frighten him.'

'Me? As if I would . . .'

*

276

Luckily Rose and Simon are up for Tuesday too so I spend most of the weekend planning what I'm going to cook and making trips backwards and forwards to Waitrose because I keep changing my mind. I have warned them all that the food isn't exactly going to be cordon bleu – it has to be stuff that I can make in advance or prepare in the short time I'll have once I get home from work. I settle on monkfish tails marinated in lemon and rosemary. Dan is making the dessert – a baked cheesecake – and William has offered to bring something home from his Food Technology class, which is on Tuesday afternoon, for the starter, although I'm not so sure that's a good idea. Zoe is torn between her natural desire to look upon the whole evening with disdain and to spend it in her room, and a seemingly almost overwhelming urge to get a look at Auntie Isabel's new boyfriend. She settles on a strategy of coming out when they first arrive for a few minutes, just to see what he's like.

'Don't pull a face if you don't like the look of him,' I tell her, and she rolls her eyes at me.

I still have to get through Monday and Tuesday at work before the big event and I feel a little flicker of excitement on my way in on Monday when I remember Mary has her audition this morning. I give her a quick call to check she's ready and that she knows where she's got to go.

By ten o'clock there's no sign of Lorna so we figure she's still holed up at home. I tell Kay not to bother with the check-up phone calls. 'She's fine,' I say. 'She'll be back when she feels like it.'

Joshua and Melanie are understandably getting a little twitchy now about when she might return so I offer up a version of my visit to her flat on Friday for Joshua's benefit: she's desperate to come back but the doctor says she needs a few more days. She won't stop working though and just relax, so it's probably taking longer than it should.

And then, privately, a slightly different but still not entirely truthful version for Melanie: she's very depressed still. It's just going to take a while for the drugs to kick in and then she'll be fine. It was true what I told Joshua, though, that she won't stop working.

I'm a little concerned myself that she's not appeared. All the lying is driving me crazy and I know that if at any point Joshua asks me straight out exactly what is going on with Lorna I'll end up telling him. My mother always told me that if you tell a lie it escalates and she was right. It takes on a life of its own and you have to tell loads more untruths to shore it up. Plus I now have the added fear that if I can't keep this up it's going to become apparent to everyone that I have been being utterly deceitful over the past week or so. I have jeopardized the reputation of the company by covering up Lorna's absence and trying to do her work myself. Even though I am enjoying myself in a way I never have before, I need Lorna to come back soon before everything gets forced out in the open.

We get through the day fairly uneventfully. Heather calls me to say where the hell is Lorna? She didn't leave her last agency – one of the top agencies if I remember

– to be ignored. I pacify her as best I can and remind her about her upcoming lunch with Niall Johnson. I ask her if there's anything I can be doing for her in the meantime and she scoffs and says no, she doesn't think so. Her tone implies that she's way too important to need the help of anyone's assistant, she needs the A team around her, but she somehow stops herself from saying it. The more dealings I have with Heather the more I decide I don't really like her. She has this imperious attitude, this way of making you feel really small. She appeared out of nowhere on our TV screens a couple of years ago, having caught the eye of some TV executive in a bar somewhere and I wonder if she's worried she could go back there just as easily if she's too familiar with the little people. As if being unimportant might just rub off.

In all the excitement on Friday I forgot to watch Jasmine on *London at Six*, but luckily Kay had the presence of mind to Sky Plus it before she left, so we watch it together now. Jasmine has nothing at all to say about the subject really, but she delivers what she does manage to come up with such conviction that she gets away with contradicting herself left, right and centre. Actually, her enthusiasm is a welcome relief from the po-faced worthiness of the other guests and I can see why it works to have her on there. I phone her to tell her well done and I promise to keep on Phil's case about future shows.

'Maybe you could be a regular,' I say. 'They know you can talk about anything.'

'That's a brilliant idea,' Jasmine gushes. 'Suggest it.'

I promise to sound Phil out, not even bothering with the whole 'let me speak to Lorna about it' preamble. I'm perfectly capable of handling this one on my own.

In the end I don't get a chance to call Phil because there's too much else to do and the day passes in a flash. Before I know it I'm walking into the mess formerly known as my kitchen where Dan and William are using every utensil we have to make a baked lemon cheesecake. I leave them having fun and phone the local Chinese for a take out.

Tuesday is much the same. I'm in a rhythm now and I don't even think about whether or not Lorna will come in. I call any of the clients I think need a bit of attention, I read casting breakdowns and, spurred on by Mary's audition, I have made a list of all the big, long-running productions – the soaps, the police and hospital shows – and I have begun to call them all to find out if they have any new – and as yet uncast – characters coming up. I'm making friends with all the production secretaries and they're all very helpful, promising to call me back if there's anything.

I get a call to say that Mary didn't get the part on *Reddington Road*, but that they loved her and they'll definitely keep her in mind for any future roles. She's gutted on the one hand, but buoyed up by their positive comments. 'It was a great idea to make that DVD,' she says, and I don't even bother trying to pretend it was Lorna's idea. I'm allowed to take some credit.

I speak to Phil who sounds quite interested in the prospect of Jasmine as a regular – only once a week, though, he says quickly, not every day. He tells me he'll have a think about it and get back to me.

By five thirty I realize I've barely noticed the day go by again and I suddenly remember I was meant to be leaving early to cook for my little dinner party. Everyone's meant to be arriving at half seven so, by the time I get home, there's just long enough to get the monkfish into the marinade and chop the vegetables before I need to get in the bath. I want to make a good impression on Luke. Not in an 'I want him to fancy me' kind of way. God forbid. No, I just want him to think that Isabel's friends look like the kind of people he would want to socialize with. I squeeze lemon juice on the smoked salmon for the (very simple) starter that I have decided to go for rather than risk giving them all botulism from something William has concocted ('eggs au gratin' apparently). It suddenly occurs to me that I haven't checked if everyone eats fish. I'm sure Rose had cod and chips in the pub the other night, but I have no idea about Simon or, obviously, Luke. I decide it's too late to worry about that now.

I bully Zoe into helping William prepare the salad and then I take myself off to get ready. I'm actually really looking forward to tonight. I'm feeling optimistic about our chances of gelling as a group. Most of all I'm looking forward to meeting the man who is responsible for Isabel's new lease of life. I wish we could fast forward a few weeks to get these first few awkward evenings over

281

with, cut straight to the 'we're all so comfortable with each other there's absolutely no pressure for us to do anything other than just get together' stage, but, nevertheless, I'm excited about the evening to come.

Rose and Simon are first to arrive and we get them settled with a drink, then Dan chats away with them in the living room while I check on things in the kitchen. Zoe pops out of her bedroom and I shake my head to indicate that it's not Isabel and Luke and she goes back in, disappointed.

Isabel and Luke turn up five minutes later. She looks gorgeous, but my eye barely rests on her for a second before moving off to give Luke the once over.

'This is Luke,' Isabel is saying. 'And this is Rebecca, of course, and Dan.'

Luke shakes both our hands. He's definitely handsome – more handsome than Alex, which pleases me. He's tall, broad and has, I notice, very thick hair. But it's the fact that he looks so . . . nice . . . that strikes me the most. He has deep-set lines around his eyes, which tell me that he smiles a lot. He looks like a man who'd be kind to you, a man you could trust.

'Nice to meet you both,' he says, 'although slightly terrifying at the same time.'

'I've told him he's on trial,' Isabel says. 'So he's going to be on his best behaviour.'

'She's not even joking,' he says, and I decide I like him.

Dinner is fun. It's relaxed and the conversation never really runs out. It threatens to a couple of times, but we get it back before it can. Luke is attentive to Isabel all evening. Just outgoing enough, but not overbearing. He tries to explain what he does for a living, but I still don't understand. I'm not really sure he does either. It's finance, anyway, moving virtual money around from place to place. It all got a bit hairy when the recession first bit, he tells us, but he hung in there and it's getting back on an even keel again now. He travels all the time to talk to other financial people about incomprehensible financial things and generally, pre-Isabel, he says, looking at her adoringly, those trips were pretty miserable affairs. Meetings and dry dinner with other men in suits. Occasionally they wanted to take him out afterwards to show him the city and that, he says, was even worse.

'I've lost count of the number of different languages I've had to learn the phrase "no, I really don't want to go to a lap dancing club" in,' he says, which makes us all laugh and reveals something rather sweet about him at the same time.

Now, he tells us, he's hoping that whenever Izz can get the time off work, she'll be able to go with him. 'If she wants to, of course,' he adds hastily.

'Try and stop me,' Isabel says, and she leans over and gives him a quick kiss.

It's so strange seeing her so intimate with someone other than Alex that I almost gasp out loud. They have a really easy way with one another. Lots of little looks and touches. I glance over at Dan and he's looking at me. We raise our eyebrows at each other in a way that I know means we both like Luke and we're delighted to see Isabel so happy. It's amazing what you can convey with one eyebrow raise when you've known someone for twenty years. I try to remember the last time he spontaneously put his hand on my knee or reached for it as we walked down the street. I can't.

'Where do you live?' Rose is saying to Luke, and he explains about Teddington.

'Oh,' she says. 'I'm sure I've seen you around . . . you're really familiar.'

'Probably when he's picking Charlie up from school,' Isabel says.

I'm worried that Luke might not want to get cornered into a whole conversation about Charlie and his ADD and the school's decision to let him stay on, so I engineer a clumsy subject change by saying, 'Rose is always having to travel for her job too,' and making her tell Isabel and Luke all about her latest trip to Kenya.

'How's work?' Rose asks later, and I fill her in on the latest and tell Luke an abridged version of the whole story.

'My God,' he says. 'How are you going to carry that off?'

'Um . . .' I say. 'I'm sure she'll be back soon and then it's just a question of making her see that it was all for her own good . . .' I tail off. It doesn't sound like much of a foolproof plan.

'What if she doesn't come back?'

I laugh nervously. 'Oh, she will; she loves her job.'

'I hope so. That's one of the craziest stories I've ever

284

heard,' he says. 'Good on you for trying to protect her. I'm not sure I could be so generous.'

I'm starting to clear the main-course plates and dishes from the table when Zoe appears and starts to help. As neither Rose nor Isabel are the parent of a teenager yet this maybe doesn't strike them as so odd, but I know what she's up to. She scrutinizes Luke and Simon as if she's trying to work out which is which.

'Hi, Auntie Isabel,' she says, and gives Isabel a hug. Rose stands up and introduces herself and tells her that the (temporary) blue streak in her hair is really cool. Luke and Simon both sort of wave so I know I have to step in and do my bit.

'This is my oldest, Zoe,' I say. 'And this is Rose's husband, Simon.' Zoe just about manages a hello to Simon although she can't quite disguise her lack of interest in him.

'And this is Auntie Izz's friend Luke,' I say, and poor Luke gets the whole force of thirteen-year-old-girl curiosity aimed in his direction.

'Nice to meet you, Zoe,' he says in his most charming voice.

'Hi, Luke,' she says, smiling, but then she doesn't quite wait until he turns away before she gives Isabel a big two thumbs up. Luke, to give him credit, pretends not to have seen, and the rest of us manage to wait until Zoe has left for the kitchen with a pile of dishes and is out of earshot before we burst out laughing.

'I think you passed,' I say to him, and then I follow her out to the other room.

'He's well nice,' she says. 'At least compared to the other one,' she adds, meaning Simon who has rather receding hair and an unfortunate pinky blond complexion.

'Well, he's making Auntie Isabel happy, that's the main thing.'

'And he's nice looking,' she says, not even joking. 'He's making her happy and he's nice looking. There'd be no point in him making her happy if he was ugly, would there?'

I don't even try to argue the point.

Five minutes later, once Zoe has returned to her room, William comes in.

'Are you Auntie Isabel's new boyfriend?' he says before I can even try to introduce him. Luckily he says it to the right man – Zoe must have described him – and the right man says, 'Yes, I suppose I am. You must be William. Nice to meet you.' He shakes William's hand, which, I know, William will like.

'Bed time,' I say to him. He looks at me in disgust. 'I know.'

While I'm out in the kitchen slicing up the cheesecake, Isabel comes in, ostensibly to get the wine to fill everyone's glass, but I know that she really wants to get me on my own.

'Well?' she says, keeping an eye on the living-room door.

'Well what?' I carry on meticulously carving the dessert.

She laughs. 'You know what.'

I put the knife down, wipe my hands on a tea towel, take my time.

'Rebecca . . .'

'I really like him,' I say, smiling at her. 'Dan does too, I can tell.'

'Really?'

'Really.'

'And he's having a good time, I know he is.'

'Maybe we could get together at the weekend? The four of us?'

'Maybe,' she says. 'I'll ask him, but weekends are difficult. He has Charlie.'

'He can get a sitter, can't he?'

'I don't think he likes to. It's the only time he really sees him, you know. And he doesn't want his wife to think he's not taking care of him properly . . .'

'Does she know about you yet, the wife?'

'No,' Isabel says. 'Luke wants to wait until the divorce is finalized.'

'Makes sense,' I say, and I hand her a couple of dishes to take in.

'Bex . . .' she says as I'm about to go through to the living room. 'I heard from Alex again.' I know she doesn't mean that he was calling to ask what time to pick up the girls.

'No, Isabel,' I say. 'Don't let him get to you. Look at how happy you are now. Plus I'd put money on the fact that he's only started doing this because you've found someone else.'

'I know,' she says. 'But I can't not talk to him because of the girls.'

'Then you have to draw up some ground rules. Tell him you're not going to answer his calls any more unless he promises to stop saying that stuff. That'll soon stop him.'

'I will,' she says, and I hope she means it.

'Don't let him mess up things between you and Luke.'

'Don't worry,' she says. 'No one's going to do that.'

I fall asleep thinking about what a fun evening we've had, how well it went. Everyone got on, no one was annoying or shy or wanting to be the centre of attention. Rose and Simon have invited us all round to theirs the week after next, and Luke left promising to try to come out at the weekend, although he doubted he'd be able to. He did offer up another evening next week, though, so it didn't seem like he was making excuses. All in all it was a really good night. Better than I could have hoped for.

25

On Wednesday, despite a mini hangover, I manage a couple more tiny coups for my little band of surrogate clients. Following my ring round I have managed to secure Kathryn her first audition in I don't know how many months. Daytime soap *Nurses* are looking for a new matron. They'd forgotten all about Kathryn, the casting assistant who calls me back tells me, till I reminded them. I take down the details, and call Kathryn at the florist's. She's ridiculously grateful and then I have to indulge her in her panic about what to wear and how to do her hair. Then *Marlborough Murder Mysteries* call to say that they've watched Mary's little DVD and would she like to come in and read for the part of Effie, sister of the handsome but cold and frighteningly clever Detective Marlborough. The role is to be a semi-regular one, popping up throughout the series. Kay and I dance a little jig of celebration around the office once I've delivered the news to Mary until Joshua sticks his head out of his office and shouts at us to shut the fuck up. Oh, and Samuel gets offered another couple of days on *Nottingham General*, this time playing a man who is suspected of assisting his terminally ill wife's unsuccessful suicide bid. I don't want to lose him the job, but I can't help asking whether that won't be strange him popping up again so soon?

'Oh no, we do it all the time,' the booker tells me. 'Our audience doesn't care. In fact, I think they like it.'

Samuel, I have come to realize, is always going to be OK. Solid and reliable. He's a good actor and people like working with him. He's never going to be a leading man, but he'll tick away nicely doing two days here and three days there for the rest of his life, as long as we remind everyone of his existence every now and again. And he's happy with that. Why shouldn't he be? He gets very well paid when he does work and he still has ample time to potter around on his allotment. He's never going to earn us a fortune, but looking after him takes almost no time or effort so everybody's happy.

Kay and I have a celebratory drink in the pub over the road at the end of the day and Kay toasts my 'new-found agenting skills'. I make my way home feeling ridiculously proud of myself, not to mention stretched and fulfilled and engaged and a host of other positive adjectives.

I wake up in a cold sweat. It's Thursday tomorrow. What if Luke's right and Lorna doesn't ever come back? Lorna's lunch with Heather and Niall Johnson is on Monday and she still knows nothing about it. I know that I have been blocking out the real implications of Lorna's absence. I allowed myself to think that I could coast along until she returned and then we could all go back to how we were. Recently I've been having too much of a good time at work to even be thinking about it at all. In fact, I don't know what I've been thinking really. I guess I haven't. And it's all about to come crashing down around my ears unless I can get Lorna back to work and doing an impression of a sane person by Monday.

I try to stop myself but I can't help waking Dan up.

'What?' he says. 'What?'

I tell him what's bothering me and all he says is, 'I thought you were enjoying doing her job.'

'I am,' I say. 'I was.'

'Then what's the problem?'

I decide he's being deliberately dense. Isn't it obvious what the problem is?

'They're expecting Lorna to be at that lunch.'

'Tell them she's still sick. It seems to have worked so far.'

'There's no way anyone's going to believe she's still just suffering from some little virus after more than two weeks. Besides, both Niall and Heather want her to be there.'

'You go in her place,' Dan says, and rolls over, pulling the duvet up round his shoulders.

'You're being stupid now,' I say, getting annoyed. 'Of course I can't go in her place. They'll cancel if I tell them she's not around and then where does that leave Heather with Mortimer and Sheedy? She's getting frustrated already.'

'Tell me what you want me to say, then we can go back to sleep,' Dan says.

'Oh, forget it. You don't understand,' I say grumpily, and then I feel bad. It's hardly Dan's fault I've got

291

myself in this mess. I rub the arm that is flopped over the duvet.

'Sorry. I shouldn't have woken you up.'

He turns over and cuddles into me. 'It's OK. You'll feel better about it in the morning,' he says.

I don't. I feel panicky, like I've suddenly discovered I'm on a roller coaster, teetering on top of a huge drop and I don't know how to get off. I can't wait to get into work to talk to Kay. She's the only person who can really understand the predicament I'm in. Consequently I'm at the office by quarter past nine and I have to sit and wait for her to arrive, counting down the minutes. The second she's through the door I start.

'Oh my God, we have to get Lorna to come back before Monday because it's Heather's lunch and Lorna has to be there because I told them she was going to be, in fact, if you remember, they thought I was her and . . .'

Kay interrupts. 'Slow down. Go back to the beginning. What's the matter?'

So, I start again only this time I try to leave the odd gap between words so that she can understand what I'm on about.

'Yes,' she says helpfully when I pause for breath. 'I was wondering how you were going to get out of this one.'

'I thought she'd be back by now,' I wail. 'How was I to know she'd just take to her bed and stay there?'

'OK,' Kay says calmly. 'Let's look at the options.' She

counts off on her fingers. 'One: Lorna comes back in the next couple of days and she's fine and she's happy to go to the lunch and grateful for the way you've saved her job and we all live happily ever after.'

'I don't think that's going to happen.'

'Neither do I. Two: Lorna doesn't come back, you tell Heather and Niall they'll have to go ahead with lunch without her there. Heather is pissed off that she's not being treated with the respect she deserves, she moves agencies again and word gets out that Lorna is suffering from some kind of long-term debilitating condition and may never return to work so all her other clients leave too.'

'Oh God,' I say.

'Three: we go round to Lorna's place on Monday, drag her out of the door and deliver her to the lunch where she sits like a drooling idiot but at least she's there.'

'That's just as bad,' I say.

Kay is still going. 'Four: we tell Joshua and Melanie exactly what's been going on and one of them takes over looking after Heather.'

'And I lose my job.'

'Really? Even though all you've been trying to do is help out?'

'Definitely. I've been lying to them, pretending to be Lorna, misleading the clients . . . Oh God, it doesn't bear thinking about.'

'Well then,' she says, 'I think we are only left with option five.'

'Run away?'

Kay laughs. 'No. We . . . when I say we, really I mean you . . . get Lorna up and back to work, convince her that everything was done for her own good and that she should never tell Joshua, Melanie or any of the clients about it and somehow turn her back into her old dynamic self in time for lunch on Monday.'

She looks at me triumphantly. 'And how do I do that?' I say.

'I have no idea.'

She's right, of course. The only thing that can save me now is to put the world back together without anyone even noticing that it had fallen apart in the first place, but I just don't know if that's possible.

Kay, practical as ever, says, 'The sooner you speak to her the more time she has to get herself back together before Monday.'

'What shall I do? Go round there again? I can't believe she'll open the door to me a second time.'

We decide that Kay will tell Joshua and Melanie that Lorna has asked me to go round to hers to go over a few work-related things. Apparently Joshua's response to this is to say, 'Oh good, I was going to call Lorna today to find out when she thought she might be well enough to come back,' to which Kay says, 'Well, Rebecca will be able to report back now,' in a way that she hopes will make him think he needn't bother.

Meanwhile I head over to Lorna's to do I don't know what. On my way to the tube I answer a call from Phil who says he has decided that having Jasmine as a regular, every Thursday night, is actually a great idea. Although

I know that I should wait until I see Lorna, given that I am on my way there right now, I tell him that Jasmine would require a fee considerably higher than her ad hoc rate as she will be keeping every Thursday night free for him from now on. To my surprise he says fine, it makes sense that a regular guest be paid more than people who just pop in. I hang up, wondering if I should have asked for even more but when I tell Jasmine she's delighted.

'Thank you. And say thanks to Lorna too,' she says.

'Of course,' I say. 'I'm seeing her in a few minutes.'

I do the 'hanging around the front door' trick again but nobody goes in or out so, in the end, I ring a few random doorbells and, when someone eventually answers, I say, 'I'm reading the meters,' and they don't even ask me which meters I mean – they just buzz me in.

I knock on Lorna's door and wait. I can hear her moving around inside so I know she's in, but there's no sign of her opening up and letting me in.

'Lorna,' I say loudly. 'It's Rebecca. I know you don't want to see me, but this is about work. It's important and I'm not going to go away. I know you think you don't care, but if I don't report back that I've seen you then Joshua is going to start trying to get in touch himself . . .'

The next door along opens and a middle-aged woman peers out at me, clearly wondering what's going on. I smile at her and try to look unthreatening and friendly and she glares at me and goes back inside without saying anything. I know that Lorna cares an awful lot about her image, her persona as a successful put-together business woman, so I think what the hell? I raise my voice even more.

'. . . And you know that he has a thing for you. He pretends it's all about work but it's not, he's gagging for it. He basically just wants to get into your –'

I don't finish because Lorna's door, which I am now leaning on, opens and I half fall into her hallway.

'For God's sake, shut up, will you?' she says. 'What are my neighbours going to think?'

'I just met one of them,' I say, trying to stand up in a dignified way. 'She seemed very nice.'

Lorna watches me as I go through from the hall into her living room. It's a nice flat, a bit makeover show by numbers but more tasteful than I would have imagined, all cream and brown and cosy fake fur. I wouldn't want to spend two whole weeks shut in here, though.

'So what now?' she says. I sit on the sofa and she remains standing, as if that might make me go quicker.

'Lorna, I haven't come here for a fight. I've come here for one very specific reason.' I've decided to cut to the chase. The main priority is to get her to go to that lunch on Monday. All the rest can wait. 'Heather has a meeting with Niall Johnson on Monday and they think you're going to be there. I just want to make sure you are.'

I look over at her and, although she's trying to feign indifference, her interest is definitely piqued. She doesn't say anything, though.

'It's a lunch. At the Ivy. Niall's very excited about Heather maybe moving across to the BBC . . .'

Finally she can't contain herself. 'Who set this up? Joshua?'

Here goes. 'I did. I . . . I thought you'd only be away for a couple of days and Heather was getting really arsey about you not having done it and I couldn't get hold of you . . . We kept trying to ring you, remember?'

'So you thought you'd score some brownie points? I'm sure Joshua and Melanie are very impressed.'

'They don't know. Well, they know about the lunch, but they think you set it up . . .'

She doesn't acknowledge that. Instead she says, 'Well, you'll just have to rearrange it. I doubt I'll be well enough to come back on Monday.'

There's clearly absolutely nothing wrong with her. Physically at least.

'The thing is, it was the only date they could both do for weeks and . . . and I think Heather is feeling un-loved. I think she might leave again if this doesn't happen . . .'

'Then tell them to go ahead without me.'

'This is such a great opportunity, Lorna. Think about it. You get a foot in the door with Niall. How many agents do you think are gagging for the chance to sit down with the Controller of Entertainment Commissioning at the BBC? I don't think even Joshua's done more than meet him for five minutes at a cocktail party. And maybe Heather gets a big new contract. That'd be great for Mortimer and Sheedy; we need the income. Plus Niall said he really wants you there . . .'

She sighs. 'What time is it?'

I look at my watch. 'Twenty past ten.'

'Not now,' she says impatiently, 'the lunch.'

'Oh. One o'clock. Will you go, then?'

'Maybe. I'll see how I feel.'

That's something, I suppose, although if she wakes up on Monday morning and decides she can't face it, isn't that even worse than if we cancelled now? I know I can't really push her any more, though. There's one other thing I have to make her aware of.

'Um . . .' I say, and then I don't really know how to continue. Just get it over with, I decide. 'Niall . . . well, Niall thinks that he spoke to you on the phone . . .'

She looks at me stony faced. 'He what?'

'He . . . When I called I said I was you because I thought he wouldn't take the call otherwise . . .'

'You impersonated me?'

'No . . . sort of . . .yes. It was just one phone call.'

She sits down on the arm of a chair like this is too much for her to take in.

'And Joshua and Melanie were OK about that?'

I hear myself gulp. 'They don't know. They think you've been working all this time not just . . . sitting here. I thought that was better . . . for you, in the long run.'

'You've been doing stuff behind Joshua and Melanie's backs? Talking to the Entertainment Controller?'

I nod reluctantly. 'I had to. I felt bad for you. I felt like you'd been used by my friend – my ex-friend – and so, yes, I've been trying to help.'

She stands up again, a new fire in her eyes. 'Well, let's see if they really think you were helping or whether they think you were behaving completely unprofessionally. Trying to further yourself somehow while risking my reputation and theirs. I'm sure they're going to understand that you were doing it all for the greater good. They won't think it was all a big power trip or anything.'

The old Lorna is starting to reemerge before my eyes. The floppy little poor-me version has been cast aside and the mean girl is back. I am not going to let her bury me.

'How on earth do you think this was a power trip if I told him I was you? And I didn't pretend to anyone that I was representing the clients so I don't know how you think I thought I was furthering myself. I told them all I was working on your behalf. I even pretended to go away and consult you when really you were ignoring all my attempts to make contact because you were so wrapped up in yourself and your own problems.'

'All? You told them all? Who's *all*?'

OK, so now I have to own up to the rest of it, the stuff I was hoping to save until she came back to work where somehow I could maybe convince her that she had done it before she went off sick.

'Jasmine's going to be doing a regular spot on *London at Six*, Samuel's got a little job on *Nottingham General*, his second, actually, Kathryn's got an audition for *Nurses* and Mary had an audition for *Reddington Road* but she didn't get it, but now she's had another one for *Marlborough Murder Mysteries*, which would be even better. I couldn't reach you so I just dealt with it all, yes.'

299

She looks at me, incredulous. 'You've done deals for them? Jasmine and Samuel?'

'I had to. If I'd kept asking for advice, then Joshua and Melanie would have realized that I wasn't able to get hold of you. For God's sake, Lorna, I thought I was doing the right thing.'

She gets up. 'OK, you can leave now. You can tell Joshua and Melanie I'll be back this afternoon. I need to come in and sort this mess out.'

There's no point arguing with her. I came here to try and get her to come back to work and I've succeeded. I've given her the one thing she needed to propel her off her couch and into the office – ammunition against me.

'Lorna,' I say as I get up to move to the door. 'I know we don't get on, but please think about this before you say anything. You'll see that I was trying to help, that I didn't want you to lose your job.' I hear a noise and I realize it's the shower running. She wasn't even listening to what I had to say.

I head back to the office deflated. I even think about just going home and hiding, but that would make me as bad as Lorna so I decide I have to face the music, whatever that music might turn out to be. Kay is distraught on my behalf and can't stop apologizing for having suggested I go round to Lorna's.

'It would all have come out sometime,' I say. 'It might as well be now.'

I consider heading Lorna off at the pass and going in

and telling Melanie my side of the story before she gets here, but I wouldn't even know where to begin. Kay lets them both know the good news that Lorna is coming back, and I clear out my few bits and pieces from her office and just sit and wait to see what will happen.

'I'm sure Lorna must be really grateful about how you've kept everything together while she's been gone,' Melanie says as she's passing through reception and I nearly laugh it's so ridiculous. 'I'm glad because I know the two of you haven't always got on so well.'

At about half past one Lorna breezes in and is greeted like the prodigal daughter by both Joshua and Melanie. Lots of concern and 'we were so worried' and 'are you sure you're completely better?'.

'Can you bring me all my clients' files,' she says to Kay without even bothering to say hello. 'I need to see what's been happening in my absence.' She gives me a meaningful look as she says this and I'm angry with myself because I feel my face going red. I have to remember I've done nothing wrong. Well, technically of course, I have, but for the right reasons. There's an important difference. I have mitigating circumstances.

'Oh, Rebecca's kept it all bubbling along,' Joshua says jovially. 'I think she's quite enjoyed herself.'

'Oh, I'm sure she has,' Lorna says. 'But I'm back now.'

She spends most of the afternoon shut up in her office. Twice she calls Kay to come through, but it's only to make her a cup of tea. Her phone line is lit up for long periods, but Kay says that when she goes in there Lorna does actually seem to be talking to people this time. She doesn't know who. I feel sick waiting to see what she's going to do next. At one point Joshua goes into her room for a few minutes but when he comes out again he seems quite jolly so it doesn't look like she's said anything.

Mary rings for me and I tell Kay to tell her that Lorna's back and to give her the option of speaking to her instead, but she says, no, she'd like to talk to me, but it's good that Lorna's back. She fills me in on her audition at *Marlborough Murder Mysteries*, which sounds like it went really well. She sounds so excited and I'm so excited for her, but I feel I should be saying, 'This is nothing to do with me any more; Lorna's your real agent.'

When she's hung up I try to get on top of my work for Joshua and Melanie, my real work, but I'm finding it hard to concentrate. Finally at about four o'clock Lorna calls me and asks me to go into her office. I consider saying, no, go away, leave me alone, but I know I can't really. I walk in there trying to look as blasé as I can. What? What could be wrong?

Lorna is sitting at the table looking like a primary-school child propped up on cushions behind the teacher's desk. I hover in the doorway hoping that she's just got some annoying but simple request that she should really be asking Kay to do. She leaves me standing there, sweating, for a while and then says:

'Come in and sit down please.'

I do as I'm told and I wait for her to speak.

'So, I just want to get this straight,' she says. 'Jasmine

302

is going to be on *London at Six* every Thursday and this –' she holds up a copy of the agreed terms; there hasn't been time for them to get the contract to us yet, it's been such a rush – 'is the deal?'

I nod miserably. This feels like a trap.

'Samuel is on *Nottingham General*?'

'Yes.'

She holds up another sheet of paper. 'And the terms are all settled?'

I nod again, too scared to actually say anything.

'Mary has been for an audition for *Marlborough* and Kathryn has one tomorrow for *Nurses*? And Joy Wright Phillips tells me she is writing again because you told her to do two hours every morning before she did anything else and it's working.'

'Is it? That's great,' I say before I can stop myself. Lorna ignores me.

'And Heather, of course, we know, has a meeting with Niall Johnson on Monday.'

More nodding. I'm waiting for the punchline.

'How about Craig? No commissions from Miramax or promise of his own season at the Bush?'

'He's still writing his first draft,' I say, refusing to rise to the bait. 'He seems fine, getting on with it.'

'And this is you just covering for me while I was off sick? Keeping things ticking over?'

'Exactly.'

'Not you trying to make yourself look good? Trying to carve out a little niche for Rebecca Morrison while I was away?'

303

Ah, so this is where we're going.

'I told you, obviously not, since I let everyone think I was reporting back to you about everything and acting on your instructions.'

'And, what? When Joshua or Melanie notice that my clients seem to be doing well you can hold your hand up and say, "Actually, that's nothing to do with Lorna, that's all down to me"?'

'Why would I do that? Like I said, I'd rather they didn't know anything about it; it's better for both of us.'

'Yeah, right. So it was altruism made you work so hard for no credit?'

'No, Lorna, it was some kind of misguided guilt. I see now that I should have just let you drown. In fact, no, I should have put my foot on your head and made sure you sank.'

She smirks at me. 'Make me a cup of tea, would you?'

'I don't work for you, ask Kay.'

'I'd hate for Joshua and Melanie to think that you had got so above yourself you wouldn't even make me a cup of tea.'

'You know what? You tell them whatever you want to tell them. I'm past caring.'

I turn to leave the room. 'Oh, and, Lorna, go fuck yourself.'

Well, it's hardly Oscar Wilde, but it made me feel better.

26

In a way it's true that I'm past caring what Lorna does to me. So maybe I lose my job, but that wouldn't be the end of the world. Apart from the fact that we need the money, of course. But I could temp. I can type, I'm fairly personable. Actually, the idea of temping has always filled me with horror, the new faces and strange places every week, but I'd cope. Maybe I'd even grow to like the fact that I didn't have to spend so much time with anyone that they drove me crazy. And the truth is, I realize, that it's going to be hard to go back to my job being the way it was. I don't think I can be happy just passing on messages and filing now I know how much I enjoyed doing more than that. Now I know that I was good at it.

I know I shouldn't, but I call Kathryn to go over the details for tomorrow because I can't imagine she's on Lorna's list of priorities. Until I know that Lorna is actually back and firing on all cylinders I fully intend to keep an eye on all her clients.

'You did as much as you could,' Dan says when I tell him everything that's happened later. 'You tried to help her because you're nice, and because you felt bad about getting in the way of her and Alex, and she's basically thrown it back in your face. It's her problem, not yours.'

'It's mine if she tells them.'

'Why would she do that? You made her look good, doing deals from her sick bed and caring enough about her clients to be ringing round getting them auditions while she should have been recovering. She looks like Employee of the Year.'

He's right, I know he is. But it doesn't make me feel any better.

I call Isabel to take my mind off things and indulge in a bit of vicarious romance. She's getting a little twitchy about the fact that their relationship doesn't seem to have moved on since their trip, though. They haven't spent a night together since they came back and she's worried that if they go on like this they'll start to lose the closeness that was developing between them while they were away.

'We had our first fight. Well, not really a fight, just a few words, you know.'

'He might just be a bit scared of commitment after his marriage breaking down,' I say. 'God, if that's the only thing that's wrong with him, that he likes his own bed, then I really don't think you've got anything to worry about.'

'He loved you, by the way. Both of you.'

'What's not to love?' I say to make her laugh.

Then she tells me that when they got back from their date last night – to hers before Luke had to go back to Teddington – Alex had been hanging around outside.

He tried to make it look like he was just out walking the dog – he took the dog with him when he left, claiming that he was the one who had the time to walk him; still, at least he left the kids – but it was obvious he wasn't.

'What did you do?' I say, incredulous.

'I introduced him to Luke. What else could I do?'

'No wonder Luke went home. He probably thought Alex would pop up at the breakfast table if he stayed.'

'I think Alex just wanted to get a look at him. Which is flattering, I suppose.'

'Psychotic more like.'

'A lot of what went wrong with our marriage was my fault. I regret that, you know. I think I thought if he really loved me he'd have gone out to work, made more of an effort to support us, but maybe I was wrong . . .'

This doesn't sound good. I need to get her off Alex and back on to the wonders of Luke before she does anything she regrets. 'Isabel, don't end up going back to him because you feel sorry for him. Give this thing with Luke a chance.'

'I know. I will. It's just hard, that's all. All the girls ever say to me is when is Dad moving back in?'

'Of course they do, but that's no reason to go back to an unhappy marriage. Where were they, by the way, while all this was going on?'

'Oh. At a sleepover. Unlike me.'

'You'll sort this overnighting thing with Luke and then it'll all be perfect. Trust me – you need to stick to your guns.'

*

'Oh God,' I say to Dan when I get off the phone. 'I think Izz is thinking of going back to Alex. Should we tell her the truth?'

'No,' he says. 'It's nothing to do with us. Let's keep out of it.' And then he thinks for a moment and says, 'What about Luke?'

'I know. That's what I said.'

'I like him. He seems good for her.'

'I said that too, well, more or less. And you know what really bothers me about all this? Alex doesn't really want her back. Not properly. He's just feeling alone and rejected and he thinks that would make him feel better.'

'It's still not up to us to tell her that,' Dan says, and I say I suppose he's right.

I stagger through to the weekend, avoiding Lorna as much as I can, waiting for the axe to fall. She seems to be coping pretty well; at least, she's giving the impression of it, which is good enough for now. At one point I hear her telling Joshua that Mary has got the job on *Marlborough Murder Mysteries* and isn't that brilliant? He congratulates her on finding Mary her first paying job, and such a good one.

'That's dedication,' he says, walking through reception on his way to the kitchen. 'You're even getting your clients work when you're off sick.'

'Oh well . . . you know me. I hate just lying around doing nothing,' she says.

I look at her to see if she'll even look at me and, to

give her credit, she does, just for a moment, and she looks a little guilty. I have no doubt that it's more because she's been caught out in front of me than because she feels bad. I'm not sure guilt is in her repertoire.

'How did you even get them to see her with nothing to show them?' Joshua says, and I wait to see how she'll respond to that one. I haven't told her about filming Mary because she never really gave me a chance.

'Um . . .' she says, looking uncomfortable. 'Well . . .'

I don't know what's happening to me but I can't just let her flounder there. Maybe I'm just hoping to shame her with my kindness.

'Lorna had me and Kay put her on DVD, didn't you, Lorna? We just got her to read something, that's all.'

She can't keep the surprise off her face as she looks at me. But there's also nervousness there. Is this a trap? Of course she would think like this because I can't imagine her ever doing anything kind for anyone unless there was a catch. I raise my eyebrows to try to convey that it's the truth.

'Mmm,' she says, and this time she genuinely does look embarrassed at taking the credit right in front of me.

'Well, you should be very pleased with yourself,' Joshua says, and Lorna says nothing.

Later I ring Mary who is hysterical with excitement and gratitude. 'I know you had a big hand in this,' she says, which goes a long way to making me feel better. Even despite Lorna having to assume the glory I am so pleased for Mary, so genuinely happy for her, that I get a real buzz from her reaction. It carries me through the afternoon. I feel like I've eaten Ready Brek. It's just as well because without that feeling the rest of the day, comprised of typing in the blanks in a contract, arranging a couple of meetings and doing some filing, would be insufferably tedious. I'm finding it hard to believe that until a few weeks ago this was how I spent my days. And I was happy. At least, I thought I was.

We're seeing Rose and Simon again on Saturday night, but first Isabel and I are meeting to go to Westfield for some Christmas shopping. After we've trailed around unproductively for an hour or so we decide that sitting at the champagne bar is much more fun, even though it's not even midday and neither of us can afford to drink champagne.

'I had a long talk with Alex this morning,' she tells me. 'He came to pick the girls up for ballet. I told him I was serious about Luke. And I meant it. I am. You were so right, he's good for me in so many ways and I'm happy when I'm with him. Really happy. In a way that I can't ever remember being with Alex.'

Thank the lord. 'How did he take it?'

'Well, he said he was upset but, do you know, I'm not sure he was really. It almost felt like he's going through the motions, like he doesn't know what else to do with his life so he thought he might as well see if he could get back with me.'

That's exactly right. 'It wouldn't surprise me. I don't think he's stable enough at the moment to know what he really wants.'

310

'And it's funny. It's Alex being around that's really made me realize that I want Luke. That and your tireless campaigning.'

'I like to provide a service.'

'I'm going to introduce him to the girls. And then, if they get on – which I know they will – I think I might ask him to spend Christmas with us. Him and Charlie. Unless Charlie is with his mum, of course.'

I couldn't be happier. For Isabel and, if I'm being honest, for myself. I lean over the table and give her a hug, nearly knocking everything on to the floor.

'You're going to be happy this time. I know you are.'

Rebecca and Daniel, Luke and Isabel. It works perfectly.

I can't believe what I'm hearing. She's got it wrong, she must have. Or else there's an innocent explanation. I can't think what that could be, but I'm sure there is one.

Rose has just put her drink down and said, 'Oh, I know what I meant to tell you. I remembered where I'd seen Luke before.'

'Oh, right,' I say, expecting her to say that she'd met him through work or Simon had played football with him once or something.

'My sister lives in Highgate and he lives on her street. I've seen him with his wife . . .'

'They're separated,' I say quickly.

'Well, I thought I remembered him saying he was separated, and, of course, he was all over Isabel, but, the thing is, Rebecca, I've seen them together recently. Like last week.'

'They have a kid. He was probably visiting him.' So he told Isabel they couldn't stand to be near each other. He was probably just exaggerating a bit. Big deal.

Rose looks at me like she's about to tell me someone's died. 'They were holding hands.'

I look at Dan like he might be able to help me understand what she's telling us. He looks as clueless as I feel.

'Maybe it's his . . . I don't know, his sister or something.'

'Why would he walk down the street holding hands with his sister?' Simon says, and he's got a point although I don't acknowledge it.

'It's not his sister,' Rose says gently, realizing she's upset me more than she anticipated. 'He lives there. With his wife and their child.'

'And you're sure about this?' I can't take it in. Luke walking down the road holding hands with his wife. The wife that he told Isabel he could barely stand to be in the same room as. And then it hits me. Of course, that's the reason he can never stay the night. It's not because of work or his fear of commitment. It's because his wife would want to know where he was. Now I think about it, it suddenly seems so obvious. It makes sense of the fact that he can't meet up on the weekends too. He's been using his son as an excuse but, in actual fact, what he should have been saying is, 'My wife wouldn't like it, really, if I told her I was going off to see my mistress.'

Oh God. That word. Isabel is a mistress.

'I take it Isabel has no idea?' Rose is saying, and I struggle to tune back in.

'No. God, no, of course not.'

'She'll be devastated,' Dan says, stating the obvious.

'Well, don't worry,' Rose says. 'I'm not going to say anything. I'll let you decide how you want to handle it.'

I look at Dan. We've – well, let's face it, I've – spent so much time protecting Izz from the full horror of Alex's behaviour and steering her towards Luke that I have never really even considered whether that was the right thing to do. I just wanted her to be over Alex. I just wanted her to be happy again.

'I'm going to have to tell her,' I say. 'I don't think she'd ever forgive me if I didn't. You're definitely sure it's him?' I say to Rose and she nods.

'Definitely.'

She would find out eventually anyway, of course. Luke would duck her invitation to spend Christmas, he'd continue to run home every night and claim childcare duties every weekend. Of course, he'd have to avoid introducing Isabel to Charlie too. Sooner or later she would have realized that something wasn't right and confronted him. Maybe he was hoping that eventually she'd get bored of the relationship not moving forward and she'd just dump him, or perhaps he intended to finish with her before it all got too serious. Sadly, it may be too late for that in Isabel's case. With my encouragement she's latched on to Luke as the great white hope for her future. She's finally got over Alex and fallen head first into something new that I've helped convince her is the answer to all her prayers. I have no idea how I'm going to break it to her that her new relationship is a sham, but I know that I have to do it straight away, before she lets herself get in any deeper.

I can't believe that Luke took us all in. He had us all falling for him, not just Izz. But how could he do this to her when she was so vulnerable? He probably does it all the time, sweeps lonely women off their feet and then disappears out of their lives mysteriously one night before they're on to him. I could kill him. I'd enjoy it. But dealing with him has to come later. I need to think how to tell Isabel first.

Needless to say the news rather takes the shine off the evening. We still have a nice enough time, we all get on, but my heart, at least, isn't really in it.

'I hope this doesn't send her running to Alex,' I say to Dan when we're getting ready for bed.

'If it does, it does,' he says like some kind of wise Chinese philosopher. 'Let her do whatever she thinks is best for her, OK?'

'I know, I know.'

On Sunday morning I take William round to Isabel's with strict instructions to keep the girls amused while their mum and I have a chat. At least I can be sure that Luke won't be there. He'll be tucked up in bed with his wife, reading the papers or smiling at her as she brings him bacon and eggs. She's surprised, but pleased to see me. I try not to look like the bearer of bad news, but she knows me too well and she picks up pretty quickly that something is wrong.

'Rebecca?' she says. 'Are you OK?'

'Of course,' I say in return. 'I'm fine.'

I wait until William has gone up to the girls' attic room and Isabel is putting the kettle on, and then I say, 'Actually, everything isn't fine.'

She looks all concern for me. 'Bex, what is it? It's not Dan?'

I launch straight in. For both our sakes I just have to get this over with as quickly as possible.

'Luke's married.' Well, there's one way to break it to her gently.

Isabel looks at me, confused. 'What?'

'Luke. He's still with his wife. Rose saw them together in Highgate.' I hesitate and then deliver my sucker punch. 'Holding hands.'

'When?'

'Last week. That's where she recognized him from. Do you remember she said . . .? Anyway. He lives near her sister.'

Isabel sits down. 'No, she's got it wrong. It must be his wife's new boyfriend. Luke said she had a new boyfriend.'

'I don't think so, Izz.'

'But . . .' she says, 'how can he still be with her? I see him three or four times a week . . .'

'But never overnight or at weekends . . .'

She looks up at me as she takes that in. There's no denying it makes sense.

'Oh God,' she says. 'How could I be so stupid?'

'He's very convincing,' I say, sitting down next to her. 'He had us all fooled. If you think about it, though, he had it all worked out. His job means that he works late sometimes so his wife isn't going to question it when he's not home till ten thirty. He travels a lot and who's to know if he has a woman holed up in his hotel while he's away? He couldn't have kept it up for long, though.'

'But he came over to yours. Why would he risk that if it was such a carefully worked-out operation?'

I've been thinking about this overnight. I couldn't sleep, of course. 'Because I think he really likes you. And I don't think that was ever part of the plan.'

'I've been so stupid,' Isabel says. 'So fucking stupid.'

'I'm really sorry.'

'It's hardly your fault.'

'No,' I say, 'but I encouraged you. I told you to go for it. I told you he'd be good for you.'

'Oh God,' she says. 'I'm meant to be seeing him tomorrow night. What shall I do?'

'I don't know. I'm all out of good ideas. But I'll come with you, if you want, if you decide to go ahead and see him. I'll stand in your corner and cheer you on. Although I can't guarantee I won't feel like I have to tell him what I think of him.'

'Is it better on the phone or in person?' she says. 'Obviously I can't phone him today – he always told me he'd call me at the weekends, so he could do it when Charlie wasn't around. He said until I'd met Charlie properly he didn't want him wondering who his dad was talking to. It sounds lame now, doesn't it, but it made sense at the time. I thought he was such a nice bloke to be so worried about his son like that.'

'Well, if you see him, there's a danger he'll win you round somehow, after all, we know now how manipulative he is. But if you phone him you risk him putting the phone down on you before you've said all you want to say.'

'I need to see him. I want to see the look on his face when I tell him I know. And I want him to have to explain himself.'

She decides to leave the arrangements as they are — that they will meet at half past six in the little bistro up the road. I offer to come again and she says no, she'll be fine and, besides, she doesn't want to alert him to the fact that anything's wrong before the time is right.

'I might just tell him I'm going to go back to Teddington with him to stay the night, see what he does,' she says. We spend a few minutes coming up with more and more elaborate revenges we could take on Luke, which seems to cheer her up until she suddenly seems to take in exactly what this all means and her mood crashes.

'Why are you crying?' Nicola demands when she comes in looking for something.

'Because I told her Justin Timberlake was gay,' I say, and Isabel manages a smile.

'He's not, is he?' Nicola asks nervously. Nicola loves Justin Timberlake. Natalie, on the other hand, is more a Rihanna girl.

317

'No,' Isabel says, and laughs. 'He's not is he, Rebecca?' She gives me a look.

'No,' I say. 'I was just teasing.'

'Well, don't,' Nicola says sharply. 'It's mean.'

I spend most of the day round at Isabel's while she alternately feels fired up and then torn down. At one point she says, 'Oh no, I told Alex I'd moved on forever,' and I can't decide if she's upset because she doesn't want him to think she's still not over him or if she's wishing she hadn't turned him down so finally. I start to worry that she's going to decide to go back to him after all, a knee-jerk reaction to her latest disappointment, but I decide to say nothing. I've said enough, really, on the subject of Isabel's relationships.

27

Lorna is all dressed up and ready for the big lunch. I'm still keeping out of her way although I'm desperately curious to know how it goes. She's being unbearably smug and self-important around the office and she makes sure she drops in something about 'lunch with Heather and Niall' at least every ten minutes in her conversations with Joshua or Melanie and the orders she barks to Kay. She still seems a little unstable to me, a bit manic. I hear her telling Melanie about the 'brilliant' weekend she had, which seems to have involved clubbing and eating out, shopping with friends and, rather randomly, bowling. I know she's lying. I know she will have spent the whole two days holed up in her flat, hoping vainly that Alex would swing by on a white horse and sweep her off her feet. Actually, I don't expect she would have cared what colour the horse was.

I'm hoping that she remembers Heather's agenda, which is to find a more highbrow project, something where she can show off her brains as well as her beauty. Not too highbrow, obviously. Just something where she can maybe say something without having to have it written for her once in a while. Lorna's only role in the lunch, really, is to stop Heather committing to something she'll later regret and to keep reminding Niall how great she is, how talented, how smart. And, let's not forget, how popular. (Her current shows, *Celebrity Karaoke* and *High Speed Dating*, pull in more than seven million viewers each, taking twenty-eight and thirty-one per cent of the audience share respectively; *Heat* apparently sells five per cent more copies than usual when she's on the cover, etc.) I have all the facts and figures memorized if she wants to hear them, but I don't want to go in there to be insulted by her, so I write what I think is relevant on a piece of paper and give it to Kay to hand to her.

'Tell her you compiled it,' I say. 'That way she might take some notice.'

'I already know all this,' she apparently says to Kay when she looks at it, but she folds it up and puts it in her pocket anyway.

About forty minutes after Kathryn's audition for *Nurses*, just as I am putting on my coat, I get a call telling me that she has got the job. It's a year's contract, a rare bit of stability in an insecure world. I pass the details on to Kay, gutted that I can't tell Kathryn the good news myself.

As (bad) luck would have it I am just going out to get some lunch as Lorna is getting in the lift. I think about saying, 'It's OK, I'll walk,' but that would be such a pointed and obvious insult that I decide I can't. We stand there in silence, both counting down the floors from five to ground, willing it to go faster. As she steps out I decide to take the moral high ground and I say, 'I hope it goes well.'

She manages to say thank you, which, I suppose, is something. I follow her out on to the street, deciding that whichever way she walks I'll go the opposite, so we're not doing that awkward 'walking down the street pretending we don't know the other one is right there' thing. She turns to the left and, just before I step out I hear her say, 'Oh my God,' so I look to see what she's seen and there's Alex, standing there, leaning against the window of the shop next door.

'Oh, hi,' he says, and then he sees me, and he looks straight past Lorna who has stopped dead still, and he says, 'Rebecca.'

'What do you want?' I say. I can see Lorna's bottom lip trembling and tears are welling up in the corner of her eyes. It's like that moment when you know a toddler is going to kick off because he's dropped his ice cream and there's nothing you can do to stop it.

'To talk to you. About Isabel.'

Lorna is rooted to the spot, waiting to hear whatever it is that he has to say to me. All I can think is that she needs to get going if she's going to get to the Ivy on time.

'I don't have time. Neither do I have anything to say to you, to be honest. Come on, Lorna, I'll walk with you.'

She doesn't move and Alex doesn't seem to be going anywhere either. I can't just walk off and leave them there; I need to know she's going to get to where she needs to be, so I end up standing there too, waiting to see what will happen next.

'Alex . . .?' Lorna says.

He looks at her briefly then turns back to me and says, 'She told you that I asked her if I could come back?'

I nod and Lorna lets out a gasp like an over-acting soap opera extra.

'And I meant it,' he carries on regardless. 'I've realized that these past few months . . . It's all been a mistake, a big old clichéd mid-life crisis, if you like. I had always had a thing for you . . . always thought I was in love with you I guess . . .'

I cannot believe this man. Right in front of him is a woman whose heart he has well and truly broken and he's barely even noticed she's there. And not only is she there but she's very obviously falling apart.

'I really don't want to listen to this, OK?'

I go to grab Lorna's arm and she shrugs me off. We've now attracted a little audience comprised of the people who work in the shops up and down the street, which, I'm sure, will do the professional reputation of Mortimer and Sheedy no end of good.

Alex isn't stopping. 'But because I knew . . . I thought . . . I could never act on it, I put it out of my mind and I was happy with her, I really was. Until . . . well, you know, it all got too much. But I should have stuck it out – I realize that now. It was as good as it was going to get and everything since has been a mistake.'

'No . . .' Lorna says, or should I say sobs.

Alex finally looks at her. 'Oh, come on, Lorna, you must have known it wasn't serious.'

If she wasn't already crushed, that one lands on her like a ton of bricks and she crumples under the weight. I need to do some damage limitation and get rid of Alex as quickly as I can.

'What do you want from me?'

'She listens to you. At the moment she's saying no, but I know you could persuade her, convince her I've changed, that I just want my old life back with her and the girls. I miss my kids, Rebecca. And just think, given time, it could be the four of us again. I know Dan would come round once Izz and I were back together. We could have our little group back, our family. Think how much you'd like for that to happen.'

Actually, what I'd like to happen is for me to punch him right in the face. Unfortunately now isn't the right time so I just say, 'I think I should keep out of it. Now just go. Please. Do the right thing for once.'

He hesitates for a moment and then he says, 'OK. But think about it at least. Everyone deserves a second chance.'

'Fine,' I say. Whatever. I just want to get away, or more to the point get Lorna away, at the moment.

Alex makes a move as if to hug me, but I step back. 'Thank you,' he says. 'I'll see you soon. See you, Lorna,' he adds, like he was talking to a vague acquaintance.

He goes, thank God, and I am left with the mess formerly known as Lorna Whittaker. She has mascara all over her face so I get hold of her as if she was a small child and I use a tissue to wipe it off.

'If you walk really quickly, you can still be on time,' I

say. I don't know how else to handle the situation other than to try to pretend that everything is normal.

'I can't go,' she says. 'I need to go home.'

'No, Lorna,' I say firmly (bad dog). 'You have to go to this lunch first. Then you can go home.'

'I can't.'

'OK. The thing is you have to. After that you can go home for a week if you want to, I don't care.'

'Rebecca, I can't.' I think it might be the first time she's ever used my name without it being pointed, without her then giving me a dressing down about something or other. 'Look at the state of me.'

There's no doubt about it, she does look like a mess. The runny mascara has escaped again and her hair has sunk into a lank helmet in sympathy. I know her statement is more about her emotional well being than whether she looks good or not, but I don't feel equipped to be the one to have to deal with that now, so I start fussing at her face with a tissue again. She grabs hold of my hand and looks me straight in the eye, which is disconcerting to say the least. 'I don't know what to do,' she says. 'You have to help me.'

'I will. Just get the lunch over with –'

'No. I'm never going to be able to get through the lunch.'

'I'll walk you there. Then you just need to sit there and smile for an hour and a half and kick Heather under the table if it looks like she's agreeing to something stupid.'

'I can't,' she says again, and I look at my watch. This is madness.

'Shall I see if either Joshua or Melanie can go instead?'

'No! I don't want them to think I can't cope. You were right, what you said when you came round to my flat, my job is all I've got really. I can't risk it.'

"What, then? I don't know what to suggest.'

'You could go instead of me. Say I'm ill again . . .'

'Come on, Lorna. Who sends an assistant when they can't make lunch? It'd be an insult . . .'

'OK. Come with me. I can say I'm not quite up to speed because I was off for so long. Please, Rebecca. I'll be OK if I've got some moral support.'

It's ridiculous. Niall will think she's got a power complex, taking her assistant to a fairly informal lunch when he would never dream of doing the same. But I don't know what else to do to get her there so I say yes, fine, let's go.

On the way she starts talking about Alex. 'I don't understand what's happened to him. We used to be so close.'

I don't feel like now is a good time to be talking about this, especially as I can hear the crack in her voice that tells me more tears aren't far off.

'Let's think about Heather,' I say, trying to sound upbeat and positive, which is anything other than how I actually feel. 'What kinds of things do you think she should be doing?'

'We'd even talked about moving in together . . .'

I refuse to be drawn in. 'Maybe something like *Countdown*, but at prime time? Or *Crimewatch*? Is that what she wants? I mean, he's hardly going to ask her to front *Newsnight*, is he?' I look at her. She's gazing off into the distance, barely watching where she's walking, so I carry on before she has a chance to talk about Alex some more. 'Or does she have ideas of her own? Because that would be where the big money was, wouldn't it? Owning the formats?'

She shrugs. Luckily it's a short walk and, just before we turn down West Street from St Martin's Lane I stop her and give her the once over, dabbing stray mascara with another – this time used – tissue I find in my coat pocket. I just about refrain from asking her to spit into it first.

'Just smile,' I say. 'And nod every now and then. It'll all be over in about an hour or so.'

Heather is already there so we take a seat in the bar. I'm waiting for Lorna to explain what I'm doing there, but she doesn't so I say, 'Lorna asked me to come along because as you know she's not been well the last few weeks and I've been sort of covering for her . . .' It's barely an explanation but it's all I have. Luckily Heather isn't really interested in anyone other than herself and the little ripple of excitement her presence is causing among a group of middle-aged women at another table, so she doesn't really react. In fact, she doesn't even ask Lorna how she is. I'm grateful for her lack of manners, though, because if she did Lorna would probably tell her and that wouldn't help matters at all.

'So,' I say to Heather. 'Maybe we should have a quick

chat before Niall gets here about what exactly it is you want to do . . .'

'I've been over and over this with Lorna,' she says petulantly. Lorna looks at me, wide-eyed.

'Yes,' I say. 'She said that you want to move on to something a bit more grown-up, a little more substantial. I just wondered if you had any specific thoughts. Because we have a few ideas,' I add, talking off the top of my head.

'Well, I don't see why Terri Sanderson gets all the good jobs,' she says, naming another young female presenter whose shows aren't exactly Nobel Prize-worthy.

'Right . . .' I say, with no idea what I am going to say next. Thankfully Niall walks in at that very minute so it's air kisses all round. I manage to introduce myself and, though he looks a little bemused, he's polite enough. He and Heather basically only have eyes for each other, which suits me. I sit back and try to relax a bit, keeping one eye on Lorna.

At the table Niall and Heather talk about mutual acquaintances and who's hot and who's not right the way through the starter. I have no idea when is the appropriate time to start a conversation about work or who is meant to initiate it. At one point Niall asks Lorna how she is and she stares down at her plate and mutters something about being fine.

It's all rather awkward, but as soon as the main course is delivered Niall says, 'So, you're thinking of leaving ITV?' and I tell myself to at least concentrate so that I can step in if the conversation takes a wrong turn.

Heather looks at Lorna as if she's expecting her to chime in at this point, which, of course, isn't going to happen. I take a deep breath. What's the worst that can happen?

'Well, Niall,' I say, and he almost jumps. I can see him thinking, Who the hell is she again?, but I carry on regardless. 'Heather feels like she's being pigeonholed at ITV. Isn't that right, Heather?' Luckily Heather nods, so I carry on. 'She brings in a great audience for them, as you know, so it suits them to keep her doing that kind of mainstream Saturday night, family stuff where it's all about the ratings.' I rattle off the facts and figures that I looked up to give to Lorna and he nods slightly impatiently as if to say yes, I know all this already. 'The thing is,' I say, in an effort to wrap up, 'Heather doesn't just want to spend her time reading an autocue. She's capable of so much more than that and she'd like to branch out to do other things.' I sit back. That's all I've got. Really.

'Like what?' Niall says. He looks at Heather and Heather looks at me.

'Um . . . like . . .' I raise my eyebrows at Heather as if to say, 'This was all your idea, what is it you're so desperate to do actually?'

She shrugs.

'. . . like documentaries.'

Niall almost laughs but he manages to stop himself and pretend he was choking on his water. 'You want to do documentaries?'

'No,' Heather says testily, 'not documentaries.'

'Not exactly documentaries,' I say, trying to rescue the

328

situation, 'but . . . you know, those shows where you see behind the scenes, where she can interview people and show off a bit more of her personality. Like . . . backstage at *Britain's Brightest Star* . . .' I add, clutching at straws.

Niall, as ever, looks at Heather rather than me. 'You want to do back-up shows? Someone else fronts the show and you do little inserts or a support show on BBC3? That doesn't feel like a big career move to me.'

Heather glares at me. For God's sake. I wish she'd speak for herself. Surely she must have some idea what she's capable of?

'Not back-up shows, no. More like . . . What Heather was thinking of was more like . . . I know, say there was a new series, a new talent show to replace *Britain's Brightest Star* because surely it can't go on forever . . .' I realize that dissing the BBC's flagship show is probably not the most sensible idea I've ever had so I add, 'Or maybe it could run in the summer when *Brightest Star* isn't on, anyway, Heather could front it but, also say there was a show mid week. Where they did a catch up on all the training and what had happened in the house since last week's live programme. Sort of like *Big Brother*, but then they have the talent show on the Saturday. Heather would be great at being in the house, getting to the real stories behind the contestants, finding out who hates who and getting them to spill the beans on who they think their biggest rival is or who is getting on their nerves.'

I'm on a roll now and everyone seems to be paying attention so I carry on. 'In fact, you could do it twice a week, say on a Tuesday and Thursday. It'd be a real event.

Eight o'clock, BBC1. Maybe you even introduce a mid-week heat so one person doesn't even get to the Saturday show. The audience votes them out based on what they've seen of the rehearsals and what they've behaved like in the house. If they're a pain in the arse, they don't even get to compete. So you'd still have Heather doing what audiences love to see her doing, but then you see another side to her too. That's it, isn't it, Heather?'

'Exactly,' she says, smiling finally. 'That's exactly the kind of thing I'm talking about.'

'That's really not a bad idea, actually,' Niall says, addressing me directly for the first time. '*Britain's Brightest Star* meets *Big Brother*. That's really not bad. Is this your idea?'

I'm so tempted to say yes. I'm so proud of myself I want to bask in the glory, but I have to remember the job at hand. 'Well,' I say. 'We sort of all came up with it together.'

'So you'd be prepared to break your ITV contract if, say, we wanted to look at doing this next summer?' Niall says to Heather who is positively animated now.

'Oh yes,' she says, and I remember why I'm here and jump in. 'Well, we'd have to talk about it further, first. The deal would have to be right. I mean, Heather's ITV contract is very lucrative and –'

'Of course,' Niall says. 'We'll get an offer together and we can meet up again in a few weeks to discuss it.'

He's looking at me now so I say, 'Great. Lorna, you'll be properly back in action by then so I can set something up with you and Niall . . .'

Lorna nods half-heartedly.

'Oh, I think you should be there too,' Niall says. 'You seem to have the clearest idea of what it should be.'

'Oh yes,' says Heather, my new best friend. 'Rebecca has to be there.'

I look at Lorna, expecting her to be glaring at me – how dare you steal my job, you bitch – but she gives me a small smile of what I think might be encouragement. I nearly fall off my chair.

'Of course,' I say. 'I'd love to.'

28

I'm so full of my own marvellousness that I completely forget about Isabel and Luke until it's too late to ring her and wish her luck. There's no doubt that the lunch went well. Niall seems as excited by the idea of *Big Britain's Brightest Brother*, as I am now calling it in my head, as he is by the prospect of Heather fronting it. Heather is buzzing with excitement and gratitude, and she seems to have forgotten Lorna's flakiness and the fact that I am completely unimportant, because as we say goodbye she says, 'Let's all go out for a drink one night to celebrate, the three of us,' and I smile and say, 'Great,' despite the fact that I can't think of anything I would rather do less.

Lorna doesn't mention going home again so we sort of drift back to the office together. We don't speak on the way, but that's fine because I have so much going on in my head I wouldn't really be capable of holding a conversation anyway. Niall Johnson, the Controller of Entertainment Commissioning at the BBC, likes my idea. *My* idea that I came up with on the spot is probably going to be on the television. Of course, no one will know it was my idea, I'm not about to start fighting for format fees and credits because the point is I shouldn't have been at that lunch anyway, the point is that it's our job at Mortimer and Sheedy to get good jobs for our clients even if that involves coming up with the ideas ourselves. The point is that when – if – that programme ever airs *I* will know and that will be enough.

I'm not sure how we are going to play it back at the office because Joshua and Melanie are certain to want to know how the meeting went and do we tell them about my involvement or not? I'm assuming not. To tell them would create even more questions needing answers. I decide to leave it to Lorna.

I settle down to type some letters, but it's hard to concentrate. Lorna shuts herself in her office and a few minutes later I hear Joshua tap on her door and go in. I wait with bated breath for him to come out again but then Melanie walks through reception and says to Kay, 'Do you know how the Niall Johnson meeting went?'

Kay knows the truth. Well, she doesn't know the details, but I muttered to her about having had to go to the lunch when I first got back. She looks at me and I shake my head, trying to tell her not to mention the fact that I was there.

In the end she plumps for complete ignorance and says, 'No, Lorna didn't say.'

I keep my head down, hoping Melanie will go away but she hangs around talking about nothing with Kay until Joshua comes back and says, 'Sounds like it went well. Apparently Johnson is going to come up with a proposal for Heather based on some programme idea she wants to do that he likes.'

'Wow,' Melanie says, 'that's great. We'll need to keep it quiet for a couple of months, obviously . . .'

'Obviously,' Joshua says. 'Lorna's hoping she can negotiate a big new three-year deal for her off the back of this. Plus Heather will own a share of the format by the sounds of it. It could earn her a fortune.'

'And us, hopefully,' Melanie says, putting into words what's really on Joshua's mind.

'Congratulations, Lorna,' she adds, spotting Lorna on her way to the kitchen. 'It sounds like you handled that really well.'

'Thanks,' Lorna says, smiling. She doesn't look at me.

The rest of the day goes by in a blur and it's only when I'm on the tube on the way home that I remember I was going to call Isabel. By the time I get off and have a signal again it's too late. She's meeting Luke at six thirty and I don't want to ring in the middle of their confrontation so I send a text that says, 'Good luck. Call me as soon as it's over,' and I go home and wait nervously for her to let me know how it went.

Dan is as anxious as me so we try to distract ourselves by offering to help the kids with their homework. It doesn't really work because Zoe's idea of getting assistance is to leave the room and hope we just do it all for her, which is against my principles, and William thinks that children whose parents oversee their homework are 'lame' and he flat out refuses our offer.

Dan helps me with the tea and we try to talk about

other things to take our minds off it. To be fair he's really keen to hear about my day, especially when I get to the part about having to go to the lunch. He makes a big show of being proud of me for saving the day as he puts it. Plus he claims to like my idea, but I think he's just being kind. Dan hates reality TV.

By half past seven I'm really starting to worry. How long does it take to say 'I know you have a wife. It's all over'?

'You don't think he's talked her round, do you?' I say to Dan.

'Who's talked who round?' William says, scraping the last bit of ice cream off his plate noisily.

'No one,' Dan says, and William rolls his eyes.

'Yeah, right.'

'No,' says Dan, looking at me. 'I don't think so. Maybe she didn't want to bring it up right away. Maybe she was trying to give him a chance to say it first.'

'So there is something,' William says. 'Who's she?'

'Duh,' Zoe says. 'Thick boy.'

'It's grown-up stuff,' I say. 'Which means it's none of your business.'

'Then why are you talking about it in front of us?'

He has a point but luckily, at that moment, my phone rings and it's Isabel so I take it into the kitchen to answer it.

'Well?' I say before she can even say hello. 'Are you all right?'

According to Isabel she and Luke had met in the bar area of the little restaurant where they were supposed to be having dinner. She waited until she'd got a glass of wine because she wanted some Dutch courage. Meanwhile Luke had chatted about his day like nothing was wrong. He seemed so relaxed, she tells me, so unfazed by being out with her in public that for a moment she started to believe that we'd got it all wrong.

'I mean,' she says, 'I thought, why would he have agreed to meet my friends?'

'Because he thinks he's invincible?' I offer up. It has been bothering me a little that Luke was happy to be so indiscreet. The only way I have been able to rationalize it is to believe that he has supreme confidence – arrogance, actually – that has allowed him to believe he will never be caught. His family don't live close by any more and Charlie will be leaving the school in the summer; he must have figured he might just get away with it. Or maybe his wife is one of those women who would just put up with it if she found out, rather than have to start a whole new life on her own. Perhaps he does this all the time and she sits in their house in Highgate waiting for him to come to his senses again.

Anyway, Isabel tells me, she knew that she couldn't weaken so she waited until she'd had a few sips and she'd asked him how his weekend had been.

'Great,' Luke had said. 'Me and Charlie went Christmas shopping in Richmond on Saturday and yesterday I took him to the little cinema up the road. They were showing a rerun of *Willie Wonka*. He loves that film.'

'And then what? You take him to school on a Monday morning and then your wife picks him up in the afternoon? Is that how it works?' Isabel asked, trying to sound casual and not like she was conducting an inquisition. Luke, she says, had the good grace to look a little nervous under questioning.

'Yes,' he said, and he tried a little laugh, 'that way we don't have to see each other more often than necessary.'

Isabel says that at this point, in the face of this blatant lie, she nearly lost it, but she decided to see how far she could push him, how easily he could look her in the eye and deceive her. She decided, she says, that if she could witness him behaving that badly then it might help her to get over him more quickly.

'It must be hard,' she'd said to Luke then, 'disliking each other so much, but still having to deal with each other because of Charlie.'

'Hard is an understatement,' Luke had said. 'Like I told you before, we can hardly bear to be in the same room together, let alone speaking.'

'You never told me why you split up . . .'

I interrupt her telling me the story. 'Good one, Izz.'

She carries on.

'You never told me why you split up. Did you just fall out of love with each other or did one of you do something bad? I'm guessing something must have happened because of how much you seem to hate each other.'

Luke, she says, clearly has an answer prepared for the eventuality of this question ever being asked. And it's one guaranteed to put him in a good light. Or, at least, to put his wife in a bad one. Although the irony is laughable.

'She was seeing someone else,' he'd said, assuming a martyred expression.

'Oh God, how did you find out?' Isabel had asked him, all concern.

'I found messages . . . text messages from him, and I confronted her. She tried to deny it, but I knew that I was right and, eventually, she had to admit it was true. She chose him over me when it came down to it.'

'You poor thing. I can't imagine how awful that must feel. Thinking you know someone, that you love them, and then finding out they've been deceiving you all along.' At this point, she tells me, she looked him right in the eye but he didn't even have the decency to flinch.

'It was,' he'd said instead. 'But then, if it hadn't happened, I wouldn't have met you . . .'

Isabel wasn't finished. 'It must have been soul destroying. It would be like . . . oh, I don't know . . . me finding out that you weren't really separated or something. That you'd been telling me all this time that your marriage was over but it wasn't . . .'

She'd nearly laughed at this point, she says, not because she felt happy, far from it, but because the whole situation was so ludicrous. Luke's confident front had dissolved somewhat after this and apparently he had tried to change the subject and brought up something banal about work. Isabel had had no intention of letting him off the hook, though.

'I mean, I can't really think of anything worse, can you? Than being deceived by someone like that. Being forced to become something you would never knowingly become. Like a mistress. Because I would never – not in a million years – agree to be anyone's mistress.'

She'd paused here, having laid her cards squarely on the table, to give him one final chance to confess, but he'd chosen not to take it, asking her if she'd like another drink instead, getting up from the table and picking up their glasses. This had made her really angry. It was as if he thought that if he could distract her for a minute then she would forget all about what she had been saying. Clearly Luke had no intention of ever doing the honorable thing. In fact, she suspected that he might go up to the bar and just keep walking. Run away rather than face the music. She'd decided to go in for the kill.

'Because that's what I am, aren't I? Your bit on the side?'

Luke had sat back down very quickly. He had tried to tell her that he'd never meant for it to turn out this way. He'd been feeling unhappy, he and his wife were going through a bad patch, it was the first time he'd ever done anything like this (yeah, right, she says). He'd told her that he'd meant to break it off ages ago, but he had found that he really liked her. In fact, he had realized he was falling in love with her and he hadn't been able to. He told her all this like it was meant to make her feel better. There were tears on both sides. Then he said to her that he really had been thinking about leaving his wife since he fell for Isabel and she decided that she had to leave, quickly, before she got taken in again by his, very convincing, bullshit.

'It was awful,' she says. 'It's scary how easy it would

339

have been to just carry on, to ask him to really leave his wife.'

'You've done the right thing,' I say.

'I know. But that doesn't mean I'm happy about it. I'm on my own again. I've been completely taken for a ride by someone I genuinely cared about. I mean, I thought he was my gateway to a new life. God, I've been stupid . . .'

'Come round. We're not planning on doing anything, just watching TV . . .'

'I think I will,' she says. 'I don't feel like being on my own at the moment.'

So, Isabel, Dan and I spend the rest of the evening lounging around on the sofas in our living room. Every now and then she gets a bit tearful and one of us will give her a pep talk and bring her tissues to mop up her tears. I haven't yet told her about Alex's plea to me and I'm not sure what to do. The last thing I want would be for her to take Alex back. Not just for my own selfish reasons, although I know it must seem like that. I just don't believe that it's what he really wants or that, even if he does, their marriage would be any better this time round.

On the other hand, I've learned my lesson. It's nothing to do with me. Isabel will have to decide for herself what she wants and in order to be able to do that she needs all the facts. And by that I mean *all* the facts. So, if I tell her that Alex wants her to know that he genuinely feels he's made a mistake and that he's desperate to give their relationship another try, then I have to also tell her the full truth about his declaration of love to me and even about all the other women. Give her both sides of the story and absolutely no advice, no trying to sway her in either direction. And I'm not sure I'm capable of that even if I did decide it was the right thing to do.

I decide to wait, talk it over with Dan later. There's no rush. Isabel isn't in the right state of mind to make such a big decision yet anyway and I can't imagine that Alex is going anywhere.

Rebecca and Daniel. And Isabel. It's not so bad.

Lorna is looking good. It's like she somehow had a makeover in the middle of the night. Her clothes are ironed, her nails are polished, her hair while still a bit of a mess is at least washed. When I walk past her office at twenty past nine, on my way to my reception area, she seems to be tidying up, throwing piles of old papers on to a heap in the middle of the floor. I can't be sure if this is a good sign or if she's actually become manic so I sneak past without saying hello.

There's a big bunch of flowers on my desk with my name on. I open the card and flush with pride as I read the message which says 'I can't thank you enough. Love Kathryn.' I arrange them in an old vase and sit and admire them. No one has ever sent me flowers at work before. Or, at least, for not-work-related reasons.

A little later Lorna phones through to me and asks me to go into her office. Although this is the second time this has happened in the past two days it is not a normal occurrence. Lorna knows that as far as I'm concerned I don't work for her and she's hardly going to want to see me for a girly chat. I mutter about being in the middle of something and tell her I'll come through in a minute. I take my time, making myself a tea, and then I say to Kay, 'If I'm not out in ten minutes, send help.' She laughs and wishes me luck.

Lorna's office is now looking as scrubbed up as she is. She sits behind her desk and motions for me to sit on the other side.

'Rebecca,' she says. 'I think I should say thank you for the way you've been covering for me.'

I sit there open-mouthed. Did she just thank me?

'That's OK,' I manage to say.

'You did a good job,' she says.

I make as if to get up. 'Well, you're back now . . .'

She's not finished. 'And for yesterday. If you hadn't been there, that lunch would have been a disaster. I just want you to know that I appreciate it.'

'Right . . . thanks.'

'Anyway,' she says, 'like you said, I'm back now and I'm feeling much better.'

'Good,' I say. 'I'm glad to hear it.' She does actually look much better although, of course, we both know that this time yesterday she was a basket case, but it seems neither of us is going to mention that. I try to make a move again. Lorna coughs, which makes me jump. This whole conversation is making me feel very uneasy.

'I spoke to Alex last night,' she says, and this time I

don't mind sitting down again because I want to hear what she has to say.

'And . . .?'

'I went round to his flat and waited outside till he got home so he had to talk to me. And you were right. He wasn't ever in love with me. He was in love with you, just like you said.'

'I'm sorry, Lorna.' I mean it, I do feel bad for her.

'Actually, you know, now he's finally admitted it, it's OK. I can move on. I just have to get over feeling stupid . . .' Her voice cracks. I seem to be destined to be surrounded by disappointed crying women at the moment. I don't know what to do. Comforting her would feel like an intrusion so I just sit there.

'I'm going to concentrate on work,' she says, once she's composed herself. 'And I'm very grateful that I still have that work to concentrate on. So that's why I asked you to come in really. To tell you that.'

'Well, if it makes you feel any better, I enjoyed doing it. I really did.'

'It seems you're good at it,' she says, and smiles. At least, I think it's a smile. It's hard to tell with Lorna, she does it so rarely. She could just have wind.

29

I've had an epiphany.

I couldn't sleep in the night, thinking about Isabel and Luke and Lorna and Alex and the big old mess that is our lives. Then I started feeling sorry for myself. I'm finding work mind-numbingly boring now I'm back to my old routine. Don't get me wrong, I still love Mortimer and Sheedy, but I feel like I've lost something. Like I'm capable of so much more. I was thinking over the buzz I got while Lorna was away, trying not to feel resentful about the fact that I am not going to be given any credit for anything I achieved – my own decision, I know, but it still bothers me, nonetheless – when I suddenly realized that I don't have to answer phones and type letters for the rest of my life.

The thing that was always holding me back was my own perception of myself. I never believed I was confident enough or capable enough to do more. I hid behind protestations of wanting an easy life and no responsibility when really, underneath all my front, it was fear that held me back. But it's different now. Now I know I can do it. I just have to figure out who's going to give me the chance. On paper I have no experience, just six years of admin.

I can't help myself – I have to talk it over with Dan.

I shake him awake and he groans and tries to roll over away from me.

'Dan,' I hiss. 'Are you awake?' I know that's the one thing I can say that will guarantee he'll wake up enough to talk to me.

He rolls back. 'Well, I am now,' he says testily.

'I think I want to have a career. Not just a job. Not just filing and typing and calling people to tell them other people want to speak to them.'

'Good for you,' he says. 'Night.'

'What do I do? If I apply to other agencies, they'll just see me as someone who's been an assistant forever. Why on earth would they trust me with any of their clients?'

'Sweetheart,' he says. 'I have no idea. Talk to Melanie about it. I'm sure she'll be able to give you some advice.'

'Am I being stupid?' I say. 'Should I just shut up and get on with what I'm doing?'

'Definitely not,' Dan says, suddenly wide awake. 'You'd be brilliant and, if it's what you want, then you have to go for it. We just have to figure out the practicalities. Maybe there's an agents' training school you could go to.'

I laugh. 'With modules in inflating CVs and schmoozing.'

'I think you're a natural,' he says. 'You're bossy and you like telling people what to do. I'd give you a chance.'

We talk about it for a little while more before I realize that I really should let him get back to sleep. There's no way I'm dropping off any time soon. I feel elated. Nervous and excited at the same time. I have no idea if

I'm going to be doing the right thing, putting myself out there, leaving my cosy work set-up, but at least I'm doing something.

I take my time trying to get up the courage to talk to Melanie in the morning. I'm worried it will sound like I'm resigning, which I am in a way although not quite yet. I want to test the water first, see what might be out there. I don't want to try to run before I can walk. I might have dredged up some courage from somewhere, but I'm still not *that* brave. I confide in Kay and she hugs me and says it's a brilliant idea and, even though no one else knows it, she knows that I'll make a great agent because she's seen me in action.

'Most of Lorna's clients would probably leave and go with you if they knew the truth,' she says.

'That's not how I want to do it, though,' I say.

Lorna is beavering away in her office, back to her old efficient self. She phones through to Kay every few minutes with another piece of business and, from what Kay divulges to me, it seems like she's gone into overdrive to prove she's back on track. I'm glad for her. Although a big part of me thinks that my life would be much simpler if she could just get back with Alex and keep him away from Isabel. I shouldn't wish him on her, though. Slightly alarmingly she seems to be checking up on the work I did while she was away, having Kay set up calls with first Phil Masterson then Marilyn Carson and then Jasmine, Mary, Samuel, Craig, Joy and Kathryn in quick succession. Could she still be plotting my downfall even as she seems to be trying to be a bit more gracious? I wouldn't put it past her. I'm tempted to listen in on her calls, but I decide my new professional self wouldn't stoop that low. Oh well, let her try. I'm out of here anyway. Fretting about what Lorna is up to focuses my thoughts and I finally get up the courage to go and knock on Melanie's door

'Have you got a minute?' I say, when she looks up. I know she'll say yes, she always does, even when she's snowed under.

'Sure. Come in.'

I go in and shut the door behind me, which at Mortimer and Sheedy always signifies that something serious is going on.

'What's up?'

I sit down. 'I . . . you know I love working here . . .'

'That doesn't sound good,' Melanie says. She puts her pen down as if to prove to me that she's concentrating on me and nothing else.

'I've never wanted to work anywhere else. You and Joshua are like family to me.'

'Are you telling me you want to leave now?' She looks worried.

'No . . . Well, I don't know. Eventually, yes.' Come on, Rebecca. Spit it out. 'The thing is that I think I want to be an agent myself. With my own clients and stuff.' I look up at her to see if she laughs at the ridiculousness of what I've just said, but she doesn't. 'Only, obviously, I have no real experience and I was hoping you could give me some advice, you know, on what I should do next.' This suddenly doesn't seem like a good idea, asking my current employer how I can get a better job probably isn't the cleverest thing I can do.

'I thought you didn't want any responsibility. You always said so . . .'

'I know. But now I do. Or maybe I always did, I just didn't want to admit it to myself.'

'Well, you know it can't happen here?' she says. 'We've just promoted Lorna and we're only a small company.'

'Of course.' The minute she says that there's no chance of my being promoted at Mortimer and Sheedy I realize that I have been secretly hoping that that was exactly what would happen. The idea of having to go somewhere else, to start again, scares the shit out of me. I feel absolutely deflated suddenly and she must be able to read it on my face.

'I wish we'd known you had these ambitions before . . .'

'I didn't even know it myself. Sorry . . .'

'You know we'll hate to see you go, but I'll do whatever I can to help you. I've always thought you were capable of so much more.'

She tells me she'll have a think about where might be good for me to apply. She knows a few people who she can talk to, she says. She and Joshua will give me a fantastic reference, it goes without saying. I thank her and I tell her again that it's not that I want to leave Mortimer and Sheedy, it's not like I'm unhappy, I just need to do this for myself. In fact, if nothing comes up then I'll happily stay here, doing what I'm doing, for the rest of my days. Melanie laughs and tells me she understands completely.

'I'll mention it to Joshua,' she says, 'prepare him for the worst,' and I feel sick, like I've set something in motion and now I'm not going to be able to stop it even if I wanted to.

It's only a few days till we shut down for the Christmas break. Two whole weeks of no work and overindulgence. Traditionally Dan and I always have Alex and Isabel and the girls over for a big celebratory dinner on the twenty-first with a few random other friends, whoever we are feeling well disposed to at the time, and then the four of us plus kids all get together again on Christmas Eve.

This year we haven't organized anything, but as the day draws nearer William starts asking who's coming and when are we going to start decorating the house, and it makes me realize that more than anything the kids need a bit of stability. I mention it to Dan and he says of course we should go ahead and we shouldn't let Alex's bad behaviour get in the way of us all having fun. He doesn't quite sound like he's convinced by his own words, but I figure it'll do us all good so I tell Isabel it's on, as usual.

We decide to invite Rose and Simon and I tell Dan I'd like to ask Kay along too. I get the impression she's dreading Christmas, although she'd never admit as much. Her eldest has decided to spend the holidays with his new girlfriend's parents and her youngest isn't coming home till Christmas Day when it'll just be the two of them. In keeping with our own little established traditions, we will be serving sausages and mash with trifle for dessert – I can't remember when or why this became the official twenty-first of December menu but now it would seem wrong to change it – and pulling homemade crackers, which with everything that's been going on I haven't even given a thought to this year.

I set aside tomorrow lunchtime to go to Fortnum & Mason to buy the little gifts to go inside, and I break the news to Zoe and William that they will have to spend Tuesday and Wednesday evenings on the production line. Dan and I will make two in secret for them after they have gone to bed. I write a list of ingredients for Dan to buy at Waitrose after work tomorrow and then William and I climb into the tiny storage space we call the loft, even though we are on the third floor of a six-storey block and it's really just a cubby hole built into the suspended ceiling in the hall, and dig out the decorations. We spend a happy hour or so putting up the tree while William tries to convince me that buying him a chemistry set for Christmas would be a real investment for his future as a mad scientist as opposed to an irresponsible and potentially lethal thing to do.

Rose sounds delighted when I call her. I think she has been a little nervous around us since she told me what she knew about Luke, that she might have put her foot in it. Isabel says that, of course, she just assumed that it would be on. It's the twenty-first of December, it's tradition, what else would be happening?

'Have you decided what to do about Christmas yet?' I ask, not for the first time. If I'm being honest, I'm worried that Alex is going to use the holidays to try to crowbar his way back into her life. On the other hand the girls will want to see him, of course they will; he's still their father. I've thought about suggesting to Isabel that she tell him he can come over either before or after lunch, but not for the actual meal itself. Preferably before when he is less likely to have had a few glasses of wine too many, although that way there is always the danger that he will get there and then refuse to leave and Isabel won't want to cause a scene in front of the twins. Anyway, I haven't offered up my suggestion because I am trying to live by my new rule of keeping out of things that really don't concern me.

'No. It's hard to have a rational conversation with Alex at the moment,' she says. 'I'm just playing it by ear.'

That's a recipe for disaster in my book, but I don't say so. Instead I say, 'You know you and the girls would be really welcome to spend the day with us?'

'Thanks. We might take you up on that. I just don't know . . .'

'It's OK,' I say, thinking of the turkey I've ordered that will never feed seven of us, 'you don't have to give us any notice.' I add 'frozen free-range turkey crown' to Dan's shopping list although I have little hope they'll have any left.

I can hardly breathe. Joshua has me in a bear hug. To say I'm in shock would be an understatement. Kay is

351

laughing while Lorna, who is looking for something in the script pile, just looks horrified.

'I can't believe you're leaving us,' he cries, mock distraught. 'What are we going to do without you?'

'You're leaving?' Lorna says, sounding genuinely surprised.

'Maybe,' I manage to say from the depths of Joshua's armpit somewhere. He lets me go just before I pass out from lack of breath.

'Rebecca has discovered her inner ambition,' he says to Lorna. 'She's got fed up with typing up my letters and making me coffee.'

'No,' I say. 'It's not like that . . .'

'About bloody time too,' Joshua goes on, laughing loudly to make it clear he's joking.

'You should have seen her face,' Kay says once they've both gone back to their rooms. 'It was priceless.'

Now I have made my announcement I feel like I should be seen to be doing something about it. I start making a list of the other agencies. I can't imagine going to work for one of the big successful companies. They're too corporate, too showy. And God knows why they would even think about employing me either when they have their own thrusting young assistants champing at the bit to be promoted. So that leaves the smaller – for that read less successful – outfits. The Mortimer and Sheedys.

I don't know where to start there are so many of them. And what are the chances I'll approach one just as they're thinking of expanding? Let alone how would I then convince them to hire me? I'm starting to despair a little. Why didn't I just keep my mouth shut, keep my stupid ambitions to myself? Now I'm going to have to deal with the embarrassment of failure – or at least of never really having had the guts to try – on top of everything else.

Having made the list I decide that at least I've done something, so I try to think about what I might put in the crackers instead. The gifts are always small but personal, and I usually think about them well in advance. Kay is easy. She's always losing her keys around the office because every time she gets them out of her pocket her keyring falls apart. I write down 'Kay: key ring', and then sit staring at the piece of paper for a couple of minutes. Kay is beyond thrilled, by the way, to have been invited to our little Christmas do. She's heard so much about Dan and Isabel that she can't wait to put faces to the names and I think, to be honest, she's just glad to be getting out of the house for the evening. I indulge her in five minutes of chat about her boys. The ways she has of justifying the fact that she's hardly going to see them over the holidays breaks my heart, actually.

I tell her I'd like to take the early lunch and I'm just putting my coat on, ready to go off to potter around Fortnum & Mason, looking for cracker gifts, when Melanie pops her head round the door and says, 'Rebecca, I've spoken to a few people. Carolyn Edwards at Marchmont, Edwards and Wright said they're thinking about expanding in a year or so's time, maybe. They're looking for a new assistant, so she said you could go in and meet if you were interested. You'd be well placed when they did want to expand . . . It's difficult, you know, because we know you're brilliant, but for other people, if they don't know you at all . . .'

She runs out of steam and looks at me apologetically. Great. The only choice seems to be that I move sideways, take the same job as I'm doing here somewhere else and then try to work my way up. I kick myself for all the years I've wasted. I feel too old to be starting again, hoping that someone will spot my potential eventually and give me some more responsibility. 'OK. Thanks,' I say, and I try to sound grateful.

'How's the career hunting going?' Dan says when I get home from work, laden down with bags of goodies for Thursday night.

'Oh, you know . . .' I say, and I change the subject.

30

Joshua, Melanie and Lorna have been shut in Joshua's comfortable office for nearly an hour now. At one point Melanie calls through to Kay to take them in a fresh pot of coffee and, she says, they all sit there in silence when she pours it out and clears away the dirty mugs. I've somehow managed to make Kay as paranoid as I am and she's convinced that they are discussing her inefficiency and the best way to get rid of her.

'I don't think that'd take them an hour,' I say, laughing. 'Lorna would just say, "I want to sack her," and they'd say, "Fine."'

'That makes me feel so much better.'

'It'll be strategy,' I say. 'They're plotting how to win more clients and take over the entertainment world.'

Nevertheless, I'm anxious about what they can possibly be talking about for so long. Maybe, now they know I'm thinking of moving on they're deciding whether to cut their losses and get someone in to replace me right away. After all, what loyalty do they owe me now, the ingrate who's throwing their years of support and generosity back in their faces?

When Melanie sticks her head round the door and says, 'Rebecca, have you got a moment? We'd like to talk to you,' I nearly have a coronary.

'Come in, come in,' Joshua says genially when I reluctantly edge my way through the door. 'Sit down.' He's smiling at me so I try to smile back and manage a kind of snarl. I can't even look at Lorna who, I imagine, will be revelling in whatever awful fate is about to befall me. I'm tempted to throw myself at Joshua screaming, 'I don't want to leave, don't replace me,' and, if I thought it wasn't already a fait accompli, I probably would. Mortimer and Sheedy is my second home. Where else am I going to work where they'll remember William's birthday or let me go home early because Zoe's in a school play?

'We've been talking about you,' Joshua says as if I hadn't already worked that one out. 'Lorna's been telling us some very interesting stories.'

He waits as if he expects me to say something, but I'm struck dumb. I was never any good at being in the headmaster's office. I just want this to be over with.

'So, the idea for Heather's new game show came from you, I gather?' he says, and I nod because it seems to be expected of me. 'They definitely want to make it, by the way, isn't that right, Lorna?'

'Next summer,' Lorna pipes up. 'Once we've got her out of her ITV commitments.'

I'm starting to get a little confused about why I'm in here. Do they just want to show off about how successful they're going to be once Heather's big new BBC contract kicks in next year?

'And she also told us that you were at the lunch with Niall Johnson,' Melanie says. I look at Lorna. She's doing that strange smile type of thing at me again. I look away. Never smile at a crocodile. 'And that you basically took charge of the situation because she was a little . . . under the weather.'

I grunt and look at my feet like a fourteen-year-old who's been accused of smoking in the stationary cupboard.

'Plus we've heard all about what you did for her clients while she was off sick. They were all very impressed with you apparently.' When Melanie says this I manage to look up at them and see all three of them beaming at me like proud parents.

'Now,' Joshua says, attempting a more serious note. 'Obviously we can't condone you keeping us in the dark and telling us that you were acting on Lorna's instructions when we now know that you weren't, but . . . it's obvious that you thought you were doing it all for the right reasons, not only for Mortimer and Sheedy, but for Lorna's sake . . .'

'. . . Which is good because, as you know, Joshua and I have always worried that the two of you didn't get on,' Melanie interrupts.

'And so we, that is Lorna really but Melanie and I think it's a great idea, have come up with a proposal for you that we hope you like.'

There's a big pregnant pause again and this time I know that something good is coming next so I allow a smile to start to creep over my face.

'What?' I say. 'What proposal?'

Joshua takes a big breath like he's about to address a

meeting and says, 'Well, Heather is going to take up a lot of Lorna's time from now on. And she's going to be earning us a lot of money. Obviously there's also Mary and Craig, who Lorna feels very passionate about. As you know, Mary has got a big break . . .'

'Thanks to you,' Lorna says, and I can't help myself, I smile at her. It's a strange sensation.

'. . . and we need to keep up that momentum for her. Craig is going to need a lot of attention to help him rise in the ranks and Lorna feels she'd like to take the time to build up her roster some more herself, use the contacts she's making, that kind of thing, you know?'

I nod impatiently. I daren't speak because I don't want to sideline him. I want him to get on with it. What proposal?

'And, of course, Melanie and I feel that with the Heather coup she should absolutely be given the freedom to do that. So . . . what that means is that Lorna is not going to have time to look after the voice-over work, nor does she feel she can put her full energies into working with Jasmine or Samuel or Kathryn or, indeed, Joy. We don't want to keep pushing them around from pillar to post, of course, but Lorna has spoken to the four of them and, given what they now know about what has been going on here over the last few weeks, they have all said that they would be delighted – in fact, in Kathryn's case 'ecstatic' – to be represented by one Rebecca Morrison.'

He sits back and takes in my reaction. I know that my mouth is wide open, but I can't remember how to shut it.

'Obviously,' Joshua continues, 'four clients and arranging a few voice-overs does not quite an agent make, but we thought that maybe you wouldn't mind being paid the same as you're on now until we can help you build it up a bit more. Or until one of your clients gets a major highly paid contract, which, given what you did for all of them in a couple of short weeks, isn't out of the question.' He smiles at me warmly and I want to hug him. Luckily I contain myself.

'Yes. I mean no. Of course I don't mind. Really?'

'Really,' Melanie says. 'We'll have to start looking for a replacement for your old job right away, of course. We thought you and Lorna could share Kay if that's agreeable.'

I'm not sure I believe this is really happening. 'Absolutely. That's if . . . Lorna, you're OK with it?'

'It was Lorna's suggestion,' Joshua says. 'We just have to hope Heather's new contract is as big as we hope it's going to be, otherwise we're all buggered,' he adds laughing.

I feel sick with excitement. Suddenly I know how Lorna felt. Why she was so pleased with herself. I want to shout out of the window. 'Look at me, I'm AN AGENT!'

'I'm . . . I don't know what to say. Thank you. Thank you so much. And I don't care if you pay me the same forever, I just want to do the job and do it well and –'

'Steady on,' Melanie says. 'Joshua will hold you to that.'

The moment over, Joshua busies himself with something on his desk and that's our cue to leave.

'We'll all have a glass of champagne at the end of the day to celebrate,' he says to our retreating backs.

Lorna is sloping back off to her office.

'Lorna,' I say, and she stops. 'I'm gobsmacked. I can't thank you enough.'

'It's OK. I doubt I'd still have my job if it wasn't for you . . .'

'No. It's not OK. You didn't have to do what you just did and I'm so grateful, so unbelievably, completely and eternally grateful.'

She smiles at me shyly again and I think what the hell and, before I really know what I'm doing, I have got her in a hug. It's a bit like hugging a skeleton and there's a moment when I worry that she might snap in two, but I go for it anyway. When I break away she looks flushed, but she also looks happy. It makes her look like a different person.

'Thank you,' she says.

'Actually,' I say, before I can stop myself, 'we're having a little Christmas do tomorrow night, me and Dan. Only a few of our friends and their kids, but if you'd like to come? Kay's coming . . .' What am I doing? Five minutes ago we hated each other, why is she going to want to come and spend time at my house?

'Really?' she says, and I say, 'Absolutely.'

'Then I'd love to.'

The next day and a half goes by in a haze of champagne drinking – first Joshua then Dan and then Isabel insist on toasting my success – and excited planning. I'm full of ideas about the heights I can take my motley crew of clients to. I'm bursting with energy, bouncing out of bed at six thirty in the morning, getting in to work by eight. I haven't felt like this for years, since . . . In fact, I don't know since what, I'm not sure I've ever felt like this before. Lorna continues to be friendly but reserved and, as always when people are nice to you, it's impossible not to be friendly back. I think I've slightly alarmed Dan, Isabel and Kay by inviting her to our little soirée but they understand that I wanted to do something nice for her, something to show that I'm truly grateful.

Kay sets to work trying to find my replacement. Luckily Amita has accepted another position, but Kay calls the two graduates, Nadeem and Carla, and asks them if they want to come and interview for a different but surprisingly similar job, which they both nearly bite her hand off to do.

On Thursday afternoon Kay pushes me out of the door at four thirty, telling me that no one wants to eat at half past nine because I wouldn't leave work in time to cook. The kids have finished decorating the flat and are happily dressing the table, all attempts at being too cool for school forgotten in the pre-Christmas excitement.

'Why is Lorna so horrible?' William asks as he's placing the traditional angels in front of all the place settings.

'She's not,' I say, and hope that for once he'll let it be.

'But you're always saying she is. You told Dad she was a complete and utter bitch.'

Zoe snorts.

'You shouldn't be listening in on our conversations,' I say. 'And that wasn't her, that was another Lorna.'

I realize as soon as I've said this that it's a mistake. William is just as likely to say to Lorna, 'Mum knows another Lorna who she says is a complete and utter bitch,' as anything else.

'Actually I did use to think that, but I was wrong, OK? And she'd be very, very upset if she knew that I'd said it, so don't mention it, will you?' I'm so confused about Lorna that I'm not sure what I actually do think about her at the moment, but I don't want to tell him that.

'I'm not stupid,' he says huffily, and Zoe says, 'No, of course you're not,' in a way that means he clearly is.

'Mum . . .' he whines.

I leave them to it, knowing that there's no way they'll have a full-blown row this evening, Not since the year Dan threatened to make them spend the evening in their rooms after they'd committed some misdemeanor or other. He'd stuck to it too until after the starter, so they'd missed everyone else pulling their crackers and comparing little gifts.

By seven the food is under control and the place is looking – and smelling – amazing. It reminds me of a fair ground, all fairy lights and garish silver and red decorations. There are scented candles in all the rooms. The mulled wine is mulling or whatever it is that it does, the Camembert is ready to bake for the appetizer, the trifle is made and the yule log that William made in Food Technology is melting quietly in the heat of the kitchen. I rush around in the bedroom, getting changed in record time, while Dan opens the wine and pours us both a big glass. At twenty past seven Kay is the first to arrive.

'Quick, carols,' I say to Zoe before I answer the door, and Zoe rushes over to the iPod dock. We always have carols playing when people arrive on the twenty-first.

'Is Cruella here yet?' Kay asks in a loud whisper as I take her through to the living room to introduce her to Dan and the kids.

'Don't.'

Somehow Kay – who, of course, has two sons, which might go some way to explaining it – turns out to be as much of a geek as William so they bond over talking about the discovery of some obscure star or other that has been on the news for reasons I can't even be bothered to try to remember.

Isabel and the girls arrive next, turning up on the doorstep at the same time as Rose and Simon who have brought along their six-year-old daughter, Fabia. Their other two are both at a sleepover.

We adults drink pungent mulled wine and nibble on the little pre-dinner snacks I've put out, and chat about not much. Rose seems a little nervous of Isabel, given that she was the bearer of bad news about Luke, but luckily Isabel, who has good intuition, spots this and makes a big show of thanking her for saving her from making a complete fool of herself. It's all very relaxed and friendly and Christmassy, and then the doorbell rings again and there's Lorna clutching a bottle of wine. She hands it to me as I show her in.

'Do come on in.' I'm talking to her like an elderly aunt I've only met once before. The truth is I don't really know how to be around her. Well, apart from defensive, hostile and suspicious that is.

'Your flat's looking lovely,' she says, looking around at the decorations as I take her coat.

'Thanks. Come through. Everybody, this is Lorna.' You never saw a roomful of people so interested. Lorna the legend is in our home. Even Rose and Simon have been filled in on her exploits on the few occasions we've had dinner with them. I introduce her to everyone she doesn't already know and she says yes to a glass of mulled wine so I leave them all to it while I go and fetch her one and check on the sausages. Isabel follows me out.

'She's even skinnier than the last time I saw her,' she stage whispers.

'I know. Oh God, was this a terrible idea, inviting her?'

'No, of course not. It's your good deed for the year.

Only we're not having beans with the sausages are we because I don't think I could cope.'

'Shh,' I say, laughing. 'We have to try to be nice.'

And, actually, the meal is fun. Everyone coos over their little cracker presents. I agonized over what to put in Lorna's and, in the end, I plumped for a pink, glittery ballpoint pen because she always seems to be having to borrow biros off people's desks at work.

'I love it,' she says, smiling. Yes, it's definitely a smile. I'm getting more used to it by now; it doesn't scare me quite so much as when it first appeared.

'You can lend it to Heather Barclay for her to sign me an autograph,' Zoe says. 'Mum was too scared to ask her.'

'Of course I will . . .'

'And for me too,' William says, and then Nicola and Natalie say they'd like one too and Fabia adds her name into the mix, even though she probably doesn't even know who Heather Barclay is. Lorna actually seems not to mind the attention and the kids are being sweet and funny and, above all, polite, so it all helps to break the ice a bit.

It took me a long while to decide who to sit Lorna next to. God forbid I should have to spend the evening listening to her stories; I've had enough of that at work to last me a lifetime. As has Kay, even in the short time she's been at Mortimer and Sheedy. Isabel is out because of the Alex connection. In the end I have sacrificed my lovely husband because I know he'll be polite and try to engage her in conversation. On the other side I've put Rose because she's sweet and friendly and she can talk to anyone. Still, it's obvious that Lorna is feeling uncomfortable. She picks at her food, head down, speaking only when spoken to. It's a bit like having a sulky teenager at the table although when I look at Zoe messing around with the other kids at the little table in the corner I feel that's doing sulky teenagers a disservice. I decide to try to enjoy myself anyway. I've done my bit, I invited her, I can't be responsible for making sure she has a good time too.

Once we've eaten, the kids all get dispatched off to Zoe's room while we adults linger over the wine. Usually the twins will fall asleep on the floor eventually and I'm assuming that this time Fabia will go the same way too. I've left a collection of sleeping bags and quilts in there for them to fight over. We always let them play until they flake out so long as they're not too noisy. We're having fun so why shouldn't they? Dan fills all our glasses again and we're all talking about I don't remember what, something banal, when Lorna suddenly coughs loudly. It's so loud it actually makes me jump and we all turn to look at her.

'I'd like to say something,' she says. I think about rugby tackling her to the ground. She must have had too much to drink and now the recriminations are going to start all over again. I look at Dan, but he's looking as clueless as I feel. It was all going so well.

'This won't mean much to you, Rose and Simon, so I apologize in advance. You've probably heard about me, though. I'm sure Rebecca will have mentioned the way I've been behaving lately. Well, not just lately, but anyway . . .'

Thankfully Rose and Simon manage to arrange their faces into expressions that say, 'No, never heard of you, what are you talking about?'

I have no idea where this is going and no idea how to stop it.

'The thing is Rebecca and I have never got on. Have we?'

Lorna is a master of understatement. What am I supposed to say? 'Um . . . no, I guess not.'

'And I've realized lately that most of that was down to me.' OK, I allow myself to breathe again, maybe this isn't going to be so bad after all.

'I was difficult to work with, I know that. It was always important to me that I'd been there longer, how I was perceived, and you know, Rebecca, you were always right, I did use to avoid answering the phones in the hope that you'd get there first. I had a chip on my shoulder about wanting to be the senior assistant, the most important person. The fact is that I . . . I've always been jealous of you. There, I've said it . . .'

She looks at me for a reaction and I smile weakly. I don't know what to say.

'You have everything I've always wanted. A husband who loves you, children, you're clever and funny and beautiful and confident and people like you. And because of that I felt threatened I suppose . . .'

This is making me feel really awkward. Part of me

wants to ask her how in the world she ever got the idea that I was confident and the other half just wants to tell her to shut the hell up. This is meant to be a fun evening.

'Lorna, you don't have to do this . . .'

'No, I do. I'm not going to be long. I don't want to ruin your evening,' she says as if she's read my mind. 'I just need to get this off my chest while I'm feeling brave enough otherwise I never will. What I'm trying to say is that I gave you every reason to hate me; I can see that now. And in return you bent over backwards to save my job and to cover up my mistakes and I can say – one hundred per cent – that I never would have done the same for you. And you even invited me here tonight. And that's really made me think. What I'm trying to say, what I'm standing here making a prat of myself and ruining your dinner party to say, is that I've changed. Or, at least, I'm going to. And I'd really like you to believe me because I'd really like it if we could be friends. And I hope you'll accept my apology for the way I've always treated you.'

She stops abruptly. There's a stunned silence round the table. Rose and Simon are both finding something fascinating in their glasses; Kay is open-mouthed. I know I should say something, but I just don't know what. It must have taken an enormous amount of cour-age for her to have said what she just has, but I really don't know how to respond. Dan, thankfully, saves the day by raising his glass and saying, 'Well, good on you, Lorna. I don't see how anyone could argue with that.'

'I agree,' Isabel says. 'Don't you, Rebecca?' She looks at me as if to say, 'Say something,' and I know I must.

'Wow, Lorna, I don't know what to say. Actually, yes I do. Of course I accept your apology, but you need to accept mine too. If you haven't always been as nice as you should, then neither have I. You know, with the whole email thing and everything.' I pause. Maybe I shouldn't go there. 'But, you know, I may have covered for you while you were away but you've already repaid me by helping me get my dream job. So, actually, I'd love it if we could just forget everything that's gone before and start fresh. See how we get on. Deal?'

She smiles at me, a genuine smile if ever I saw one. 'Deal.'

'Thank God,' I say. 'Now can we just have another drink?'

She laughs along with the others. Dan pours yet more drinks and we all make a big effort to talk about something else. Lorna, I notice, suddenly seems much more animated, more relaxed. She obviously came here tonight with a mission and now she's accomplished it. The permanent sneer has been replaced by something much more appealing. Well, good for her. I'm not sure I could have done the same. I have no idea what will happen from here on in, whether we really will manage to bury six years of animosity, but I'm certainly willing to give it a try.

The tension broken, we start to have a really fun time. Everyone gels; no one is left out. Lorna actually does have some funny stories – and not ones which revolve around how brilliant she is either. Simon proves to be a great mimic, not a talent he's displayed before, and he does hilarious but affectionate impressions of all of us. (Me flustered – 'Is this OK? Are you enjoying yourselves? Does anyone need anything? Oh God, it's shit, isn't it?') Lorna asks me to show her my impersonation of her – the one I did for Niall Johnson – and I risk it all by agreeing. I throw myself into it, the big eyes , the breathless enthusiastic delivery, and she laughs so hard she's wiping tears from her eyes.

At one point, I remember, I take a chance and say, 'Lorna, when we shared an office did you used to eat noisy food just because you knew it annoyed me?'

'No!' she says, indignant. Then she laughs. 'Well, not at first anyway.'

If I dare to say so myself, we're all having a great night.

The doorbell rings.

Dan and I both look towards the clock on the wall. It's gone ten, well past random cold-caller time.

'Who's that?' I say, slightly pointlessly, because there's no way he could know.

'I'll go,' Dan says, and gets up.

'It's probably the woman from downstairs to tell us we're being too noisy,' I say to the others. 'She has to get up early.'

Nevertheless we all strain to hear what she's going to say. Even though the flat is quite small, it's hard to make out what's being said except for the fact that the person

Dan is talking to clearly isn't the woman from downstairs unless she's had a sex change.

There's a short exchange and then I hear footsteps coming along the corridor and the front door closing. Dan comes in first, looking apologetic.

'Sorry,' he starts to say, but someone else comes in behind him and cuts him off.

Alex.

He's brandishing a bottle of champagne.

'I couldn't miss the traditional twenty-first of December Christmas celebration at the Morrisons,' he says. He sounds drunk. He's not slurring, but he's got that brashness in his voice, the same as when he came to the office. 'I knew you'd all be here.'

He looks around the table. Smiles at Isabel. 'Ooh, the Rottweiler,' he says when he sees Kay.

He introduces himself to Rose and Simon. 'Alex . . .' he says, holding out his hand as if they were all at the same business dinner.

They both shake warily. They've heard enough to know who Alex is, but, of course, not all the complications that go with him.

Then he spots Lorna sitting next to Rose. She's gone white, her former relaxed mood shattered.

'OK,' he says, looking at me, 'now I'm really confused. I know you needed to make some new friends, but this is ridiculous. You hate Lorna. You told me so yourself a hundred times.'

Dan steps in. 'Alex, that's enough. You weren't invited. You shouldn't be here . . .'

'Of course I was invited. This is what we do every twenty-first of December. Then on the twenty-fourth you come to us. New Year is in a restaurant early and then home to one of our places, alternate years, before midnight. We spend Thursday nights round here, Mondays at ours, on Friday we go to the pub and every other Saturday we go out for a meal. Once a year, in the autumn half term, we all go away together. No one else is ever invited to any of these rituals except tonight's. Rebecca has our whole lives mapped out for us, the four of us and our four children. That's how it works, isn't it Rebecca?'

I hate him. 'I think you should leave now.'

'I've only just got here,' he says, and he sits himself down in Dan's chair, which just happens to be next to Lorna. She looks like she might be sick.

'You will have eaten sausages and mash then trifle. There will have been carols playing when everyone arrived and a personalized cracker for everyone. Rebecca doesn't like change.'

We all sit there paralysed by our middle-class reluctance to cause a scene. Finally I feel like I should say something. 'Alex, I know you're still pissed off with me . . .'

He laughs. 'Don't flatter yourself. I'm not here to see you. I'm here to see Isabel.'

All eyes turn to Izz; Rose and Simon wide-eyed and curious, Lorna pale and shaky, Dan furious but at a loss what to do. Isabel looks at Alex, waiting to hear what comes next. Personally I have no interest in anything

Alex might have to say. I just want him to leave us all alone.

He leans forward towards her. 'Isabel, I want to come back. I made a mistake. A stupid, terrible mistake and I regret it so much you wouldn't believe. I know that I should never have left you and the girls. And I know that the way I've behaved since with Rebecca is probably unforgivable.'

I'm aware of Rose and Simon's heads whipping round to look at me like they're following a tennis match. I look at the table.

'But I was wrong about Rebecca. God, was I wrong. And you know I never loved Lorna . . .'

Whip. Two heads turn in Lorna's direction. I look at her too. She looks shaken, but this isn't news to her any more so she's holding it together.

'. . . and what I've come to realize is that actually it's you I love. I've loved you all along. I just went crazy for a bit, that's all. Call it a mid-life crisis. Whatever. It's over. And I want to say that if you'll have me back then I want to come back. We can get over this, Isabel, please . . .'

He finally shuts up and we all look at Isabel. I can tell that she's moved, that she's thinking about it. Her whole experience with Luke has left her vulnerable and the devil-you-know security of her marriage probably looks pretty inviting to her at the moment.

'Alex . . .' she says quietly. 'I don't know what to think.'

I know it's none of my business. I know I should

keep out of it. But what kind of a friend am I if I let her fall back in love with him without knowing the full picture. If, once she knows the extent of Alex's betrayal of her, she still wants to take him back, then that's her funeral. She's a grown woman; she can make up her own mind. But at the moment he's not playing fair.

Before I can say anything the door opens and in walks Natalie, looking cute in her SpongeBob pyjamas and rubbing the sleep out of her eyes. We all sit there in silence, some of us – me included – even plaster smiles on our faces as if to say, 'Look, Nat, we're all having a great time.' She's too tired and disorientated to notice the tension and she folds herself on to Isabel's lap like a cat.

'I can't sleep.'

'Do you want me to tuck you back in?' Alex says, and Natalie is suddenly wide awake, flicking her head round to find the source of the voice.

'Dad!' She flings herself at him as if he's been found at sea after a five-year absence. 'You didn't tell me Dad was coming,' she says to Isabel, accusing.

Isabel tries to make light of it. 'I knew he was going to get here late. I didn't want you refusing to go to bed because you wanted to see him.'

'I'll get Nicola,' Natalie says, her first instinct always being to share everything with her twin.

'No,' Isabel says, and she leans over and gently takes hold of her arm to stop her running out of the room. 'Dad's got to go in a minute and you'll see him again soon, both of you.'

374

Natalie sighs, a loud theatrical sigh. 'When are you coming home?'

'Sooner than you think, maybe,' Alex says, and Isabel says, 'Alex . . .' a warning shot across his bows.

Natalie's face lights up. 'Really?'

'Well, it's up to Mummy,' Alex says, and the rest of us swap looks, open-mouthed. It's unthinkable that he would give Natalie hope like this and then put Isabel in the firing line if it doesn't work out.

Isabel picks Natalie off his lap. 'It's up to both of us,' she says. 'Daddy and I. We have lots to talk about, but either way you'll see him soon. Whatever happens he'll still be coming over to visit. And, who knows, maybe one day . . .' She tails off and whisks her daughter out of the room before Alex can say any more.

We sit in stony silence for a moment and then Dan says, 'Fucking hell, Alex, that was a bit much.'

Alex ignores him, helps himself to a glass of wine in somebody's empty glass, smiles at the blank faces round the table. I want him to leave, of course I do, but I don't actually know how to achieve that. Asking him to go isn't likely to work. I don't want a fuss, a noise, disturbing the neighbours and, more importantly, the kids. Plus, deep down, there's something in me that wants to see this played out once and for all. And it can never be a bad thing for Isabel to be reminded how manipulative he is, how scheming and fucked up and insincere.

She comes back in, looking pleadingly at Alex. 'Don't ever do that again, bringing the girls into it, giving them false hope.'

'But it's not false, is it? Not necessarily, anyway. You're thinking about it, aren't you, Izz?'

Isabel looks around at us all. 'I'm not having this conversation here. It's so . . . inappropriate.'

'Actually, we should probably get going,' Rose says, raising her eyebrows at Simon.

'No . . .' I say. I don't want the evening to end like this, our guests bullied out of our home.

Dan says, 'I think it's Alex who should leave.'

Alex ignores him, looks at Isabel. Rose reluctantly sits back down.

'You won't talk when I pick the kids up; you won't talk on the phone. It might be inappropriate, but I don't know how else to get you to listen to the fact that I'm sincere. I want to come back.'

'Alex, I'm still trying to work out where our marriage went wrong. You left without me ever having realized you were unhappy. What does that say about us? You made a pass at Rebecca, for God's sake, my best friend.'

'I've told you,' he says, 'that was a mistake. A tiny, momentary blip. I was drunk. I didn't know what I was doing. I was so confused. I regretted it immediately.'

OK, that's my cue. I can't sit here and watch him spin her this line. I take a deep breath, cough, here goes. I'm about to speak up when Dan gets there first.

'A momentary blip? Except that you told her you'd been in love with her for years. And you repeated it the next day. You begged her to leave me.' He looks at Isabel apologetically. 'That's the real reason we fell out.'

Isabel looks confused.

'I didn't want you to know that. Ever,' I say. 'But Dan's right. If you're going to get back with him, then you have to know exactly who he is, what he's capable of.'

'OK,' Alex says. 'Like I said, I was confused. I said all sorts of things.'

'And you told me that your marriage had been dead for years.' We all look at Lorna who has piped up from the other side of the table. 'You told me that you'd never really been faithful to Isabel anyway. Sorry, Isabel . . .'

Alex interrupts. 'Hold on. Don't you join in. Half of these people hate you, remember. They've been laughing at you behind your back for years.'

'You're a user, Alex,' she says. 'It took me a while to see it, but it's true.'

'Isabel,' he says. 'Don't listen to them.'

She looks at him, a slight frown on her face. 'Is that true, what Lorna just said?'

'Of course not. They're all jealous or they've got a grudge against me. They'd rather get back at me than see you happy . . .'

'So, it's not true?'

Dan speaks. 'Alex, if you really want Isabel back, now's the time to come clean . . .'

Alex says nothing.

'So, it is,' Isabel says.

Dan looks at the table, not wanting to say any more.

'I'm so sorry, Isabel,' Lorna says again.

'You haven't got anything to apologize for,' Izz says. 'In fact I should thank you, all of you, for preventing me from making the same mistake twice. You think you want me back, Alex, maybe you do or maybe it would just be convenient – you'd be back in the fold; life would eventually go back to how it was. But how am I ever going to trust you again? You had the chance then to say, "Actually, it's all true, everything they're saying, but I'm different now," but you didn't take it. You lied to me all the way through our marriage and you're still lying to me.'

'Come on,' he says. 'Don't do this.'

'Sorry, Alex. I was wavering because I missed you and it's scary being on your own. But you've just made up my mind for me. You can still see the girls, I won't ever be difficult about that. But we'll go back to our fixed arrangement, no turning up out of the blue or calling me on the off chance. We're never going to get back together. Not ever.'

I lean over and give Isabel a hug. She's shaking.

'Oh, and, Alex,' she says. 'Get a job.'

'Definitely time to go now, mate,' Dan says.

Alex stands up. 'You all fucking deserve each other, you know that?' he spits as he leaves.

We sit in stunned silence for a moment.

'Blimey,' Simon says eventually. 'This is better than a night in front of the TV,' and we all laugh nervously, despite everything.

'Are you OK?' I say to Isabel, and she says, 'Do you know what? I feel absolutely fine. I don't have to pine for him any more because I've realized I never really knew him.'

'How about you?' I say to Lorna, and she smiles and says, 'Ditto.'

Kay goes off to the kitchen and comes back with another bottle of wine. 'Fuck it, let's all get drunk,' she says, so we do and we laugh a bit too loudly at things like we're trying to prove we're all OK, and then we sing carols and turn the iPod speakers up way too loud and this time the neighbour really does come up to tell us off.

31

I wake up next morning fully clothed, sprawled across the bed. I have a hazy memory of phoning taxis at about four in the morning and swearing undying love for all my guests as the night drew to an end. The clock says nine thirty so I am already late for work. I try to call out for Dan, but my furry tongue is stuck to the roof of my mouth so I peel myself off the bed and sway towards the door. It hits me like a speeding truck that we have a house full of other people's kids and a responsibility to get them off to school on time (too late) and well fed. It might be the last day of term but that doesn't mean they can roll in any time they (or their parents) can be bothered. The flat seems very quiet. I make it to the kitchen in one piece. It's surprisingly clean considering the carnage that went on. In the middle of the table is a note. It seems that Dan got up early and, with the help of Zoe, got all the kids washed, dressed and breakfasted and out of the door on time. He (Dan) has already called Melanie on her mobile to say she probably shouldn't expect either me, Kay or Lorna to show up until very late today because we were all downing shots until the small hours and she, the note tells me, laughed and said they'd cope.

'Don't forget to look in the living room before you leave,' the note says, enigmatically. Even though there's no prospect of me feeling up to going out any time soon, I can't resist a mystery so I shuffle over to the living-room door and open it. The smell hits me first, heavy with alcohol like an empty pub. The room is dark, but I can just about make out two comatose figures, one on either sofa. Of course. Kay and Lorna opted to sleep where they were, in their clothes, rather than even attempt to go home. It's all coming back to me now. Isabel spent the night on the spare bunk in William's room. (All the girls, of course, stayed with Zoe. 'Stay in a boy's room? No way! That's gross.') Only Rose and Simon actually made it through the front door.

I tiptoe to William's room. The beds are made, no sign of Isabel. She always was good at getting up the morning after a night before while I would lie in bed moaning for hours. So I put some coffee on, open the living-room curtains and then the windows even though it's four degrees out there. Mumblings from under the two quilts.

Kay surfaces first. Groans, looks at her watch, panics.

'It's OK,' I say, laughing. 'They know we're going to be late in.'

She crawls out from under the cover, make-up all over her face, hair standing on end.

'Oh God,' she says. 'Oh God. What did I do? No, don't tell me.'

There's something about seeing someone suffering even worse than you that takes the edge off a hangover. Maybe it punctures the psychological dark cloud that hangs just above your head. 'I wasn't the only one' or

381

even just 'I wasn't the drunkest'. Anyway, seeing Kay looking so rough seems to perk me up.

'You were fine,' I say, as if I even remember. 'We were all as bad.'

Lorna is still out cold, head back, mouth open, breath rattling in her throat.

'Lorna,' I say. Nothing.

'Lorna.'

'Lorna.'

Kay laughs. 'Lorna.'

'Lorna.' I raise my voice slightly.

'Lorna,' Kay says.

I start laughing. I can't stop, deep in out-of-control hangover hysteria. 'Lorna.'

A couple of minutes of this and we're both crying with laughter. We clutch on to each other like two giggly thirteen-year-olds. Every few seconds one or other of us says, 'Lorna,' she doesn't react and that sets us off again. I realize that I could keep doing this all day and then I remember that we do all have jobs to go to so, reluctantly, I walk over and shake Lorna gently.

'Lorna,' I say, and she opens her eyes and says, 'What?' which Kay and I find hilarious for some reason. Lorna looks around confused, takes in where she is.

'What's so funny?' she says in a groggy voice.

I start a little production line. Shower, coffee, toast, make-up. None of us is capable of moving very fast and even the most routine of jobs feels like climbing a mountain. We have a ten-minute detour when I try to lend them some clean clothes and the sight of size-eight

382

Lorna in one of my size-eighteen tops nearly finishes us off. By ten forty, though, we're ready to go, although we all look like we haven't slept in a week and the other two look like they've been dressed by goodwill. As we stagger to the tube station I call Isabel to check she's still in one piece. She's at work already, although when she got there she realized she was wearing odd socks under her jeans. One of them, she thinks, might be William's.

'I'm trying to pretend it's a quirk,' she says. 'But no one's buying it.'

'It was fun, wasn't it?' she adds. 'Apart from Alex.'

'It was,' I say. 'It really was.'

And I mean it. I can't remember the last time I laughed so much.

'Ask Kay and Lorna if they want to come on Christmas Eve,' she says rashly. 'And Rose and Simon.'

'Great,' I say. And I mean that too.

It's the last day at work before the Christmas break, which always means a little drinks party in the office in the afternoon. I have never felt less like anything in my life. All of the clients are invited and there's usually a pretty good turnout as there always is when there's free drink on offer. Melanie and Joshua were a little surprised to see the three of us crawl in together. Lorna's and my antagonism has never been a very well-kept secret in the office and, despite our dishevelled and unprofessional appearance nearly two hours late, their smiling faces give away how pleased they are to see that their children are playing nicely.

Nothing much happens at this time of year anyway. Half of the businesses in London have already packed up for the holidays. The phone barely rings all day. I sleep sitting up in my chair for most of the rest of the morning and then Joshua and Melanie take us out for the traditional Mortimer and Sheedy Christmas lunch at Rowleys over the road.

The three of us are terrible company, grunting monosyllabic answers and guzzling bottle after bottle of sparkling water. Eventually Joshua insists that we all have a glass of champagne. The idea of it turns my stomach but after a couple of sips I perk up. Great, so now I'm becoming an alcoholic. Everyone toasts my promotion and then Lorna's success with Heather and finally Kay for fitting in so beautifully. The three of us toast the two of them for being the best bosses in the world. A bit of an exaggeration maybe, but who cares? Joshua makes the same little speech he always makes at our Christmas lunch, basically telling us we're all wonderful and that Mortimer and Sheedy is going to take over the world next year and then we walk the fifty yards or so back to the office cosseted in a cloud of mutual respect and affection.

The drinks party is from four thirty till six thirty. It's a very informal affair, cheap champagne and beer in coolers on my desk and a few bowls of Pringles dotted about the place. No one dresses up. Clients and selected friends of the company like Marilyn Carson stop by on their way home from work or Christmas shopping or on their way to the theatre, have a quick drink, wish us all a happy holiday and go on their way again. There's always one person – generally a client who hasn't worked for a while – who arrives at four thirty on the dot and has to be forced into a taxi at half past six, a bit worse for wear. This year, Kathryn arrives first so I wonder if it's going to be her. She hugs me so hard I start coughing and Kay hands her a glass of champagne as she tells us how much fun *Nurses* is, even though all she's done so far is have a costume fitting, and how she's having the time of her life.

'And it's all thanks to Rebecca,' she keeps saying. I sneak a look at Lorna to see if she's irritated by this apparent snub, but she's smiling along with the rest of us, so I relax and accept the compliment. Kathryn does look fantastic, animated and glowing, more alive than I've ever seen her, and I allow myself a little pride in her transformation.

By five fifteen the room is buzzing. Gary McPherson has been and gone, arriving with one of last year's *X Factor* runners up on his arm and announcing that they're getting married. There are loud congratulations all round. Kay, who reads the gossip magazines, whispers to me that she had no idea Gary and Anastasia were going out and I explain to her that they've probably only just met, but both know their stars are waning and they need to cash in on the big magazine deals before the offers slip away. I tell her too that Gary will without doubt invite all his ex-co-stars from *Reddington Road*, even the ones he has always professed to hate, to the wedding and Anastasia will be hastily renewing contact with all the other *X Factor* contestants she ditched as losers as soon as the show finished, because they will be paid big bonuses for each famous face who attends the ceremony and agrees to be photographed. They may even get the cover if she can persuade the winner to come along. Gary tells us we'll all, of course, be invited, and I tell Kay not to get too excited. He'll never remember, not unless one of us makes the papers in the meantime and could therefore make him a few quid more.

'God,' she says. 'It's an education working here.'

My other new charges come by to wish us Happy Christmas – Jasmine, with a new boyfriend in tow, and Samuel who has already finished his second little stint on *Nottingham General* and tells me he needs a job.

'Have you ever met Marilyn Carson?' I say, and he tells me he hasn't so I take him over and introduce him. My mind is already whirring with ideas about how to keep him in work.

Mary and Craig both stop by and, at one point, she tells me quietly that she almost wishes Lorna had handed her over to me too, because she knows she has me to thank for *Marlborough Murder Mysteries*. I tell her to wait and see, that now Lorna is back on form she'll be unstoppable, but the compliment still fills me with pride. Craig is puffed up with importance about his first ever commission. It starts filming two weeks after the Christmas break – they don't hang around in soap land – and they have already indicated that they'd like him to write another. I let him have his moment of showing off. I figure we're all allowed those.

Someone arrives – a woman – who I don't even recognize.

'God, is that Joy Wright Philips?' Lorna says, going over to greet her. Joy has never been to a Christmas party. Ever. Well, not since I've been here anyway. I've only actually met her once and that was years ago and I remember she was quite dour. Lorna brings her over to introduce her and Joy gives me a big smile and shakes my hand and says that she's writing, she actually genuinely is. She writes in bed every morning – only allowing herself to move to get a cup of tea – two hours, without fail and with no other distractions. She's making progress, she says. She has an idea she thinks will work. She's thinking the Bush or the New End, somewhere small. She'd love to come in and talk to me about it in January. I tell her that I'm absolutely delighted she's over her block. I have no idea, really, whether she can actually write, it's been so long, but I'm thrilled she's inspired and actually putting pen to paper again – or finger to keyboard, I suppose – and that I had something to do with that.

'I'll show you what I've done so far,' she says, 'and don't be afraid to tell me if you think it's crap.'

We have chosen Nadeem as our new assistant to help Kay out. He's as in love with our world as we are and so keen to learn and do well that we know he's going to fit in perfectly. And it'll be good to have a boy about the place to balance out all those hormones. He turns up at the party with a big smile on his face, eager to meet everyone and to learn, and Kay takes him under her wing straight away. He's the same age as her oldest son.

387

Heather, of course, does not come. She's far too important to drink warm, weak champagne in an attic near Piccadilly. But she does send over a massive bunch of flowers for Lorna, which makes me think she's forgiven her for their shaky start, and a smaller bunch for me, which was sweet of her. I look forward to telling the kids that Heather Barclay sent me flowers. I remind myself to remember to take the card home for Zoe.

It's all over in a flash. There are no drunks to throw out. We lock up and leave the mess, knowing that the cleaner will be in tomorrow. Outside, we all hug each other and wish each other nice things. Kay and Lorna both shout, 'See you Sunday,' as they go. It's a veritable love in.

I stop off on the way home and buy treats for Dan, steaks and lemon tart and chocolate truffles. I know that I have a tendency to take him for granted. There is no way I would have slept in this morning, however drunk I had been the night before, if I hadn't known deep in my subconscious that he would get up early, however bad he felt himself, to look after the kids. Dan has always been the stable one at the centre of our group. He's like a combination of the best bits of all of us, rock steady and reliable like Isabel, funny like Alex, loyal like me, but with none of our bad bits. It's easy to overlook him, to wonder whether, maybe, there's something or someone more exciting over the horizon, but once you've noticed he's there it's impossible to imagine you might ever want anything different.

388

OK, so we might no longer be in the throes of infatuation, we might have our routines and our cosy rituals, but, I've decided, that's no bad thing. A four-year-old brief moment of madness aside, he has never let me down. I know that doesn't sound like a very exciting quality but, actually, it's the most important one I can think of. He puts up with my insecurities and he never lets me down. He's the solid ground at the centre of my world and I need that. Everything else might be shifting, but as long as I have Dan there, gorgeous, reliable, kind, thoughtful, funny Dan, then that's fine, I can cope with that. Even come to enjoy the changing landscape.

When he comes out of the kitchen to say hello I nearly suffocate him with a hug.

'What was that for?' he says.

'I just felt like it,' I say. 'I love you.'

'I should hope so. I'm your husband,' he says, laughing. And then I kiss him. Properly, not like we're mum and dad saying our polite goodnights, but deeply and passionately, like we used to. He's a bit slow on the uptake, but then he cottons on and he kisses me back and it almost feels like it did when we first met. Better, in fact. Until that is I am dimly aware of the sound of the door opening and I hear a disgusted thirteen-year-old voice saying, 'I am so going to need therapy now.'

32

It's Christmas Eve, the traditional gathering round at Isabel and Alex's except that, this year, of course, there is no Alex. Isabel has told him he can see the girls in the morning so long as he comes with his parents, who always visit their granddaughters on Christmas Day, and leaves when they do. Alex, apparently defeated, agreed without a fight. She knows that he won't cause a fuss with his mum and dad around. Even Alex has boundaries, it seems.

Tonight, I know, was always going to be hard for Izz, however much of a brave face she's been trying to put on, so I volunteer to spend the afternoon helping her get everything ready and we manage to laugh, get angry and even cry at different points in the afternoon as we talk about everything that has gone on these past few months. It's like a Stanislavsky master class.

At one point Isabel says to me, 'I don't know how I would have got through it all without you,' and we have a big mushy moment, my best friend and me, which is thankfully broken by the twins running in and telling us that William is refusing to be dressed up as a Christmas fairy and what are we going to do about it? Wonders will never cease.

Now we're all sitting round the table. Isabel and Dan,

Kay and Lorna and the four kids. I look around. It's like the Walton family only a bit less nuclear. Lorna and Kay have turned into some kind of a double act with Kay telling her to 'for the love of God shut up' whenever she rambles on without letting any one else join in, and to 'eat something for Christ's sake' when she spends too long pushing her food round her plate. Lorna just laughs and says, 'Oh sorry,' and either stops talking or takes a big mouthful, and I realize maybe that's how I should have handled her all along. In turn she has taken to saying, 'Really, Kay, I didn't realize you had children,' whenever Kay launches into another long and rather pointless story about one of her sons.

Is Lorna ever going to become my new best friend? No, of course not. No one could replace Isabel or even come close. I'm sure Lorna will still get on my nerves sometimes and me on hers. But I know how to deal with her now and, most surprisingly of all, I actually like her. I do.

I can't wait to go back to work in January and launch my glittering career. I can't wait to spend tomorrow, just my lovely husband, my imperfect but adorable kids and me, celebrating Christmas, just our little family. I even can't wait for New Year's Eve, the most overrated night of the year, when the five of us adults have agreed to meet up again to enjoy hating the whole thing together. We might invite Rose and Simon along, we might not. I'm easy.

Rebecca and Daniel and Isabel. Sometimes Kay and Lorna. Sometimes Rose and Simon. It might just work.